SHADES
OF PASSION

VIRNA DePAUL

SHADES OF PASSION

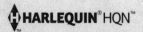

Recycling programs
for this product may
not exist in your area.

ISBN-13: 978-0-373-77742-6

SHADES OF PASSION

Printed in U.S.A.

PROLOGUE

THE MAN CAME TO BETH just when she needed him most.

Just when the pain of existence became too sharp to bear.

She looked into eyes that morphed into rich landscapes, green hills and golden sunsets that stretched far beyond the back of his head, going on for an eternity.

Those eyes beckoned her, promising an end to her suffering. Tempting her with not just peace, but infinite joy. Love. Acceptance.

Only there was love here. Hope.

Hadn't someone told her that? Someone she trusted? Believed? Hadn't she said the world was beautiful?

The man held out his hand. In his palm lay a pink satin ribbon. "The world can be beautiful," he said. "Depending on which direction you travel."

I've traveled so long, Beth thought. *I'm tired.*

"I know you're tired," the man said. "Come with me. I'll carry you. I'll let you rest."

His voice matched the hypnotic beauty of his eyes. It was a deep rumble that resonated throughout her body, enveloping her in a comforting hug the same way her mother's arms used to wrap around her. But her mother, her champion, was gone now. Cancer had taken her. It had eaten away at her insides and left Beth alone, with only her father for company. She didn't want her father. She didn't trust him.

There was another woman, though. Another woman who fought for her. Wasn't there?

Beth struggled to remember, but her vision tunneled, focusing her attention on the long length of ribbon in the man's hand. She reached out and stroked it. It felt smooth. Soft. And when Beth pressed the ribbon against her lips, the memory of her mother's kisses made her weep.

"You're not alone," the man said. "I'm with you. Part of you. Part of everyone. I'll bring you to your mother. She's waiting. All you need to do is trust me."

Beth's tears dried up, and her grief turned to resolve. *Trust me. Trust us. Trust me.*

The man's visage blurred. Morphed into one of a female with blond hair and green eyes.

I know her, Beth thought. *She's helped me. She can help me again.*

I'm part of everyone, the man had said. *I'm part of you.*

Which meant Beth wasn't alone. Not anymore. And she never would be.

Not if she trusted *him*.

Following the man's instructions, Beth held the ribbon between her hands, then looped it around her throat.

"It will hurt at first," the man warned.

Beth hesitated. Where had the woman gone?

"Don't fight it. It's like being born again. You'll close your eyes and sleep for a time. But when you wake up, I'll be there. And so will your mother. You'll finally be happy. No one will hurt you ever again."

"I hurt," Beth whispered. "I don't want to hurt anymore."

So she did what the man said until she couldn't breathe. Until she felt pain. Until she felt fear.

But just as he promised, it didn't last long.

I'm being born again, she told herself as the darkness closed in.

And this time, the world will be beautiful.

CHAPTER ONE

Simon Granger's father had always measured a man's worth by his ability to man up. Didn't matter how tired or angry or sick or sad he was—a man did what he had to. Otherwise, he was worthless. No, less than worthless. He was nothing but a bag of bones taking up space.

That's why, the day after his ex-girlfriend Lana Hudson was murdered by a serial killer, Simon showed up for work just like always.

Now, six months later, he still worked. He testified in court. Occasionally he even socialized with the other members of the Special Investigations Group, a division of the California Department of Justice.

He did what he had to. No complaints. No excuses. But this…

This was harder. Much harder.

So hard that he'd put it off.

So hard that he wasn't sure he could actually do it. But his father's voice prodded him.

Don't be a wuss, Simon. All that counts in this world is a man's actions. Do the right thing and it doesn't matter what you feel. You, the man, what you do— that's what counts. That's what's real.

As usual, playing back his father's words spurred him into action. This time, he didn't stop until he stood by the grave site. He studied it with an odd combination of regret and relief.

It was in a good spot, in the shadow of a willow tree, covered with the thick green lawn that sprawled across the cemetery grounds. The place emanated peace. He could almost feel Lana standing beside him, her hand on his shoulder, a soft smile on her face as she thanked him for coming.

The gravestone suited her. It was polished. An elegant marbleized cream. The epitaph, however, made him flinch. Underneath her birth and death dates, it read:

Lana Hudson
Beloved Daughter
Taken by a Soul in Pain but
One Better for Having Met Her

He wanted to wipe out any mention of the "soul" that had taken Lana from them. It seemed obscene that a tribute to Lana's life would include any mention of the man who'd killed her. But the epitaph hadn't been his call. As a man Lana had briefly dated, Simon had no right to override her parents' wishes. That was especially true given he couldn't dispute the epitaph's overall message—that Lana had blessed every life she'd touched, no matter how dark that life had been.

"Hi, Lana. Sorry it's taken me so long to visit. Things have been busy at work and..." He cringed, imagining how Lana would have called him out for his lameness if she'd still been alive. "Yeah. Well, you know why I haven't come by. I was pissed as hell at you. I—I still am. But I loved you, babe. And I miss you. I couldn't let another day go by without telling you that."

A faint breeze encircled him and he closed his eyes, imagining her arms holding him close. They'd fought before she'd been killed. Fought because she'd taken risks to help a criminal and Simon hadn't approved. Hadn't understood. He still didn't.

But that didn't matter. Not anymore.

Lana was gone. She'd taken part of Simon's heart with her. Without it, there was no joy in life. No hope for it.

Still, he'd do what he had to. He'd do his job.

Whether he did it from a desk or on the streets, he'd do his part to make sure that men like the one who killed Lana got what they deserved. A fast-track ticket to hell.

The breeze that had wound around him suddenly stopped, and he heard its absence as a sigh of disappointment. He imagined Lana's voice chiding him. Urging him to be compassionate. To understand that not all killers were evil. That bad things sometimes happened due to pain, not hate.

As he always did, Simon tried to hear the truth behind her words. But he couldn't. Like the soul immortalized in her epitaph, he was better for having met Lana. Yet even *she* hadn't been able to work miracles.

Crouching, he placed the flowers he'd brought against her tombstone.

And as he walked away, he was bleakly aware that he hadn't felt that gentle breeze again.

Two days later, Simon sat on a wooden bench in the foyer of the Welcome Home homeless shelter in San Francisco's Tenderloin district, waiting for the director, Elaina Scott, to come out of a meeting. To pass the time, he opened the file he held, reviewing what he knew about the victim, a previous resident of the shelter.

It wasn't much.

Three days ago, Louis Cann had been stabbed to death in Golden Gate Park. Normally, the homicide would have been handled by the San Francisco Police Department. In fact, SFPD had already conducted most of the preliminary investigation. Yesterday, however, things had changed. And that was putting it mildly, Simon thought with a mental snort. Now, a prostitute named Rita Taylor claimed she'd seen Cann's killer walking away from the crime scene—wearing a patrol cop's uniform.

Talk about a conflict of interest.

Which was why SIG had been assigned the case. SIG was the state equivalent of the FBI, with jurisdiction over every law enforcement agency in California. The team of five special agents assisted with some of the most complex investigations, but one of their primary duties was to handle cases that other agencies couldn't due to some kind of conflict.

Unfortunately, even with the preliminary work conducted by SFPD, the meager contents of the file Simon held were just that. In addition to Rita Taylor's statement, he knew the victim's identity and that Cann had often stayed at Welcome Home. He also knew that Cann had once served in the military, that he'd fought in Desert Storm and that at the end of his tour he'd managed a fast-food restaurant. Within a year, he'd been living on the streets. He'd been doing so for over ten years and would probably have continued right on doing so if he hadn't been killed.

He didn't have a record of significant problems with the police, and the few volunteers and street people that had known him had denied knowledge of anyone wanting to hurt him. In fact, every person that had been interviewed had said the same thing: Cann kept to himself. He didn't have friends. He didn't want them. He talked to no one. Who would want to kill someone like that, especially when that person had nothing worth stealing?

In other words, everything in Simon's file amounted to a major dead end.

There was no reason to believe that interviewing the shelter director would result in anything new, but this was his case now and Simon wanted to make sure nothing important had been overlooked the first time around. After he was done here, he'd reinterview Rita Taylor, check with SFPD about patrol officers on duty near Golden Gate Park three days ago and then spend the next few days conducting even more interviews— of patrol officers, park vendors or other employees who might have been in a position to see anything, and anyone else he could think of. A whole lot of legwork for what was probably not going to be a lot of payoff.

Didn't matter. His job was to pursue every lead, weak as it may be, and that's what he was going to do.

He flipped through the crime scene photos, settling on the close-up shot of the Semper Fi tattoo on Cann's left biceps. He couldn't help thinking how pathetic it was that Cann, a man who'd once served his country, had ended up living on the streets. Dirty. Wizened.

Dead.

Bags of bones taking up space.

It's what Simon's father would have said if he was here. And despite knowing it was wrong—or at the very least, politically incorrect—Simon would have had to agree with him. He wasn't exactly proud of his thoughts, but he wasn't a fraud and he wasn't a liar, either. While it was true that justice should be blind, that didn't mean it had to be ignorant, too. Even so, any personal feelings he might harbor about individual weakness didn't affect the way Simon did his job.

Simon sought justice for a lot of people and that included the ones he didn't necessarily like, as well as the ones he'd privately characterize as weak. To Simon's way of thinking, homelessness was the ultimate sign of weakness. Criminals were weak, too, but at least criminals still fought for something, even if it was something selfish or depraved. The homeless no longer fought for anything, even their own dignity.

Or did they?

Had Cann fought for his life in the end?

If so, they'd found no evidence of it. No defensive wounds to indicate he'd resisted his attacker. Which meant he'd most likely been taken unawares. Even the expression on his face at the time his body had been found suggested it. He looked slightly surprised. As if he couldn't quite believe what had happened to him. But in that startled gaze, Simon saw something else. An unspoken plea for justice. A haunted yearning for Simon to find his killer.

That desperate, desolate expression was something Simon had long ago become familiar with. He'd seen the same expression on the faces of every murder victim he'd ever encountered. He'd even seen it on Lana's face, too, he thought grimly, blinking rapidly to drive the disturbing memory away.

And damn it, he didn't want to see it anymore.

Not like that. Not like this, he thought as he shut the file with a snap.

Hopefully he wouldn't have to. Not once he closed this case, anyway.

Visiting Lana's grave had helped him make the decision he'd been struggling with.

He couldn't do this much longer. One way or another, Simon's days of working the streets were coming to an end. His choices were either early retirement or a move to management, and despite everything, he wasn't ready to leave the job altogether. Then again, he could always do private security. A lot of former cops did, including Lana's father, and they made an extremely good living doing it, too. Gil Archer had made it clear that Simon could work for him anytime he wanted, but Simon wanted balance. Off the streets but not *completely* off the streets. That left management, only this time—unlike eight months ago, when he'd walked away from a captain position because it hadn't been exciting enough—he'd have to make it stick. If he could convince the brass to give him another shot, that is.

Understandably, Commander Stevens was reluctant to stick his neck out for Simon again, especially when so many other qualified applicants were jonesing for a cushier gig with increased pay. Still, Simon figured if he solved this case, Stevens would owe him big-time. Hell, the mayor would probably be so grateful he'd speed the promotion along, cutting through all the civil service bureaucratic red tape Simon had had to navigate last time.

Unfortunately, closing this case wasn't exactly going to be a walk in the park. So far, they'd managed to keep Rita Taylor's accusations locked down, but that wasn't going to last long. While he was trying to win over Stevens and the mayor, Simon's actions would be scrutinized like crazy—by a public wanting to make sure a guilty cop didn't get away with murder, and by his fellow officers who'd be judging his loyalty and his ability to protect one of his own. And that wasn't even counting the press. The minute Rita Taylor's statement got leaked, the higher-ups would have a shitload of reporters riding their asses.

And that meant they'd be riding Simon's ass, too. Hard.

A homeless man—a homeless *ex-marine*—dead. The only suspect a possible cop.

Things weren't looking good for a city that was already suffering negative publicity from recent police encounters with the homeless. Simon's involvement would either make him a scapegoat or a hero. It was up to him to make sure the latter occurred.

A minute later, a sound made him look up.

A bewhiskered man wearing a filthy khaki jacket and equally dirty green-and-white-checkered golf pants made his way down the hall, coming toward him, placing each foot in front of the other equidistant, murmuring numbers to himself. After a moment, Simon realized the man was counting steps, making certain not to step on the black tiles and only stepping on the white ones. Even with twenty feet between them, the man stank—the perpetual stench of homelessness.

Each city's homeless had a particular odor. New York's stank of the subway—engine grease and urine. In San Francisco, the pungent odor that surrounded the homeless had a different scent—urine and pine. Probably because so many hung out in Golden Gate Park, and despite what had happened to Cann, that wasn't likely to change.

The man drew closer and Simon wanted to pull back, away from the increasing wave of stench, but the slats of the bench kept him trapped. When the man reached Simon, he stopped walking. Stopped counting. As if waiting for something. But what?

At first, Simon thought the guy had made him for a cop. That he was going to ask him a question. Maybe even share something about Cann. But then…

Oh, hell.

Simon lifted his foot from the white tile.

"Forty-two," the man murmured as he stepped on the tile, then continued walking and counting, reaching fifty before opening the outer door and leaving the building.

After the man left, Simon stood to stretch his legs and scanned a large bulletin board on the wall. It was covered with flyers announcing everything from AA meetings to pleas for volunteers to an upcoming fundraising gala to benefit the mentally ill. The price of admission? Four hundred dollars a plate. It was being put on by the San Francisco Golf Club and Simon had seen the same flyer before—at work. The event would be attended by some of the city's wealthiest philanthropists and politicians, and Commander Stevens had mentioned that with all the bad PR the police had been receiving lately, the mayor wanted a few officers to sit at his table. Free of charge, of course, but Simon still wondered how many volunteers Stevens had managed to line up. Most cops Simon knew, Simon included, would hate putting on a monkey suit and rubbing elbows with a bunch of socialites, even if it was for a good cause. But because Simon wanted Stevens and the mayor on his side come hiring time, because he wanted that captain position, he'd volunteered anyway.

Still, something about seeing the fundraising flyer here—in a homeless shelter, for God's sake—bothered him. It didn't take a genius to figure out why. Hell, the residents who stayed here could probably live a year on the cost of one night's admission to the gala. Even worse, most of the money raised wouldn't go directly to places like this shelter, but toward providing a bunch of rich people a gourmet meal and a night's entertainment.

It just seemed wrong somehow. But, he reminded himself, it was a good cause and the homeless would benefit to some degree. It wouldn't make a bit of difference in the grand scheme of things, of course, but—

The door next to the bulletin board opened and a pretty Asian woman who looked to be in her mid-twenties stepped out. Wearing a skirt and an ivory blazer, she looked as overdressed in these surroundings as Simon did in his slacks, button-down shirt and suit jacket. She smiled, nodded at Simon, then walked away.

The receptionist he'd spoken to earlier poked her head out of the office. "She's ready to see you, Detective." She beckoned him in and Simon put thoughts of the fundraising gala out of his mind. He walked into the receptionist's office, which served as an intake room for those wishing to stay at the shelter. In the corner, a silver-haired man in a pale blue polo shirt watched as a younger man, dressed more casually in jeans and a graphic T-shirt, spoke to a stooped-over woman of indeterminate age and swimming in a tattered, faded sweater. The man in the polo shirt looked familiar, but Simon couldn't place him before the receptionist drew him to another closed door, knocked, opened it for Simon and waved him inside.

Despite the shabby walls and chipped trim, the space seemed homey, softly lit. He'd noticed earlier, while sitting in the foyer, that the scarred vinyl floor appeared well kept, and no cobwebs or dust bunnies were in sight. Indoor plants covered most surfaces. To those without one, this place must feel like a home, even if it was just a temporary one. But to Cann, this would never be home again.

Seated at a cluttered desk sat a woman, probably early fifties, with salt-and-pepper hair and glasses. Pictures of kids sat haphazardly with files on the desk and a diploma from Harvard hung on the wall. The shelter director. Probably some trust-fund baby do-gooder, he thought, then mentally winced.

It was exactly what he'd thought about Lana when he'd first met her.

Only the do-gooder part had been accurate.

After a moment, the woman looked up and gave him a tired smile.

"Ms. Scott?" he confirmed.

"Please call me Elaina. What can I do for you, Detective?" she asked.

"I'm Special Agent Simon Granger, but the title of Detective works, too. I'm with the Department of Justice, and I'm here about Mr. Louis Cann. I understand he stayed here this past month?" At her silent invitation, he sat in the chair next to her desk.

"Yes, but I already gave the local police a statement, and the officers interviewed the residents who were staying here at the time. They all had alibis at the time of the murder, as did my entire staff. Furthermore, none of us had seen Mr. Cann that day or had information about who might have attacked him. Given that, I'm curious why you're here. And why DOJ is involved in the murder of a homeless man."

"I'm afraid I can't talk details, but rest assured I'm trying to find the person or persons responsible. As you indicated, the residents that happened to be here for questioning have been cleared. There's no evidence that any of them had a vendetta against Louis Cann. But a lot of people come in and out of this shelter. I'm wondering how often Cann stayed here in the past year. If he had run-ins with past residents. A grudge can last quite a long time. Maybe you'd be willing to give me your roster from the past few months along with the registration documents of those occupants? It'll increase the scope of our investigation. Give us more to look into."

Scott picked up a pen and tapped it against the surface of her desk. "You mean it'll give you more water to cast your net into. Sounds like a fishing expedition, Detective."

That may be, Simon thought, but at least he was willing to fish. The news was plastered with accusations that the police didn't care about the homeless or, more specifically, the mentally ill, yet here he was, doing his best to find Cann's killer.

But he was also inferring that another homeless

person might be the murderer, he realized. Suspecting she might take offense to that—as unwarranted as that offense might be—he said, "Look, the roster would help. But I'm not limiting my investigation to past residents. I also plan to talk to park employees and past employees of this shelter who might have associated with Cann."

Jesus, he thought. That probably sounded even worse to her. Like he was accusing her previous co-workers of murder. But so what? Investigative work was about following every lead, regardless of whose feelings might get hurt in the process. Basic civility was one thing, but he couldn't worry that his questions would be taken the wrong way. That kind of political tiptoeing would be more important when he was back in management, but right now, he had to keep his mind focused on what was best for the investigation. "Listen," he began, but Scott shook her head.

"I'm sorry, but unless you have a subpoena, I'm afraid I can't give you a roster or documentation on the shelter's residents. Unless the resident signs a release, those records are confidential. And as I'm sure you can guess, no one signs a release."

Right, Simon thought, then tried again. "I apologize if my requests seem clumsy, but I'm trying to find a killer and that means potentially keeping your past and future residents out of harm's way. Doesn't that count for something?"

"Of course it does, but—"

"Besides," Simon continued, "we both know that under the law, confidentiality is waived in certain circumstances."

"Yes, I do know that. But this isn't a situation where

a client is threatening suicide, has threatened to harm a third party or where child abuse has been disclosed. Now, I'm sorry, but I really can't see how I can be of more help. And before you go hunting down that subpoena, I will say any information I'd have on Mr. Cann would be minimal. Dare I say even useless to you? But do what you feel you need to. Most of the residents the police talked to have already moved on, but I believe there are one or two left who knew Mr. Cann. You're obviously free to inquire whether any of them is willing to talk with you."

Simon's mind automatically rebelled at that suggestion. "Given the statements I've already reviewed, and unless they've suddenly stopped drinking, taking drugs or hallucinating, the chances of me getting anything useful from them isn't exactly high, now is it?"

Elaina Scott's brow furrowed but she said nothing.

"I don't mean to be insulting, but I'm trying to call things the way I see them. You know as well as I do that your…*residents*…often don't make the most reliable of witnesses. Most of them are…" He hesitated, trying to be polite, but Scott *tsk*ed anyway.

"Crazy? Pathetic?" she guessed.

Simon shrugged. "Mentally challenged," he said.

"That's correct. But mental challenges don't make them pariahs or murderers, Detective."

"But it does make them extremely inaccurate reporters," Simon said. He stood. "And the truth is, I can't solve Mr. Cann's murder without more than I have now. If I'm fishing in the dark, it's because I have to. In a murder investigation, we often rely on people who were close, either emotionally or physically, to the victim, and that includes people the murder victims lived with."

"Does it also include cops who should have been protecting the murder victim rather than killing him? Or are they subject to some kind of immunity?"

Her loaded comment surprised him, but he was careful not to let it show on his face. He simply stared at the woman and she eventually smiled, but it was a smile hardened by suspicion and experience.

"I work on the streets, Detective. I hear plenty. Mr. Cann's murder is still a topic of conversation around here. I've heard the rumors that a cop has been implicated. Yet here you are, focusing your attention on residents of this shelter. On people who've worked here."

"Because I'm looking to find the truth. No matter what that truth is. You can bet I take accusations of a cop's involvement in Louis Cann's murder very seriously. And yes, despite what I said about inaccurate reporters, I'd like to speak to your current residents about Mr. Cann if they're willing to speak with me, whether they were interviewed by SFPD before or not. Before I do that, however, do *you* know anything that can help me?"

She appeared startled by the way he'd turned the tables on her. "Like what?"

"I don't know. Something. *Anything* that will give me more insight into who Mr. Cann was. Whom he associated with."

"He was a loner, Detective. He kept to himself. That's how he preferred it."

"Right." Simon swiped his hands over his face, then sighed. "Too bad. It's a little difficult to find out who murdered a man who apparently never associated

with anyone else." Simon remembered Cann's Semper
Fi tattoo and again wondered what had brought the
man to the point where he'd been living on the streets.
"Funny how Mr. Cann managed to spend four years
in the military surrounded by people only to get out
and, by everyone's account, never talk to another living soul again."

"That's not uncommon for a man who served in
battle, Detective."

"What do you mean? How did a former marine come
to be in a homeless shelter, Ms. Scott?"

She visibly hesitated. But after assessing Simon for
a minute, she seemed to come to a decision. She sat
forward. "I'm not a medical doctor. I'm afraid you just
missed her. She left my office before you came in.
But my best guess? You've heard of post-traumatic
stress disorder?" When he tipped his head, she continued. "We have many former military personnel come
through here, Detective. The local clinics can't recruit
volunteers to provide counseling fast enough. PTSD
is a severe illness and is cropping up more and more
among our returning military. It affects some of these
young men and women so severely they can no longer function in society. I suspect if you go through
Mr. Cann's military records, you'll find a diagnosis
of PTSD."

"I've asked for those records, but getting that kind
of thing isn't easy, especially when that person is already dead. Next of kin tends to fight us on exposing
skeletons they'd rather keep buried. Too bad Cann's
family didn't do more to help him while he was alive."

Scott just smiled sadly and shook her head. "It's not
that simple, Detective. I wish it were. Truth is, many

homeless people have loving families who've tried to make a difference and simply can't."

Maybe, Simon thought. He'd certainly heard that line before. But he couldn't help thinking that if someone *he* cared about suddenly became homeless, he would make damn sure he didn't stay that way. "The doctor who was here before me. She's a psychiatrist?"

Scott shook her head. "A family practitioner that minored in psychology. But she just started pro bono volunteer work at a mental health crisis clinic. She stopped by to introduce herself to me and put up a flyer."

"Right. Another flyer," Simon murmured. "Any chance Cann saw her? Or any other counselor that you know of?"

"No. Like I said, this is the first time I've seen her. And Mr. Cann never mentioned seeing a counselor or dropping in at a clinic." Scott sighed. "The truth is, I know almost next to nothing about Mr. Cann, Detective, and he didn't keep me appraised of his comings and goings. We provide food and shelter here when we can. In order to meet our requirements, our residents have to provide basic information and follow some rules designed to keep everyone safe. Other than that..." Scott shrugged.

Right. Other than that, he had exactly what he'd had before—a big fat zero. "Is there anything else you can tell me about Cann?"

"Just that he didn't deserve to die."

"I agree with you." When she just continued to look at him, he asked, "You don't believe me?"

"I believe you're a dedicated cop. You want to do your job and do it well. But you have obvious biases against the mentally ill. I sensed you withdraw even as I used the word *PTSD*. But it doesn't matter. I want the person who killed Mr. Cann found as much as you do. Probably even more so. I promise that if anyone does turn up with new information, we will contact you right away. Now, are you ready to see if any of our current residents will talk with you?"

He sighed.

Strike one.

More and more, he thought, this was a ball game he hated playing. But for now, at least, he *was* playing.

"Yes, Ms. Scott. I'd appreciate your assistance with that."

THE NEXT DAY, BACK AT SIG headquarters, Simon glowered at the man in front of him.

Liam "Mac" McKenzie, SIG's lead detective, stared back without flinching. "I see you're not thrilled with the idea, but my hands are tied. Elaina Scott was crystal clear in her opinion that you shouldn't be handling the Cann murder. She said your obvious dislike for the homeless, and in particular, the 'mentally challenged,' was quite apparent."

Damn her, Simon thought. When he'd interviewed the few Welcome Home residents who'd been willing to talk to him yesterday, the interactions had gone smoothly. They hadn't provided anything useful, but he'd been respectful and professional, just as he always tried to be. Scott must have still been pissed by the conversation they'd had in her office. Or maybe she just hadn't believed him when he'd said he took accusations of a cop's involvement in Cann's murder seriously. "Come on, Mac. Since when does a bullshit complaint like this warrant pulling me off of a case?"

"I never said you were off the case. I said I want you to get some help. With the case and…off of it. DeMarco will assist. You've both been handling some tough cases lately with no time off to speak of. Consider the partnership a chance for a well-earned break."

"And while DeMarco's assisting, my well-earned break is going to consist of spilling my guts to some stranger?"

Mac sighed. "It's called grief counseling. You need it."

"That's your opinion."

"As well as Commander Stevens's. Why do you think it was so obvious to Ms. Scott that you're uncomfortable with mental health issues? Anyone who has them and anyone who talks about them?"

"Not everything is about Lana, damn it."

"In this particular case, it is. It's about Lana. It's about you. Are you really surprised? We've been at you to get some help. There's a reason we're all worried about you."

"Like?"

"Like it's been over six months, yet you still leave the room if someone even mentions Lana's name."

Of course he did, Simon thought. Despite managing to visit her grave site the other day, hearing Lana's name immediately caused a flood of memories to swirl through his mind. The last time they'd made love. The last time they'd laughed together. And the last time they'd argued just before she'd died. Yeah, they had been broken up before she'd been killed, but it wasn't what he'd wanted. He'd still cared. Lana had still mattered. His insides felt like they were being squeezed in a vise, but he carefully kept his expression clear and his voice neutral.

"What's there to talk about, Mac? Lana and I dated for a while, and dealing with her death's been tough." He shrugged. "Life goes on."

"Who do you think you're talking to, man? Lana didn't just *die*. She was *murdered*. Violently. Yet you can't seem to acknowledge that, can you?"

He glanced away, shoving the ache rising from his chest back down where it belonged, to the deep, dark place behind his ribs. He narrowed his gaze on the paper-filled trash can two feet in front of him. "Dead's dead. What the hell difference does it make how she died? Elaina Scott's accusations aside, tell me one thing I've messed up on the job. If you can't, then I don't need to see a damn shrink."

"You haven't messed up. Not yet. But it's coming. This is just a preventative measure. You're not sleeping, Simon. You look like shit. And your grim reaper attitude has everyone ready to slit their wrists whenever they're in the office with you."

Fuck. The desire to kick the trash can grew almost overwhelming. "Who's complaining? Tyler? DeMarco? I saw the same shrink you guys did after Lana died and he cleared me for duty. The department has no right to impose mandatory therapy sessions."

Mac shook his head. "No one's complaining. Yes, you've been cleared for duty. And no, this counseling isn't mandatory. You won't lose your job if you don't see it through."

"No. But I'll be stymied. Relegated to having an 'assistant.' Or I'll work the less choice assignments.

Great. That's just great. Thanks for backing me up on this one, Mac."

"Damn it, just listen! You're hanging by a thread, Simon. You know it. We know it. And Commander Stevens knows it. No one's wanted to push you, but this is where that ends. You want this case? You want the other ones that are coming down the pipeline? The big ones? See a shrink for regular counseling or take some time off before deciding to do it, but either way…"

"Yeah," Simon growled. "Either way I'm gonna end up lying on some quack's couch trying to convince her I'm not too much of a basket case to do the job we do, when only a basket case would want the job in the first place."

Mac grinned. "You still have a sense of humor. Show the shrink that."

"I wasn't kidding. What we do is fucked up, Mac, and you know it. It's what makes Lana's *murder* just another day in the life."

"So why are you still here then?"

"I won't be. Not for long. It was a mistake coming back to SIG. I've known that for a while now. I was gonna wait before requesting a transfer, but this little dictate has just speeded my decision along."

"A transfer?"

"I want back in management."

"You tried management. You didn't like it."

"Maybe I didn't give it enough of a chance."

"I remember Lana telling you that. What? Now that she's dead, you feel guilty enough to do what she'd have wanted you to?"

Simon smiled tightly. "Nice try, Mac, but I don't feel guilty for her death. She put herself in a killer's sights, and then she walked right up to him. She was careless despite the warnings I gave her. I'm not blaming myself, and that's exactly what a shrink will tell you."

Mac nodded. "Then you have nothing to worry about. If you want a shot at another management position, you need to prove you're stable enough for it. That's going to mean another psych evaluation eventually anyway. Might as well get it done now."

Simon blew out a disgusted breath. "Might as well. It'll probably take a while to get scheduled—"

"I made an appointment for next week. See this for what it is, Simon. Stevens and I are doing you a favor."

"Yeah," Simon grunted. "Thanks heaps. So what do I do in the meantime?"

"You'll continue working the homeless murder case with DeMarco. Close it, see the shrink and you'll get considered for management. Hell, I'll even recommend your promotion myself. I'll do everything I can to make it happen for you, Simon. But you have to work with me."

Simon knew he didn't have a choice. If he wanted a shot at a promotion, hell, if he wanted to continue working—and he *needed* to continue working—he had to appease Mac and Stevens. Volunteering to attend some damn fundraiser wasn't going to be enough. Even solving Cann's murder might not be.

He didn't blame himself for Lana's death, but he sure as shit didn't want spare time on his hands.

Whether he blamed himself or not, spare time meant time to think about Lana. Time to think about how she'd cried and pleaded with her killer before she'd died. And time to wonder if some part of *her* had blamed Simon for failing to save her.

CHAPTER TWO

UNBELIEVABLE, DR. NINA WHITAKER thought as her boss, and she'd like to think her friend, continued to pace in front of her. *She just won't give up.* Karen was determined to pull Nina away from her geriatric dementia patients in order to deal with politics and policing issues. Never mind that those things had once been Nina's passion. They were in her past for a reason.

Almost three years ago, she'd sold her carriage house in Charleston, South Carolina, and moved across the country. Her goal had been to heal and start over, but in running from her past, she'd also been forced to leave behind one of her greatest accomplishments—convincing the Charleston law enforcement community to embrace greater mental health training and oversee the formation of a Mental Health Intervention Team. At one time in her life, Nina would have run with that success and continued to advocate the same kind of change in every city across the nation.

The death of her patient Beth Davenport had changed all that.

After Beth died, Nina had decided to leave crisis work, policy reform and decisions of life and death to others, and instead focus on a quieter though still worthwhile existence. Now, Karen wanted Nina's help convincing SFPD to adopt the same MHIT training model that Charleston had implemented. Unfortunately, she was no longer content with Nina acting as a source of information on the topic. She wanted Nina to rally for funds. To talk to the police. To act as the program's spokesperson.

She couldn't do it, Nina thought.

She wouldn't.

Stay strong. Don't give in.

But despite her inner pep talk, Nina could feel herself being swayed by Karen's words.

"Another homeless man's been hospitalized after resisting arrest. That's two this week. Both those men were mentally ill, and both times they didn't understand they were being arrested. It wasn't that they were resisting arrest—it's that they didn't understand reality. We can put a stop to it, Nina. What's it going to take before you're willing to get involved?"

Hell freezing over? The fact that it was a question, even in Nina's own mind, further signaled her weakening resolve, but she managed to shake her head. Karen was an expert manipulator, but Nina was a psychiatrist. While that didn't mean she was wholly immune to being manipulated, she had the advantage of knowing it was happening. Not only that, she was a realist. Give Karen an inch and soon Nina would find herself fully immersed in the trap she'd worked so hard to free herself from. "I'm sorry, Karen, but you'll have to be content with the help I've already given."

There. That was good. She sounded firm. In control.

But Dr. Karen Harper, the chief administrator for San Francisco Memorial Hospital's Mental Health Division, remained unconvinced. Like a predator scenting weakness in its prey, she moved closer. "Do you want

someone to die?" She paused, hands on her hips, looking down at Nina over the tops of her glasses, which
were a dark navy blue the exact shade of the top she
was wearing. "A transient? Maybe even a cop? Because it's happened before and it could happen again. It
will happen again. It's just a matter of time. I'm trying
to do everything I can to stop it, and with all the bad
publicity the police have had with the homeless lately,
this is as good a time as any to push. But in order to
make the police listen to me, I need your expertise on
this, Nina. Please."

Please.

The word wasn't normally in the hospital administrator's vocabulary. It just proved how desperate Karen
was for Nina's help and how passionately she believed
in the MHIT program. Obviously, Nina believed in it,
too. It could help the city's police reduce violent confrontations with not just the homeless, but all mentally
ill suspects. It could help save lives. But becoming immersed in that kind of advocacy again? It just wasn't
something Nina could afford.

Helping others without actually being responsible
for whether they lived or died. That's all she wanted.
That's why she'd left her home and chosen to work with
geriatric dementia patients in the first place. It wasn't
a job without its own pain. She genuinely liked her patients. She tried to help them through their suffering,
and eventually she grieved their passing. The fact remained, however, that when the end came, it usually
wasn't a surprise. She was prepared. What Karen was
asking of her came without that type of assurance, and
she wanted no part of it.

Nina knew herself. Her strengths, but most of all her weaknesses.

What Karen was asking would play into every single one. If she started trying to save lives again, she'd feel duty-bound to save them all, and her failure to do so would eat away at her. Reminding her of the other lives she'd failed to save.

Two lives in particular.

"We've talked for hours," Nina reminded her friend. "I've given you the information you need. The statistics. You're more than capable of educating police officials about Charleston's Mental Health Intervention Team program and the benefits the city has seen—"

"Not without the support of the program's creator and chief advocate. With these latest claims of police brutality, higher-ups from the SFPD have finally agreed to meet with me. However, I suspect it's just a political tactic to appease the press. They want to show the public the police aren't taking our concerns lightly. But no matter how much you've prepared me, I can't anticipate all the questions that will be asked. And I don't have first-hand knowledge of how the program was implemented. Having you by my side at these meetings will lend us credibility we just can't get otherwise."

She was right, but Nina told herself to stand firm. Nina was a treasure trove of information when it came to police interaction with the mentally ill, but she could help Karen without becoming personally involved. "I'm sorry, Karen. You knew when you hired me where I wanted to focus my efforts. If my services haven't been valuable to the hospital then—"

"I didn't say your work here isn't valuable, Nina.

And yes, you were very clear that you were no longer interested in public policy work. That you wanted to focus your practice in the geriatric department. But I thought…" She shook her head and blew out a breath. "I guess I thought you wouldn't be able to help yourself. The work you did in Charleston was so important."

"And it's work you'll implement here, too," Nina said softly. "It didn't happen overnight in Charleston, either. I'll continue to be a resource to you. But I don't want to be directly involved. It took over my life, Karen, and I'm just starting to get it back. This isn't the kind of thing you can just dip your toes into. It'll consume my time."

It'll consume me, she thought.

"All right. Thank you for hearing me out," Karen said. "Please…let me know if you change your mind."

It was only when Karen left Nina's office that Nina spotted the folders her boss had forgotten.

Or more likely, the ones Karen had deliberately left behind.

She could guess what was in them. Articles about recent confrontations between police and the homeless, most of who were mentally ill or challenged and therefore more prone to intense reactions if the particular responders didn't know how to deal with that person's condition. Too often police didn't understand what was happening in a schizophrenic's brain, or how mania could induce psychosis in someone with bipolar disorder. Threats only revved up those people's minds—made things worse, not better.

She told herself she wasn't going to fall for Karen's obvious ruse.

Less than thirty minutes later, she opened the folder

and scanned the papers inside. Each article had a common theme: that someone—suspect, civilian or police officer—had suffered personal injury or death because a confrontation with a mentally ill suspect had escalated when it probably hadn't needed to. Several articles also included statistics.

That people with severe mental illnesses were killed by police in justifiable homicides at a rate nearly four times greater than the general public.

That ten to fifteen percent of cases where law enforcement officers acted with deadly force could be considered premeditated suicides.

That people with mental illnesses killed law enforcement officers at a rate five point five times greater than the rest of the population.

The facts went on and on.

She'd seen thousands of articles just like these. It's what had spurred her to seek change in South Carolina—a task made far easier given she'd had her father's political influence behind her— and the positive effects of that change continued to bear fruit even today. San Francisco, while more liberal than most cities, still had to function with limited funds, which meant reluctance to provide training that appeared extra rather than essential. Police routinely received training on how to handle mentally ill suspects, but it was usually subpar, barely covering the basics. What if Karen was right and Nina could convince San Francisco officials to take them seriously and make positive changes as a result?

She closed her eyes as guilt prodded at her.

It was one thing to make a lifestyle and career choice, but something else entirely to stand by and do nothing when she had the ability to help society as a whole, and one particular community specifically. What harm could it really do to act as Karen's consultant, and talk to police about starting a Mental Health Intervention Team in San Francisco? If she could help even a handful of police officers truly understand that those experiencing a state of psychosis could be subdued without resorting to violence, didn't she have an ethical duty to do it? No, she wouldn't be able to help everyone, but helping even one person...

Someone like her former patient, Beth Davenport...

Or someone like her sister, Rachel...

Pain rippled through her. Oh, God, Rachel. She still missed her every hour of every day.

What would Rachel want her to do?

She withdrew her purse from the drawer of her desk and took out the small cloth rag doll that had been Rachel's. She knew what carrying it said about her. That it was an unhealthy attachment brought on by lingering guilt.

A crutch.

A way to punish herself.

It didn't matter. The doll was the last tangible connection she had to her sister. She wasn't giving it up.

With a sigh, she put the doll back in her purse, stowed the purse in the drawer, picked up her phone and called Karen. "A phone call," she said when the other woman answered. "Maybe a meeting or two. But that's all I'm committing to. And you owe me drinks when this is over."

"I'll take it. Thank you, Nina. You won't regret this. Drinks are on me—I promise."

Nina hung up. But even as she did, she had the unsettling feeling she'd soon be regretting a lot of things.

CHAPTER THREE

LESTER DAVENPORT HAD made many mistakes in his life. He hadn't taken school seriously. He'd taken alcohol far too seriously. And he'd been a terrible husband. So terrible that his wife had ultimately left him, just as he'd always known she would, then up and died anyway, leaving him to deal with his daughter's grief as well as his own.

His biggest mistake, however, had been entrusting his daughter—his sweet little Beth—to the care of the Charleston mental health system. He'd known his daughter had deserved better. Not a county hospital, but the best that money could buy. He should have done whatever it took to get her out of there.

Only he hadn't had that kind of money. And his daughter had suffered because of it.

Now, as Lester imagined that suffering—the kind of pain his daughter must have been feeling to have done what she had—he sobbed so loudly the sound hurt his ears. Hands shaking, he reached for the box of cards he'd bought at the grocery store. He picked one at random—they all sported puppies, so it didn't matter—and began to write.

Beth had loved puppies.

Beth! his mind cried as he wrote.

His sweet Beth.

After a few days in the hospital, she'd started to get better. He'd seen it in her eyes. The last time he'd visited her, he'd talked about bringing her home. How wonderful it would be—just the two of them together again. This time, he'd promised, he wouldn't mess up. They were going to have a fresh start.

As he'd talked, Beth hadn't spoken a word.

She'd seemed to get worse after that.

He'd seen it. Why hadn't they?

They'd left her alone. His sweet daughter. Even after they'd known what she wanted—to end her pain, to leave this world—they'd left her alone with the means to accomplish her goal.

A damn teddy bear. One that Leo, her hoodlum of a boyfriend, had brought her. Lester had never liked the kid. He'd done his best to keep Beth away from him, but the hospital staff hadn't been smart enough to do the same thing. They'd taken the teddy bear away from Beth, but they hadn't thought to check Beth's mouth. That's where Beth had hidden the ribbon.

After Beth had died—no, after she'd killed herself with the ribbon that had been tied around the damn teddy bear's neck—Lester had wanted to kill Leo. He'd thought about it. Planned it. Had been this close to ending Leo's life.

But then he'd realized the kid couldn't really be blamed.

No, *she* was the one to blame.

Beth's doctor.

Nina Whitaker. The daughter of a wealthy politician who'd played at helping others when she hadn't known what the hell she was talking about.

She'd said Beth was going to be okay.

That she'd take care of her.

She'd lied.

Then she'd left.

She'd thought she could run and leave her mistakes behind her, right along with Beth's memory.

But she couldn't.

She wouldn't.

Every year, Lester made sure of it.

Every year, he sent her a card.

Every year, he reminded Nina Whitaker that Beth was dead—and that it was her fault.

CHAPTER FOUR

SEVERAL DAYS AFTER BEING told he had an appointment with a shrink, Simon pulled into San Francisco Memorial Hospital's parking lot. If he drove a little faster and slammed his car door a little harder than normal, so be it. Normally, he was cool as ice, unflappable and disciplined enough to work a case for hours, days, even months—whatever it took to get the job done. But he was here under protest and he was pissed and he didn't care who knew it.

Damn it, he had interviews in the Cann murder case to conduct. At least, he *should* be conducting them. Instead, he'd been forced to hand off a few of them to DeMarco just so Simon could spill his guts to some stranger. If his fellow SIG members had thought he was surly before, they'd better watch the hell out. Work was supposed to be his escape, but ever since his conversation with Mac, all he could think about was Lana.

Not good. He needed to burn off some of his anger and frustration before he met with Dr. Kyle Shepard or he might just find himself on a leave of absence from SIG before he was ready for it.

As he made his way to the hospital's main entrance, the sound of female laughter caught his attention. To his right, two women were getting into a convertible Bug. They smiled flirtatiously when they caught sight of him, but he felt no surge of attraction toward them; that worried him. They were young and pretty and he felt *nothing?* It was as if Lana's death had killed his ability to be attracted to another female.

Hell, who was he kidding? He hadn't been attracted to another woman well before Lana's death. And since they'd broken up before she'd died, it had been over eight months since he'd even had sex.

That couldn't be good. Simon was an extremely sexual man and like many cops, he relied on an active sex life to balance out the stress of his career. Before Lana had died, despite the fact she'd still been grieving her dead husband, Johnny Hudson, he'd been focused on her for close to two years. He could barely remember being attracted to a woman before her. After she'd died, well…romance was the last thing on his mind. It hadn't escaped his notice that of the SIG team members, he was the only one who was currently single or not getting any. Mac had his wife, Jase had Carrie and DeMarco was constantly hooking up with some new woman.

No wonder Mac and Commander Stevens were worried about him. He'd obviously been ignoring his baser needs too long.

Maybe when he was done talking to Dr. Shepard he'd go to McGill's Bar, a local cop hangout. Pickup joints and one-night stands weren't his style, but he could probably do with some physical relief. Sex with no emotional commitment. It wasn't pretty, but not much about his life was.

Without another thought for the females in the convertible, he continued forward. When he caught sight of another woman getting out of her car, however, his gut immediately clenched.

He froze. His first thought was…*she looks like Lana.*

His second thought was…*something's not right with her.*

His cop senses went on alert.

He knew immediately why she reminded him of Lana. She was blonde. Not just pretty. Gorgeous. Elegant. Like Lana, she was the kind of woman you couldn't help noticing.

So Simon noticed.

And this time when he was confronted with a good-looking woman, he felt an unmistakable stirring of attraction.

He studied her more closely. Her resemblance to Lana was only superficial. Her face was more angular, her features sharper and her eyes were almond-shaped, suggesting she had some exotic ancestry. Her body was also different. Where Lana had been slim and athletic, this woman's curves were more lush. Her hips wider. She looked tidy, pulled together in a silk blouse and tailored skirt.

Her car, on the other hand, was god-awful ugly. An old Ford station wagon in a faded eggplant color. The contrast between her beauty and the car's run-down junkyard condition didn't connect. That immediately made him edgy. He didn't like things that didn't make sense.

He told himself he was being ridiculous.

Driving a beat-up old car wasn't a crime. Maybe she spent her money on hair salons and fancy clothes rather than what she drove.

With a shake of his head, he walked until he was right next to her. Before he could pass her, she turned and brushed against him. Innocent as it was, the brief contact caused both of them to jerk back. She dropped her bag, spilling its contents on the ground.

"Sorry," she muttered. He crouched down to help her, frowning when he saw the small, crudely sewn rag doll, just about four inches tall, lying amid her keys, wallet and—

She stepped closer and crouched beside him. He couldn't help noticing the graceful sweep of her slender calves. To his utter surprise, his fingers itched to touch them. To determine for himself if they were as smooth as they looked. Disturbed, he jerked his gaze away and somehow ended up knocking heads with her.

She gasped.

"Shit," he muttered.

She raised a hand to briefly rub her temple. Her eyes were green. Soft and pale just like her creamy skin and her golden hair. "It's okay. I wasn't looking where I was going. I—"

Her gaze flickered to the ground. Abruptly her words cut off and her face turned bright red. Simon looked back down at the contents of her purse. He noticed something he hadn't seen before and felt heat spread through his body; not to his face but someplace farther south. The word *Sextuplets* blazed up at him.

Was that—?

She snatched up the DVD case and shoved it back into her purse, then threw in everything else before standing. He straightened far more slowly.

He swiped a hand across his face but obviously didn't do a good enough job of hiding his smile.

"Not a word," she said and started to walk away.

Her voice was like another punch in the gut. It was a bit gravelly. A rocker chick's voice inside a woman who looked like an angel. He fell in step beside her.

She didn't look at him. When they reached the front entrance and passed through the automatic sliding doors, she paused in front of the Information counter. He followed suit.

Her gaze met his and her chin tilted up. "A patient gave it to me. She's an older woman and she has a collection and I didn't want to hurt her feelings—"

He pressed his lips together and managed to keep a serious expression on his face. He nodded. "Right. She collects porn and thought for some reason you might be interested. I wonder what made her draw that conclusion?"

She narrowed her eyes, trying to look threatening but only managing to look adorable. The tendrils of attraction he'd been feeling exploded into something hot and wild. It took him by surprise, so much so that she'd already moved toward the lobby elevators before he noticed. He followed.

She frowned at seeing him standing next to her again.

"What?" he said. "We're in a public hospital and I have a doctor's appointment."

It had been a while since he'd met a woman who blushed so easily.

"Of course," she said.

"Are you one?"

"Am I one what?"

"A doctor?"

"Yes."

"Then you shouldn't be so embarrassed about getting caught with a skin flick in your bag. The human body and what it needs to survive is nothing new to you, right?"

She smiled tightly. "Right. Excuse me…"

She turned and walked away.

He cursed himself for driving her off. "Weren't you going to take the elevator?" he called.

"Yes, I *was*."

He watched her go with more than a little regret, but he was smiling when he got into the elevator. Too bad he couldn't have run into the doctor at McGill's. He'd have spotted her and he'd have done his best to bed her. Because despite his musings in the parking lot, he was definitely interested in having sex again.

And suddenly she was the only one he was interested in having it with.

NINA ACTUALLY FANNED herself as she took the stairs up to the sixth floor. Whew.

That was one handsome man. Not pretty-boy handsome, either.

Manly man handsome.

Manly man *sexy*.

And given the way he'd reacted to seeing the porn she'd had in her purse, he had a sense of humor, too, which merely made him more attractive.

She cringed at the memory of him seeing that DVD case, but at least it had distracted him from Rachel's rag doll. She'd noticed the brief surprise on his face when he'd glimpsed it and she'd once again wondered whether her inability to get rid of the doll represented a bigger problem than she'd thought. She didn't need an object to remember her sister, after all. Especially one that her sister had been cradling on the night she'd…

Swallowing hard, Nina shook her head. No. She wasn't going to deal with that particular memory right now. Especially not today. It was the third anniversary of Beth Davenport's death and Nina had no illusions about what was in store for her today. Last year, Beth's father, Lester Davenport, had proven how resourceful he was, once again tracking down her place of work and mailing her one of those hideous cards of his. Before the day was over, she'd probably get another one. Until then, she would damn well think about something else.

Someone else.

With determination, she thought about the man from the parking lot again.

He wasn't quick to smile, but when he did, the expression softened his intimidating, almost grim countenance into something mischievously boyish. It made her think of playing tickle-tag along the ocean shore or dancing the salsa at a hip city club or resting her head in his lap while she read a book in Golden Gate Park. In other words, it made her think of all the things she'd like to do with a partner, yet her life had become her work and she rarely dated, and she hadn't yet met a man she could picture herself doing all those things with. At least not before him…

Given he was a complete stranger, that was either pathetic or a sign that she was ready to explore dating again. It was all a matter of interpretation.

The question was which interpretation she was going to choose.

Having reached the sixth floor, Nina pulled open

the stairwell door and headed toward her office. And just like always, once she immersed herself in work, thoughts about what might be possible in any other aspect of her life faded away.

HIS LONG LIMBS SPRAWLED out in front of him, Simon tried to put the pretty doctor out of his mind and waited for his appointment with the shrink to start. As more and more time went by, he found himself thinking about her and wondering if he should track her down. Then what?

Despite that porn DVD in her purse, she didn't look like a woman into casual sex, which meant she probably *had* gotten it from one of her patients.

When he caught himself smiling, he shook his head. He had to focus here, not think about some intriguing woman and the equally intriguing contents of her purse.

Impatiently, he glanced at his watch. It was already twenty past the hour. Rising, he strode to the receptionist's window. She was another pretty blonde and she was talking to…

His eyebrows lifted in surprise.

The pretty doctor.

Simon waited as the women continued their chat, then cleared his throat.

They looked up. The blonde doctor's green eyes widened in recognition.

Simon nodded. "Hello again." Their gazes remained locked before he managed to turn his attention to the receptionist. "Do you know how much longer Dr. Shepard is going to be?" Simon asked.

"It shouldn't be too much longer."

"Right."

He felt the gaze of the other woman on him and looked back at her. She smiled.

She had an incredible smile.

Attraction once again morphed into something else. Desire. Need.

He made up his mind to ask her out. Maybe she wasn't into casual sex, but he could always get lucky, right?

Then he noticed the badge now hanging around her neck.

Nina Whitaker, MD, PhD. Psychiatry, Psychology.

A psychiatrist.

Just like Lana. Only Nina Whitaker was a twofer. An MD *and* a PhD.

She'd truly made it her life's work to help the mentally ill.

Air left his lungs and the damned pain wormed its way upward again. Silencing a swearword, he turned away without returning her smile.

AS THE TALL, BROODING man stalked away from the receptionist's window, Nina reached past Sandy to close the sliding Plexiglas window.

"God, isn't he gorgeous?" the receptionist gushed.

That, Nina thought, is an understatement. For the second time that day, the brief glimpse of the man had gotten her motor running. "Gorgeous, sure, but he also has a major chip on his shoulder." Her heart had nearly exploded out of her chest at seeing him again, but despite the renewed spark of interest in his eyes, she hadn't missed how his expression had grown disdainful once he'd seen her name tag. "What's his name?"

"Simon Granger. Isn't that just hunky?"

The strong name fit him, she thought. "Who's he here to see?"

"Dr. Shepard."

Ah. That made sense. Kyle worked primarily with military and law enforcement. And since Simon's hair was on the longer side, that meant… Nina nodded. "He looks like a cop."

"Yep. You wanna talk to him? Who knows? Maybe he could be of service." She grinned. "Seriously. Didn't you say your meetings with the police chief had stalled?"

More like hit a brick wall, Nina thought. Karen had been wrong. Even given Nina's experience with establishing the MHIT program in Charleston, she was having little luck convincing San Francisco officials that spending time and money to train officers on advanced strategies to deal with the mentally ill would be worth it in the long run. The police chief hadn't disputed the training could make a difference for the suspects, but thought it would likely jeopardize his men more than it would help them.

"My men are trained to use force only when it's absolutely necessary to protect themselves or others. They don't need to be second-guessing themselves by considering the mental health complexities of the suspect in question. That's something that becomes relevant once the suspect has been contained and any threat he poses diminished. In the moment, it doesn't matter why someone's acting dangerous, only that he is," he'd said.

Nina had heard the same argument again and again. And in all fairness, it had some validity. But protecting police was only one aspect to be considered. Those same cops had to make distinctions between the suspects they apprehended all the time. They handled men and women and children differently. They approached things differently if someone was elderly, had an established record, or had never been in trouble with the law a day in his life. They considered how someone was dressed, how they walked, how they talked. An understanding of someone's mental condition was another aspect that should be considered when entering a situation, and glossing over it was the easy answer.

Bottom line, however, was most cops hated the idea of coddling a criminal and were resistant to seeing one in a compassionate light. Maybe it was because it made it harder for them to do their job. But that was no excuse for ignorance.

She looked once more at the gorgeous guy in the waiting room. "Too bad I don't do cops," she murmured only half-jokingly.

Sandy laughed. "You don't do anyone, Nina. Good thing I do."

Smiling, Nina straightened. She'd leave the flirting to the receptionist. As sexy as Simon Granger was, he was still a cop. One who obviously disdained what she did for a living. "I'll be on the geriatric floor."

"Ms. Horowitz still there?"

Nina pictured the elderly woman who'd gifted her with the DVD Simon Granger had seen and who had a penchant for Old Hollywood lingerie, even when she was hospitalized. "For a little while longer, I think. Then the family will likely call hospice."

"It's hard to imagine a life as vibrant as hers coming to an end."

Nina frowned. She tried, she really tried to hold

back the dual images, the first of her sister as she lay in her coffin, and the second of a teenage girl with a pink ribbon tied around her neck, but it was impossible. It had been exactly three years since Beth Davenport had hung herself, but Nina knew no amount of time would make her forget the horror of finding her body.

Just like it wouldn't erase the horror of finding her sister's.

She swallowed hard, speaking only when she was sure her voice would be steady. "The end of any life is hard to imagine. But there are far worse ways to go. Ms. Horowitz will be surrounded by people who love her when her time comes. That's really all any of us can ask."

"I'd rather fall asleep and never wake up without ever having to deal with a deteriorating body or mind."

"Most dementia patients aren't aware of the infliction," Nina reminded her.

"But we are. And we pity them. That's enough. I never want to be pitied."

Nor do I, Nina thought. *But sometimes circumstances just lend themselves toward pity.*

Without her permission, her gaze once again wandered to the big man now pacing in the waiting room. The set of his shoulders and his energy-driven stride told her he wouldn't want to be pitied. Would likely deplore such sentiments more than most. Yet she'd seen the shadows in his eyes. Knew he grieved, if not another person, then some loss of self that had happened a long time ago. Her instinctive desire to soothe and heal him wasn't surprising, but the renewed surge of chemical attraction was. Her mind wanted to get to know Simon Granger better, but so did her body. Nina turned back to Sandy, who was also staring at the man. "I'm heading back to my office. Want me to see what's keeping Kyle so you can stay and enjoy the view?"

Sandy didn't take her gaze off him. "You don't mind? I'll be your slave for life."

Nina laughed. Before she left, she couldn't resist one last glance at him. He looked up, and through the Plexiglas partition, his gaze immediately collided with hers. For tense seconds, they stared at one another. Then he glanced away, leaving her to simultaneously savor and curse the sizzle of desire that once again coursed through her.

She obviously needed to get out more. Find someone fun, have herself a little frolic and stop drooling over the patients. Problem was, she rarely socialized so finding someone fun to frolic with was a little difficult.

As she approached Kyle's office, an athletic young man with curly blond hair was just leaving. He wore a short-sleeved T-shirt that revealed brilliantly colored tattoo sleeves. A particularly gruesome tattoo caught Nina's attention—a skull with a unicorn in its mouth. Philosophical statement? Evidence of personal frustration over bipolar tendencies? Or both?

She almost rolled her eyes at her mental questioning.

Sometimes a tattoo was just a tattoo.

The man was saying goodbye to Kyle. "I'll check out the clinic you told me about. Thanks, Dr. Shepard," he said before turning and catching sight of Nina. He smiled before walking away.

In spite of his disturbing tattoo, he seemed…carefree. Happy.

Which was good, of course, but a little unusual for one of Kyle's patients. Kyle specialized in PTSD, and his clients typically had the same brooding quality as the man pacing restlessly in the waiting room.

Kyle stepped into the hallway. "How's it going, Nina?"

"Good. Sandy sent me to check on you. Your next patient's getting a little restless."

He nodded. "Thanks."

When Nina got to her own office, she noted that her in-box was still empty and checked her watch. Looked like she and the police officer in the waiting room were both being a little impatient. If she'd read him accurately, he was obviously waiting to be seen by a doctor he had no respect for. Not uncommon with cops who were reluctant to show weakness or reach out for help, even though doing so was key to their continuing ability to do their jobs.

And she? She was waiting for her annual present from Lester Davenport, of course. The deliberate reminder of his daughter's death and the part Nina had played in it.

Nina didn't need the reminder. She knew the significance of today's date.

And she blamed herself enough as it was.

Still, ten minutes later, when the mail finally arrived, Nina's hands were shaking. When she saw the envelope with the familiar handwriting on it, her breath stuttered in her chest.

And when she opened up the envelope and withdrew the card inside, she closed her eyes and thought, *No.* She obviously hadn't blamed herself enough. Like always, Davenport's note caused pain to run through her like a thousand razor blades, but this time, there was something else added to the mix.

Fear.

Because Beth's father wasn't content with angry words anymore. This time, he'd included threats.

Several of them.

But all of them amounted to the same thing.

His daughter was dead.

And he wanted Nina dead, too.

CHAPTER FIVE

SIMON FIGURED DR. KYLE Shepard was a middle-aged man's version of Little Orphan Annie. It wasn't a particularly attractive combination, but it probably lulled most people into a false sense of security. They'd be too distracted by the doc's garish red hair to pay any attention to how he was trying to siphon out their most private thoughts.

Not Simon.

His guard was up and would stay that way. He wasn't taking any chances when it came to his job, but he didn't need some stranger prying around in his head, either.

"So, Detective Granger, you're here because you're a trauma survivor."

It wasn't a question, but given the way the doctor paused, he clearly expected Simon to respond.

"I'm here because my superiors ordered me to be," he drawled.

"And how do you feel about that?"

He smirked. He couldn't help it. Why the hell did shrinks always lead with that damn question? What the hell difference did it make how he *felt* about a situation he couldn't change? "I don't feel anything about it. I'm here. I'll cooperate. All I want is to get back to work."

"All you want? But that isn't true, is it? You want Lana Hudson to be alive, don't you?"

Simon stared at the redhead, thinking he'd underestimated him. Shepard had gone in for the kill mighty fast. Faster than Simon had expected. "What I want and what is possible are two different things. What I want is irrelevant."

Dr. Shepard nodded. "With respect to Lana, or with respect to your life in general?"

The temper that had been simmering below the surface suddenly flashed. Simon leaned forward in his chair. "Am I here for full psychoanalysis? Because, frankly, I thought I was here for grief counseling given a serial killer tortured and killed my girlfriend."

"Ex-girlfriend," Dr. Shepard said mildly. "Wasn't she?"

Simon sat back. "She's dead. Can't get any more 'ex' than that."

"Why had you two broken up?"

He'd known that question was coming, and he didn't pull any punches or try to hide the ball. He knew perfectly well why Lana had broken up with him and he'd made his decisions knowing it would happen. "She didn't like the fact I'd gone back to work the streets after taking a management position. She didn't want to be involved with someone with a death wish, not when she'd already lost her husband to the war."

"Do you have a death wish?"

He gazed steadily at the doctor. "I'm not afraid of death."

"That's not what I asked."

Simon said precisely, "I don't wish to be dead."

"Have you ever? As a teenager? When you were in the military?"

Dr. Shepard stared at him with an intensity that, if Simon didn't know better, implied he knew his deepest, darkest secrets. Instinctively, he slammed every defensive wall he possessed in place. "No."

"Then what do you wish for?"

He forgot about why he was there—to safeguard his job—and blurted out the first thing that came to mind. "Right now, I'm wishing this appointment was over and I was back at work."

Several tense seconds of silence followed his response. Great, Simon thought. Now he'd gone and pissed the guy off. But damn it, he didn't want to be here. He shouldn't have to be. He—

"Work is important to you. Why?"

Simon pinched the bridge of his nose. Why was this guy asking questions when the answers were so damn obvious? But fine, Simon thought. The sooner he gave the doc the answers he wanted, the sooner he could get out of here. "I make a difference there. I like to think I keep the bad guys on their toes. I delay them a bit."

"Delay but not stop them completely?"

"No one can stop them. Not all of them."

"Can they be healed? Some of them?"

Dr. Shepard's question automatically made Simon think of the doctor.

Nina Whitaker.

She'd reminded him of Lana in more ways than her cool blond looks. She'd had that same watchful gaze, intense yet filled with compassion, as if she could see every scar that lay underneath his skin and she wanted to kiss them all. Make them better. The idea of her kissing him anywhere made him shift in his seat and wrestle with the attraction that had tried to pull him closer even as he'd mentally sneered at her chosen profession. He ran a hand through his hair, painfully aware that he hadn't answered Dr. Shepard's question. And that he didn't want to. "Why are you asking me that?"

"Lana was a psychiatrist. Some might say the reason her killer got close was because she was trying to help him. What did you think about that?"

He remembered the fight they'd had the last time he'd seen her. He'd been scared for her. He'd wanted to protect her. But she hadn't wanted that. She'd wanted to heal a criminal more than she'd wanted to protect herself. Or him. So when he answered, he answered truthfully. "I thought she was a fool."

"One that deserved to die?"

The feeling of denial was emphatic and swift. "I didn't say that."

"No, you didn't. But do you believe it?"

Did he? The least constructive emotion Simon felt when he thought about the way Lana had died was anger. At the man who'd killed her. And, like he'd felt at her grave site, even anger at her for placing herself in a killer's sights. But he didn't *blame* her. He knew she'd been doing what she felt she had to. "No. I don't."

Dr. Shepard nodded. "Okay, let's talk about the incident that led to her death. What do you know about it?"

For the remainder of the hour, they discussed how Simon's fellow SIG detectives, Carrie Ward and Jase Tyler, had been working a case trying to track down a serial killer dubbed The Embalmer. How Carrie and Lana had gone on national television and tried goading the killer into revealing himself. Unfortunately, they'd

been more successful than they could have ever anticipated. The killer had waited outside the police department and concocted a good enough story that Lana had
gone with him of her own free will. And then she'd
been killed—*murdered*—just as violently as Mac had
indicated earlier.

After rehashing the facts and discussing Simon's
"feelings" about them over and over again, Dr. Shepard
nodded. "Thank you. Our session is done. If you'd like
to reschedule, I look forward to talking to you next
week."

Simon stood. Managed to choke out, "Thanks."
Without waiting to see if the doctor extended his hand,
Simon turned and left.

He was almost to the hospital lobby when his cell
phone rang. He scowled when he saw the number of
the incoming caller on the screen.

"Checking up on me, Mac?"

"Are you still at the hospital?" Mac's voice was
strained. Urgent.

"Yeah. What's up?"

"SFPD just brought a 5150 into the E.R. There's reason to believe he kidnapped a young girl. If possible,
take Dr. Shepard to the E.R. with you. See what he can
get out of the guy as he's evaluating him."

Shit, Simon thought, replaying how rudely he'd just
walked out of the man's office. "Wish I'd known we
needed his help before I talked to him."

"Made that good of an impression, huh?"

"I cooperated," he mumbled. "Sort of."

"Just snag the doc and meet Officer Dan Rieger in
the E.R."

"On my way."

He backtracked to Dr. Shepard's office. He was able to get into the waiting room, but the door leading to the back offices was locked. The receptionist was gone, but she'd left the Plexiglas divider open. He stuck his head in and called out, "Dr. Shepard?" Nothing. "Is anyone here?"

He heard a noise in one of the back offices followed by footsteps. A woman stepped into view.

It was the doctor he'd rudely dismissed earlier. Nina Whitaker. The one that, despite himself, he'd imagined naked and lying in his arms.

Hell, he was imagining her naked right now.

"Can I help you?" she asked.

"I need a doc to come into the E.R. with me. There's a 5150 about to arrive who might know where a kidnapped young girl is."

She hesitated. "Let me find out who the on-call doc is." A minute later, she was back. "It might take a while, but someone will meet you down there."

Damn it, they didn't have time to wait. That was obvious by Mac's call. By the fact he'd wanted Simon to drag Dr. Shepard to the E.R. "This is a critical situation. You can do it, can't you?"

She hesitated. "Yes, but—"

Despite his misgivings, despite the fact he wanted to stay as far away from her as possible, it couldn't be helped. Clenching his jaw, he motioned for her to join him. "Let's go."

CHAPTER SIX

SIMON GRANGER GUIDED her toward the E.R. with a big hand cupped under her elbow. Even as she managed to keep up with his long strides, Nina tried to get through to him. "Wait a second. You're saying you want me to get information from someone exhibiting a psychotic break?"

"If that's the same thing as someone acting crazy, then yes."

She glared at him. "And you think that's easy to do?"

"Doesn't matter if it's easy or not. He supposedly kidnapped a little girl who might need medical help. We have to find out where she is. If you don't get the information out of him, then I will."

She managed to pull away and skid to a stop. The detective faced her with his hands on his hips.

"And just what does that mean?" she asked. "That you'll beat the information out of him?"

"I didn't say that. But I've been trained in interrogation techniques. If your questions don't give us the answers we need—"

"Your 'techniques' will likely escalate the situation even more."

His expression remained impassive. "Then let's hope I don't have to use them."

He turned and strode away, leaving her to follow.

As they entered the E.R., he went up to the receptionist and showed her his badge. "There should be a patrol officer here with a 5150. Officer Dan Rieger."

"Yes," the woman said, her gaze finding Nina's, who nodded. "They've already been put in a room. I'll show you to him."

She escorted them past several exam rooms to where a uniformed patrol officer was pacing in front of an open door.

"Officer Rieger? Special Agent Simon Granger. Is your perp inside?"

The man nodded. "They're taking some blood tests. He's in restraints and they gave him a shot to calm him down. We picked him up for shoplifting, but he got all agitated. Started saying we were part of the alien invasion. That he wouldn't tell us where the little girl he was protecting is."

"Are you certain he has a young girl and isn't simply delusional?" Nina asked.

"He had a young girl's jacket. And an inhaler. One of those over-the-counter kinds, so it doesn't have a prescription on it. But he said the girl was having trouble breathing and had run out of her medicine. That's what he was stealing. I gotta go with my gut on this one and say he's got some girl hidden somewhere. And if she's out of her asthma medication, we're running out of time."

Simon turned to Nina.

She nodded. "Let me see what I can do." She stepped inside the room and nodded to the nurse who was labeling a vial of blood. On a gurney lay a young man, legs and wrists restrained by leather straps, a dazed expression on his face. Possible catatonia or maybe too heavy a dose of the antipsychotic. She just hoped he was lucid enough to discuss the girl he'd taken and where they'd find her. She stepped inside and tried shutting the door.

She gasped when Granger held it open.

"I'm coming with you."

She glared at him. "No. You are not. I'll evaluate the patient and report back in a minute."

"But—"

"Let go of the door right now, Detective, or I'll have no choice but to call security and have you thrown out."

Their gazes held and clashed for several seconds and she had to force herself not to look away from the pure fury in his. Slowly, however, he released his grip on the door and stepped back. With an imperceptible sigh of relief, Nina shut the door, blocking out his scowling face.

"She a psychiatrist?" Officer Rieger asked Simon.

"Yeah." Simon stared at the door through which she'd disappeared.

"I hope she's a good one."

Despite the way she'd managed to get under his skin, Simon had a feeling she was better than good. The problem was, she could be the very best and he still wouldn't like it. If she could help them get the information they needed, great, but he knew what would happen either way. She'd already referred to their perp as a "patient." As soon as she came back out, she'd start talking about helping the guy. Trying to help the man who'd kidnapped a little girl and probably had done God knows what to her already. And when that happened, he wasn't sure he'd be able to—

The door opened and Nina stepped out.

"Can we go in and see him now?" Simon asked.

She shook her head. "That's not a good idea."

"Why?"

"Because he's indeed having a psychotic break. He doesn't know where he is but he feels threatened. The doctor gave him Haloperidol, a quick-acting antipsychotic, but he's still having delusional thoughts. Right now, he needs to get his brain activity settled. He's operating in a vastly different reality than we are."

"So what are you going to do?" Simon growled. "Light incense and sing Kumbaya?"

She narrowed her eyes in warning. To Simon, sass and intelligence had always been an alluring addition to physical beauty. This woman had all three in spades. Too bad they had a life-or-death situation at hand. If the situation was different, and despite what she did for a living, he might be up for exploring what made Nina tick.

"If that's what it takes," she said. "You want the information, don't you? The only chance I have of getting it is to establish trust with him and make him feel safe. And the only way I'm going to be able to do that is if I know he's actually going to *be* safe."

"Meaning what?"

"He looks like he's been roughed up." She glanced pointedly over his shoulder at Officer Rieger.

Simon didn't jump to any conclusions. He knew better than most how dangerous a cop's job was. It was easy to judge a cop's actions once danger had passed, but unless you'd been in his shoes… "I don't know anything about that," he said softly.

"No, but he does."

"He resisted arrest," Officer Rieger clipped out.

Nina glared at the young officer. "He thinks we're all aliens who want to suck out his brain. Of course he resisted."

"You're bartering with me for promises of leniency?" Simon asked, his expression and tone incredulous. And pissed. "When what I'm asking for is information to help save a little girl?"

She returned her gaze to his. Bit her lip as if contemplating his words, then shook her head. "Wanting a man to be treated with basic respect is not the same thing as asking for leniency. I'll do everything I can to get you the information. But you involved me, which means Mr. Callahan is now my patient, and that means I'll be doing whatever is necessary to make sure he's treated with dignity."

"Mr. Callahan, huh? Yes, let's think about his needs instead of the little girl he kidnapped. At least you've got your priorities straight, Doc," Simon sneered.

"I need to go in now. But this is going to take a while. And I can't promise anything."

"Nothing but taking good care of your patient, you mean?"

Her back stiffened and she paused with her hand on the door, but she didn't turn back around. Instead, she said softly, "I'm well aware of what's at stake, Detective. Don't think for a minute that I'm not." She stepped back into the room and shut the door with a decisive click.

An hour later, Simon was about to barrel into the examination room when Nina finally stepped out. She looked flushed, her expression pinched, but she immediately locked gazes with him. "I have something. I can't know for sure, but..."

"What is it?"

"He grew up in a house in Pacifica. 180 West 27th Street. He said it's the place he always felt safe. Safe to be who he truly is. Safe from the aliens."

Without taking his gaze off her, he snapped, "Rieger?"

"Yes, sir."

"Let's go." To Nina, he said, "Keep talking to him." He handed her a card. "Here's my cell. If he says anything to make you think we're headed in the wrong direction, call me."

"I will. Good luck. I hope you find her."

"I hope so, too."

They found the girl in the basement of Michael Callahan's family home. She'd been tied up and was dehydrated, her skin ice-cold and turning blue. Her pulse was thready and her breathing labored. She was exhibiting signs of exposure, shock and an asthmatic attack. Simon carried her out just as an ambulance pulled up in front.

"We've got it from here, sir."

As he stared at the girl, Simon thought of Lana. Despite what he'd told Mac earlier, he had the sudden thought that he'd failed her. Had he failed this girl, too? Waited too long to get to her? Should he have muscled his way into that examination room and beaten the location out of her abductor?

"Sir, please. Give her to me."

Simon reluctantly gave the girl to the medic.

He followed the ambulance to the nearby hospital.

And he stayed until the doctors told him the little girl would be okay.

CHAPTER SEVEN

A WEEK AFTER THEY'D found Rebecca Hyatt, the little girl Michael Callahan had kidnapped, Simon sat at his desk in SIG's detective pit. He finished typing up his report on the Cann murder, stuck it in the folder and filed it along with the other "as-of-yet unsolved" crimes that would be occasionally looked at but otherwise relegated to the back burner. Between Simon and DeMarco, they'd followed every lead and interviewed everyone they could think of, patrol cops included, but had come up empty. Add the fact that their only witness, Rita Taylor, had recanted her statement about Cann's killer being a cop—she now insisted that what she'd thought was a police uniform might actually have been that of a city bus driver or air-conditioning repairman—and it was time to move on to the next case. First, however, he had to do the final report on the Michael Callahan incident.

In front of him laid the daily newspaper from the day after the event. He'd seen the article when it had come out. He'd kept a copy to add to the file. Now, he skimmed the article again and cursed.

Doc Finds Child but Public Suspicion of Police Continues

The article was chock-full of information. First, it detailed several recent incidents between police and mentally ill suspects, some of whom had been homeless, and all of whom had claimed police brutality. Next, it referred to the murder of Mr. Cann, a homeless veteran, and the "rumor" that a cop had been responsible, though thankfully it didn't identify Rita Taylor as a potential witness. Finally, the article touched on Rebecca Hyatt's rescue, though again the reporter had been smart enough not to include the little girl's name.

He'd had no such qualms about Simon. Or Nina Whitaker. Or Officer Rieger or Michael Callahan. According to Callahan's parents, their son was schizophrenic and hadn't meant to harm anyone, and they were grateful Nina had been able to work with him to find the girl's location; funny how people didn't mind exposing skeletons if doing so meant it might keep a loved one out of jail.

Taking everything into account, the article had managed to do what the reporter had intended: make San Francisco law enforcement look like a bunch of blundering fools who couldn't distinguish their asses from a hole in the ground without the help of a damn shrink.

Yes, Nina Whitaker *had* helped them find the little girl, but the newspaper made her sound like a miracle worker. Worst yet, a miracle worker whose involvement was necessary in order to overcome the shortcomings of local police, when the only shortcoming in this particular situation had been Michael Callahan's. As much as Nina would say that shortcoming had been caused by illness, it was no excuse. Even assuming Callahan *had* been trying to save the little girl from aliens? He'd almost killed her. Besides, the only one who'd ever know if Callahan really believed aliens had been after the girl was Callahan. What a crock. Simon had seen enough to know that Callahan had probably been motivated by far less altruistic desires.

Slapping the newspaper clipping on the top of his "To Be Filed" mound of paperwork, Simon started on the final report. Unfortunately, it didn't have his full attention. His mind kept wandering back to Nina, just like it had all week.

She was beautiful, sure, but she had a strength and spirit that eerily reminded him of Lana's. On the one hand, that called to him. On the other, it made him sick. He couldn't help thinking that the same spirit he admired was going to get her in trouble one day. Maybe not in as much trouble as it had gotten Lana, but...

Move on, Granger, he told himself. Lana and Nina Whitaker were both in his past. He needed to focus on the present and the future, and do his job—keeping people safe from the criminals Nina Whitaker wanted to heal and treat.

He'd just finished the final report on the Callahan incident when he felt an itch between his shoulder blades. When he looked up, he thought he must be hallucinating. First he'd read about her in the paper. Then he'd struggled to keep her from his thoughts.

He needn't have bothered.

Nina Whitaker stood in front of him.

Shit, he thought, but his curse was mostly in response to the way his body immediately zinged to life. Feigning an annoyance he wasn't really feeling, he stood and walked up to her.

"What can I do for you?"

She cocked a brow at his curt greeting. "I'm here for an update," she said mildly.

He pressed his lips together, knowing he should have

called and updated her as soon as they'd found the girl. It would have been the professional thing to do. Unfortunately, since she made him feel anything but professional, he'd figured it was better to be safe than sorry. But now that she was here… "You were right. We got to her in time. Rebecca Hyatt. I should have filled you in. I apologize."

There was none of the relief he'd expected to see in her expression. "I already know that," she said. "When you failed to call me, I tracked down the information on my own. I found out her name and what hospital she was admitted to. I also know her mother fainted before seeing her and that her father caused quite a scene, too. By all accounts, despite the fact his daughter was found and is going to make a full recovery, he blames me for the delay in getting to her. According to him, if I'd let the police handle the situation, we wouldn't have wasted time coddling a criminal and you would have gotten to his daughter much sooner. I'll be lucky if he doesn't file a lawsuit against me." She paused, but only to suck in enough breath to continue. "Then, of course, there were all the news stories covering the event. Some more favorable to me, some not. So like I said, I already knew what happened. I meant I'm here to give *you* and your commander an update."

For some reason, his instinct was to apologize for the behavior of Rebecca's father, when he'd probably have felt the same way if he'd been in the man's shoes. Confused, he scowled. "An update on what?"

"On my patient."

Her patient. Michael Callahan. He crossed his arms over his chest. "What makes you think I give a fuck what the status of your *patient* is?"

Her expression softened. "Michael didn't mean to hurt her. Aliens, remember? He thought he was helping her."

"And I'm sure that's exactly what his defense attorney is going to argue at trial. Will you be testifying on his behalf?"

"I imagine so. And I imagine that makes you hate me even more, doesn't it, Detective?"

He paused. It would be easier if she thought he hated her, but for some reason, he didn't want that. "I don't hate you," he said grudgingly.

"Just my job."

He didn't bother denying it. "Well, you've given me the update. So I guess you can go now. Thank you for your help."

"If you really want to thank me, have a drink with me."

He couldn't have been more surprised if she'd suddenly stripped down in front of him. It didn't matter that he'd sensed she was attracted to him, too. He'd done absolutely nothing to encourage her. And she obviously thought, with good reason, that he was a redneck cop who'd use muscle to get results when reasoning failed. He narrowed his eyes suspiciously. "Why? We already established I don't respect what you do."

"Is that a requirement for having a drink with me?"

"Not usually. But then again, having a drink is usually a prelude to something else. You offering me that, too?"

He'd simply been trying to goad her, but the way she blushed and looked away had his body hardening. Yeah, she was attracted to him. But was she receptive to doing something about it? He'd never have pegged her as an easy lay, but maybe…

She lifted her chin defiantly. "A prelude to having sex, you mean? I'm afraid that's not what my invitation is about."

He shrugged, not surprised that he'd misread her. "So what is it about?"

She imitated his shrug. "You interest me. You seem to be a smart man, yet your bias against the field of mental health treatment seems unreasonable."

That wasn't quite how Elaina Scott had put it, but close enough. "So you want to analyze me?" Of course she did. For all he knew, she'd compared notes with Dr. Shepard. He knew that would be illegal, but people broke the law all the time.

"I prefer to think of it as 'getting to know someone better.'"

"And then what?"

"Does there have to be anything else?"

There did if his body had any say in the matter. He stepped closer, wanting to rattle her and liking the fact he did. Her breath escalated and she inadvertently took a step back. He studied her slowly. From her pale, glossy hair, down to the tidy but curvy length of her body and ending at the shiny black pumps she shifted nervously.

When he met her gaze again, her eyes were slightly dilated.

"I just like to keep my options open," he explained. "I don't like what you do for a living, but you're damn easy on the eyes. Who knows? Maybe I could do something for you this time around. I'd make damn sure you enjoyed yourself in bed with me."

"I'm sure you would. But it takes more than the promise of pleasure to get me into bed with someone."

"And it takes more than someone wanting to get to know me better to get me to go for a drink with a *shrink*." Deliberately, Simon stepped back.

She smiled tightly and nodded. "I understand. Then I suppose it really is time to go, Detective Granger. Goodbye."

She turned to leave, looking as shocked as he felt when he reached out to stop her.

"Wait."

She stared at his hand for a second and so did he. His grip highlighted the differences between them. Him, big and rough. Her, soft and smooth. Powerful and delicate. Male and female. Suddenly, he longed to press the rest of his flesh against hers, chest to chest, hips to hips—to see how that looked, yes, but more important, to feel it. To feel *her*.

He whipped his hand away and took a step back.

To her credit, she didn't smirk or comment on his retreat.

"Michael Callahan is still in the hospital," he said. It was a statement, not a question, and even though he hadn't meant to sound critical, she obviously interpreted his words that way.

She pursed her lips then nodded. "He was held on a seventy-two-hour hold for evaluation, but under the law can be kept for an additional fourteen days for treatment."

"Even though he's going to prison the second you're done with him?"

She gave him a chiding look. "He'll only go to

prison if he's deemed competent. And only then if he's convicted—"

Simon snorted. "He gave you the information that led us to that little girl. He'll be going to prison eventually."

He didn't say the words *if I have anything to do with it* but they echoed around them nonetheless.

She sighed. "Maybe prison is where he'll end up. Maybe not. And whether you or I think he deserves to be imprisoned is irrelevant. It's up to a jury, one that's been given all the facts, including those about Michael's psychotic break at the time he took the little girl."

"Right. And you're going to be the one to tell them those facts. Don't forget to bring your box of Kleenex while you're at it."

She narrowed her eyes. "Look, I know you're—"

"Simon, you going to introduce us to your friend?"

Nina's head whipped around at the sound of Jase Tyler's voice. The handsome, sandy-haired Texan stood several feet away. Beside him, Carrie Ward, fellow agent and Jase's girlfriend, struggled to keep her expression serious but her curious gaze bounced between Simon and Nina as if she was watching a tennis match. A *very* interesting tennis match.

"Dr. Nina Whitaker," Simon bit out. "Meet Special Agents Jase Tyler and Carrie Ward."

The trio shook hands.

"Sounds like you and Simon were discussing the pros and cons of rehabilitative therapy. You a shrink, Dr. Whitaker?"

Nina cautiously turned to Carrie. "I'm a psychiatrist,

yes. Do you have an interest in rehabilitative therapy, Detective?"

Carrie smiled. "Working with this bunch? I need all the help I can get."

That startled a laugh out of Nina, and Jase and Simon looked at each other. Despite himself, Simon had to forcibly stop himself from smiling, too.

"Seriously, whether I'm interested in rehabilitative therapy depends," Carrie said. "Whose rehabilitation are you discussing?"

Nina hesitated, but Simon crossed his arms over his chest and leaned back against his desk. Granted, Jase and Carrie weren't as touchy about shrinks and therapy as he was, but as fellow cops they knew how often criminals tried to excuse their actions with claims of mental illness. "She's treating Michael Callahan."

"The guy who kidnapped that little girl." This time it was Jase who made the statement, not Simon, but his tone was clearly critical.

Nina lifted her chin. "I'm here to speak with Commander Stevens. If he decides to fill you in, you can discuss your disdain for my profession then. Outside my presence."

Jase stared at her, his expression blank, before he tipped his head. Simon saw the gesture for what it was—a small sign of respect. The same respect he felt for Nina. They couldn't help it. They worked in a male-dominated, often violent world. The fact that Jase and Carrie's relationship was going so strong was testament to the fact that, despite his previous dalliances with drop-dead gorgeous but fragile women, Jase was instinctively drawn to strong women who kept their soft hearts more under wraps. Just like Simon usually was. And Nina Whitaker was definitely a strong woman. In many ways, however, in ways that related to her patients, Nina's soft heart was on display for everyone to see, whether they liked it or not.

"It was nice meeting you, Detectives," she said to Jase and Carrie. Then she turned to Simon. "Goodbye, Detective Granger. I'd say it was a pleasure, but we'd both know I'd be lying."

Jase made a choking sound that obviously communicated his amusement.

As Simon watched Nina stride out of SIG, Carrie elbowed Jase.

"Looks like you made less of an impression on her than even Simon here," she said.

The other man grinned at her. "I no longer want to make a good impression on women. Just one particular woman."

Though they immediately separated, walking to their respective desks, Carrie couldn't hide the pleased blush that colored her cheeks. Knowing how much the two had gone through to be together, the sight pleased Simon, but he couldn't let them see that. "Jesus, I'd tell you both to get a room, but you're already living together. Give me a break, would you?"

He threw himself into his chair, trying to convince himself he could actually concentrate on work after seeing Nina Whitaker again.

Jase laughed. "Funny. That's exactly what Carrie and I were saying to each other before we interrupted you and the doc."

Simon frowned. "What the hell are you talking about?"

"You two were generating more heat than a five-alarm fire. Too bad she's…well…you know."

Simon grunted, but Carrie interjected, drowning out the sound.

"Too bad she's what? Smart? Beautiful? Has a backbone?"

Simon swiveled around to stare at her. "Did you miss the part where I said she's Michael Callahan's shrink?"

"Nope. I didn't. Did you forget that Lana did a lot of good before she was killed?"

Simon's heart twisted. Stunned silence echoed around them.

"Jesus, Carrie," Jase said.

But Carrie just continued to look at Simon. "I'm not trying to be cruel, Simon, but you can't blame every psychiatrist for what happened to Lana. She was good at her job. What happened to her was the work of one man, and one man alone."

"A man Lana thought was sick."

Shadows suddenly appeared in Carrie's eyes, giving her a haunted expression. "Brad Turner *was* sick. Sick enough to dismember a woman. Sick enough to peel the skin off another—" Her voice rose a notch before she tamped down her emotions.

"Carrie," Jase said softly, but Carrie shook her head.

"No. I'm okay. Lana isn't. Because of Brad Turner. But maybe if someone had listened to her, or *someone like her,* earlier, maybe Brad Turner would've gotten help long before he met Lana. Maybe he wouldn't have killed the women he did. And maybe Lana would be alive today. Have you ever thought about that?"

Simon had no doubt that his face must look as

haunted as Carrie's just had. At least, that's how he felt. Haunted. And nauseous. He rose and walked toward the door, hoping it didn't look like he was stumbling.

"Simon, wait."

Simon froze, but didn't turn around.

"I—I care about you. We all do. We're worried and—"

Simon turned toward her. "Don't be worried. And for God's sake, don't care about me. All it's gotten me so far are weekly appointments talking to a man about how I *feel* and what I'd do differently if I could. But no more. I'm through with 'not-really-mandatory-but-essentially-mandatory' counseling. You can tell both Mac and Commander Stevens that. Worry and caring? No, thanks. I don't need it, Carrie, and frankly, I don't want it."

CHAPTER EIGHT

"You want me to shadow Simon Granger?" Nina asked Commander Stevens in disbelief. "You can't be serious. I'm a psychiatrist, not a cop."

"And that's exactly the capacity in which we want you to serve, Dr. Whitaker. I'm not asking you to go into overtly dangerous situations with Detective Granger. He's not a street cop, but an investigator. His casework is controlled and he's not an adrenaline junkie. To the contrary, he's put in for a return to management."

"And you want me to determine whether he's fit for that position? Is that why you sent him to see Dr. Shepard in the first place? Because I'm not going to spy on someone and report to you about him without his knowledge."

"That's not what I'm asking," Stevens said. "Simon is seeing Dr. Shepard for counseling. He's going through a difficult time…"

Nina held up her hand. "Please don't say anything more. It's not appropriate for you to disclose Detective Granger's personal business to me without him knowing it."

Stevens hesitated then said, "Fine. But you're wrong. I'm not asking you to shadow Detective Granger so you

can evaluate him. At least, not any more than you'll
be evaluating any other cop that works for the city."

"I don't understand."

"We've discussed your desire to establish a Mental
Health Intervention Team within San Francisco P.D."

"*Discussed* is one way of putting it. I've asked for
your assistance in having that program implemented.
Given the information I got from Michael Callahan and
the favorable press it's brought to the department, I was
hoping you'd see the benefits of what I'm proposing."

"I'm open to hearing more about it, of course."

"But?"

"But you're assuming this program will benefit us
based largely on public outrage at the way certain matters have been handled. I don't think it's appropriate for
you to recommend changes based on incidents you're
learning about third-hand or by subjective sources.
The program you started up in Charleston was based
on extensive research, third-party observations and
case studies."

"That's right. But that was when the program was
in its infancy, before it had any kind of track record. It
took years to accumulate that data. Now we have concrete statistics showing that the MHIT program has
benefited the Charleston Police Department and—"

"But those stats are based on where the Charleston
Police Department started out. And based on the ini-
tial data you collected, which indicated the program
was warranted in the first place. I'm asking for that
same foundation. That you not judge the compassion
or competency of our men when you haven't even witnessed it yourself."

Taking a deep breath, Nina leaned back in her chair. "Tell me what you have in mind."

"Simon has several open cases, including one concerning a murdered homeless man, but they're all inactive right now. Barring additional activity in those cases, he's ready for a new assignment. However, that can wait a week. In the meantime, you can work together. He'll monitor dispatch and accompany you to calls that will be handled by a patrol officer. He'll assist and you'll observe SIG and the SFPD in action."

"But why Detective Granger?" she asked, perturbed. "Won't he object to babysitting me?"

"That's irrelevant. Simon's been working one tough case after another. He's due a lighter assignment. Plus, he's applying for a promotion to management. Better he get used to the idea of politics and suffering for the cause now. Finally, I consider your MHIT proposal fairly critical. At least, that's what you're arguing, isn't it? That we absolutely need to give some thought to broad prevention instead of simply focusing on what's already in front of us?"

Hoisted by her own petard, she thought. *You had to give Stevens points for persuasiveness.* "Yes, that's what I'm advocating."

"Then this is my offer. You'll get the chance to evaluate how San Francisco law enforcement personnel interact with those experiencing mental illness. Complete a detailed report with your findings, and I'll set up meetings with the appropriate people so you can make your recommendations."

What Stevens was offering was both insanely difficult and far too easy. It made Nina wonder what he was *really* after. She narrowed her eyes as a thought occurred to her. "And what if my findings aren't favorable to the police? What if certain departments want them suppressed? Or if they make it even more difficult for me to attain police cooperation?"

"Part of the benefit of being with the Department of Justice is that we oversee every law enforcement agency in the state. I'm not out to hide anything. However, despite what you and your colleagues think, I have faith in our officers and believe they handle confrontations with all suspects well and to the best of their ability. I'm not saying you'll be able to convince me otherwise, but I will give you a fair shot. Who knows? Maybe we can compromise on training that's amenable to both of us."

"I won't skew my results to make you look good," she warned.

"I'm not asking you to. But I must also warn you that this type of arrangement is highly unusual. You'll be signing waivers of liability forms all night. You have to go into this with your eyes wide open. If anything were to occur, Simon will protect you with his life. I have no doubt about that. But you are still a civilian putting yourself into potentially dangerous situations. If you're not willing to take this kind of risk for the program you're advocating, then—"

Commander Stevens's phone rang. "Excuse me a moment," he said before answering. His facial features relaxed slightly at the caller's greeting and his expression reminded Nina of how different—how wonderful—Simon looked when he allowed himself to relax, too.

"I have a few more things to wrap up," Stevens said to the person on the phone, "but I'll be ready to tee off at six as planned. Yes, I'm looking forward to the gala, too. Four officers will be in attendance, including one from SIG. Yes. Yes. I'm actually just finishing up a meeting here. It's with the doctor I told you about. The one that..." Stevens glanced at Nina and held up a finger, indicating he'd only be another minute.

She nodded and averted her gaze, only half listening as Stevens described how Nina had assisted with Michael Callahan. She was sure his flattery was deliberately timed.

As he'd probably intended, Nina thought again of the *other* people—citizens and police officers alike—who might be better off if the city implemented advanced mental health training and increased practical assistance for law enforcement. She thought of Beth and Rachel. Rebecca Hyatt and Michael Callahan. She even thought of Mrs. Horowitz, who'd passed away two nights before and how, in spite of being prepared for the end, Nina had cried anyway.

She'd known this would happen. She'd become personally invested. She'd risked the peaceful life she'd made for herself in exchange for the challenging task of helping and saving others, and she knew exactly why she had. Because she truly believed the MHIT program could help people. And because her peaceful life had ceased to be enough for her.

Coincidentally or not, her restless feelings and lack of fulfillment had started the day she'd met Simon Granger.

She just wished she hadn't asked out the man she was about to trail. He probably thought she'd lied about where she'd gotten the triple-X movie she'd dropped from her purse and would be expecting her to come on to him at every turn. Well, she could control her baser instincts. And obviously he didn't want to have anything to do with her romantically.

The problem was he wasn't going to want anything to do with her professionally, either.

It was going to make things uncomfortable for both of them.

But Nina wasn't going to take the easy way out again. Not this time.

"I'm willing to take the risk," she said quietly. "When does this assignment start?"

SIMON STARED AT COMMANDER Stevens until the normally unshakable man's left eye twitched. He didn't make the mistake of viewing it as weakness. Fact was, Stevens didn't enjoy playing the heavy, especially when it came to his own men. The twitch evidenced that. But it didn't change the fact that Stevens *would* play the heavy if it was necessary.

Simon just wasn't going to make it easy for him.

"No. Absolutely not. I don't want to spend any more time than I already have with that woman." He refrained from childishly saying, "And you can't make me," but just barely. "I have a job to do, and babysitting a shrink isn't in my job description."

"You've always been good at your job and that's why I need you to do this. You already know the local police are under fire because of repeated confrontations with mentally ill subjects. And despite Rita Taylor's recent backtracking, there's still plenty of talk on the street that someone saw a uniformed police officer fleeing the scene of Mr. Cann's murder. Now, Michael Callahan's family is making allegations of police brutality."

"What?" First Rebecca Hyatt's father blamed Nina for how she'd handled the situation; now Callahan's family was blaming the police? On what basis? But then Simon recalled Nina's comments about bruises and Officer Rieger's claim that Callahan had resisted arrest. Simon cursed.

"DOJ has been asked to step in as an objective party," Stevens continued. "To determine whether local law enforcement can benefit from the type of training Nina Whitaker is proposing. Between you and me, this is a formality. The mayor's ready to cave. Training *will* be ordered. It's just a matter of how much of it we'll have to suffer. It's going to depend on whether we can convince Dr. Whitaker that we're not the brutalizing apes the press has made us out to be."

Simon shifted restlessly. A brutalizing ape was probably exactly what Nina Whitaker thought he was. "So assign her to some patrol officer at SFPD. Or if DOJ needs to be involved, an intern. Hell, I don't care who you assign her to, so long as it's not me. Unless—" His frown darkened. "Are you still concerned I'm unfit to do my job because of what happened with Lana?"

"I never accused you of being unfit, Simon. Just… troubled. I think you're internalizing a lot and that you can benefit from talking to someone about it." Stevens held up his hand. "I know. You've made it quite clear that you're not going to see Dr. Shepard again. Ultimately, that's your choice. But if you're as well adjusted as you say you are, if you don't really have the biases against the mentally ill that Elaina Scott accused you of, then you should have no problem with this assignment. That's particularly true since you want to be in management. The city is suffering a public relations nightmare right now. Think how grateful the higher-ups will be if you facilitate a partnership with Dr. Whitaker in a way that benefits both sides. So that no one comes out looking like a bad guy, especially us."

"So this is about making us look good? Is she aware of that?"

"She's agreed to do an objective assessment."

"And if her objective assessment is that we're all in fact brutalizing apes, what's that gonna do for my promotion possibilities?"

"I suppose that's a risk we're all going to have to take. Welcome to the world of politics. You ready to play with the big boys?" When Simon remained silent, Stevens slapped his open palm on his desk. "This discussion is over. Today's Tuesday. Beginning Monday, Dr. Whitaker will shadow you for five days. You'll take her out on SFPD calls so she can see how the beat cops relate to the public. She'll make observations as a consultant for a proposed project between the hospital and the police. To the extent she makes observations that aren't favorable to the force, I'll have your back on that. That's all I can promise. But bottom line, you want my support so you can get that captain position? I guess you need to decide how much you want it."

Simon rose. "I don't want it this bad. Is that all? Sir?"

They stared at one another before Stevens sighed and sank into his chair. "Give it some thought, Simon. She's going to shadow someone. If not you…" He shrugged.

"Not me is my preference," Simon muttered as he left. Not yet ready to return to his desk and what were sure to be questions from his fellow SIG detectives, Simon walked to the SIG break room. He froze in his tracks when he saw Nina Whitaker there, nursing a cup of coffee. He couldn't help it. He stalked up to her and got in her face.

"What the hell are you trying to pull?"

SPECIAL AGENT BRYCE DeMarco was standing in front of the vending machines just outside the SIG break room when Simon strode right by him. The other man didn't even bother to say hello, but DeMarco didn't call him on it. From the looks of him, Simon was distracted. Again.

He was entitled. The guy had been going through some heavy-duty shit lately. Hell, they all had. DeMarco felt like he'd been put through the ringer ten times over. Then bludgeoned with a hammer. Then cut into pieces and fed to sharks.

He still couldn't believe Lana was dead. She'd been a good woman. A good friend. DeMarco missed her like crazy. He could barely stand to think about the way she'd died—at the hands of some violent sicko who had ensured her final minutes on this earth had been filled with pain and terror.

Unfortunately, as much as DeMarco grieved Lana's passing, his own brand of trouble had started rearing its ugly head long before she'd died and he was still dealing with the aftermath. He was having trouble sleeping, and when he did sleep, he had nightmares. He found himself getting pissed off easily, when normally he was pretty easygoing. Hell, DeMarco hadn't even tried to bed a woman in God only knew how long because the last few times he'd tried he hadn't been able to get it up.

All that had been going on for months, well before Lana had died.

Ironically, the only person he'd told about his problems had been Lana. And the only reason DeMarco had finally decided to confide in her was because he'd trusted her. Respected her. Liked her.

He didn't feel the same way about her replacement.

Not that the new staff psychiatrist was a bad guy, at least DeMarco had no reason to think that, but he was a stranger nonetheless.

No way was DeMarco going to admit to nightmares and fucking impotency to a man he didn't know. Even with Lana he'd held back. Still, talking to her about what had happened in New Orleans six years ago had helped.

Until, that is, he'd gotten the call last year.

Now, the nightmares were worse than ever.

Sometimes, when the horrible images wouldn't leave his mind, he wished—

He looked in the direction that Simon had disappeared.

Sometimes he just wished he could talk to one of his friends about what had happened. About how much it was messing with his head. But the timing to talk to someone, someone who knew him and cared about him, was always off.

Last year, when DeMarco had been called to New Orleans for his "family emergency," Jase and Carrie had been smack-dab in the middle of a complex serial killer case. And afterward…after that same serial killer had murdered Lana…well, everyone had been on edge.

DeMarco would have felt like the biggest pussy in the world if he'd gone crying to his friends after that. He'd told himself he'd start to feel better. When he hadn't felt better, he'd told himself he'd reach out eventually. Only too much time had passed. Reaching out now seemed foolish. Weak.

His friends had problems of their own without having to deal with his shit.

No, he was fine. Tired. Stressed. But he'd deal.

Just like he always had in the past.

With a sigh, DeMarco punched the coins into the vending machine, grabbed his chilly soda and started to walk away.

He paused, however, when he heard Simon's angry voice coming from the break room.

NINA STARED AT THE ANGRY man looming over her and inwardly cringed. A cup of coffee before driving home had obviously been too much to ask for. Calmly, she set her coffee cup down. "I assume you've spoken with Commander Stevens?"

"Are you trying to prove something here?" he all but snarled.

"Not at all. I'm assuming you're talking about our new partnership? Because that wasn't my idea."

"This crock of shit program you're trying to institute sure is."

Nina took a shallow breath and urged herself to remain calm. "It's not a crock of shit. We've been trying to get this program in motion for months. I talked to the chief of police about it before I ever met you."

"That's supposed to make me feel better?"

"It's not supposed to make you feel anything. But I am wondering why the thought of working with me bothers you so much."

"Two reasons. One, I don't like you."

He wasn't telling her anything she didn't already

know. Yet she couldn't help it—his words hurt her. Why? She barely knew him and his dislike was irrational, not based on anything she'd actually done. "You don't know me well enough not to like me. You don't like what I do. There's a difference."

"Not a big one."

Nina crossed her arms over her chest. "What's your second reason?"

"You're right. I don't like what you're trying to do. Force your mumbo jumbo beliefs on cops. We know what we need to do. We rely on our training and our instincts."

"And being more educated about what is motivating other people can't help you with those instincts?"

"When someone's dangerous, it doesn't matter what's motivating them."

"But it matters how you treat them, doesn't it? If you knew someone was being coerced into doing something, wouldn't you treat them differently than someone who is intentionally causing pain to others?"

She could see her words gave him pause. For all of two seconds. Then he shot back with, "It might impact how I *feel* about doing something, but it's not going to change what I'd be doing."

"I think you're lying to yourself about that. You really think you would have been objective and neutral with Michael Callahan if you'd questioned him? No. And he would have retreated. Closed up. You wouldn't have gotten the information that you needed to find Rebecca Hyatt."

"I disagree with you. I would have gotten it."

"By force?"

"If necessary."

As she stared at him, she wasn't sure she believed him. She had little basis for how she felt, but she had some. Before he'd known she was a psychiatrist, he'd been charming. Funny. In the emergency room, although he'd challenged her several times, he'd allowed her to take the reins and handle Michael Callahan the way she saw fit. And then there was the picture she'd seen in the paper. The one of him standing in the hospital waiting room as he waited for news on Rebecca Hyatt. His expression had been fierce...and worried. His actions along with his job told her he was a complex but decent man. But even complex, decent men could lose control when they were pushed.

"Thankfully," she replied softly, "using force wasn't necessary. Because I was there. Because I've been trained to deal with people like Michael when he's suffering a psychotic break."

"How long did you spend in school? We can't all have that kind of medical training."

"But you can have more than you do now."

"At what cost? You don't think we're overworked enough? While we're spending time learning to be kinder and gentler to people who are endangering others, crimes are being committed. And people are getting away with them."

This was pointless. Neither one of them was going to change the other's mind. Not today. "It's fine if you disagree. In the end, you're not the one making the decision about the benefits of the program. But we need to work together. And I hope you won't make it any more unpleasant than it has to be."

He smiled tightly. "I wouldn't place much hope on that if I were you."

As he watched her walk away, Simon wrestled with his anger, but also his attraction to her.

It was the same attraction he'd felt for her at the hospital.

The same attraction he'd felt every time he'd seen her.

It had been tempered by wariness then anger and now resentment, but it was still there, impossible to ignore. And it wasn't one-sided, either.

But like him, she did a great job ignoring it.

Because it was the professional thing to do? Or because he was being such a major asshole?

On some level, he knew that was exactly how he was acting. Fuck, he might as well have thrown himself on the ground and beaten the floor with his fists. Elaina Scott had called to complain about him with far less reason. Could he really blame Nina if she did the same thing?

Simon sighed and ran his hands through his hair.

Asshole-ish behavior aside, he really was at a loss.

He knew he wasn't getting out of this partnership anymore than he'd been able to avoid seeing Dr. Shepard that first time. While that hadn't ended badly, he also knew if he spent any significant time around Nina Whitaker, things were gonna get complicated.

He'd had more than enough complications for a lifetime. Dating and then losing Lana had wreaked havoc on his life. He'd entered a kind of stasis after her death. He'd focused on his work. Been content with being by himself. But suddenly his body wasn't content with that any longer.

It wanted her. Nina.

Yet even if he allowed himself to have her, she'd made it more than clear that *she* wouldn't allow it.

With that thought, another followed. He straightened and grinned.

He had to agree to this partnership, but nothing the Commander said could make *her* participate in it if she didn't want to. If she decided she didn't want to work with him or requested someone else, that couldn't be blamed on him, now could it?

CHAPTER NINE

THE DAY AFTER SHE AGREED to participate in Stevens's shadow program, Nina called Karen about Stevens's offer. Of course, Karen was thrilled and generous with her compliments despite the fact shadowing Simon had been far from her idea. Nina told her boss that several times, but it didn't seem to matter to the other woman. Nor did Nina's concerns about her current patients and the appointments she'd have to miss. Karen assured Nina that she'd look into it and would call Nina back in the morning.

Sure enough, Karen called Nina's office the next day. "It's all been arranged. Dr. Anderson and Dr. Rodriguez will work together to cover your geriatric duties over the next week. Now, I promised you drinks. Tell me where you'd like to go. Later, you can fill me in on how next week goes."

Nina envisioned Karen toasting a victory far too prematurely. "The drinks you promised were conditional on the police giving the program the green light, remember? That hasn't happened yet, Karen. And we don't know if it will."

"I know that," Karen reassured her. "I'm sure Stevens and his bosses are hoping this little exercise will work out in their favor somehow. The question is, why does Commander Stevens think you're going to be

swayed by this unconventional hookup? Is your little
tête-à-tête with Detective Simon Granger a strategic
one on Stevens's part? Is there something you want to
tell me, perhaps?"

Karen couldn't know about her attraction to Simon
Granger, but Nina blushed at her deliberate choice of
words and insinuating tone anyway. "I can't possibly
speak for Commander Stevens, but he did say Detective Granger had the extra time on his hands." Pathetic,
Nina thought. Even to her own ears she sounded less
than convincing.

Karen laughed. "Right. Extra time. And extra sex
appeal. The guy's gorgeous!"

Nina blinked. "How—?"

"I looked him up on the internet," Karen confessed.
"Along with the rest of the SIG detectives. They have
their very own webpage. The best of the best. Nice.
And I must say, all the men on that team are fine. I can
see you and this Simon Granger together. You, with
blond hair and green eyes. Him, brown hair and—
What color are his eyes? I couldn't tell on the com-
puter screen."

"I couldn't tell you," Nina said, even as she thought:
gray. Like slate, but not as hard. Or smoke, but not as
insubstantial. A nice metallic color that could be cool
or warm, depending on his mood. Masculine but in-
viting. The color made her think not of clouds during
a storm, but shade from a blistering heat. Protective.
Sheltering…

"It doesn't matter," Karen said, jolting Nina from
her thoughts. "You'd make a striking couple."

Nina was too horrified to talk at first. She'd been
composing a mental poem about the color of Simon

Granger's eyes, and Karen had them practically married. Not good, she thought. So not good.

Her voice was stiffer than she intended when she finally responded to Karen's teasing. "I'm not looking for a hookup, Karen. And certainly not one with a cop who thinks my job is a joke. Because he does. And despite this little partnership that Stevens has arranged, you know most of the police think what we do is a joke, too."

"Maybe," Karen said. "But they also don't know who they're dealing with. You'll bring them around, Nina. You did it before and you'll do it again."

Once more, Nina squirmed at Karen's words. Her boss sounded a little too confident in Nina's abilities and that confidence made Nina decidedly uncomfortable.

She'd once had that same confidence in herself, but that had been ages ago. When she'd truly thought she could make a difference and not suffer for trying to do so. Now she knew that making a difference came with huge responsibilities. And consequences. She didn't want the pressure of making lifesaving decisions. That's why she'd left Charleston and began working with her patients in the first place. But yet here she was, literally about to plunge back into the fire. So be it. But she didn't want Karen thinking she'd misled her. And she didn't want her to take too much for granted, either. "I'll do the best I can, Karen. I'll shadow this cop. I'll make my recommendations. But then I'm out. Whether Stevens supports the MHIT proposal or not, I'll have done all I can do. I want your promise that after my week as Detective Granger's shadow is over, you'll handle things on your own from now on. Deal?"

Her words were met with a tense silence. A full minute later, Karen spoke, her voice slightly stiff and far more professional than when she'd teased Nina about Simon. "Okay. If that's what you want. I appreciate you doing this for me, Nina. I'm sure plenty of other people will, too. Goodbye."

Nina winced. "Karen—"

Static buzzed on the other line.

Quietly, Nina hung up the phone. Damn it, she hadn't meant to offend Karen or hurt her feelings. They weren't overly close, but Nina had always considered Karen a friend. Friends met for drinks. And teased each other about good-looking men. It didn't always have to be about work between them and that wasn't even what Nina wanted. But the fact still remained she was feeling pulled between her desire to live a safe and content life, and her instinct to seek a bigger payoff even if it might be at the potential expense of her peace of mind.

All it took to sway her in favor of peace of mind was thinking of the last card Lester Davenport had sent her. And the ones he'd sent before. Because he blamed Nina for his daughter's death.

Just like Nina's father blamed her for Rachel's.

Nina gasped and threw down the mental gates on her thoughts. Where the hell had *that* thought come from? She hadn't talked to her father in months, but their relationship was fine. Sure he'd been upset with her when she'd left Charleston, but that had only proved how much he loved her. He didn't blame her for Rachel's death. Not really. Those things he'd said to her twenty years ago had been said in grief. He'd apologized again and again. And Nina had forgiven him. She'd forgiven herself—

She jolted at hearing her own labored breaths and at feeling the sting of tears in her eyes. Angrily, she swiped them away. It was a major failing of hers that she cried easily. *Stop it right now, Nina. You're letting your thoughts get away from you. Lester Davenport's card shook you more than you anticipated, that's all. But he's done what he needed to do.* She would do the same.

She'd been happy before getting that latest card. And she'd been content with her job before Karen had started riding her about the MHIT program.

She'd call Karen back and arrange to have drinks, she decided. But she wouldn't back down about the job. She'd committed herself to the shadow program for the upcoming week but after that it would be business as usual. She'd find her peace and contentment again.

No one, not Karen, not Lester Davenport and not even Detective Simon Granger, was going to stop her.

CHAPTER TEN

LESTER DAVENPORT PICKED up his pace as he walked down the hospital corridor. In one hand, he held a bouquet of flowers. In the other, a stuffed puppy doll. He smiled as he imagined Beth's joy upon seeing his gifts. He imagined her throwing her arms around him. And he imagined her telling him she loved him.

"I love you, Daddy."

She hadn't said the words in so long. Not since she was a little girl. Certainly not since her mother had left him. And especially not since her mother had died.

She'd blamed him for that. Even though Nadia had been diagnosed with cancer well after she'd divorced Lester, Beth had still blamed Lester for her mother's illness. She'd told him so herself and she'd said other hateful things. Things that had made Lester say hateful things back. Things that, at one point, had even goaded Lester into slapping her.

But he'd apologized for that. Over and over again, he'd apologized. Beth had never said she'd forgiven him. Before she could, Nadia had died. And after that, Beth had gotten sick, too. She'd begun to hurt herself, saying she wanted to join her mother. Then she'd been admitted here. To this hospital.

At first, Lester hadn't liked it. Hadn't liked the staff, especially Beth's doctor, who'd asked questions suggesting Lester was to blame for his daughter's illness. But eventually, Beth had started talking to him again, and Lester's feelings about the hospital and Beth's doctor had changed.

When Beth's doctor told him Beth was doing better, he started making plans to bring her home. He was going to throw a big party for her, to celebrate their fresh start. They were going to be a family again and Beth would forgive him for everything. She'd tell him she loved him again, he just knew it.

He was still smiling as he approached the nurses' station outside Beth's room. As he got closer, however, his gait slowed. People were shouting. Medical personnel were scrambling around. There were police there, too. And was that…?

Yes. Yes, it was. Leo. Beth's boyfriend. But what was he doing here?

The punk was sitting in a chair, sprawled out disrespectfully. When he caught sight of Lester, he grinned, waved and then pointed his finger at something.

With a feeling of dread, Lester's gaze followed the line of his finger.

Shock slammed into him like a ton of bricks. His stomach heaved with nausea and his fingers grew numb. The bouquet of flowers and the stuffed puppy doll fell. As soon as they hit the ground, the flowers withered and died, but the puppy doll came to life. The puppy began running around Lester's legs. Barking. Nipping. Trying to get his attention.

But Lester's attention was too focused on the horrific sight before him.

Beth hung right in front of him now, suspended by a pink ribbon tied to the ceiling. Her eyes were open but empty. Her head lolled to the side as if she no longer had the strength to hold it up. As if she no longer had the life…

She was dead, he realized. She'd hung herself with that pink ribbon. But where had she gotten it?

Lester tore his gaze away from his daughter and looked around for help.

The nurses. The police. Even Leo. Everyone was gone.

Where had they all gone?

"Dr. Whitaker?" he called out even though he had no reason to believe she was here. But she was Beth's doctor, after all. She'd said Beth was getting better. So where was she?

She needed to cut Beth down. Needed to bring her back to him, just like she'd said she would.

"Dr. Whitaker, where are you? Beth's tried to hurt herself again. You need to help her."

He started running, or at least he tried to, but no matter how fast his legs pumped, he gained no ground. It was as if he was running in place or on some kind of treadmill and Beth's body stayed exactly where it was, swaying in front of him.

Suddenly the pink band around his daughter's neck lengthened. Like the stuffed puppy doll that Lester had dropped, it came alive. It swirled through the air, reaching out, winding itself around Lester's body and throat, hissing like a snake.

It was going to kill him, Lester thought, but as much as he wanted to be with Beth, he didn't want to die. No, no, his mind screamed, he didn't want to die. But he couldn't escape, either.

"Dr. Whitaker," he screamed again. "Dr. Whitaker!"

A shrill ringing sound ripped through the air, jolting Lester Davenport out of his nightmare. For a second, he continued to struggle for breath. Continued to believe he was being choked by the same ribbon that had taken Beth's life. Then he realized he was simply trapped by bedding. That during his struggles, he'd pulled the twisted sheet tight against his neck until it felt like a noose. Desperately, he untangled himself from its grasp and scrambled out of bed.

The phone rang again, but he didn't even look at it.

He covered his mouth with his hands and sobbed. Then he ran into the bathroom and emptied his stomach into the toilet.

Long minutes later, he staggered out, returned to the bed and sat down. His bleary eyes took in the empty beer bottles littering the floor. He grabbed one that was half-empty and chugged down the contents. He swiped his hand over his mouth, then fell back. Just as he did, however, the phone rang again.

Flinging his hand out, he grabbed the receiver and dragged it to his ear.

"Hel—hello," he croaked.

"Mr. Davenport?"

He frowned at the unfamiliar male voice on the other line. "Yes, this is Lester Davenport."

"Mr. Davenport, this is Rick Shannon with the *San Francisco Reporter.* I've been trying to contact you about your daughter, Elizabeth."

Images from his nightmare once again swirled around him, making his stomach heave again. He swore he could actually hear that damn dog yapping. The pink ribbon hissing. He pulled himself up to a sitting position. "My daughter is dead," he said.

"Yes, I'm aware of that, Mr. Davenport, and I'm very sorry for your loss. I've read the articles from three years ago. I know what happened."

"Then why are you calling?"

"Because I was hoping you could give me some additional information that wasn't in the papers. About what happened to your daughter. And about your daughter's doctor at the time, Dr. Nina Whitaker. You told reporters that you blamed her for Elizabeth's death."

"That's right," he spat out. "She *is* responsible. I'm not retracting that statement, so if that's why you're calling you can—"

"Actually, that's not why I'm calling. I'm calling because I believe you. And I'm afraid Nina Whitaker is going to hurt someone else. Because of her actions, a little girl named Rebecca Hyatt almost died the other day. The police are trying to make it seem like she actually helped the girl, but I think we both know that's a lie. Wouldn't you agree?"

"Yes," he said quickly, even though he had absolutely no idea what the guy was talking about. But of course Nina Whitaker had endangered another girl. After Beth, it had only been a matter of time. "Absolutely I agree. Tell me more."

By the time Lester hung up the phone, he felt stronger. Between the drinking and his grief, he'd barely managed to hold on to sanity. But now things were different. The dream had been a sign, as had that phone call. He had a purpose now.

Damn Nina Whitaker. She obviously wasn't taking his cards seriously.

She'd let Beth die. According to the reporter on the

phone, she'd let her own sister die, too. Lester wasn't going to let her endanger another girl.

Even if that meant he had to go to California to stop her.

CHAPTER ELEVEN

ON ANY OTHER SATURDAY, Nina would have slept in and risen leisurely to have a cup of coffee on her back patio. Instead, despite a restless night, she woke at the crack of dawn, feeling aroused and surly. She immediately knew the cause: her dreams of Simon Granger. They'd plagued her all week, no matter how hard she'd tried to purge him from her thoughts. And even when she was awake, she thought of him often, and those thoughts were always accompanied by a vague feeling of anticipation.

Damn it, the man was sexy and intriguing and infuriating and he was going to be trouble. Moreover, she had no illusions that he was going to take the assignment to work with her sitting down. He was going to push back; it was only a matter of when and how.

Instead of sitting around and stressing about it, however, Nina decided to take a drive. Maybe to the ocean, she thought, which never failed to clear her head of troubling thoughts. She dressed, packed a day bag and had just poured herself a cup of coffee when there was a knock at her door. She frowned and again thought of Simon Granger.

It would be easy for him to find out where she lived. She'd suspected he'd push back against Stevens's machinations. Had his offensive begun already?

Deliberately, she took a minute to fix her coffee the way she liked it. Then, bringing her cup with her, she looked through the peephole but saw nothing. She opened the door. There was an innocuous-looking letter sticking half out from beneath her welcome mat.

She seriously doubted Simon Granger would leave her a note rather than tell her face-to-face exactly what he thought of her and her proposed plans for the city.

With a sigh, she knelt down, picked it up and walked back into the house.

Juggling her coffee cup, she pulled the piece of white parchment paper out of the envelope, a small smile on her lips as she imagined it to be a love note from Simon. The kind that kids passed around in school that proffered two boxes—check yes or no—to the question whether the recipient liked them. She and Simon didn't like each other, that was obvious, but she was honest enough to admit they were attracted to one another.

When she glanced at the paper, she wasn't expecting to see the note she'd imagined. But she wasn't expecting to see what was actually there, either.

She died and so will you.

Her mug of coffee slipped from her fingers.

As SIMON SAT IN HIS parked car across the street from Nina Whitaker's home, he again thought of contradictions. Of puzzle pieces not quite fitting into place. Although he couldn't see it, he'd bet her ugly car was parked at the end of her long driveway, muddying up the hoity-toity aesthetics of what was an honest-to-goodness mansion.

The woman worked as a shrink at a public hospital but apparently she was loaded. Either that, or she was boffing a really rich sugar daddy, but he just couldn't make himself believe that about her. More and more, he was fascinated by what made her tick. And that very fascination should have him even more determined to get her the hell away from him by any means necessary. Instead, he was here, prepared to lay his proverbial cards on the table.

He recalled his plan to seduce her. To use their mutual attraction to get her to quit the absurd partnership they'd been forced into.

As soon as he'd had the thought, another had started to form and it had kept at him until he'd had to accept it: he couldn't do it. He'd never crossed the line, but he had no problem intimidating suspects when he needed to. On the other hand, he'd never used sex to intimidate an innocent woman and he wasn't about to start now. That wasn't his style, and moreover, he didn't really need to stoop that low to accomplish what he wanted with Nina.

The fact of the matter was he *was* attracted to her and she was attracted to him. Since both of them seemed equally determined to fight that attraction, things were going to naturally be uncomfortable between them. If she was prone to caving, which he doubted anyway, she'd probably cave on that basis alone. Given that, playing the heavy with her seemed overkill.

Plus, there was the simple matter of what she was trying to accomplish. Although he could accuse her of caring too much and having too much faith in the ability of men to change, the fact remained she was trying to do something good. He simply didn't agree with her methods or that change was necessary. If that was the case, if he truly believed in the competency and training the city had already provided to law enforcement, why not give her a fair shot, let her make her recommendations to Commander Stevens and let the cards fall where they may? As misguided as he considered her goal, he really didn't have enough information about what she was suggesting to back up his opinion. What he needed to do was stop reacting to her in a knee-jerk manner simply because of what had happened to Lana. He doubted she could say anything that would win him over, but he supposed he owed her the opportunity to try. Otherwise, he would be no better than the close-minded man Elaina Scott had accused him of being.

Getting out of his car, Simon strode toward her front door. Given the length of the driveway and walkway, it took a minute. Not only was her house located in San Francisco's ultraposh Pacific Heights, but the symmetrical, redbrick and gray-shingled residence was smack-dab in the middle of the Gold Coast area, so called because the houses in it were even more fancy than those in the normally fancy-pants neighborhood. Unlike most of her neighbors, however, Nina didn't have a gate blocking access to her residence, but she did have the same spectacular view of the city at the rear of the house. Despite its size and majesty, complete with topiaries, boxwood hedges and rosebushes, Nina's home managed to appear welcoming. That impression was aided somewhat by the butt-ugly car that was indeed parked in the driveway; it took the snobbery of the house down a notch or two. Or twenty. Simon grinned. He'd bet that just the idea of it being driven on their street drove her neighbors crazy. He wondered if any of them had ever had the nerve to say anything to the elegant woman who drove it.

He lifted the heavy metal knocker resting against the arched solid wood door and announced his presence. As he waited, hands in his pockets, he heard shuffling from inside. For a second, he wondered if she was going to ignore him, but that didn't seem to jive with what he knew about her. She wasn't a coward...

She slowly opened the door. Even wearing jeans and a sweater, she looked as classy and elegant as her house. From his vantage point, he could just make out wood-paneled walls, herringbone pattern wood floors, exposed beam ceilings, a redbrick fireplace, period light fixtures and diamond-paned windows. He couldn't help his low whistle.

"Nice place," he said. "Not what I'd expect for a shrink. Not one that works at a public hospital, anyway."

Her lips pressed together, but instead of reacting snappishly, she simply shrugged. "I imagine I don't fit a lot of your preconceptions about psychiatrists. Maybe you'll figure that out over the next week while we work together."

She said it lightly but firmly, establishing that despite any thoughts he might have of trying to run her off, it wasn't going to work.

Nope, he decided. He couldn't imagine her neighbors commenting on her choice of vehicle. Hell, she probably intimidated them to the point they told her they loved how quirky it was. He suppressed a smile and nodded, amazed that being in Nina's presence could make him feel edgy but lighthearted, too. Even a little relieved. It was quite an alluring combination. Too alluring. "Maybe I will," he finally answered her.

She appeared surprised by his easy acquiescence.

He smoothed a hand over his hair. "Can I come in for a second so we can talk?"

She stepped back and he stepped in. The place was big, and every foot of it gleamed and shone like a high-priced jewel.

"Seriously, your home is beautiful," he said. *Like you,* he thought.

She looked startled, as if she truly thought him incapable of civilized conversation. For a horrifying second, he wondered if he'd actually complimented her looks out loud, but no...

She said, "Thank you. It belonged to my grandmother. I was lucky enough to inherit it from her and I pretty much work to pay the taxes. Hence the car I drive. Can I get you something to drink?"

"No, thanks." He studied her, and the attraction he felt for her bloomed as strongly as ever. By the way she was holding herself, ramrod-straight yet a bit fidgety, she sensed it, too. Might as well come right out and acknowledge it, right? "What I wanted to say is...I'm attracted to you."

Her eyes rounded comically.

He seemed to be giving her one shock after another, and, man, it gave him a thrill. Deciding he was having too much fun, he forced himself to say, "But I don't want to be attracted to you. That's why I don't want to work with you. I thought about seducing you to drive you away, but I decided not to."

She gave an incredulous laugh. "Well, that's mighty big of you, Detective Granger."

He grinned, liking how she looked and sounded when she laughed. He bet he'd like it even more if she laughed with genuine joy rather than mockery. "Not really. Honestly, I think if we spend any significant time together, it's gonna happen on its own."

"It?"

He raised a brow. "You want details? 'Cause they say anticipation is half the fun."

She sucked in an enraged breath. "Well, you're certainly full of yourself." As soon as the words were out of her mouth, she pressed her lips together. Probably expected him to comment on how she'd soon be full of him. But he wasn't that tacky. Either that, or he just didn't want to be too predictable.

Shrugging, he leaned against one paneled wall, his gaze wandering to the entry table and framed pictures next to him. His eye caught on a picture of a teenage Nina laughing with a girl that looked remarkably like her. A sister, perhaps? Probably. She was pretty, too, but even though she smiled in the picture, her gaze seemed troubled. It was a notable contrast to the happiness in Nina's eyes. In the picture. Not now. Now she was looking at him with wary expectation. As if waiting for him to acknowledge something. What had she said? Oh, right. That he was full of himself.

"Actually, I wish it was just a matter of being conceited. But I'm just a realist. I don't want to act on the attraction. Neither do you. But regardless, if we spend the next week together, it will happen."

Her pupils dilated but she raised her chin rebelliously. "And that's not enough to scare you away?"

"I guess some part of me still likes to live dangerously," he said softly. He frowned at his choice of words. Feared that she'd catch his meaning—that part of him no longer liked to live dangerously anymore. Feared that she'd wonder what had caused a change in him and maybe even question him on it. And he did not want to talk about Lana with this woman. Not now. Not ever. Quickly, he asked, "Do you? Like to live dangerously?"

"Not particularly." She paused several seconds, as if weighing her next words. "How long have you been here, by the way?"

"Outside, you mean? Not long. Why?"

"Because I'm wondering something. You're trying to scare me away with this silly idea of us 'doing it.' Maybe you'd try scaring me away a different way, too."

He straightened and scowled. "What do you mean?"

She pursed her lips, as if she was weighing something over in her mind, then she shook her head. She even waved her hand in a gesture of dismissal. "Oh, nothing. It's just, you've suddenly shown up being all charming and honest. It's thrown me for a bit of a loop."

"You find me charming like this? I'll have to keep that in mind."

He caught it. Just the hint of a smile before she wiped it away. It made him wonder how far he'd go to see it again.

"What I mean is, I have to wonder if you're luring me into some kind of trap even as you deny doing so. If you're pretending to put all your cards on the table even as you stack the deck against me."

"Well, no matter what I say you're not going to believe me, are you?"

"I suppose not."

"Right. So we're going to be professionals about

this. Whether we want to be or not. We'll give this shadow program a real chance, and let the rest take care of itself. No hidden agendas or dirty tricks. Deal?" He held out his hand for her to shake.

Warily, she clasped it.

He immediately frowned. "You're cold as ice. And you're shaking. What's wrong?"

She quickly pulled her hand from his. "I guess that's just what I do when I'm around you. Probably overcome by all those images of us 'doing it.' But don't worry, by the time we start working together, I'll have it under control. Good day, Detective. I'll see you on Monday."

CHAPTER TWELVE

SIMON WALKED OUT TO his car but abruptly stopped. Something wasn't right. He couldn't say what, exactly, but his gut was telling him not to leave. The few times he'd failed to listen to his gut had resulted in danger. Most recently, his gut had told him that Lana's actions had put *her* in danger. It had told him to stay with her. Watch her. Protect her. He hadn't done that. Instead, he'd let his pride and his anger affect him. He'd walked away from her, which had given her the opportunity to walk straight into a serial killer's arms…

Shit. Thoughts like that didn't support his comments to Mac, and what he'd thought was his honest belief, that he didn't blame himself for Lana's death. He wondered what Nina Whitaker would say about that. That he truly held himself responsible? Whatever her response would be, and however much it would anger him, he wasn't going to ignore the unsettled feeling he was having now.

Doubling back to her front entrance, he knocked on the door. She didn't answer. He tried the handle, but the door was locked. Frowning, he considered the possibilities. She could have hopped in the shower. Or more likely, stepped out onto the patio to take in her spectacular view.

He went around the side of the house. The backyard was a mess—piles of brick and earth, the place obviously undergoing some sort of landscaping. But she wasn't on the patio. After hesitating briefly, he tested the small patio door next to the kitchen, and found it unlocked. Not smart of her but lucky for him. He inched it open and called out, "Nina. It's Simon."

Again, no answer.

Alarm crawled up his spine.

Where the hell had she gone?

"Nina?"

He stepped in. Kept calling her name as he checked one room after another. He didn't draw his gun, but he was acutely aware of the weight of his off-duty piece in his pocket holster. He positioned his hand at the ready, prepared to use the weapon if he needed to.

In the living room, he startled a large tortoiseshell cat with large white rings around its eyes—like a clown face. The cat hissed, then dove under the couch. He scanned the area, noting the impressive main-floor kitchen. Next to the kitchen were two doorways, one leading to an informal dining area, the other leading to a huge pantry and food prep area that was as big as the kitchen and dining area in his own apartment. Everything was neat and tidy, but the airy rooms only served to highlight how little space one tiny female would occupy. He wondered if the sheer size of the house made her feel as lonely as he imagined it would.

He didn't like the idea of her being lonely. Hated it, in fact. It just didn't seem fair. She obviously had a huge heart and a tremendous amount of courage—the way she'd placed herself in front of Michael Callahan, protecting him despite Simon's derision and aggression, spoke to that. Who protected her? Who brought her joy? Pleasure?

And what the hell business was that of his? His increasing obsession with her bothered him. It made him want to turn around and get the hell out of there. But then he remembered how cold her hand had been. How she'd been trembling. Almost as if she'd been scared. And how she'd obviously been trying to hide that from him.

He found the idea of her being scared even more disturbing than the idea of her being lonely.

He was heading toward what he figured was her bedroom when she stepped out, her gaze on a piece of paper. She must have caught sight of him from her peripheral vision because she glanced up. And screamed.

Simon held his hands out, palms up, surrender style. At the same time, he noted the look of wild fear in her eyes. She was wearing earphones and blasting music. Her fear was understandable given he'd startled her in her home. But he still couldn't shake the feeling that she'd already been frightened before that. "Whoa. It's just me."

She ripped her earbuds out of her ears. "What the hell are you doing in here?"

"I'm sorry. I knocked. Called out. You didn't hear me."

"So you just decided to come inside?"

"I thought something was wrong."

"What? Why?"

"I don't know. Just a feeling. Something told me you were in danger."

It was quick, but he saw her expression flicker.

He narrowed his eyes. "Maybe I wasn't too far off the mark. What's going on, Nina?"

"Nothing." But she shifted, unsuccessfully trying to hide the paper she was holding behind her.

"Don't lie to me. What is it? Did you get bad news?"

She stared at him, trying to decide whether to trust him, then shrugged. "I got a note from someone who's angry with me. It was a little disturbing."

"By disturbing, do you mean threatening? Let me see it."

She took two steps back. "No."

"Why?"

"Because it's a private communication."

"By all means. Let's protect the privacy of someone who's threatening you. Damn it, there's no patient here that you need to protect. And if someone's frightened you, you shouldn't be protecting him at all."

"It isn't so much what was said that frightened me as the fact that it was left on my doorstep. I—I don't like knowing someone who's angry with me knows where I live, especially since my house alarm is broken. But I'm sure it's nothing."

"You can't know that. Let me see it. Please."

He knew it was the *please* that finally did it. If he'd pushed, if he'd ordered, he had no doubt she'd do her best to keep the note away from him. As it was, she hesitated, sighed and then tried to hand him the note.

"Hold it out for me," he said. "So I don't get my prints on it."

She did. Simon's jaw clenched as he read it.

"Do you have a Ziploc bag you can put it in?"

She hesitated. Nodded. Quickly got an oversize plastic bag from the kitchen and put the letter inside. Only then did Simon take it from her.

"Do you know who left it for you?"

"No." But again there was that slight hesitation.

"Doc?"

"I don't know. I automatically thought of one person, but he's on the other side of the nation. Or at least he should be." She rubbed her forehead, then shook her head. "No. It can't be him."

"Him who?"

She opened her mouth. Shut it. "Nope. I'm not accusing a man of something like this when I don't have proof that it's him."

"What if the proof is the fact that you end up hurt? Proof is the police's job to find. Or maybe it's just that all psychiatrists would rather risk their lives and the lives of other people to give dangerous criminals the benefit of the doubt."

"So we're back to your disdain for my job?"

He could have said they'd never left it, but he didn't. "Nope. We're here. With you scared. With someone threatening your life. And with you not willing to tell me about it. Yet you forget. We're supposed to work together. Haven't you considered the fact that someone threatening you might be a threat to me, as well? To your patients?"

She bit her lip, obviously taking what he said seriously. "You're right," she said quietly. "I'll tell you. But I want your word you're not going to go off half-cocked, hunting down someone who might have simply let his emotions get the better of him and written down something that he shouldn't have. It doesn't mean he has any intention of acting on it."

"I promise not to go off half-cocked. I'm not much for half measures anyway. When I do something, if I 'do it,' I make sure I go in all the way."

The sexual innuendo was unmistakable and deliberate on his part. At worst, he wanted to distract her; at best, he wanted to make her smile. The fact she didn't smile let alone call him on his statement told him she really was scared. But she wasn't stupid. She narrowed her eyes, searching his face for humor, and he was careful to keep his expression blank.

"Have a seat," she finally said. "I have to get something, and then we'll talk."

NINA WENT INTO HER STUDY, shut the door and leaned back against it as she tried to get her racing heart to slow down. Simon had scared her, yes, but she was feeling off balance for another reason altogether. Because of the letter she'd received yes, but also because...well, she'd thought he was sexy before...

When he acted all firm and protective of her? Wow.

She'd been tempted to throw herself in his arms and gobble up all that manly strength and protection he was offering her. As much as that made her feminist ideals howl in shame, it was only natural to want to be taken care of at times. She knew that. She just couldn't let herself give in to those feelings and actually rely on him. At least, not for anything more than his professional advice or protection.

She moved to the drawer where she kept the three cards she'd accumulated over the years. Again, she hesitated. She believed Beth's father was essentially harmless, but finding the letter on her doorstep had been a deviation from his routine. It was troubling, and Simon was right. She might be willing to take chances with her own safety, but she couldn't do that with others. It was best to show him the cards, maybe even let him ask a few questions, rather than be stupid or prideful about it. It might go a long way to showing him that she wasn't careless or a complete bleeding heart. Go a long way to getting him to trust her. She wanted to help people, but she didn't want to endanger herself, emotionally or physically, to do it. Since they'd be working together, it was important he know that.

She took a deep breath before walking toward the kitchen. She'd get more Ziploc bags. Put the cards inside before she gave them to—

She passed the living room and, at the sight in front of her, she stopped abruptly.

Simon Granger was sprawled out on her couch, his knees splayed casually open. One arm rested against the back of the couch, while the other encircled her cat, Six. It struck her how big he looked, how masculine against her chenille sofa, and next to her curved-leg coffee table and end tables. When he saw her, he straightened and she mentally shook herself. Rushing to the kitchen, she retrieved six of the largest Ziploc bags she had. One at a time, she placed each card and each envelope inside a separate bag, spreading each card open first so he could easily view both the outside and inside. As she did so, she was acutely aware of his gaze on her and the way her hands trembled slightly.

Finally, she sat next to him, taking care to keep several feet of breathing room between them.

"What's its name?" Simon asked.

"What?"

"Your cat."

"Oh." She sighed. "Her name is Six."

He nodded. "On account of her having six toes on her left hind leg."

She let out a light laugh. "You don't miss much, do you?"

"Nope," he said.

"Well, I know it's not the most original name, but it was better than the name the shelter gave her."

"Which was?"

"Clownface. I just couldn't do that to her."

"Yep," Simon said, grinning. "Six is *such* a better name." His grin faded, though, when he glanced at the cards in her hand. "Come closer and let me see that," he said, patting the empty cushion next to him. "And tell me about this threat."

She hesitated, then shifted closer. His heat and solid strength washed over her. Comforted her. The relief almost made her dizzy. She was used to being by herself. To living in this great big house with no one for company but Six. It rarely bothered her and most of the time she enjoyed her independence.

But it was comforting to know she wasn't entirely alone now. Not in this.

She hadn't told anyone about the cards she received because she hadn't wanted her past to play any role in her life in San Francisco. Maybe it was time to tell someone. And Simon obviously wanted to help. "Every year I get a card from a patient's father. It marks the year of the patient's death. She was a teenage girl named Elizabeth Davenport. Beth. She came to me after her mother died. She was suicidal. Suffered from acute depression and delusions. And despite my best efforts, she ended up killing herself."

"That's rough. I'm sorry."

She nodded and held out the cards. "Her father blamed me. Quite publicly. He couldn't tell reporters enough about how I'd screwed up and cost his daughter her life."

"Did he ever try to hurt you? Physically?"

"One night he cornered me in a parking lot. He screamed at me. At one point, he grabbed my arm. But one of my colleagues chased him off. I never saw him again after that."

"But you heard from him."

"Yes. Three times. The third the most recent—the day you and I met. The third anniversary of Beth's death. I—I didn't really take it seriously. And I assumed that would be the last I'd hear from him. At least for another year."

"Until you received the letter today."

"Maybe it's a coincidence?" Her question sounded weak to her own ears. "Granted, it could be from Beth's father, but it's not consistent with the cards I've received. Plus, he's always handwritten his notes. This one is typed."

"He threatened you in the recent card he mailed you. Why not up the ante? Why not come here and prove he's serious? That doesn't sound like coincidence to me. It sounds like cold-blooded intent—at the very least, intent to scare you. And he obviously succeeded."

He read over the three cards she'd handed him, his face darkening with each one. He picked up a pen and small pad of paper he'd placed on the coffee table. "What's his name and where does he live?"

"Lester Davenport. He lived in Charleston, last I heard."

"That's where you lived before moving to San Francisco?"

"Yes, but I also lived in Seattle for a while before finally deciding on San Francisco."

"And he found you in Seattle, too," he said, noting the Seattle address on one of the envelopes he held. "Do you know how?"

"No, but I'm a licensed professional who works with the public. I imagine it wouldn't be too difficult to search for psychiatric practices on the web. After all, you found out where I lived, right?"

"I have access to public records that a normal person doesn't. You need to make an official complaint," he said.

Her chest went tight. "I—I don't want to do that."

"Why not? Even if he didn't threaten you with the letter, the cards are sufficient. Right now they're just written threats, but someone with a vendetta will often escalate their behavior with no warning whatsoever. There's a real threat of actual harm, and you need to take that seriously."

"I do. I admit the letter I received this morning scared me—I'm still scared—but we don't know that Lester Davenport left it. Even if he did, it doesn't mean he'll really hurt me. I met him before Beth killed herself. He brought her to me because he wanted to get her help. I honestly think he's just a father in mourning. Beth was his only daughter and before she committed suicide, her mother died of cancer. Lester lost everything he loved in a matter of months. He's stuck in the grief process. People say things when they're hurt and grieving that they don't mean. That they'd never say otherwise. I think he simply needs to vent, and I don't want to take legal action because he acted rashly and end up causing more problems for him."

She sounded almost desperate to make him believe her. And she knew why. Knew she was making excuses for Lester because she was also making excuses for her own father, the same man who in his grief had told Nina it was her fault Rachel had died.

Simon watched her carefully, as if aware something in her past was driving her to defend Lester Davenport. Hell, he could have been a therapist himself given the way he was studying her.

Finally, he said, "You know it's him, Nina."

She shook her head. Then somewhat contradicted the gesture by saying, "Maybe. Part of me might suspect it's him. But I can't know it. And neither can you."

He grunted. Stood abruptly, which dislodged Six and caused her to prance away. "Will you at least let me check it out? Have the letter processed for fingerprints? Make some inquiries. Unofficially?"

Unofficially. That she could handle. And like he'd said—they'd be working together. He might not be thrilled by that fact, but he obviously took his job seriously and would feel compelled to look into the situation whether she gave him her permission or not. She was a witness and a potential victim, that was all. Just another part of the job for him. He was attracted to her, but that wasn't the same as caring about her. After all, he'd told her flat out that he didn't even like her. She had to remember that. "That's fine. Just keep it off the books."

He nodded, and tucked his pad and pen into his inside jacket pocket.

She stood, as well. "Thank you again."

He stared at her. Then to her surprise, he stepped closer, raised his hand and lightly gripped her chin. "Thank you for confiding in me. Despite the issues we have between us, I wouldn't want anything to happen to you."

She jerked at his words. His words negated her earlier thoughts. Made it sound like he really did care about her. Probably just more games to manipulate her and get what he wanted out of the shadow program, she thought. But she'd play along. "Are you always this straightforward?"

"Honestly? I'm usually not this talkative. Just ask anyone I work with. But when I do talk, yes, I try to be a straight shooter."

Yes, that was more than apparent. She wondered if he knew how utterly attractive that made him. More attractive than he already was, which was obviously considerable.

She bit her lip.

She was already playing along. Now that her fear and worry about the letter had been dissipated slightly, she found all she wanted to do was luxuriate in this odd connection she felt to him. Despite the "issues" he'd referred to, he was a good cop. A good man. One who said he was attracted to her and one who'd already verbalized his utter certainty that, if they worked together as planned, they'd eventually end up "doing it." Having sex. Sex she hadn't had in a good long time. Sex she hadn't wanted to have in a long time.

But that had obviously changed. Her body wanted sex. With this man. The sooner the better.

Of course, that couldn't happen, but he'd already shown a propensity to flirt. To tease. Maybe he'd be willing to do it a little longer. Maybe flirting with him—maybe even kissing him—would stabilize and reinvigorate her as much as she'd been hoping her planned trip to the ocean would.

"So," she said, reaching up to lightly trail her fingertips against the outer wrist of the hand he was touching her with. She liked the way his eyes immediately darkened. "Were you being honest when you said you're attracted to me? When you said something happening between us is unavoidable?"

"Yeah. I was." He frowned and pulled his hand away from her touch. Interesting. Despite having more than his fair share of chutzpah, was he actually scared of the very attraction he'd just copped to? Actually scared of little old her?

"But that doesn't mean you don't have a say," he explained. "I think you're attracted to me, too, but if you don't want anything to happen, all you have to say is no and nothing will."

"But you doubt my ability to say no?" She smiled slightly. "You're very perceptive, Detective."

He narrowed his eyes. Those same eyes that had caused her to wax so poetically in her own mind when Karen had asked about them. Steely gray, they should have been remote. Hard. Instead, they reminded her of velvet. And how much she loved the feel of velvet.

"Meaning?" As if against his better judgment, his hand slowly lifted again. Instead of cupping her chin this time, he cradled her cheek in his palm.

Her breath quickened and she moistened her lips. His lips parted slightly as he watched her.

"Meaning, we aren't working together. Not yet. If 'something' is going to happen between us anyway, maybe—" When she paused, he swiped his thumb slowly against her lower lip. Automatically, she gasped at the pleasure that small touch brought her.

He shifted ever closer, brushing her body with his. "Maybe…what?"

"Maybe we should—grab the bull by the horns, so to speak."

He smiled, not just with his mouth, but with his eyes. Eyes that were focused intently on *her* mouth. "Exactly what part of me—or you—is the bull is this scenario?"

"What I mean is, maybe we should try to defuse any tension by satisfying our curiosity now. Our curiosity about kissing," she amended quickly. "Not anything more. But a first kiss? That's bound to be on our minds. Considering we're attracted to each other, I mean."

"Right." His gaze remained on her mouth. "Seems reasonable," he said.

"Right. Especially because—well, maybe what we're anticipating won't live up to the fantasy. That's almost always the case. If we kiss, chances are we'll see this—this—"

"Connection?" he asked.

"Yes, chances are we'll see this connection between us isn't anything special."

He brought his gaze up to hers. He looked doubtful, then amused, but simply said, "Hmm. I'm willing to give it a try if you are." He arched a challenging brow.

She swallowed hard and said, "I— Yes. Yes, I am."

"Good."

Instead of lowering his head and kissing her right away, however, he continued to stare into her eyes. He rubbed his thumb against her lip again. His stare combined with his gentle touch had her trembling. It was so much better than trembling with fear, the way she had been when he'd first arrived.

"There's just one little problem, though," he said.

She struggled to concentrate. "What's that?"

"What happens when a kiss blows our mind? What happens when it isn't enough? Because I'm pretty certain that's what's going to happen."

"You are?"

"Yeah."

"Well, you've been so honest with me. And I have to be honest in return. We can't sleep with each other. It would complicate things. But this…maybe we can have this. And hope that'll be enough?"

He didn't agree with her. She hadn't been expecting him to. And though she'd said the words, though she'd meant them and knew they had to be said, she didn't quite believe them herself.

"Well, here goes…" he said.

And covered her mouth with his.

KISSING NINA WHITAKER felt fresh.

New.

Like he'd never kissed a woman before, and for a man of Simon's experience, that was saying something. It troubled him at first. Made him hold back. But when she seemed to melt—her mouth parting, her body relaxing into his—he couldn't hold back anymore.

Groaning, he opened his mouth, slanting it to get at her better. Deeper. His tongue didn't so much invade as it took with confidence of its welcome. She'd admitted she wanted him. Hell, she'd initiated and justified this kiss even as she'd warned him he couldn't have more. That thought grated at him. Spoiled the pleasure he was experiencing more than he wanted to admit. But he forced himself to push his agitation away.

Here. Now. They could have this, she'd said. And he was going to take advantage of every last second of it.

God, he'd missed this. The closeness of a woman. Her softness. Her scent. They highlighted his strength and cautioned him to be gentle even as they urged him to let down his defenses. Yet even as he wallowed in the familiar feeling of intimacy, he was acutely aware, once again, that this was different. She felt different. Tasted different. Smelled different.

Better than anything or anyone he'd ever had before.

Her tongue tangled with his, rubbing almost shyly against him, and he lowered his hand to the small of her back, urging her closer. Her breasts pressed against his lower chest, and though he'd thought something about her car and then her house didn't quite fit, that wasn't true for their bodies. They fit. Divinely.

He was breathing fast and his skin prickled and he wanted more. He wanted to strip her. He wanted to pick her up and carry her to her bedroom. He wanted inside her. Now.

"Simon," she gasped, and he became aware of her hands, not pulling him closer but holding him away. He pulled back. Or tried to. His body didn't cooperate the way he was expecting it to.

Not that he could blame it, really.

His hands had fallen even lower to cup her ass and his lower body was pressed tightly against hers. That warm, sweet juncture between her thighs cradled his erection and without his conscious thought, he was pushing into her, as if he could get through the barriers of their clothing and into her warm moist heat by sheer will. Her eyes were wide. Slightly shocked.

And he felt that same shock rippling through him.

Holy fuck. What was this? He'd been planning on enjoying a kiss. He'd been looking forward to challenging her statement that a kiss wouldn't lead to anything more. But he hadn't been expecting to be swept away by his own passion for her. Forget passion. By his own *need*.

He couldn't need her. He wouldn't.

But he wasn't an idiot, either.

Working together was going to be damn difficult. Even more difficult than he'd anticipated.

Forcibly, he uncurled his hands from her flesh and took a step back.

He cleared his throat. "You said we can't sleep together because it'll complicate things, right?"

Slowly, she nodded.

He took a deep breath. Released it. "I think we already hit complicated and dove straight into a fucking mess."

CHAPTER THIRTEEN

ON MONDAY MORNING, Simon pushed back from the old newspaper articles he was reading and cursed.

Nina Whitaker wasn't just rich. She was connected. Well connected.

She was the daughter of Charles Whitaker, a former governor of South Carolina.

He shouldn't be surprised, he thought. Even without the Pacific Heights mansion, she screamed class and pedigree and affluence more than any woman he'd ever met.

Yet part of him had been surprised. Because of the car she drove. Because of the porn flick she'd been carrying when he'd first met her. But mostly because of what she was trying to accomplish. Why wasn't she in South Carolina, using her father's connections to make the differences she sought, he wondered. But he already knew the answer to that.

First, she'd already accomplished what she wanted in South Carolina. Her MHIT program had started in Charleston and was now firmly established there.

Second, she was running.

And with good reason.

She'd told him about Elizabeth Davenport, her patient who had committed suicide, but Nina hadn't told him about her sister. The sister who had committed suicide years before her patient had. There hadn't been the same amount of press coverage there'd been on Elizabeth Davenport's suicide, likely because, unlike Lester Davenport, Nina's father had swept everything under the rug. But the brief reference to the event and her sister Rachel's subsequent obituary hadn't been difficult for Simon to find, either. All he'd had to do was conduct a search of Nina's and her father's names, and it had come up. Anyone who cared to look for it could access information about the tragic event. One article had even included a picture, not of Rachel, but of a teenage Nina, sitting on the stoop of a house, looking scared while police officers and medics talked close by.

He recalled the photograph he'd seen in her foyer. The picture of her laughing and embracing a girl that looked eerily like her. A girl that had to have been her sister. What had losing that sister cost her? Especially given that her sister hadn't died because she was sick or murdered, but because she'd *chosen* to die. Chosen to take her own life, regardless of the fact that Nina had obviously loved her.

He barely knew Nina, yet it made no difference. His heart ached for her.

He generally thought of psychologists and psychiatrists as bleeding hearts and, given Nina's background, it was probably truer than normal. She'd made excuses for Lester Davenport's actions, writing them off as grief over losing his daughter. It was a grief she and her family were intimately acquainted with and explained why she'd been so reluctant to cause Davenport trouble without concrete proof he'd left that letter for her. Hell, she hadn't wanted to cause him trouble even assuming he *had* left the letter. She'd suffered tragedy

early on in her life and it was no wonder she was trying to make positive changes for those suffering from
mental illness. With that kind of emotion driving her,
how could she possibly see that her well-meaning compassion and yearning to help a disadvantaged group
of citizens could be dangerous? To other civilians. To
cops. To herself.

And just what was he going to do about that?

He was still contemplating the question when she
walked into the SIG detective pit. His gaze took her
in hungrily, but the visual stimulation wasn't enough.
He wanted to touch her again. Explore her body, inside and out.

"Detective Granger," she greeted him, her voice
breathless.

He looked up in time to catch her blushing and
he knew immediately she was remembering the kiss
they'd shared. He didn't have to remember. It hadn't
left his mind for one freaking second. She must have
seen the rush of desire that washed over him because
she glanced away and shifted uncomfortably.

"Am I—" She cleared her throat. "Am I dressed ap-
propriately?" She wore heather-gray slacks, a purple-
and-black top and a purple sweater. Black ballet flats
with a jaunty ribbon completed the elegant package.
"We didn't really talk about it, but I assumed slacks
would be fine. Do I pass muster?"

Right. As if his gaze had been roving her body simply to assess her clothes rather than to appreciate the
woman underneath. But whatever. He could give her
that illusion. He leaned back in his chair and steepled
his fingers against his chest. "You look fine," he said,
and thought, *No truer words have ever been spoken.*

She looked amazing. And he needed to stop thinking about how great she looked—how much better she'd look if they'd just made love—and focus on the day ahead. "Have a seat. I'd like to go over some things before we head out."

She nodded and took a step toward the chair beside his desk. Before she could sit, however, two men walked into the room. Commander Stevens and Gil Archer.

Lana's father.

Simon couldn't help it. He stiffened, something that Nina obviously noticed.

Her features grew quizzical and she turned to face the other men. They were about the same age, fit despite their graying hair and both wore suits. The only striking difference between them was that Gil was a few inches shorter than Stevens.

Commander Stevens held out his hand. "Good morning, Dr. Whitaker. It's good to see you. Do you have any questions I can answer before you and Detective Granger head out today?"

Nina glanced at Simon. "We were just about to sit down and discuss what he has in store for me." Her gaze shifted to Gil Archer, who was just holding out his hand to Simon.

"It's good to see you again, Simon," he said quietly.

"Likewise, sir," Simon said, though he could barely speak past the lump in his throat. Gil Archer had always been unfailingly polite to Simon, before, during and after Simon's personal relationship with Lana. He'd never said anything to make him think that he blamed Simon for his daughter's death, but it didn't matter. Even during the best of times, when Simon knew he wasn't to blame for what had happened, he had trouble remembering that when in her parents' company. He didn't see them often, but because Stevens and Archer were old friends, it happened on occasion. At least Lana's mother wasn't here. The last time he'd seen her, she'd vacillated between being catatonic and sobbing over the loss of her daughter. Of course, that had been at Lana's funeral…

Aware that Nina's gaze was bouncing back and forth between them, Simon cleared his throat. "Mr. Gil Archer, this is Dr. Nina Whitaker."

Archer nodded and smiled. "Of course. Dr. Whitaker." He held out his hand, cradling Nina's when she placed it in his. "You're the psychiatrist Stevens has been telling me so much about. Not to mention that I read about you in the paper. Commendable work helping Simon find that little girl. Rebecca Hyatt's grandfather is a member of my golfing club. Very appreciative. And very wealthy. We both donate considerable amounts of money to worthy causes each year. Between you and me, I'm sure he'd be happy to donate funds to the proposed program Stevens will be considering. If it moves forward, of course."

"Of course," Nina said mildly. "That would be wonderful. And do you feel the same way, sir?"

Archer glanced at Stevens and laughed appreciatively. "Watch out, Stevens. This one will have you agreeing to a number of things before you know it." He turned back to Nina. "Do I feel the same way? I believe I do. My daughter, Lana, was a psychiatrist and I couldn't have been more proud of her. Funny," he said, tilting his head. "You even look a little like her. Isn't that right, Simon?"

Simon shifted uneasily. He'd thought the same thing when he'd first met Nina, but oddly enough, he'd stopped seeing the resemblance since then. At some point, he'd stopped comparing her to Lana. In fact, he realized suddenly, he'd stopped thinking of Lana altogether. At least, he'd stopped torturing himself with thoughts of her like he usually did. Mostly what he'd been thinking about the past few days had been *her*. Nina. The kiss they'd shared. And how much he wanted to kiss her again.

Instead of agreeing with Archer, Simon said, "It was good seeing you, sir. Commander. But as Nina said, we were just sitting down to get started."

"Right. Right," Archer said. "I suppose we should get going. I was just checking with Stevens here to see if he had any recommendations. We're a little short-staffed at work and getting bigger and bigger contracts every day. If you're ever interested in extra pocket change, Simon, or know someone who is, just let me know."

Pocket change? For the most part, Archer paid big bucks, which was why so many cops had signed on with his firm after taking early-retirement packages.

"Gil runs one of the biggest security firms in the city," Commander Stevens explained to Nina.

"I do, but as I said, I'm a big supporter of mental health professionals. In fact, I'm on the Board of Directors of the San Francisco Golf Club and we're sponsoring an upcoming fundraiser to raise funds for those with mental illness. I believe you'll be attending, Simon?"

"That's right, sir."

"Perhaps, Dr. Whitaker, you can join us, as well?

Maybe you can even be a featured speaker, talk about this extra training you're proposing, so we can waive the entry fee? Shall I send you an invitation?"

She nodded and smiled, but was probably just being polite. Any idiot could see she'd stiffened up ever since Gil Archer had told her she looked like his daughter and had turned to Simon for confirmation.

Stevens and Archer left, and Nina finally sat down.

Her gaze rested heavily on him, but he tried to ignore it as he took his own chair. "So, have you done a ride along before?"

She paused, then nodded. "I have. In Charleston. Not over the course of several days, the way I'm going to do here. But I did a day here and there."

"Did anything interesting happen?"

She shrugged. "Not really. Some traffic stops. Nothing terribly dramatic."

And had that disappointed her? he wondered. Had she been craving excitement? Adventure? Was that what this was really about? But no, she hadn't been any more thrilled with this partnership than he'd been. And despite their kiss, or maybe because of it, she probably still wasn't.

"We'll head over to SFPD where you can watch some of the intake procedures. We'll also keep track of specific calls and respond to the most interesting ones. We'll just be observers. Patrol will handle the action. I know you've got a job to do, but so do I. The main thing we're going to be focused on is your safety. You're not going to do anything to endanger yourself. Is that clear?"

She raised a brow. "I had no plans to do so, so that's comforting."

"I just want to make it clear—this isn't about you trying to save anyone."

Now she frowned. "The program I'm advocating is all about preventing harm and saving lives, but I wasn't planning on diving in front of a bullet for anyone today. Not even you."

"It's not me I'm worried about."

"Then whom, exactly, are you worried about? And what makes you think I'd endanger myself to help a total stranger?"

When he didn't immediately answer, her gaze flickered down to his desk and the papers there. He knew the instant she figured out what they were—old press coverage of her sister's suicide—when her face paled. He didn't like the flash of pain on her expression and immediately wanted to shove the papers into the trash. Away from her view. But he forced himself not to. He had a point to make. An important one. Her past was painful, but it was best he knew about it. Best *she knew* he knew about it.

"I'm sorry about your sister," he said softly. "About Elizabeth Davenport, too."

"But?" she asked snappishly.

"But a woman on a crusade is a dangerous thing. That's why we need to discuss these things now. Before we hit the road."

She said nothing else. She refused to say anything else. And he refused to give in to his sudden urge to shift guiltily, as if he'd done something wrong. To counter the feeling, he went on the offensive.

"You told me about Elizabeth. Don't you think you should have told me about your sister, too?"

Her eyes widened. "Why? The only reason I told

you about Beth was the threatening note. It was relevant. Rachel's death…isn't relevant to anything at all."

She was lying. He knew it and so did she. Something like that would be relevant to everything she did, but before he could respond, she stood. "Besides, telling you would have been too easy. It would have deprived you of the pleasure of doing your little detective thing, right? I knew you'd look into it anyway and find out yourself."

But her last words didn't ring true. She'd been truly blindsided by the fact he'd dug up information on her sister. Or maybe she'd just been blindsided by the fact he was making her talk about it.

"My little detective thing, huh?" he asked softly. "I don't know if you've noticed, but there's really nothing little about me." She blushed and he'd bet she had to forcibly stop her gaze from dropping to his crotch. Not so much to admire him, but to put a curse on him. "Besides, sounds like rationalization to me."

"I'm nothing if not rational. Believe me, your warnings are unnecessary. I don't have a death wish and I don't plan on endangering myself to help strangers in some misguided attempt to save my dead sister. Is that what you wanted to hear?"

"Yes," he said quietly.

"Great. Then how about you tell me something now?"

"What is it?" he asked warily.

"Who in your past endangered herself to help others? Your mother? Your sister? No, your girlfriend." He stiffened and she nodded. "Was she a psychiatrist? Is that why you hate my profession so much?"

"Yes, she was my girlfriend. Well, ex-girlfriend, but

still. And yes, she was a psychiatrist. And while *hate* is too strong a word, I admit I'm leery of those in your profession because she died and she didn't have to. She was murdered by a serial killer she was trying to help."

"Let me guess. We're talking about Gil Archer's daughter. Lana. The one he said I look like."

"We're talking about Lana, yes. And as to whether you look like her?" He studied her while she held herself stiffly. "You're both blonde. Pretty. But different," he finished lamely.

"Yeah. I'm alive. But apparently I'm paying for her mistakes. You grew to distrust her, so now you distrust me. You distrust all psychiatrists. You probably distrust anyone with a mental health issue. Heck, anyone with anything you perceive as a weakness at all. So how do you handle your own weaknesses? Or do you simply expect yourself to be Superman?"

"Don't," he snapped. "Don't psychoanalyze me. I'm a cop and you have a history—"

"A history that's my business."

"That's where you're wrong. It's your business so long as it doesn't affect me. That being the case, I just want to make sure we're clear on what this next week is going to look like. That's all." He stood and shrugged into his jacket. "You ready to go?"

"No," she said quietly. "You're coming down on me because I withheld my past, or so you think. Don't do the same thing. My sister's suicide was a tragedy and sure, it could conceivably impair my judgment. But what do you call your girlfriend's death? What about the fact you admitted it affects how you think about psychiatrists and I'm betting probably affects how you think about the mentally ill, as well? You want to question me about my past? You can expect the same thing in return."

Simon's jaw clenched. "Fine." He sat back down again and held his arms out. "What do you want to know?"

Her eyes widened slightly before she asked, "How—how long ago did she die?"

"Six months ago. Next question."

"Were you there when it happened?"

"No. But I saw her afterward and I know exactly what he did to her. Given how often I imagine what really happened, I might as well have been. Next question."

She shook her head. "I—I'm sorry."

"And like I said, I'm sorry about your sister. We've both had to deal with tragedy. I'm just trying to make sure we don't have to deal with more."

"Fine." She stood. "Have I alleviated your concerns?"

Since she obviously wasn't going to ask any more questions about Lana, he relaxed slightly and stood, as well. "Not by a long shot. But I'm hoping we'll get there. I—"

"Hey, Simon."

Simon looked up at the sound of DeMarco's voice. Nina glanced up, too, and for a second he saw appreciation flicker over her face. Mentally, he scowled. Maybe she went for the tall, dark and Latin-lover kind of guy, and DeMarco was certainly that. He clenched his fists when Nina smiled secretively.

"What's so funny?" he growled.

She started. Looked up at him guiltily. "Nothing.

I was just thinking about something my friend Karen said."

"Uh-huh."

DeMarco stepped up to them. He glanced at Nina, then back at Simon with a quick yet not so subtle waggle of his brows.

"Hey, DeMarco. We were just heading out."

"Whoa. Not so fast. Aren't you going to introduce me?"

Simon sighed. "DeMarco, this is Dr. Nina Whitaker. She's going to be shadowing me for a few days."

"Doctor. As in medical doctor or—?"

"Doctor as in a shrink. I mean, psychiatrist," he said when Nina glared at him. "She's advocating some further training for the department."

DeMarco turned a curious gaze on Nina. "Training in what?"

"Expanded training on mental health consumers and de-escalation techniques," she replied. "But more than just that. Part of the program consists of establishing a Mental Health Intervention Team. Training dispatch to route certain calls to that team rather than patrol."

"That right? Sounds fascinating. Tell me more."

"I'm not sure we have time…" She glanced at Simon, and he jerked his chin, indicating she should go ahead. If he was going to give her a fair shot at changing his mind about the merits of the MHIT program, he needed to know more about it. For the first time, he found his curiosity outrunning his skepticism.

"The pilot program I helped launch in Charleston was actually modeled after one formed in Australia. The program has four key aims—reducing the risk of injury to police and mental health consumers during mental health crisis events, improving awareness by frontline police of both the risks involved in dealing with mental health consumers and the strategies to reduce potential injuries, improving collaboration with other government and nongovernment agencies in the response to and management of mental health crisis events, and reducing the time taken by police in the handover of mental health consumers into the health care system."

DeMarco nodded and hummed. "Sounds ideal. But then again, around here we tend to focus more on reality than the ideal, don't we?"

"Meaning?"

"Meaning, we're short on manpower and funds already."

She smiled tiredly, as if she'd heard the same argument over and over again. "And that's justification for failing to implement effective policies? Policies that can improve what you do?"

"Not a justification. Just an explanation. There's a difference, you know."

"Really? Thanks for pointing that out to me," Nina said lightly. "But seriously, many of the police officers in Charleston were skeptical, too. At first. But afterward, the results are unassailable. Self report data has evidenced a reduction in the number of times that medical attention has been required for a member of the public as a result of officers being MHIT trained. Also, MHIT training has increased police officers' confidence when dealing with a mental health problem or a drug-induced psychosis. Qualitative data from Charleston Health staff working specifically in mental health has—"

She stopped speaking abruptly. Simon, who'd been fascinated by what she'd been saying, blinked and glanced at DeMarco. The other man was smiling, as if he, too, found Nina fascinating. And attractive.

Simon felt an immediate sense of possessiveness and had to bite back a warning for the other man to back off.

Nina shook her head. "Sorry about that. As you can probably tell, give me an opening and I'll run with it. I've talked to so many people about supporting the program, including donating to the cause, that I've pretty much memorized the spiel."

"It's a great spiel."

"She already persuaded Gil Archer to donate a chunk of change," Simon said.

DeMarco whistled with admiration. "I'm ready to reach for my checkbook right now. Maybe when we have more time you can tell me more."

Nina just smiled politely while Simon bit back a growl.

DeMarco laughed, then turned to Simon. "We haven't hung out in a while. You wanna get a drink sometime this week?"

Simon's shoulders relaxed. Why was he getting upset over DeMarco's flirtation with Nina? Like Jase, the guy pretty much flirted with anything that moved. "Sure. Let's touch base in a few days."

DeMarco nodded. "Will do." He held out his hand for Nina to shake. "It was nice meeting you, Dr. Whitaker."

"Likewise."

Humming softly, DeMarco settled in at his desk.

Simon shook his head when he recognized the melody, "Me and My Shadow."

As Simon and Nina walked to his car, Simon abruptly asked, "So what was it that your friend told you? And why did it make you smile when you met DeMarco?"

She stumbled slightly, which just piqued his curiosity more. She didn't answer until they were inside the car and he turned toward her, obviously waiting for an answer. "She—um—commented that she thought your team was particularly blessed in the good looks department."

"Right," he snorted and started the car engine. "And DeMarco confirmed that in your eyes?"

"Sure. He's a good-looking guy. Nice, too."

Simon pulled out of the SIG parking lot. It required a key card to enter, so Nina's wreck of a car was probably a few blocks away on the curb or in a public parking lot. "He is nice. And he seemed to like you."

"What's not to like?" she said mildly. "Except in your case, my career, of course."

"Look, I'm trying to be open-minded, I promise. I listened to your spiel, as you called it, back there, didn't I?"

"And?"

"And I can't argue with your good intentions," he acknowledged. "That's not what this is about. Like DeMarco said, it's more about practicality. Reality. That's all."

"Why don't we just agree to disagree on what's practical or realistic?"

"Fair enough."

After several minutes of silence, Simon tapped his

palm on the steering wheel. "We'll be together for the next few days, but I want you to know, if you ever need anything and I'm not around, you can always contact anyone on my team. Commander Stevens. Our lead detective, Mac, is away on a case, but there's Jase or Carrie, who you met the other day. Or even…DeMarco."

She seemed surprised by his non sequitur, but nodded. "Thank you. Does that include a date to the fundraising gala Gil Archer was talking about? Because if DeMarco's free…"

He shot her an exaggerated scowl.

Nina snorted. "I'm joking. Sheesh."

"Please, don't joke about the gala. I'm not exactly looking forward it. At least if you were there, that would be a step in the right direction."

Her eyes rounded at that before she glanced away, trying not to look pleased. "Oh. Well…good. So…does that mean you don't hate me anymore?"

"I never said I hated you. I said I didn't like you. And you were right when you corrected me. It's your career—or more accurately, certain aspects of your training—I don't like, not you."

When she remained quiet, he said, "I might as well keep my reputation as a straight shooter, don't you think?"

"Yes," she said quietly. "That would be good."

"So. Funny that your first attempt at teasing me involves going on a date with DeMarco. Is that called verbalizing an unconscious desire in your line of work?

She blinked dramatically. "Why, Detective Granger, if I didn't know better, I'd say you sound jealous."

He grunted. Then shrugged. "I do, don't I?"

When he said nothing else, she shook her head in amazement. "Straight shooter, right?"

"What can I say? I hate lying, even to myself. Doesn't mean I have to like it. Just like I didn't like DeMarco flirting with you. Maybe I'm just old-fashioned. We have kissed, remember? And despite your stated feelings on the matter, well, as far as I'm concerned, the jury's still out on whether we'll be doing more."

She opened her mouth to reply, then shut it.

"No comment?" he asked. "No insisting that our kiss got me out of your system like you were hoping it would?"

"How about I change the subject and say DeMarco's lucky to have you."

He looked at her chidingly, but gamely responded, "Yeah? Why's that?"

"It's obvious you're friends and he looks up to you. But it's also obvious he uses his humor as a mask. What you do, it's hard. You must rely on each other to stay grounded."

Simon thought about it. Although he didn't ask for help often, he'd never doubted the other SIG members would be there for him if he needed them, but did they feel the same about him? Did DeMarco? DeMarco's flirtations with Nina aside, he'd been quieter lately. More engrossed with his work. Maybe even...troubled?

Was that why DeMarco had asked to have drinks with him? Did he need to talk some things out?

He made a mental note to check in with his friend when they got back.

"So...when I saw him the other day, Commander Stevens commented that you've got your eye on a management position. Is that—is that right?"

"Sure. It's a promotion. More responsibility. More pay. Why not?"

"You seem to love what you do right now. You seem to be good at it."

"Can't stay in one place too long or a person will grow complacent. I made the move last year, but got bored. Transferred back. It—it probably wasn't the wisest choice."

"How come?"

Simon glanced at her. "Are you psychoanalyzing me again, Doc?"

"Not at all. I'm just…trying to get to know you better. You intrigue me."

He grinned. "Yeah? Well the feeling's mutual."

They stared at each other for several seconds before he looked away and concentrated on the road again.

"So you got bored and wanted back on the streets, but what changed? You want to be bored again?"

"Maybe," he said, clearly surprising her. "What? You weren't expecting that answer?"

"Honestly, I wasn't expecting you to answer at all."

"As we've already discussed, Lana dying has had a huge impact on me. I suspect you already guessed that. I cared about her. I loved her. And I hate that I couldn't save her. Of course I don't want to be that helpless again. I want more control in my life. Control I'll have a better chance at maintaining if I'm a captain rather than a detective. For example, the fact that we're having to work together right now? That wouldn't be happening if I was management."

"Good point. Although one subject to debate. Commander Stevens indicated this would give you a better idea of what management was actually like."

Really? Simon thought, wondering which one of them was right. But in the end it didn't really matter. The fact was, even though he hadn't wanted to work with her at first, he was enjoying her company immensely now. And that included the conversation they'd just had about his career decisions and how they'd been affected by Lana's murder, no less. How the hell had that happened? When had he decided that Nina wasn't an opponent, but a smart, beautiful woman whose company he enjoyed enough to let down his guard. When had it become so natural for him to tell a woman he barely knew that he liked her and was thinking about kissing her again?

It had begun when he'd visited her home, he realized. When she'd joked with him about their "doing it." And his respect for her had been growing by leaps and bounds ever since.

Fortunately, before he could think about it too long, a call came through on his radio. He listened to the dispatcher's communication with the patrol officer. Then he switched lanes. "We've got our first call," he said abruptly.

SITTING AT HIS DESK, DeMarco was supposed to be working some leads in a carjacking case but he was growing more and more frustrated with each minute that passed. He'd felt fine when he'd been talking to Simon and his doctor friend, but now for some reason his mind kept wandering. And not to Nina Whitaker, the woman who'd just walked outside with Simon. Hell, that would have been understandable. She was a damn good-looking woman. Smart, too. If he was merely thinking that or about getting her in bed, he wouldn't be worried. Distracted, but not worried.

Instead, DeMarco kept thinking about the murder of that homeless man, Louis Cann, and how he and Simon must have missed something even though he knew damn well they hadn't. And what was worse, DeMarco kept thinking that the Cann case file was calling out to him.

He didn't mean that his instincts were urging him to look at the file.

He meant the file was literally calling out to him from the file cabinet across the room.

"Hey, DeMarco," it was saying in a voice eerily reminiscent of Bill Cosby. "Come and get me. Open me up and I'll show you what you're missing."

DeMarco gritted his teeth and willed the voice to go away. Instead, it continued calling to him. He felt a fine sheen of sweat break out on his body.

Abruptly, he whirled around, wondering if Jase Tyler, their resident jokester, was messing with him. Jase was at his desk all right, but he was talking to Carrie. They both looked up at his sudden movement.

Jase raised a brow. "Hey. You okay, DeMarco?"

DeMarco swallowed hard. "What? Yeah, of course I am."

He turned back to his desk. Blinked rapidly and tried to focus on the papers he'd been reading. The letters were all swirling around. And that damn voice was still calling to him.

Get the fucking file, he told himself. Then the damn voice will shut up.

Slowly, DeMarco stood and made his way to the file cabinet. Acutely aware that Jase and Carrie were watching him, he opened the right drawer, found the file and reached for it. His hand hovered over the file almost fearfully, as if he expected the damn thing to leap out and bite him. He forced himself to pick it up.

A sudden clanging across the room made him jump. He whirled around and shouted, "What the fuck?" Automatically, he reached for his sidepiece.

"Whoa, DeMarco," Carrie said, holding up her hands. "I just tossed my soda can in the trash."

"Jesus, Carrie. You startled me."

When she and Jase just stared at him, he shook his head.

"Damn it, I'm sorry. I think—I think I should go home for a little while. I'm not feeling well."

"You want me to drive you?" Jase asked.

DeMarco shook his head. "No. But thanks. I'll be fine."

But even as he said it, DeMarco knew he was lying. Because he was holding the Cann file now. And it was still calling to him. This time, however, it wasn't taunting him about a dead homeless man named Louis Cann.

It was taunting him about Billy Dahl, the teenage boy DeMarco had shot six years ago in New Orleans.

WHEN SIMON AND NINA arrived at the modest little house off of Mission Street, the patrol car was already parked outside. Simon explained that he'd assess the situation first and would return for her only if he determined it was safe. Even so, he said, "Stay here," before exiting the car and entering the residence. To her surprise, he returned a few minutes later and got back in the car.

Silently, he started the engine and reached to put the car in gear. She stayed him with a hand on his arm.

"What's going on? Is the situation already over?"

He gave a curt shake of his head. "Officer Harrison has it under control. At least, he will."

"But you don't want me to go in," she confirmed. "Who's the suspect? Is he exhibiting signs of mental illness like the dispatcher thought?"

"It's a she. And yes, there may be a mental health issue involved."

"Then why shouldn't we go in?"

The muscle in his jaw ticked. "Look, I just think it would be better if we wait for the next call."

When she merely continued to stare at him, he finally sighed. "It's a teenage girl. A suicidal teenage girl."

"Oh."

He nodded. Said softly, "We'll take another call."

Because she'd told him about Beth. And he'd read about Rachel. And he didn't think she'd be able to handle it.

Was he right? The minute he'd said the words *suicidal teenage girl* her heart had nearly exploded out of her chest. Now her mouth was dry and her hands clammy. *Keep it together, Nina. This isn't about them and it isn't about you. It's about a different girl who might need you.* Or one down the road who might benefit if the MHIT program got the green light.

She cleared her throat. "No. It's okay. If this is clearly a mental health call, it's best I—I see how Officer Harrison handles things."

He turned to look at her, his eyes grim. When he made no move to exit the vehicle, she did it herself. She heard him curse lightly before opening his own door again. They followed the sounds of voices through the front door and the adjacent hallway. A middle-aged woman wearing a pink housecoat and turquoise flip-flops stood in an open doorway. They could hear the low murmur of a male voice in the bedroom and hysterical female sobs getting higher and higher.

"This is Anne's mother," Simon said and although Nina nodded at the woman, she couldn't help wondering what the officer and Simon were thinking, letting the woman stand there in full view of her daughter. For all they knew, the mother had upset the daughter and her presence was continuing to do so. When they peeked inside, Nina immediately stiffened.

The uniformed officer was talking to a teenage girl, telling her everything was going to be okay. The girl, however, had backed herself into a corner, a sure sign that she needed space, but Officer Harrison hadn't gotten the clue. When he took a step closer, his hand on his weapon—maybe his Taser—the girl flinched and shifted, giving Nina a good view of the long-bladed kitchen knife in her hand.

Anne's mother moaned as her daughter stabbed repeatedly at her thigh, nicking herself so that her light Capri pants grew spotted with blood.

"What's he doing?" Nina asked. "He needs to back off."

He looked at her like *she* was crazy. "She's harming herself. He's going to disarm her so we can transport her to a hospital under a 5150 watch. Standard procedure."

"He's only making things worse. She's a wall walker. He needs to back away."

"He can disarm her easily enough."

"And risk someone getting hurt in the process? Trust me, Simon. Ask him to back away."

Simon looked at her, seemed to struggle with himself, then said to Officer Harrison sotto voce, "Officer, return to the hallway, please."

Officer Harrison looked confused but backed toward them. Immediately, the girl stopped stabbing herself.

"Leave me alone," she screamed. "I just want to die. I can't live like this. Can't live—" She jabbed the point of the knife in her thigh again. Now the blood trickled down her leg instead of dotting her capris. The situation was escalating as Anne's mind took her further and further into a deep, dark place.

"Can I talk to her?" Nina asked Simon, pushing back the constriction in her chest.

He nodded, his lips so tight they lost color, but he didn't take his eyes off Anne.

"Anne," Nina called out gently, "I'm not with the police. I'm a doctor and I just want to help you. Will you talk to me?"

It took her a few tries, but within minutes she had the girl's attention. Anne's breathing started to slow and she inched closer toward Nina. Suddenly, however, she froze.

"I don't want to talk to them. To the men. You come in and I'll talk to you."

Nina glanced at Simon, who this time met her eyes. He shook his head.

She turned back to Anne and said, "My friend is afraid you might accidentally cut me with your knife. If he stays in the doorway, will you put it down?"

Shakily, the girl did as she asked, placing the knife on a small television console.

Nina moved forward, but Simon grabbed her arm. "The knife's still within her reach."

"It's okay. She's calmed down. She's not going to hurt me."

"You're not going in there. Have her come out."

"She wants me to come in. As a show of trust. It's okay. She's calm. Willing to talk. I know what I'm doing, Simon. I do this for a living, remember?"

"So do I. You're not—"

A loud thud emanated from the front of the house and Simon automatically glanced that way. Praying she was doing the right thing, Nina pulled out of his grip and walked inside the room with Anne.

Simon's low but vicious curse made her wince, but she put all her attention on Anne and calming the girl down. She'd made progress and was moving toward the doorway with her when a man's harsh voice drifted inside the room.

Anne let out a guttural cry, a low moan that started deep in her throat and carried through the room, ending with Anne screaming, "Don't let him near me!"

A man, overwhelmingly large and with a face full of rage, tried to push past Simon, who held him back. Quick as a snake, Anne grabbed the knife with one hand and Nina with the other.

The young girl was much stronger than she'd looked. Her grip was tight as she held the knife at Nina's side.

"I can't let him near me," Anne choked out.

When the blade pierced fabric and the cool metal met her skin, Nina fought to keep her knees from buckling.

SIMON'S HEART THUDDED in his chest at the sight of the frail, desperate-looking teenager holding a knife to Nina.

"Stop this, Anne. You're such a bad daughter! I'm your father and you will listen to me. Damn it, put the knife down."

Fucker. Didn't Anne's father realize his daughter was about to blow? That this time she wouldn't just be hurting herself, but someone else? Simon shoved the man back with his shoulder and into Harrison's iron grip. Without turning his focus away from Nina, he ground out, "Harrison, get Anne's parents out of here. Now."

When Officer Harrison and Anne's parents were gone, Simon turned back to Anne.

She was trembling and breathing heavily. Nina, despite her best efforts to remain calm, looked scared.

"Listen to me, Anne. You're frightening Nina. You need to let her go now."

"I don't want to see my father." Anne whimpered, her eyes wild.

"No one's going to make you see him," Simon said. His gaze assessed the distance between him and Anne, and he weighed the risk of Tasering her while she still held Nina.

Nina obviously sensed his intentions. "It's okay,

Simon. Just stay back. Remember what I said about giving Anne some space. She and I are going to talk. Can you take a few steps back?"

He frowned, his gaze on the knife at her side. He was so damn angry with her he could barely see straight. She'd deliberately disregarded all his earlier warnings about not placing herself in danger, and damn it, he'd let her. He'd trusted her. Let down his guard because he'd known how shaken she'd be at Anne's situation, and that had shaken him, as well.

But while she had a knife to her side at the moment, that knife hadn't been there before Anne's father had called out. Fact was, she had been making progress before the man had shown up. She and the girl had been walking toward them, the girl's face relaxed, her breathing even. She'd calmed the girl down once. Maybe she could calm Anne down again.

His instincts told him he'd trusted her for a reason. They told him to do it again. Finally, he determined he had no real choice.

Simon took several steps back, but he didn't leave.

"Your father," Nina said, even though her gaze remained locked with Simon's. "He scares you, Anne?"

The girl sobbed. "Yes."

"Okay. I understand. But he's gone. Simon won't let him inside. And I don't scare you, do I? We were talking. Getting along. You don't want to hurt me, do you?"

Anne shook her head. "No. Just—just keep my father away from me. I don't want to see him. I can't breathe when I see him. He tells me what to do. What to eat. What to wear. What to say. Where to look. It's like he's choking me. I can't live. Not like this."

"Okay. I'm going to help you. I promise. But you need to let me go. Can you do that? Please."

After a tense prolonged moment of silence, she lowered the knife and released her death grip on Nina. Instead of immediately leaving, however, Nina turned back toward Anne.

"Thank you, Anne. Now, let's put down the knife and walk on over to Detective Granger. He's a good man and he's going to make sure your father doesn't interrupt us again."

CHAPTER FOURTEEN

NINA SPENT SEVERAL HOURS talking to Anne. Although there was no evidence that her father was guilty of anything more than being a controlling asshole, he had no say over what happened next. Anne had tried to hurt herself and was legally required to be evaluated by a mental health professional. One that wouldn't be Nina, since she would technically be classified as a witness. Nonetheless, Nina made sure the girl had her phone number along with the names of several counselors that Nina respected. Officer Harrison then drove Anne to the hospital, but before he did, Anne gave Nina a prolonged hug. The entire time, Simon stayed close, restless energy radiating off him like a raging fire.

Nina fought back gruesome memories of Beth and Rachel. This time, she'd helped. This time, no one had died. She'd been lucky. Lucky that Simon had decided to trust her and let her handle Anne as she saw fit. And lucky that things had worked out.

Simon, however, didn't look like he felt lucky. He just drove, grim-faced and stiff.

Finally, the tense silence between them suddenly became too much for Nina to bear. She placed a hand on his thigh, forcing herself not to flinch when the muscles there bunched along with those in his jaw. He was vibrating, she realized. With residual anger? Fear? Both?

His girlfriend had been killed by a serial murderer. Simon believed that the reason she'd been killed was directly linked to her chosen profession. Anne hadn't been a serial murderer, but she'd turned out to be a threat to Nina nonetheless. Had Simon thought of Lana in that moment? Had he wondered whether he would be responsible for yet another woman's death? Because there was no doubt in her mind that Simon blamed himself for Lana's death, just as he blamed himself for letting Anne Stanley get too close to Nina.

"Do you want to talk about what happened back there?" Nina asked. "Why Anne felt she had no choice but to use me as a shield?"

The leather wrap on the steering wheel squeaked as Simon squeezed harder. "I don't really care why she went all wacko with a knife. That's her business, not mine. I care more that she endangered you, and that you undermined my authority. That you refused to listen to me when I told you not the enter that room. This isn't a fucking game, Nina. These are life-and-death situations, situations I'm trained to handle—"

"I'm trained to handle them, too. We simply disagreed about how to handle this particular situation. But you did the right thing by listening to me, Simon. And listening to yourself. Your gut told you to give Anne a chance."

"My gut was swayed by you!" He slapped his hand against the wheel. "And look what happened. You were almost killed."

"That's an exaggeration—"

"Her knife pierced your fucking skin!"

"A slight cut. Nothing more. I wasn't truly hurt. No, in this particular case, de-escalation didn't work, not perfectly. A bad thing almost happened. But it didn't. Even if it had, it doesn't mean what we did wasn't warranted. We can do everything by the book and still have horrible things happen. You know that. You can't stop trusting your instincts because things don't go perfectly."

"My instincts are exactly what you're trying to stop me and other officers from listening to."

"That's not true. The training I'm talking about will simply enable your men to have more information to work with. To assess the situation with. The way Officer Harrison was crowding Anne was making the situation worse. You instinctively knew that and—"

He cursed and suddenly swerved the car to the side of the road. He turned toward her, his arm against the back of the seat. "Instinct only goes so far. What if my instincts are telling me two different things?"

"Then you make the most reasoned decision that you can."

"What if my instincts are telling me to pull away from you and pull you closer at the same time? What if they're saying to back away because I don't like your profession or the fact that you're willing to endanger yourself the way Lana was? But what if they also refuse to let me forget the feel of your mouth under mine? Or the feel of your body pressed against me? What if they want me to kiss you again? Right here? Right now?"

She stared at him, her body trembling, her heart racing. She licked her lips and tried to think. "Again, you do the best you can. You reason things out. We're attracted to each other and right now that attraction's been heightened by the adrenaline spike we encountered back there. But we're working together, and you don't respect what I do, so reason tells us that you should follow your instinct not to kiss me."

"And you always do the reasonable thing?"

She smirked. "Oh, come on. After the way I dared you to kiss me the other day, you're actually going to ask me that question?"

"Dare me to kiss you again," he whispered, his gaze flickering to her lips.

And God, how she wanted to. The words were on the tip of her tongue, but she ruthlessly held them back.

She shook her head. "I can't. It—it wouldn't be professional."

For a minute, he looked at her as if he wasn't convinced. As if he was going to pull her into his arms and kiss her and maybe even do more. Instead, he took a breath, turned away and quietly pulled back onto the road.

They were silent for several minutes, each unwilling to risk breaking the tension between them lest it unleash a tidal wave of emotions and desire.

"I called a friend of mine in Charleston," she finally said.

He glanced at her.

"Molly's husband is a cop. He—he did some checking around, and he says Beth's father is still there. A neighbor of his said she'd seen him just last night."

He grunted. Then said, "I know. I put out feelers about him and was told the same thing. I also got a call earlier. While you were talking to Anne. There weren't any fingerprints on the letter but yours. But Davenport could have hired someone to deliver the letter and that person could have worn gloves while doing so. Or he could have flown to California and back in one day. It doesn't sound like my source or your friend's husband saw him for themselves. I'll call the local P.D. and have a patrol car stop by and try to contact him directly. I'll also double-check travel records when we get back to the office."

"That seems like a lot of effort. I know how busy you are. How short-staffed. That isn't necessary."

He turned a dark expression on her. "Yes. It is."

As they got closer to SIG headquarters, he asked, "You want to come in or—"

"No, I think I'll just head back home."

"Where's your car?"

"Down a couple of blocks in a public parking lot."

It didn't take long for them to reach Nina's old clunker. He turned the ignition of his own vehicle off but didn't remove the key.

"Thank you. I'll see you tomorrow? Same time?"

He nodded.

She shoved the passenger-side door open and walked to her car. Behind her, she heard him call, "I'll follow you home."

She stopped and shook her head, turning around to face him. "That's not—"

"Necessary. I know. But I'll do it anyway."

Remembering the scare she and Anne had caused him, she shrugged. "Suit yourself," she muttered.

But when she tried to start her car, the engine wouldn't turn over. Groaning, she rested her forehead against the steering wheel for a second before she sensed him standing next to her door.

"Want me to jump you?" he asked.

Her head snapped up. He was smiling again. Showcasing that fabulous sense of humor of his despite the tense circumstances they'd just experienced. His smile loosened the tight muscles that had clenched inside her stomach ever since the confrontation with Anne Stanley.

"Sounds wonderful," she said.

He grinned full-out now, making him look years younger. Then his gaze flickered to the backseat of her car and he stiffened. "Shit."

With a frown, she began to turn, but he reached out and stayed her. "Don't look."

She kept her gaze straight ahead even as she asked, "But why?"

He yanked open the back door and leaned into the car. "Someone left something for you."

"What?"

He hesitated.

She whirled around in her seat to look, but Simon's large shoulders blocked her view.

"What is it, Simon?" she demanded.

"A dead cat."

"What?" she gasped out. "What does it look like?"

Had Six crawled into her car and died of heat exposure? She'd never forgive herself if she had.

"Nina, I'm sorry. This cat looks exactly like yours. Down to its sixth toe. It's your cat."

"Oh, God," she moaned. "I don't remember leaving the windows open. I don't know how she could have gotten in here."

"She didn't climb into the car on her own," Simon

ground out. He turned and faced her, and for the first time she could see Six. She wasn't simply dead, she was bloody. "Nina, someone used your cat to leave you a message."

NINA HAD FELT BONE-CRUSHING, mind-numbing grief before.

Losing her cat didn't make her feel anything like she'd felt when she'd lost Rachel. Or when Beth had committed suicide. But it still hurt.

In her gut. In her soul. She ached for the small animal that had been her companion. But even more so, she hated being reminded humans could do such horrible things. And she hated the fear that had seeped into her very being. Fear at what might happen next.

"You shouldn't be alone," Simon insisted even as he pulled up in front of her house. "Let me take you to a hotel. At least until I can talk to Charleston P.D. I need to know for myself where Lester Davenport is. I need to know he won't get to you."

For a moment, she didn't understand what he was saying. He wanted her to go to a hotel? Some clinical impersonal space filled with strangers? She cringed at the very thought. "No, Simon." She tried to explain her desire to be in familiar surroundings. Her need to feel safe in her own home. Reassured that her life wasn't going to implode due to the actions of one sick individual. But instead she said, "I'm not going to run. Besides, you can't be sure Lester Davenport left my…my cat there for me to see. I know he's hurting and fixated on his daughter's death, but he—he's never done something like this before. Nothing so violent."

"He left you a letter telling you that you were going

to die! 'She died and so will you.' That's what he wrote and he was obviously referring to his daughter. It makes sense, Nina. More sense than hiding your head in the sand."

"Refusing to let myself be scared out of my own home is not hiding my head in the sand. I'll be fine." She opened the car door and stepped out.

"Do you have a security system?"

"Besides my locks, you mean? I told you my house alarm is broken, remember?"

"Damn it." He slapped the steering wheel in frustration and stepped out of the car, as well. "Fine. Then I'll stay, too. I'm sure I've never slept in such luxurious accommodations before. It'll be a good experience for me."

He said it with confidence and humor, probably hoping to distract her, but she wasn't going to give in. She couldn't. Giving in would lead to more giving in, which could very well lead to her collapsing altogether. She couldn't let that happen. She was strong. She would survive this even if Six hadn't. And she was going to have to do it without the comforting presence of Simon Granger.

"No, Simon. We both know that's not a good idea."

"Damn it, you're stubborn."

She snorted and arched a brow, as if to say, "And you're any different?"

"Fine. At least let me go in. Check to make sure the place is secure."

She narrowed her eyes at him. "And then you'll leave?"

"If that's what you want, yes."

She shook her head. "That's not good enough."

"Why? Afraid you won't be able to resist me?"

"That's exactly what I'm afraid of," she said softly. "I'm—I'm not stupid. I'm shaken by what's happened. It would feel good to let myself be comforted…"

He reached out and smoothed her arm. "Then why won't you let me comfort you?"

"Because today established we're not good for each other, Simon. I asked you to trust me. You did. Things didn't go as well as they could have and that made you angry with me."

"I was angry that you were put in danger. Justifiably angry!"

"But you were also angry with me. Angry that I put myself in danger. Part of you still is. Aren't you?"

His expression turned decidedly mulish. "I can be angry with you and still comfort you."

"But eventually you're going to be so angry with me you're not going to want to comfort me. And then where will I be? Yearning for something I should never have allowed myself to have in the first place. No, I can comfort myself. I've grown quite good at it."

She was unlocking her front door when he called, "How good are you at comforting others?"

She froze. "What?"

"You don't think I'm shaken by what happened?" He walked toward her, not stopping until the tips of their shoes almost touched and she had to crane her neck to look up at him. "I watched Anne Stanley get close enough to you to end your life. Someone's threatened you several times on paper. Now some psycho has been bold enough to put a dead cat in your car? Hell, *I'm* shaken." He smoothed his palms up and down her arms, probably not missing how she trembled. "I could use some comforting, even if you can't."

"Simon—"

"It's been a rough year for me, you know," he said.

Because his girlfriend—his psychiatrist girlfriend—had been murdered by a serial killer? Was he actually bringing that up, actually copping to the difficult time he'd been having as a result, in order to play the sympathy card to get inside her house? Or was it possible that Anne's behavior and finding Six really had shaken him? That being closer to her would make him feel better?

"You're ruthless," she accused.

"Ruthless? Normally, I'd agree. Right now I need some TLC. Sex would be the ultimate, but I'm not asking for that. A cup a coffee will do. I'll come in. I'll take a quick look around. We'll talk. And when you're ready for me to leave, I'll leave. Sound good?"

It sounded like both a temptation and a mistake.

Nina knew once she got Simon inside her house again, she wasn't going to have the strength to ask him to leave. Not until she gave him the comfort he'd been asking for, and took some for herself, as well.

But she invited him anyway.

He checked the house while she made them coffee. When he was convinced everything was clear, they sat on her sofa, chatting civilly until Simon's cell phone rang. He answered but kept his gaze on her as he spoke to Jase for a few moments, then hung up. "You were parked near security cameras. We should have been able to get the guy on tape. The bastard didn't wear a disguise, but he didn't have to. He knew where the cameras were. Knew the angles well enough to keep his face hidden. We can get a general sense of height but not weight. He was wearing a bulky jacket with a hood. Baggy pants. And, Nina—"

She didn't like how he hesitated. Or the concerned look he gave her. "What?" she prodded.

"Your patient. The one who committed suicide. Her name was Elizabeth, but you've called her Beth. Beth Davenport, right?"

"Yes, she preferred Beth. Why?"

Simon leaned forward and held her arms, as if trying to brace her for what he had to say. "The coroner's a friend of mine. He took a quick look at Six. She had the initials *BD* carved into her fur."

Shock hit her like a slap in the face.

She swallowed back bile. She knew humans could cross the commonly established lines of decency for myriad reasons, grief being one of those reasons. She knew how dark a person could go in the throes of despair. Sociopaths and psychopaths weren't the only people out there capable of carrying out horrific acts— one only had to look at the Nazis to know this to be true. But she still found the idea of Lester Davenport trying to pay her back for his daughter's death by killing and mutilating her cat to be beyond repugnant. "Do you still think Beth's father hired someone to come after me?"

"If your friend's husband was right about him being in Charleston, then yes. The cat was still…warm. She hadn't been dead that long."

She nodded and blinked rapidly, suddenly overwhelmed with sadness.

Coffee and civility forgotten, he pulled her into his

arms and she didn't even bother resisting. She allowed herself to cry. Briefly.

Sooner than she wanted to, she swiped at her eyes and straightened. "I moved here to escape death…and I know she's just a cat…but…but she was my cat. And—and seeing her that way…all I could think about was…was…"

"Was your sister?"

She nodded. "My sister. And Beth. I found her, you know. So I understand the pain Beth's father is feeling. Why he would be angry and want vengeance. Do things that are out of character—"

Simon pulled back sharply. "Don't try to justify what he's done by the fact that he's grieving. Not anymore."

"I'm not justifying it. I'm explaining it. There's a difference, remember? At least, that's what DeMarco said. Even if he is responsible for this, it doesn't necessarily make him a monster." Or did it?

Simon stood and began pacing, running his hands through his hair in obvious frustration. "Jesus. Just what would make him a monster? If it wasn't a cat he killed and mutilated, but a person? Would you believe he was a monster then?"

Right now she just wanted her cat back. No. That wasn't true.

She wanted Beth to be alive.

She wanted her sister to be alive.

She wanted to believe it wasn't Beth's father doing such horrible things to frighten her, but a random act of violence that would stop as suddenly as it had started. "I'd believe he was dangerous and that he needed to be stopped, but whether I'd think he was a monster? I'm trained to see beyond a person's actions. To not judge a person for his actions alone."

"Then you obviously need new training."

She sighed. "So it's begun already. I guess I wasn't as much comfort to you as you thought I'd be."

"You're still wearing your clothes. That might be why." He said the words stiffly, but she saw them for what they were. Another attempt to lighten the tension between them. She appreciated his effort, even if it didn't quite work.

"You said you'd leave when I asked you to. I think it's time."

"Is that really what you want? Because I don't want to leave. And you didn't really ask me to."

"My mistake. I'm asking now."

He seemed to struggle with himself, and she wondered if he would really fight her on leaving. And what she'd do if he did.

But he nodded. "Fine. Lock the door behind me."

She followed him to the door, but before he opened it, he turned. "I'm sorry but I can't leave without one more thing."

"What?"

"This." He kissed her. Gently. Thoroughly. As if the kiss could blast through their differences and everything that stood between them. When he pulled away, they were both breathing hard and he rested his forehead against hers.

"You managed to do it anyway, you know."

"Do what?"

"Comfort me."

This time, she was the one to smooth her palms across his arms. He was big, roped with muscle, and for a second he felt so good, so safe, that she wanted to say she'd changed her mind and beg him to stay. Instead, she simply said, "If that's true, then I'm glad."

"I'm not. Because you were right."

"Right?"

"It's just going to be harder to do without it when you're gone."

CHAPTER FIFTEEN

THE NEXT MORNING, SIMON was back at Nina's house, standing on her porch with coffee, bagels and a friend. Nina recognized the other man immediately.

"Detective DeMarco. How nice to see you again."

DeMarco smiled and tipped his head in a gentlemanly gesture. "Nice to see you, as well, Nina."

"I was expecting to meet Simon at SIG but—" She closed her eyes. "Oh, right. I forgot I left my car…" She smiled brightly rather than let her thoughts linger on why the police had impounded her car and taken Six's body, as well. She'd have to make arrangements to have her cremated… "Are you going to be joining us today?" Even as she asked the question, she noted that Simon, just like yesterday, was wearing standard detective garb—slacks, a button-down shirt and a jacket. DeMarco, on the other hand, was wearing a casual shirt and jeans.

"Actually, it's my day off. Simon here asked me to shore up your security seeing as you don't really have any and he couldn't do it himself today. If I can't fix your current system, I'll install a new one. It'll be basic but reliable. Is that okay with you?"

Her startled gaze jerked first to Simon, then back to DeMarco. "He needn't have bothered you. After—

after what happened yesterday…" She paused, assuming Simon had filled DeMarco in.

DeMarco nodded.

"After what happened," she explained, "I scheduled an appointment with a security company for this Thursday."

"Well, I'm already here. No sense having them come all the way over when I can get the job done today. Assuming you're okay with that, of course."

She sighed. "Why wouldn't I be? I'm not a fool. Someone's threatening me. I need better security." Now she looked at Simon. "I just wish Detective Granger had seen fit to talk to me before he bothered you."

"It's no bother. Simon and I are friends, not just coworkers."

"Well, thank you. I appreciate it. Please let me know how much I owe you. And—" she interrupted his automatic denial "—I'm afraid I can't let you continue unless you're willing to bill me for both your expenses and time."

DeMarco grinned. "No problem."

She looked between them suspiciously. It had been a little too easy to get his acquiescence.

"We need to stop by SIG on our way out," Simon said. "I want you to look at the video surveillance we have. It's grainy, but you might be able to catch something that we couldn't."

"Sounds good."

When they got to SIG, Jase Tyler greeted her warmly, as did Carrie Ward. Simon took her to a small room with a television screen and DVD player and played the security tape. It showed exactly what he'd said it would. A man wearing a bulky jacket, the hood covering his head, his back to the camera, his arms cradling what she knew to be Six's body and then depositing it into her backseat after he'd easily popped the driver's side lock.

"I can't tell whether he's wearing gloves," she said.

"He must be. We had them dust for prints while I drove you home, remember? They've come up empty so far."

Just like the threatening letter. "Right. Well, I'm afraid I won't be much help. I don't see anything in the video that you haven't."

"It was a long shot, but one I needed to explore anyway."

"Of course," she said.

As they left and walked back to his desk, Simon said, "I haven't heard back from Charleston P.D. yet. And while I've done some preliminary searches, I haven't found any evidence that Davenport has traveled to California in the past few days. I'll obviously keep checking on that."

"Thank you."

"I wish I could do more. In fact…I was thinking. Do you want me to make arrangements. For Six, I mean?"

He'd taken her by surprise again. "You'd do that?"

"Of course. Have you thought about how you wanted to…?"

"I'm going to have her cremated. I'm not sure what I'm going to do with the ashes yet, though."

"How about I have someone from the coroner's office take care of it? I promise I'll entrust her to someone reliable and you can pick up her ashes when you're ready."

She hesitated. Then said a quiet, "Thank you."

He patted her arm in an absentminded gesture that, despite everything, made her smile. "Would you excuse me for a second? I want to call DeMarco."

"Sure."

A couple of minutes later, he was back, but he had a frown on his face.

"Something wrong?"

"What?" He shook his head and his expression cleared. "No. It's just…I asked DeMarco to help out at your house and we agreed that we'd get that drink he'd talked about after we were done here today. I wanted to firm up where we were going to meet, but he apparently forgot. He said he's got a date."

"And you're angry that he's blowing you off for a woman?"

"No. If I needed him, I know he'd drop everything for me."

"But?"

"But I want to make sure he knows the same thing. If he needs to talk to me, I want to be here for him."

"He knows you're here for him. You planned to have a drink with him. He's the one who changed the plan."

"I know but—" He shrugged, unable to give voice to what was making him uncomfortable.

"You're worried about him?" she asked.

His gaze jumped to hers. "A little. He seemed fine this morning. And just now on the phone, too. Yet I can't shake the feeling something's bothering him. He's worked some tough cases in the past few months. We all have. And then there's what happened to Lana…"

"Was he close to her?"

"They were friends. Everyone at SIG liked Lana."

"Well, safeguards are put in place for a reason. You

don't have to always handle things alone. You know that. You've talked to Dr. Shepard. Maybe DeMarco needs to talk to someone, too?"

Maybe, Simon thought, then blinked. What the hell was he thinking? He'd fought seeing Shepard and he had no doubt DeMarco would do the same thing. No, if DeMarco needed to talk to someone, he didn't need to see a shrink. Simon was here for him. The entire SIG team was here for him. He knew that.

He shrugged and smiled, hoping to dispel the serious nature of the conversation. "Actually, he probably just needs to talk to a friend. Either that, or get laid. Er—I mean—"

"It's okay," she said with a laugh. "So maybe seeing this woman tonight is the best thing for him, after all."

"Yeah. I'll connect with him when we get back. And thanks for not holding that comment against me."

"I'm sure you'll make others that will give me that opportunity. You're a nice man, Detective Granger."

"Not nice enough to have warranted an invitation to stay at your place last night, though?"

"Plenty nice enough. Just smart enough not to."

"It wasn't a matter of being smart. You asked me to leave. I left. But if it was up to me, I wouldn't have."

She stopped walking. "Simon, I told you before. We can't sleep together."

"Whatever you say," he said lightly.

They were almost to the outer door when a man dressed very similarly to Simon jerked his head in greeting. "Hey, Granger."

Simon nodded. "What's up, Hooper?"

"Not much. I heard you're gunning for a captain position again. Just so happens that I am, too. Maybe with me on board, things like the retired annuitant program won't be cut."

"Good luck with that," Simon said mildly. Nina heard nothing confrontational in his tone, but Hooper reacted as if he did.

"Won't need it, but can't say the same for you. You already went that route once before, right? Look how that worked out. What makes you think it'll work out any better this time around?"

Nina gasped, wondering if she was reading Hooper right. Was the man actually referring to Lana's murder?

Maybe not, because Simon just chuckled. "Fuck you, too, Hooper."

Hooper grinned, shot Nina an assessing look, then gave Simon a mocking salute before walking off.

Only when the other man turned his back did Simon allow a sliver of emotion to show on his face. He hid it quickly, but Nina saw the wave of anger wash over Simon's face as he stared at Hooper.

"Well, he's certainly obnoxious," she said lightly, wondering how Simon would respond.

His jaw remained tight but the tension eased a bit from his eyes. "He's an ass. But he's also insightful. He's just telling things the way he sees them. My last stint in management didn't actually work out very well."

"Maybe that's because you left it. Sounds like you won't be doing that again."

"Sounds like it. But who knows? Maybe I'll get there and realize I've made a mistake yet again. Maybe I'll realize running from the streets wasn't in my best interest, after all." He closed his eyes in disgust. "Shit. Forget I said that, would you?"

"I'd rather not." She knew she was pushing, but she added, "It's okay to move on to something that is safer, if that's what you really want. It doesn't make you a coward." She should know, she thought, but held back from sharing her own situation.

This time, Simon's laughter sounded harsh, without any forced cheer. "Safe was never my M.O. With work or with women. That seems to have changed and I'm beginning to wonder if I really am a coward."

"Simon—"

His beeper went off and he glanced down at it. "We've got a call. Local SFPD are at the park, dealing with a disturbance between a man and a woman. Let's go."

Nina followed him down the hall, perfectly aware that his face had reflected relief when his beeper went off. Saved by the bell, she thought, knowing he'd resent her thinking it. He'd resent the idea that he needed to be saved from anything remotely emotional.

Physical safety was one thing. He apparently thought his need to feel personally safe in his career amounted to cowardice.

She guessed that made two of them.

AFTER ATTENDING TO the call, which had been a simple drunk-and-disorderly, Nina found herself impressed with how Simon had handled himself. He'd stayed cool and calm as he'd talked to the man and his girlfriend, despite the fact that the man had gotten insulting at one point. Now, however, as she walked side by side with him back to his car, past the Scottish pines in Golden Gate Park, she took note of his intense concentration, of the tightness in his shoulders and how his hands were jammed in his pockets.

"I know you hate it when I try to psychoanalyze you, and I swear that's not what I'm doing. At least, not more than I can help. But I'm curious," she said. "How did you feel when you were talking to that drunk couple?"

Hands still in his pocket, Simon shrugged. She had the feeling he was doing all he could not to roll his eyes at her, and she appreciated that. It actually made her smile, in fact. He really was a good guy.

"I felt fine," he said.

She snorted.

He turned his head and caught her gaze with his, taking in what she knew was her best derisive expression, and then his face softened. The smile lines at the corners of his eyes grew deeper. "All right then, not *fine* exactly. The call was routine. Seemed minor from the outset. Two people in the park in the middle of the day, hollering at each other, beer cans strewn around them, no weapons in sight and so drunk they swayed when standing."

"But?"

"But as you know, something that starts out relatively minor can escalate into something pretty dangerous really fast. Drunks react quickly. You push them too hard and they can blow."

Just like someone with mental illness might. The question was whether Simon would automatically apply the same techniques to someone that was mentally ill as he would to someone who was drunk. Most cops normally didn't. Mental illness was harder to spot. Often interpreted as aggression or willful defiance as opposed to something outside the person's control.

"It's better to give them a chance to wind down," he continued. "Talking to them helps. Gives them a chance to sober up just a bit. So we talked to them. Me and the patrol officer. But even as we did so…"

"What?"

"On the streets, you can never completely let your guard down."

No. She imagined cops kept their guard up while on the streets the exact same way she and her coworkers kept their guard up while in the hospital. Even when she was working with her dementia patients, she couldn't relax completely. But she could certainly relax more than when she was dealing with a patient suffering psychosis. "Is that why you're applying for a management position?" she guessed. "So you can let your guard down during the day once in a while?"

"Didn't we just have this conversation?"

"Let's have it again," she teased.

He frowned heavily and for a minute she thought she'd angered him. Eventually, however, he sighed. "Do I want to be captain so I can let my guard down? If only it were that simple."

"What do you mean?" When he didn't answer, she changed her gait until she was close to him, then nudged him with her elbow. "Anyone ever tell you getting you to open up is like pulling teeth?"

He barked with laughter. "Yeah, well I hate the dentist. A lot."

She snorted, but didn't push. He glanced at her, smiled, then sighed. "What I meant was that making captain wasn't what I thought it would be. Oh, I knew it would come with a whole new set of challenges, of course, but I didn't think it would completely mess with my confidence, either."

She practically held her breath. What he'd just revealed was huge. He was allowing himself to be vulnerable, to appear less than totally together, and for a cop, for *him,* to do that...

"I wanted to be higher up. But when I got there, I missed the action. Missed the adrenaline—that high every cop gets when pursuing a suspect or a perp."

"That's to be expected."

"*I* didn't expect it. I was so sure of my decision. Wondering if I'd made a mistake? That shook my confidence. I'd never doubted career decisions I'd made in the past."

"Did anything else shake your confidence? Besides missing the streets more than you'd thought?"

He didn't respond. Given he was such a straight shooter, she took that to mean something else *had* shaken his confidence, but he didn't want to talk about it.

They exited the park and when they reached his car, he opened the door for her. She got in and watched him walk in front of the car, his legs long and lanky, his stride smooth. The view of his rear was a sight to behold.

Damn, but Simon Granger had one fine ass.

She couldn't help thinking of the bawdy conversations she'd had with Mrs. Horowitz before she'd died. She'd often teased Nina about needing to work less and socialize more. With good-looking men, in particular. If she was here now, Mrs. Horowitz would have tried cajoling Nina into watching that porn and then putting the moves she learned about to good use with Simon.

And maybe she would, she suddenly decided. Well, not exactly the porn part. But putting the moves on him suddenly sounded too tempting to resist.

What was the harm? He was clearly interested. And although they were connected by the job right now, she was a private consultant—not part of the police department. Once her observation period was over, she would go back to her own life. Simon would go back to his. The kiss he'd given her before had made her insides liquid. Imagine what his mouth could do to the rest of her body?

He seemed willing enough to have a temporary fling. And maybe she'd had the right idea all along. Maybe instead of fighting the attraction between them so hard, she should let it run it's natural course. It would burn out eventually. The sexual tension between them was only ratcheting higher and higher the more they resisted it.

Simon flung himself into the driver's seat and slammed the door shut, then inserted the key in the ignition and turned the car on, but instead of putting the car in gear and heading back to the police precinct, he dropped his hands to his lap and stared ahead. Her erotic thoughts were quickly swept away by concern.

"What is it, Simon?" she asked.

"Nothing," he mumbled. "Absolutely nothing."

Yet more avoidance. But he obviously didn't know her at all if he thought she'd simply take his denial and walk away like a good little girl. She gave him a few more minutes of silence, but when he still didn't pull out, she couldn't stay quiet any longer.

"Hmm," she said softly. "I can tell how absolutely

CHAPTER SIXTEEN

AFTER THE DRUNK-AND-DISORDERLY stop at the park, Nina accompanied Simon on a few other calls, all of them uneventful. At the end of the day, he drove her home, promising to pick her up in the morning and leaving only after going over the new security system that DeMarco had installed. It was pretty straightforward, which she kind of regretted since it took Simon all of thirty seconds to explain it to her and then he was ready to leave again. After an awkward hug and gentle command that she "be careful," he was gone.

She spent the next half hour mulling over their conversation at Golden Gate Park, and then mulling over their hot and heavy kiss. She'd been scared by the power he seemed to have over her. She still was. But that didn't stop her from fantasizing about that kiss turning into something more. Something that involved them both naked and horizontal. He took turns exploring first her neck, then her breasts, then between her legs. That particular spot was aching so much she was actually contemplating doing something about it when Karen called and invited her to have a drink. She figured drinks or masturbation were her two choices for the evening, and since masturbation would be a very poor substitute for the real thing...

Now, Karen listened patiently as Nina described

the calls she and Simon had experienced, and how the patrol officers and Simon had responded to the various situations. Of course, she refrained from talking about Lester Davenport or Six. There was no need to dredge up the past or worry Karen, especially since nothing else had happened and likely wouldn't. She was safe. When she wasn't home, she'd be spending her time with Simon, and when she was home, she'd be protected by the new security system DeMarco had installed.

"So there's definitely room for improvement," Nina said, "but I don't see anything that can't be easily remedied by the MHIT program."

"That's good to hear. Call me again on Friday night so you can give me another update. Now, let's move on to a juicier topic."

"What do you mean?"

"Come on, Nina. You know what I'm dying to hear about."

"Uh, no. I really don't."

"The hunk. I want to know how things are going with the hunk. I've seen pictures, remember? That Simon Granger is man candy. Has he shown any interest? Have you given him anything to go on? Put your cleavage in front of his eyes? Walked past him in the halls a little too closely so he could brush up against your boobs or your butt?"

Nina fought to keep herself from blushing. This was a side of Karen she hadn't seen before. Obviously, it was the liquor talking. She'd better be careful that the same thing didn't happen to her.

She'd done more than allow Simon to look at her

cleavage, but she wasn't about to tell her friend—and boss—that.

"I have a professional relationship with the man. Even if I was attracted to him—" she couldn't quite bring herself to say she *wasn't* attracted to him "—I can't go around seducing people I work with, now can I? How would that reflect on the hospital? On my reputation? What if someone claims I slept with him to gain his support for the MHIT program? It could ruin what little legitimacy we have in the police's eyes." For just a second, she wondered if that was exactly what Stevens and Simon were hoping for. But no, while she might have believed that at one time, she knew Simon now. She'd witnessed him in action. He was a good cop. A good man. One she wanted desperately.

Karen gulped the rest of her mojito and waved at the barman for another. "You're worrying too much. You're allowed to sleep with this man if you want. The question is, do you?"

Of course she did. Her body responded to Simon's simply by being in the same room with him. Just thinking about his mouth on hers was enough to bring back the needy ache between her legs.

"No," she insisted. "The question is how are my patients doing? Fill me in on that, would you?"

She did, and Nina laughed at some of the shenanigans her patients had been up to. It reminded her that she really did love working with them. And that once again reminded her of her conversation with Simon. He'd shared his fears. His desire for safety, for breathing room, and his concerns that it made him a coward. She, however, hadn't shared the details of her own life and fears. Hadn't confessed that Beth's death had broken something inside her. That it had literally sent her running, away from work she'd always loved, because she'd needed to feel safe. She'd wanted to work with patients who were already close to dying so that death wouldn't be a surprise. So that no one could blame her. Her failure to share all that with him didn't seem fair, especially because part of her knew why she'd held back.

They'd made such progress since the first day they'd met. She hadn't wanted to give him any reason to dislike or disrespect her again.

Frustrated, she took a bigger swallow of her drink than she'd intended to, draining it. "I'm looking forward to getting back to them," Nina said.

The bartender placed their third round of mojitos down on the table and then Karen said, "Sure. As soon as you have enough info, you can come back to the hospital." She waved at the mojitos. "We'll do this again when you're done, and one more time when the MHIT training launches. Sound good?"

Nina grinned. "Sure. So long as you remember I'm not making any promises…"

"Like I said, you worry too much."

Yeah, well, having your life threatened and your cat murdered tended to do that to a person. But the truth was, she'd been a worrier even before those things had happened. It was easy to worry when you spent so much time alone or concerned about others. Being with Simon made her worry less because he was always surprising her—with his depth, his vulnerability, his humor. Sometimes he infuriated her and baffled her, but most of the time he simply made her feel…alive. Imagine if she could feel that way every day.

And every night.

As soon as she had that thought, she pictured it. Bare skin pressed to bare skin. Lips and tongues and fingers moving. Brushing. Caressing.

Savoring.

"Whoa. Exactly what are you thinking of? Or should I say, *who* are you thinking of?"

She jolted at Karen's words. Swallowed hard. "Sorry. I guess I've had one too many drinks."

"Uh-huh," Karen said knowingly.

As Karen paid the check, Nina struggled with what she was feeling. Once again, she tried to get a handle on her feelings for Simon.

At the park, she'd been scared off by the power of her feelings for him. But she hadn't spent a whole lot of time thinking about what he wanted from her, besides the physical. Was there a chance he wanted more than that from her? That he might want the emotional intimacy that she did? That he'd want a real relationship with her, even after this week was over?

The fact he'd opened up to her earlier in the day was a point in her favor. Despite what he'd said before, he'd obviously grown to like her. He also wanted her. And wanted to protect her. She could almost convince herself that those things meant something significant.

But he still had major issues with what she did for a living. And that meant he had major issues with who she was at her core. He was also still grieving the loss of Lana Hudson. And every time he thought of what Nina did for a living, he'd inevitably think of Lana.

For that reason alone, things could never work out between them.

She couldn't forget that.

CHAPTER SEVENTEEN

WEDNESDAY AFTERNOON, Simon snapped his cell phone shut and searched for Nina. He'd picked her up at her house that morning and they'd already gone on a couple of calls before stopping to have lunch back at SIG headquarters. Afterward, a victim on one of his cases had called wanting an update.

Nina had been across the room a few moments earlier, laughing with Carrie, but now she was nowhere in sight. He was about to check the break room for her when DeMarco came around the corner, his nose buried in a file, and almost slammed into Simon.

At seeing his friend, Simon immediately switched gears. "Hey. I was just looking for Nina but I wanted to get back to you about—"

"I haven't seen her," DeMarco snapped. "Besides, what do I look like? Your personal assistant?"

Simon frowned at DeMarco's tone. Frowned even deeper at seeing his ramrod-straight spine and the quiver in his tightly clenched jaw. DeMarco's swarthy good looks were pinched with tension. He looked about ready to blow. "What's wrong? Did something happen on your date last night?"

"My date—? Oh, right. No. My date was fine."

Given the way DeMarco averted his gaze, Simon didn't buy that for a second. "You got something on your chest? Let's get that drink you were talking about. Or a cup of coffee right now."

Indecision flashed across DeMarco's face before he shook his head. "You're looking for Nina, remember? Besides, I'm fine," DeMarco said. "I'll catch you later." He strode out of the office, leaving Simon to wonder what the hell was going on.

Sure, the stress of the job got to everyone at some point, but was that what this was about? He'd never seen DeMarco quite so on edge. Maybe Nina was right. Maybe DeMarco needed to talk to someone. Not just a friend but a professional…

Just as he had the first time he'd had the thought, Simon backtracked. Unlike before, he wasn't so sure it was the right thing to do.

What? Now that he had a shrink at his side day in and day out, was he really starting to buy into the whole touchy-feely therapy thing? He wasn't an idiot. He knew mental health professionals could really help people. Medicine, in particular, could do wonders for those who needed it.

But for someone like him? For someone like De-Marco?

No. They were stronger than that.

DeMarco didn't need Simon to be all up in his business. He'd make sure they had that drink, but as for the counseling thing? DeMarco was a grown man and could make his own decisions.

He'd just started to look for Nina again when she rounded the corner, a cup of coffee in each hand, and proceeded to hand him one. "Cream, no sugar, right?"

"Uh, right. Thanks." He gulped down the coffee,

ignoring the burn in his throat, and said, "You ready to head out again?"

"Sure. I'm ready whenever—"

His cell phone rang again. "Sorry," he said. "Let me just get this."

"Sure. I'll go say goodbye to Carrie."

As she walked away, he answered his phone. "This is Simon Granger."

"Simon, it's Stevens. I'm out of the building but I just got word there's been another murder in Golden Gate Park. I need you and DeMarco to check it out. SFPD is there right now holding the scene for you in case it's connected to Louis Cann."

Adrenaline immediately started pumping through Simon's veins. Despite doing everything he was supposed to and then some, he'd hit a dead end in the Cann case. His gut clenched at the notion he might be getting another shot at solving that murder case but only at the expense of another victim. "Have they ID'd the victim?"

"Not yet. He didn't have a wallet on him."

"Was the victim stabbed?"

"Yes."

"Any witnesses?"

"Not that we know of so far."

"Any reason we should think this victim *isn't* related to Cann?"

When Stevens responded in the affirmative and explained the details, the world around Simon seemed to still. A roar louder than the surf sounded in his ears. Horror and disbelief immediately crashed through him, and his gaze automatically sought out Nina.

She was walking toward him, a smile on her face,

and he quickly averted his gaze so she wouldn't see how freaked out how he was. He didn't want to make her panic. Not until he had more facts. But he was acutely aware of his own feelings of panic. Of his immediate instinct to grab her and hustle her away someplace safe. Safer than SIG headquarters, even.

Coincidence.

It has to be coincidence, he thought.

"Simon, did you hear everything I just said?" Stevens asked on the other line, snapping Simon back to the situation at hand.

"I'm on it, sir."

He hung up but immediately started dialing his phone again. "DeMarco?" he barked when the other man answered his cell. "There's been another murder in Golden Gate Park." Nina stepped up to stand beside him. He held up a finger to indicate he'd be another minute. He thought about walking away and hiding the truth from her, but then dismissed the idea.

She'd just been smiling, but now she was staring at him, a slight furrow between her brows, her expression one of concern. She'd obviously caught on that something was seriously wrong.

And she was right. Something was very wrong and unfortunately she was going to have to hear about it eventually. It was best she hear about it now, when he had his team close by, able to help him protect her. It was best she hear it from him.

Much like he'd done with Stevens, DeMarco peppered Simon with questions. Keeping his gaze level with Nina's, he answered, "Yes. No. Yeah, same M.O. as Louis Cann. But this time, there was something else. The victim had initials carved into his back."

Nina's eyes flared and she sucked in a breath.

Simon placed a hand on her shoulder, trying to lend her his support. His strength. "The initials are *BD,*" he said quietly.

Nina turned ghostly white and swayed on her feet.

He tightened his grip on her shoulder. Coincidence, he thought again. It had to be.

BD.

The initials that had been carved into Nina's cat.

The initials that matched those of Lester Davenport's daughter, Beth.

SIMON HADN'T WANTED to leave Nina. All he'd wanted to do was hold her and do his best to wipe the fear and horror off her face, but, of course, there'd been no time for that. Knowing he had a job to do, he explained that Carrie would drive her home and stay with her until Simon got there.

She'd nodded. Said she'd understood. Tried to look brave.

And even as he'd gotten into his car and driven off, Simon had wanted to put his fist through the damn windshield.

He met DeMarco at Golden Gate Park. There, they met with the patrol officer holding the murder scene as several others kept the milling crowd at bay.

"A family of four was heading to their car after visiting the Natural History Museum," the patrol officer, who introduced himself as Ken Richards, said. "They took a detour through the Aids Memorial Grove and found the victim lying behind a massive boulder. They haven't touched him and neither has anyone else."

"Show us," Simon ordered.

Officer Richards led them onto a wooded trail and to a boulder that was approximately five feet tall and eight feet wide. Behind it, a man lay on his stomach. He was naked from the waist up, his back bloodied, the initials carved into his back jagged and grotesque.

BD.

He'd known they were there, but Simon still felt a jolt of shock. He could barely believe the same initials that had been carved into Nina's dead cat had been carved into a dead man.

What did it mean? What possible reason would Davenport have for doing this? It didn't make sense.

Unless…

His mind scrambled for any logical explanation.

Unless Davenport had been so determined to torture Nina that he'd studied up before coming to California. He could have easily seen the news coverage on Rebecca Hyatt and learned that Nina was working with the police. If he'd also read about Cann's murder, he could have decided to commit a copycat, believing the addition of the initials on this victim might get back to Nina. It was a long shot, but still a possibility.

Assuming that's what had happened, had Davenport singled out this man at random? Or was this man somehow connected to Davenport's daughter? Or to Nina herself?

Before he could even begin to answer those questions, he needed to find out this man's identity. Take photos of his face and show them to Nina. See if she could identify him or connect him to Lester Davenport or his daughter.

Since he couldn't touch the body before the evidence techs processed the scene, he scanned the area immediately beside the man's body for any clues in plain sight. The dirt around him was disturbed, indicating a struggle. The man's face was turned in profile, but he had a beard and his hair was partially obscuring his face. Despite his naked torso, he still wore boots two sizes too large, and green-and-white-checkered golf pants—

A memory tickled at the corners of Simon's mind and realization made him jerk. Black-and-white tiles, he thought. Fifty of them. "Aw, hell," Simon muttered as he took a closer look at the guy's face.

"What is it? You know something about the vic, Granger? Know who he is?" DeMarco prodded. He'd been unusually quiet. His face blank. Now his voice was stiff.

Simon blew out a breath he hadn't realized he'd been holding and straightened. "Yeah. Or, to be precise, I know *what* he is."

"And?" DeMarco prodded. "What is he?"

Simon faced DeMarco. "Homeless. And mentally ill. I saw him at the Welcome Home shelter the first day I went there to talk to Elaina Scott. He was a resident there. Same as Louis Cann."

"Shit," DeMarco said.

"Right. Shit," Simon repeated. "Between that, the similar crime scene and means of death—stabbing— the murders are connected. Except for one thing. Why the deviation with the initials?"

"Who the hell knows? And who the hell knows what BD even stands for?"

Simon just grunted. He hadn't told DeMarco or Stevens about the initials that had been carved into Nina's cat or his suspicion that the initials stood for Beth Davenport. Until Stevens had called, he'd had no reason to tell them. He'd promised Nina he'd look into Lester Davenport's involvement in those two things "unofficially," and he'd been doing so. After Stevens's call? He'd held back, not because he'd been hiding the ball, but because he'd wanted to know what all the facts *were* and put together some theories first. Now he needed to get Stevens up to speed. Then he needed to talk to Nina. Once Simon had a better handle on things, he'd tell DeMarco.

Thinking about dragging Nina even more into this disturbing nightmare made him wince. She'd already been through so much and he didn't want to scar her with this additional ugliness. Unfortunately, he had no choice. Given the initials on this man, Simon needed to find out what Nina knew, if anything, that might help them.

Once again, he wondered how it was possible the initials on this man's back could be connected to her. She was a doctor, a psychiatrist, but he'd never asked her about her patients. And he'd never talked to her about the Cann case. There hadn't been a need to. Was it possible that she worked with homeless patients? That she'd done pro bono work for the Welcome Home residents or at a nearby clinic, just like the family practitioner who'd introduced herself to Scott on the day Simon had been there?

A hundred questions continued to flash through Simon's mind even as the evidence techs showed up and swept the scene. Within an hour, they were done.

"It'll take a while before the techs get us the results of their sweep," DeMarco said, looking beat. "What's next?"

"Go home. We'll wait for a hit on who this guy is. In

the meantime, I'm gonna meet with Stevens. Give him an update. We'll start fresh in the morning."

DeMarco nodded. "Right. I'll see you bright and early." DeMarco left and Simon was about to do the same when Officer Richards called out, "Detective Granger. There's a woman here who wants to talk to you."

"Here?" he repeated. Lord, he hoped it wasn't Nina. He looked around but didn't see her or Carrie. "What's her name? Where is she?"

"She said her name is Rita Taylor."

Rita Taylor. The prostitute who'd originally claimed she'd seen a cop running from the scene of the Cann murder. The same woman who, when Simon reinterviewed her, had changed her story, saying she couldn't be sure she'd seen what she thought she had. And she was here now? At the scene of another murder victim?

"Where is she?"

RITA TAYLOR SAT IN OFFICER Richards's patrol vehicle while Simon stood next to the open door looking down at her. The exotic and curvy brunette was dressed much the same way she'd been when Simon had last seen her—in her working clothes: a skimpy tank top, miniskirt and thigh-high lace-up boots. Her makeup had been applied with a heavy hand, which simply emphasized how pale she really was beneath it. Not fair, as in light-skinned. But pale, as in upset. In shock. Scared.

"So you didn't witness this murder?" he confirmed. "Didn't see anyone fleeing the crime scene?"

"No. I told you…I was working a few blocks down. I heard the sirens. Heard what people were saying.

That another homeless man had been killed, stabbed in Golden Gate Park. Just like that first one."

Frustration ate at him. She was beating around the bush. Giving him nothing to work with. "And you what? Remembered something from before? About the cop? Or bus driver? Or air-conditioning repairman?"

She glared up at him and he held up a hand. "I'm sorry, but I'm just trying to figure out why you're here, Rita. You came to me, remember? But so far you haven't told me why."

"Do you think this murder is connected to the first one?" she asked. "That's what I need to know before I say anything else."

Simon hesitated, studied her tense posture then said, "Yes. I have reason to believe the two murders are connected."

Rita dropped her face in her hands. "Oh, God," she moaned.

"Tell me what's going on, Rita. During our last interview, you told me you weren't sure you'd actually seen a cop before. Have you changed your mind?"

Rita laughed, but there was a hysterical edge to the sound. "I've changed my mind about something. I'm just not sure if I should tell you." She took a deep shuddering breath, then seemed to make up her mind about something. "But I didn't sign up for this. For all I know, I could be next."

"What are you talking about?"

She swallowed hard. Took another deep breath, then said, "Someone paid me to say it was a cop who murdered that first homeless man."

Interesting. So she was copping to giving the police false information, despite the fact she knew she could be prosecuted for having done so. But all he said was, "Who?"

"I don't know."

"Oh, come on, Rita!" he exploded.

"I'm not lying. I swear. When all of the ruckus was going on after the first murder victim, when we were waiting for the cops to show up, a man came up to me and offered me a thousand dollars if I would just say I saw a cop leaving the scene."

"And you agreed? Despite knowing he might be the killer? You seem smarter than that."

"He didn't look like no killer. And he said he just wanted to take advantage of an opportunity. Teach you cops a lesson because you've been treating homeless people so bad lately. And you have! It's been all over the papers."

Simon swiped his hands over his face and fought to hold on to his temper. "*I* haven't been treating anyone badly, Rita. Now what else did he say? Did he just hand you the money?"

"Yes. Cash. In a blank envelope. It's all gone now."

"Why didn't you just take the money? Why'd you do what he said?"

"Because he scared me," Rita confessed. "He said he'd know if I didn't follow through. That I'd be sorry if I scammed him. So I did what he told me to. Convinced myself it would be the easiest grand I'd ever earned. And it was. I didn't even feel that guilty about it. He didn't want me to say it was a specific cop. I figured what was the harm? If a cop didn't really do it, there'd be no evidence of it. And if a cop really had…"

"But then you backed off of your story when I interviewed you. Why?"

"I wasn't expecting to be reinterviewed, especially by someone with the DOJ. When you explained who you were, I figured you knew something. I thought if I backed off a little, if I acted wishy-washy, you'd leave me alone. And you did. But I've been living in fear ever since. Wondering if what I told you pissed him off. Wondering if he's going to come after me. And I'm even more scared now. There was something about him. Even though he was wearing sunglasses, there was something about his mouth that seemed sinister when he talked to me. It gave me the creeps. Now that another murder has happened, I'm afraid he'll come looking for me. Because he wants me to lie again to you because he wants to kill me to make sure I don't tell you about him."

"But you are telling me about him. Why? And why me?"

"I don't know. Call it a sixth sense. I get a feeling with people. I can sense their light and their dark. I just know when I met you, you seemed nice. Decent. When I came over here I asked if you were here. The patrol officer said you were and…well…I figured you're the lesser of two evils."

Simon blew out a breath. "Well, you were right about that." He turned away. Paced for a few seconds before coming back to her.

"Here's the deal. You're going to need to get off the streets. You're now a critical police witness and we'll protect you. But you're going to have to cooperate, Rita. Tell us everything you know. Testify in court if we need you, too."

"You protect me, make sure I don't go to jail for lying to the cops before, and I will. I promise."

"You said you don't know who this guy was. That he wore sunglasses. What else? What did he look like?"

"Older. Conservative. Well-dressed. He carried himself well. He looked tough. And he…" She paused. Bit her lip. Looked at Simon with suddenly uncertain eyes.

"What is it?"

"He wasn't wearing no uniform, but I've seen a lot of cops in my line of work. Talked to a lot of them. Undercover ones, too. I can't know for sure, but the way this guy carried himself? If I had to guess at what he did for a living? I'd say he *was* a cop."

CHAPTER EIGHTEEN

IT WAS DARK BY THE TIME Simon had Rita Taylor under police protection and was able to get back to SIG. Once there, he went straight to see Commander Stevens.

He told him everything—about the cards Nina had received, the mutilation of her cat and the seeming connection between those two things and the murders of two homeless men. Then he told him about Rita Taylor's statements.

When he was done, Stevens looked as shell-shocked as Simon felt.

"What have you heard on Davenport?" he finally asked.

After talking with Rita Taylor, Simon had once again contacted the authorities in Charleston. The officer he'd talked to said they'd just been about to call him with a report on Davenport. They'd tried contacting Davenport at his home several times, but on each occasion, his house had been empty. In addition, they'd checked with his place of employment, a local landscape company, and verified he'd called in sick for the past three days. So far they hadn't been able to find him.

"Davenport's neighbor has said she saw Davenport in Charleston earlier this week. I'm not buying it. I think Davenport was here on Saturday morning and put that letter underneath Nina's entry mat. I think he killed Nina's cat on Monday. And if that's true, he probably killed the man murdered in the park today, as well."

Stevens sighed. "Well, you've done all you can tonight. You can start fresh tomorrow. Check additional flights out of Charleston. Whether Davenport has any documented connection to the murder vic or even Louis Cann. Keep in touch with your contact at the Charleston P.D. That kind of thing. Is Ward still with Dr. Whitaker?"

"Yes."

"And will she continue to stay with her?"

Simon hesitated. Shook his head. "I'm going to relieve her. I need to talk to Nina. Find out whether she might know anything about the murder victims. I'll make sure she has protection."

"Right," Stevens said again.

"She can't shadow me tomorrow." Simon didn't form it as a question.

"Damn straight she can't," Stevens agreed. "Shadowing you isn't a priority anymore and neither is Dr. Whitaker's proposed program. There's her safety to think about now. Plus, whether it's related to her or not, we've got two murders to solve."

"They're related to her. They have to be. I just don't know how yet."

"So you think Davenport might have been responsible for Cann's death? Even though the initials weren't part of the killer's signature?"

"Both victims stayed at Welcome Home. It's a coincidence that can't be explained otherwise. I'll simply go with it for now. Can't hurt given we'd hit a dead end in the Cann case anyway."

"You said you'd seen tonight's victim before and he appeared mentally ill to you?"

Simon rubbed the back of his neck. "Yes. And when I talked to her, Elaina Scott implied she thought Louis Cann had suffered from PTSD."

"So that seems to be another connection to Dr. Whitaker. The victims are both homeless, but also both mentally ill. She treats people with mental illness. I think you're right. There's a connection there. Find out what it is."

"I will. I—" Simon abruptly frowned as he remembered something. Something Elaina Scott had told him. And something he'd seen at the shelter on that damn bulletin board. "The day I visited her, Ms. Scott had just met with a doctor. A woman who'd just begun pro bono work at a nearby crisis center. Scott described the clinic as the drop-in variety. There's probably more than one. I think I saw a flyer or two for clinics on the shelter's bulletin board. It's possible both victims saw the same flyer and attended the same clinic. Hell, for all I know, Nina does that kind of pro bono work and saw both of them."

"But that still doesn't explain the initials. Why on one of the men and not on the other. Why—if they stand for Beth Davenport—why Lester Davenport felt compelled to carve the initials into a man and a cat."

"It could be the idea for the initials came to him afterward. Doesn't mean he's not good for both murders. Or…" Simon's brow furrowed as he reached for other possibilities. "Lester Davenport hates Nina because he blames her for his daughter's death. If Nina treated the men, killing them would hurt her."

"And if she never treated them? Doesn't even know them?"

"I don't know. But what else killed his daughter? Apart from Nina's alleged role in things? Who or what else could he blame?"

"His daughter killed herself."

"Because she was *sick*. What if in some twisted way he thinks that by killing homeless men—*mentally ill* homeless men—he's somehow eradicating the type of sickness that took his daughter from him?"

"So who they actually were was irrelevant. It's the sickness he's trying to kill. Again, it's a stretch, but it's good thinking, Simon. Keep thinking outside the box. I have a feeling it's the only way you're going to solve these cases."

Simon looked at his watch. It was almost 9:00 p.m. "I need to get to Nina, sir."

"Spend as much time as you need with her tomorrow. Consider her just another lead in this case. If she's connected to the victims, even if she doesn't consciously know it, you need to explore it. And if you don't think you can be objective here, Simon, I need to know that right now."

"Sir?"

"Correct me if I'm wrong, but I'm assuming that after working with Dr. Whitaker for three days, you've come to like her. Can't blame you, of course. What's not to like? But you need to maintain your objectivity. I haven't once heard you consider the fact she might know something about these murders and simply isn't disclosing it."

The idea of Nina lying to him about something so important floored him. "There's nothing to indicate that."

"Not much, maybe, but I disagree that there's *nothing*. She showed up pushing this MHIT program right when our public relations problems began. And right around the time Cann was murdered. We let her in close, and all of a sudden she's linked to it? And a subsequent murder, too?"

"What are you saying? That Nina is somehow orchestrating all this to make us look bad? So she can manipulate us into giving her program the green light. That's ridiculous!"

Stevens ran this hand through his hair, suddenly looking weary. "I agree. Nonetheless, the theory has been posed."

"By who?" Simon exploded.

Stevens frowned. "By me. I don't buy it, but I'm not ruling out anything. As I said, one of us has to stay completely objective here, and something tells me that person isn't going to be you. Am I wrong?" When Simon didn't answer, Stevens sighed. "Yeah, that's what I thought. Just follow every lead, Simon. Every. One. If you can't do that, I'll put someone on the case who will."

CHAPTER NINETEEN

AFTER HE LEFT STEVENS, it took Simon a minute to gather his composure. The idea that Nina knew anything about the homeless murders and was intentionally manipulating them was ludicrous. But he'd do what Stevens said. Follow every lead. Because that was his job and failing to do his job would only serve to put more suspicion on Nina.

As he drove to her house, he called Carrie and told her he was on his way.

"How is she?" he asked.

"She's lying down in her room. Trying to hold it together. But she's pretty upset."

Of course she was. God, he felt bad for her. "Take care of her until I get there, Carrie."

"You know I will, Simon."

When he got to Nina's house, it was almost ten. Carrie had left the front lights on so he had a clear path up the walkway. She opened the door as he was walking up. He filled her in on what he and Stevens had talked about, leaving out Stevens's paranoid speculations about Nina, then said, "Thanks, Carrie. I've got it from here."

Carrie nodded. "Just call me if you or she needs anything." She gave him a hug, squeezing tight.

He returned the hug as tightly as he dared. Then he went to find Nina.

He found her lying in bed, with tear streaks drying on her cheeks. Her eyes were red, her breathing ragged, and her obvious distress made his head and heart hurt. He hated that he hadn't been able to hold her as she'd cried.

But he was here now.

If she wanted him.

He stepped up to the side of the bed and hesitated, uncertain what she'd want.

"Nina—"

With a sob, she launched herself out of the bed and into his arms.

She buried her face in his neck and cried.

Her grief and fear poured out of her, and she didn't even try to stifle her sobs. She was completely outside herself, completely out of control. Nothing like the elegant, professional woman he was used to.

And also exactly like her.

He wrapped his arms around her.

Held her tight.

And didn't let go even after she fell asleep.

DeMarco barely remembered the drive back to his house after he'd left Simon at Golden Gate Park. He barely remembered anything about what they'd talked about while they'd been there. But he remembered exactly what he'd seen, and how the entire time he'd been trying to keep himself from throwing up.

For weeks, he'd been feeling more and more out of control. When he'd started hearing that damn file calling to him in the office, he'd thought he wasn't getting enough sleep. He'd gone home and started popping pills and drinking to force the issue, but that had merely made him twitchy the next day, so he'd stopped.

Aside from a royally bad mood here and some memory lapses there, he'd been getting by. Memories still haunted him, but talking folders had ceased to make another appearance. But then Simon had called him, telling him that a man had been killed with the letters *BD* carved into his back, and DeMarco's entire world had imploded. It had continued to crumple as he'd seen the horrifying evidence for himself.

He'd barely held it together at the park before making it home, downing a few drinks and collapsing in bed. He'd curled up in a ball and eventually he'd fallen asleep.

But even in sleep his thoughts troubled him.

As he slept, DeMarco's body moved restlessly beneath the sheets. At the same time, his mind fought a losing battle against a slide show of horrifying images.

First, he dreamed of two murdered men. One by one, he saw the crime scene photos that had been in Cann's file. Saw how an ex-marine, a man who'd fought for his country, a man who couldn't have been a *bad* man given that, had been dismissed by society and then disposed of as if he was trash.

Next, DeMarco once again saw the grotesque initials that had been carved into the back of a different homeless man. Though he knew nothing about *that* man, he sensed he was more than what he appeared. Even the green-and-white-checkered pants he'd worn had made him seem more pathetic. More vulnerable.

The visions in his head spun and undulated before changing once again.

Suddenly, DeMarco saw himself, six years younger, all spiffed up and shiny in his patrol uniform, walking his beat in a city that had yet to be devastated by Hurricane Katrina. The vision became reality, one steeped in familiarity.

He smelled stale beer and urine. Felt the hard, uneven pavement of the sidewalk beneath his feet. Recognized one person after another. Merchants. Streetwalkers. Juvenile delinquents and bums. Some he liked. Others he didn't. But he protected them all. And he was suspicious of them all.

DeMarco groaned, long and hard, and the sound bounced off the walls of his bedroom. Yet it didn't wake him. In some part of his consciousness, he knew he was dreaming. That he really wasn't back in New Orleans, patrolling Rampart Street and chatting with the locals.

But it *felt* real.

So the dream continued.

In a few weeks, he'd be leaving his beat behind. He was being promoted to detective, a change he was really looking forward to. He wouldn't miss seeing the people on Rampart Street, of course—not enough for it to matter. But he knew them, knew things about some of them that even their families probably didn't, and in some ways that made them part of him.

That included William "Billy" Dahl, the seventeen-year-old kid who, despite having nimble fingers and a long theft record, had a good sense of humor and loved his mother to distraction.

DeMarco had already busted Billy twice that year, once for snatching a woman's purse, and once for robbing a local grocery store—with a gun that had turned out not to be loaded. Billy had spent almost a year in juvy hall for that one, but when he'd gotten out, he'd returned to the streets. Every time he'd seen DeMarco, he'd greeted him as a friend would. They'd joke around, no hard feelings in sight. Billy had even threatened to set DeMarco up with his sister, whom DeMarco had to admit was mighty fine.

On the last night he was scheduled to be on patrol, DeMarco stumbled upon Billy's latest theft attempt.

Once again, the images in his mind morphed. De-Marco, who'd been walking and chatting with those he encountered, froze as he caught sight of Billy.

The kid had cornered a couple, tourists by the looks of them, and was shouting at them to hand over their money. DeMarco was about twenty feet away when he saw Billy waving the gun.

Damn it, Billy, he thought.

He drew his weapon. Shouted at Billy to put down his.

Billy jerked in surprise, then, to DeMarco's utter disbelief, grinned.

"Hey, DeMarco," he called out, his voice slightly slurred as if he was drunk or high. "You know the kind of guns I carry."

He turned back to the frightened woman cowering against her companion, pointed the gun at her and said, "Just give me the purse before I shoot you. I'll give you until five."

He started counting.

One.

"Billy, don't!" DeMarco shouted. "Put down the gun."

Two.

"Put it down now!" DeMarco waited for Billy to comply, but he didn't. He just kept counting.

Three.

Billy turned to DeMarco and winked.

Oh, shit, DeMarco thought. *He's trying to tell me the gun's not loaded. But I don't know that. I don't know that, Billy!*

Four.

He had a split second to make a decision.

To take a chance that he was right about Billy and put an innocent woman's life in danger.

Or to take Billy's threat seriously and shoot.

He did what he had to.

What he'd been trained to do.

He shot.

Five.

As it turned out, Billy's gun really had been empty.

CHAPTER TWENTY

NINA WOKE TO THE MEMORY of being held in Simon's arms, but the bed next to her was empty. She rubbed at her eyes, still gritty with tears, and struggled to a sitting position. She didn't have to struggle to remember what had happened. She knew with utter clarity that a man had been attacked, the initials *BD* carved into his back just like they'd been carved into Six. She knew that Simon had apologized for having to leave her, but that he'd needed to do his job; even so, she'd barely held on to her sanity in the hours afterward, despite the way Carrie Ward had tried to distract her. She knew that when Simon had finally arrived, she'd been filled with a feeling of relief so intense that she hadn't been able to stop herself from throwing herself into his arms.

And she knew that he'd held her as she'd cried for hours. And kissed her lightly before she'd fallen into a deep, dreamless sleep.

She was so grateful it had been dreamless. She'd feared her mind would bring her one nightmare after another, but Simon's embrace had kept them away.

Rising, she shuffled to the bedroom doorway and called out, "Simon?"

"I'm making breakfast. Come out and join me."

Her troubled heart momentarily lightened and she

smiled at the invitation to join him in her own kitchen.
She was glad he'd made himself at home. The few people she'd had over to the house had been intimidated
by its sheer size and grandeur. She'd felt the same way
when she'd first moved in. But now it was home to her.
Her haven.

Even so, she'd never felt as safe as she did now,
knowing that Simon was just a few rooms away.

She showered and dressed, then joined him in the
kitchen.

He was wearing the same clothes he'd worn the day
before, but he looked fresh and alert. "I used a new
toothbrush I found under your sink. I hope that's okay."

"Of course it is." She watched as he scrambled eggs
and poured them into a pan. He'd already browned
bacon and within minutes he slid a full plate of food
in front of her.

"Thank you."

"You're welcome."

"You're not going to join me?"

"I ate while you slept. It's almost noon."

"Noon? Oh, no. I didn't realize…"

"It's okay. You needed the rest."

She tried to eat, she really did, but she found she had
no appetite. Instead, she stared at the breakfast he'd
prepared while he sipped a cup of coffee.

Eventually, he rose. "At least try to eat your toast
before we go," he said gently. "I've got everything
packed."

"Packed? For what? Don't you—don't you have to
go to work? To, you know, work on the case?"

"I've already been there. Carrie came back over

early this morning and I hunted down some leads while you were asleep."

"Did—did you find out anything new?"

"Nothing that we need to talk about now," he said. "I have several patrol officers, as well as DeMarco, following up on a few things. Until they find something or I'm back on shift tonight, I'm off the clock and all yours. You like the ocean?"

Even though he'd already been to the office once, she suspected it went against his nature to delegate the smallest of tasks to others. Yet here he was doing it for a major case, and he was doing it in order to spend some downtime with her. For a second, it made her feel guilty. Needy. She should tell him she was fine. That he needn't put off his work for her, not when someone was out there attacking cats and homeless men with a knife.

Instead, she nodded. "Yeah," she whispered. "I love it."

SIMON DROVE ACROSS THE Golden Gate Bridge and headed up Highway 1, into the Mount Tamalpais State Park, where he pulled off at the secret trailhead leading to a quiet inlet up the coast from San Francisco. The waves lapped gently against the shore. He came here often to get away from life and all its attendant stressors, and he hoped the serenity of the place would soothe Nina, as well.

Before leading Nina down the rocky hill, he grabbed a blanket, a bottle of Napa Valley wine and a wine opener from the back of his car. When he got to a small spit of sand, he spread out the blanket and motioned for Nina to join him.

He needed to get his mind back in the game—to

start putting the clues together and figure out why Lester Davenport would target two homeless men to get to Nina. That was especially true given Stevens's absurd theory that Nina knew something she wasn't telling them. If Stevens harbored any suspicion about Nina whatsoever, Simon wanted them eradicated.

First, however, he needed to get Nina settled. Get some pink back in her cheeks.

"Wine?" he asked, gesturing to the bottle as Nina settled down beside him.

She gave him a half smile, and then said, "Are you planning to ply me with alcohol to distract me, Detective Granger?"

That was exactly what he'd been planning on doing. But he simply said, "Maybe. Or maybe I'm planning to seduce you to distract you and the wine is just a part of the whole evil plan." He jiggered the corkscrew into the bottle, knowing full well he wasn't trying to get into her pants but hoping she'd pick up on his humor, on his attempts to make her feel better. "Have you thought of that?"

"Believe me, I have. But we've already established you don't have to seduce me to distract me. Or to have sex with me. A simple invitation will probably do the trick."

His hands stilled and he stared at her. When she laughed, he closed his eyes and groaned. "You're good. Too good."

"I know. You should have seen the look on your face. A weaker woman would have been fearing for her virtue."

He snorted out a laugh. "One thing you aren't is

weak. But you are sexy as hell and I can only take so much. So please, keep that in mind."

"I will," she said with another smile. In the next moment, however, her smile faded. "Thank you for bringing me here. And for making me laugh. I know— I know we need to talk about things. About that man. About the initials." Nina pulled the bottle, now unstopped, out of his hands and drank from it long and hard before handing it back to him. A few stray drops of wine clung to her lips.

His cock jerked to attention. They'd joked about him seducing her, and that had been the furthest thing from his mind. But as it was wont to do in her presence, his mind suddenly detoured toward true and urgent desire before he knew what was happening.

Although he hadn't been planning on drinking himself, he took a swig of the wine, too, letting the roundness of the cabernet sauvignon melt in his mouth before swallowing. He cast a glance at Nina; her gaze was firmly fastened on his throat. When she saw he'd caught her looking at him, she averted her gaze and swallowed hard. He struggled to keep himself from tossing the bottle aside and grabbing her, kissing the hell out of her, lying her back on the blanket and getting her naked.

The wind picked up Nina's long hair and blew a strand in his face.

He tucked the strand behind her ear, staying too close for too long just to inhale her scent.

She turned her head slightly, and looked at him out of the corners of her eyes.

"Sorry," he said with a grin. "I got a little distracted."

Her expression remained serious for a few seconds,

but then she finally smiled back at him. "Wasn't that the point of coming out here?"

"Yeah. And I'd love to distract both of us in the most pleasurable way possible. But you're right. We need to talk."

Her eyes shuttered, an automatic refusal to deal with reality.

Message received. She wasn't quite ready for him to launch straight into the subject of two murdered men, so he said, "Can I ask your professional opinion about something?"

Her eyes cleared. "Sure."

"The police are taught that most homeless people are mentally ill, and I'm not an idiot—I know when someone hears voices in his head, his perception of reality is vastly different than mine. But how can someone who was once a functioning member of society suddenly get there? How does someone start believing everyone is after them? Why does he suddenly start to wear aluminum foil hats to prevent the government from invading his thoughts?"

Nina smiled sadly. "I can't teach you everything in one day—I went to school for twelve years to learn the answers to your questions, after all—but I will say that the brain is immensely complex. A lot of mental illnesses are hereditary, but they can also be induced by one's environment or experiences. A person can be completely fine and then—" she snapped her fingers "—things change. Schizophrenia, for example, usually starts in young men in their late teens or early twenties. A person might have a mild case of bipolar disorder that is suddenly exacerbated by stress. Or sometimes someone who isn't mentally ill one day undergoes a profound trauma and is thrown into an altered mental state. There are so many ways that a person's perception of reality becomes completely different from the way the rest of the world sees it."

"Can you give me a more concrete example?"

"Sure. The girl we helped, Anne, could have been experiencing some sort of altered mental state brought on by her father's controlling behavior. It's not too different from one's fight-or-flight response when cornered. Suddenly, everything and everyone is a threat. If you remember, she was calming down as I talked to her. But when her father showed up, when she heard his voice, she snapped again. She didn't *want* to hurt me, but she felt, in that moment, that she had no choice. It was either her or me."

Simon picked up a handful of sand, allowing the minuscule particles to trickle from his fingers as Nina's words settled in his mind. "What about the trauma of being homeles? Can that make someone snap?"

"It's possible. Given enough time. Or enough bad experiences."

"Have you ever worked with the homeless directly? At a pro bono crisis clinic, for example?"

"No. Never."

He nodded. Continued to filter sand through his fingers. "Can someone who is experiencing grief experience a psychotic break?"

"Someone like Lester Davenport, you mean?"

"Yeah. Someone like him."

"Someone who's grieving might not experience clinical psychosis or delusions, but his mind might not work the way it did before. Psychologists often talk to grief patients about five stages of grief—"

"I know—denial, anger, bargaining, depression and acceptance."

"Right. Depending on the severity of the stage a person is experiencing, he can start to think outside the box. He could be so driven by his grief that he does something completely out of character."

"Something like...I don't know...kill someone with mental illness because he 'blames' mental illness in general for taking his daughter away from him?"

Nina frowned. "That's an interesting question. Do you mean he views mental illness as an actual entity upon which he can seek revenge?"

"Maybe. Is that possible?"

"Anything's possible where the mind is concerned. But—but what are you really talking about? Do you think that's what Lester Davenport is doing? That he's acting out two agendas? Targeting me because I didn't save Beth. And targeting not only homeless people but mentally ill homeless because mental illness drove Beth to kill herself?"

"It's a theory. The major one I've been able to come up with based on the facts I have."

"Including the facts you discovered yesterday and today?"

He nodded.

"Tell me."

"Louis Cann and the latest victim were both residents of the Welcome Home homeless shelter. That seemed to be their main connection, despite the fact they were both stabbed in Golden Gate Park, because Cann's killer didn't leave the same signature. No initials. So today, I decided to double-check some things. Although I'd seen the crime scene photos in Cann's file, I never actually visited the crime scene myself. This morning, I did. While I was doing that, DeMarco stopped by Welcome Home and canvased nearby walk-in crisis clinics. Anyplace a resident from Welcome Home might go. He found one place advertised in a flyer on the Welcome Home bulletin board. The crisis clinic is located a few blocks from Golden Gate Park. Turns out both murder victims went there at some point."

"They told you that?" she asked with surprise.

"For confidentiality reasons, the counselors wouldn't disclose what the men had been seen for, but DeMarco got them to admit they recognized both of them. Why they were there doesn't really matter. Either they were in mental crisis or led someone to believe they were. That fits my theory about why Davenport attacked them."

"But again, how do you know it wasn't simply the location that tied them together? Maybe the killer hangs out near the clinic and was simply looking for easy prey, mentally ill or not."

"I can't dismiss that thought completely. But a crime of opportunity based on shared location doesn't go deep enough. It doesn't explain how the men might be linked to *you* and Davenport's determination to get revenge for his daughter's death. The mental illness angle does. Can you think of anything else that makes sense?"

She shook her head. "No, but none of this makes sense. Still, there's a flaw in what you just said. You said both men might be linked to me. This latest man who was carved with the initials *BD?* I understand why you think that. But with Cann, you said the initials weren't a factor."

"They weren't. That is, I didn't know they weren't until I revisited the scene. Before today, I relied on SFPD's report on the crime scene."

"And?"

"And the responding officers missed something. Something engraved in the tree right next to where Cann was found."

"The initials *BD*."

"Right."

She sat in stunned silence until he reached out, took her hand and finally said, "This isn't your fault, you know."

"I know."

"Do you?"

At SIMON'S INSISTENT question, Nina nodded. "In my head, I do. Even though I don't always feel it in my heart. You, of all people, can understand that, can't you?"

He raised her hand to his mouth and kissed it. "Yeah, I can."

She savored the feel of her hand in his for several moments before reclaiming it. She told herself that she needed to be strong. Let Simon ask the questions he needed to ask her. And ask him a few questions of her own. "Still no word on Davenport?"

"No. He's still MIA. Hasn't been to work in three days. That tells me right there that he's on the move. In California. Only I haven't been able to track down any recent airline tickets he's purchased or flights he's taken out of the Charleston Airport. Of course, he might have driven to a more remote airport, and I'm checking on that, but it's going to be a while before I can track down that kind of information."

"What will happen once he's caught? Assuming these murders are linked to him, of course."

"He'll be tried for his criminal acts. He'll go to jail. Where he won't be able to hurt anyone anymore."

The notion shouldn't have bothered her, but it did. Just a little. And maybe it was wrong, but she vocalized that fact. Someone like Lester Davenport belonged in a hospital rather than prison. "So he'll be locked up the same way anyone would? Someone who killed for pleasure rather than out of grief?"

She literally felt Simon withdraw from her.

Stiffly, he said, "It doesn't matter why someone kills. What matters is making sure they don't kill again."

"Oh, really. So you don't believe in self-defense?"

He scowled at her. "That's different and you know it."

"No, I don't. A person acting in self-defense is acting to protect his body. A person acting out of a psychotic break is acting to protect his mind. To protect the reality as he perceives it. Both are acting out of character. Granted, if a person is dangerous, the public needs to be protected, but jail isn't always the answer. Sometimes a hospital is the right choice. But to lock someone in jail for—"

"I can't believe you're going here, Nina. People don't act out of character. Our actions *are* our character."

Nina pulled back from him. "Even someone whose brain is releasing the incorrect chemicals or a disproportionate amount of chemicals, thereby telling them to do something completely out of their own character? If that's true, then you have a lot more to learn about mental illness than I thought."

"Maybe. But you seem to be saying that all mentally ill people should be given a pass. Even if they do something awful, like kill a cat. Or a human being."

"That's not what I said," she snapped out. "And not what I meant. Despite everything, sometimes you can't fight where you come from. Who you're born to be. People can do their best to help you, but it's not always enough."

"So you admit some people are unredeemable, then?"

Nina grabbed the wine bottle and took a long drink. "Sociopaths. Psychopaths. Their brains aren't misfiring—they're people who were born or made broken. No medication can fix them." She handed him back the bottle and her face grew sad. "Contrary to what you might think, I don't believe in miracles for everyone. Some things, including the way a person thinks, can't always be changed. That's the saddest thing of all."

It was apparent from the way she looked at him and her tone that she was talking about *him*. From the look on his face, he got the message loud and clear.

THEY DIDN'T TALK FOR nearly an hour.

They just sat, staring at the ocean and occasionally drinking wine.

Eventually, he turned to her and said, "I'm sorry. I was hoping coming here would make you feel better. Instead, you're angry with me." Still, having her be angry with him was infinitely preferable to her being upset or blaming herself for something she'd had absolutely no control of.

"It's not your fault," she said. "You're a straight shooter, remember? We'll just never see eye to eye on this issue, will we?"

"I don't think so." And that was something he truly regretted. He liked Nina and respected her—far more than he'd ever thought possible—and he didn't want her to think otherwise. Not anymore. Even more than that, he was attracted to her. If he'd met her under any other circumstances, he'd bed her and even date her until their time together petered out on its own. Unfortunately, it was obvious they strongly disagreed about core things with respect to human behavior, and what could be excused away and what couldn't. It was also obvious that those disagreements would make any type of long-term, intimate relationship between them difficult, if not impossible.

That wasn't just presupposition on his part—he'd loved Lana, but that love hadn't been enough to keep them together, in large part because they'd disagreed about the same types of issues that he and Nina did. What made him think a relationship with her would work out any better?

Nothing.

She smiled sadly and nodded. Trailed her fingers in the sand next to her. "I guess we're done here then."

His jaw clenched. "I guess so." Rising, he started to pack up their things.

"Unless..." Nina whispered.

Simon froze. "What?"

"Unless, despite our inability to see eye to eye

on this one issue, you'd be interested in having sex with me?"

Did his breath whoosh out of him as loudly as it sounded to his own ears? Was he staring at her as googly-eyed as he felt he was? Maybe, because she closed her eyes, almost as if she needed to block him out of her sight in order to keep her courage up.

"I know," she said with a shaky laugh. "You probably can't believe I'm propositioning you. Not now. Neither can I. But the thing is…I don't want to go back yet. I know we were just fighting. That you still don't respect what I do. Not really. But it doesn't matter. I still want you."

"No," he said quietly. "What you want is to forget."

Her eyes flew open and she nodded. "Is that so wrong? What you said earlier, about seducing me to distract me? It sounded good. It still does."

Hell yes, it sounded good. And no, it wasn't wrong for her to want it. There were, however, several reasons he should pretend this topic of conversation had never been broached. Several reasons he should bundle her into the car and drive like crazy to get her back home and away from him.

First, he'd just got done telling himself that a relationship between them wouldn't work because of the issues between them. That meant any sex they had—now or otherwise—would be a temporary affair.

Second, she had undergone significant stress and trauma in the past few days. She'd just admitted she was looking to forget her troubles by being intimate with him; if not for that, he couldn't see her agreeing to a fling. She'd told him so from the very beginning—that she wanted to keep things professional between them. If he had sex with her now, he'd be taking advantage of her vulnerability, and he liked her too much to do that.

Third, his mind needed to stay focused on the case and he didn't want to mislead her about—

"Simon," she said quietly. "I'm well aware of what the circumstances are here and what I'm asking for. This isn't a matter of you taking advantage of me, but whether you're willing to give me what I want. What I'm *asking* for. If you're going to say no, then say no. But please don't say no for any other reason than you don't want to have sex with me."

He clenched his teeth so hard his jaw hurt. "Damn it, you know it's not about that. I look at you and I want you. I look at you and all I can think about is getting naked and feasting on you, whether we're at SIG, in my car, in your house or on the beach, right here and now."

She scrambled to her feet. Took a step toward him. Froze when he automatically took a step back.

"Then do it," she said. "Do *me*. Right here and right now."

"Nina, think. This isn't what you want. Not really."

"You're wrong. It's what I want. I'll prove it to you." She started unbuttoning her blouse, her fingers shaking but determined.

Desire had him hardening and his fingers itching to brush hers away because she wasn't moving fast enough. It made him desperate to get a glimpse of more of the creamy skin that she was slowly revealing. To touch it. Lick it. Taste it.

Frantically, he ripped his gaze away from her. He looked around them. They were alone. No one else was here. But he wasn't going to have sex with her for the first—and probably last—time on a beach.

Wait, what the hell was he thinking? He wasn't going to have sex with her at all.

Was he?

EVEN AS NINA CONTINUED to unbutton her blouse, even as she stepped so close to Simon that their bodies brushed, she knew she was being exactly what she'd sworn never to be.

Needy.

She couldn't help herself.

Even with the cool ocean breeze tickling her skin, warmth smothered her. She'd shared her beliefs with Simon to give him some insight into her, but the conversation had turned too serious, proving exactly how unsuited for each other they were no matter how much she'd fantasized otherwise.

It didn't matter.

She wanted the distraction he'd hinted at—no, she *needed* the distraction. Knowing her cat had been purposefully killed and cut had been bad enough. Believing that two homeless men had been killed, the second held down and initials cut into his back, because of her? It was too much to bear. As soon as they left this beach and drove home, she'd have to deal with it, but she wasn't ready for that. Not yet.

Not now.

Not with Simon's warm body a fraction of an inch away from hers. Not when the ocean breeze carried his heady scent into her nostrils.

Now she wanted to forget everything. Everything but him.

"Simon?" she murmured. Her hand fell away from her body. She'd undone the last button, but didn't have the nerve to strip her blouse off completely. She stared at his neck, where his own button-down shirt lay open, exposing the beating pulse there.

He raised a hand and brushed his knuckles across her cheek. "What is it, Nina?"

"What do you say? Will you distract me some more?"

He stared her. Withdrew his hand, then one by one, closed the buttons on her blouse. When he was done, he said, "Let's go."

Defeat and disappointment crashed through her, and she blushed with embarrassment.

Until he said, "We're going to a hotel."

Then her blush became all about relief. Anticipation. And lust.

Beautiful, wonderful, life-affirming, utterly distracting lust.

CHAPTER TWENTY-ONE

ONCE SIMON DECIDED TO grant Nina the distraction she wanted, he approached the task with the same confidence and single-mindedness he applied to everything else he did in life. She couldn't help but imagine him putting all that focus to mind-boggling good use on her body.

It took them less than twenty minutes to find a nice hotel and register for a room. As Simon locked the door and drew the curtains closed, blanketing the room in shadows, Nina quivered. Inside and out.

Distraction. Comfort. Passion. She didn't care what word most accurately defined what was about to happen. She just knew she needed Simon.

Simon moved closer until they stood face-to-face next to the bed, their breathing loud in the quiet room. Mindful that she'd asked for this, that she needed to remind him he wasn't taking advantage of her, she placed a hand on his chest and slowly ran her fingers down, brushing a fingernail over his now hardened nipple.

Thankfully, her touch appeared to prod him into action. He stepped closer until she had to tip her head back to keep their gazes locked. Raising his hands, he cupped her face, his thumbs gently smoothing against the edges of her jaw, stretching out the sexual tension until it was almost unbearable and she couldn't stifle the whimper that escaped her. His eyes darkened and a flush rode high on his cheekbones just before he lowered his head and kissed her. Softly. Just the barest pressure, which had her frowning and moving closer. Pressing harder. He smiled, but that smile quickly disappeared when she flicked her tongue out, savoring his taste.

She needed him.

He sucked in a breath and pulled her even closer, his mouth slanting against hers. His tongue curled around hers, urging her to play again, and she eagerly complied. She hummed with pleasure, the sound turning into a disappointed gasp when he pulled away far too soon.

"Shh," he whispered and began kissing her neck, making his way downward even as he undid the buttons of her blouse. He stopped with his face resting lightly against her cleavage, and she looked down and tangled her hands in his hair. His eyes shut, he butted his cheek against her as if he was a cat—savoring the softness of her skin against his.

Nina gasped, and then arched her head back, exposing her throat to him. Sexual arousal charged through her like an electrical current. "Make love to me. Please."

A low moan ripped from somewhere deep inside him. Kissed her throat. Bit it. Sucked.

"You smell good," he murmured. "You feel heavenly. Your skin tastes so sweet. Do you taste just as sweet everywhere else?"

A warm rush of sensation sizzled straight to her core. "Why don't you find out for yourself?" she dared him.

His grin was pure masculine wickedness. With a quick efficient twist of his fingers, he undid her bra and pushed the cups away.

She hissed when he covered one nipple with his big palm and the other with his mouth. He sucked softly at first, then more deeply. She felt the tug between her thighs and whimpered. She ached. Felt empty. Longed to be filled but only by him. "Please. More," she said.

"How much more?" he said as he lifted his head.

"Everything you have. Everything you're willing to give me."

"Everything?"

She nodded. Then qualified, "For now. We can have this for now."

It was the same thing she'd said before their first kiss and she could tell he didn't like it. But she was trying to hold on to some semblance of reality. She wanted him, but she couldn't lose herself completely. She couldn't forget who she was and what she believed and how both those things would always conflict with who he was and what he believed.

She waited for him to protest. Or to agree. He did neither. Instead, he finished undressing her, undressed himself, swept her up in his arms and lowered her to the bed.

As Simon laid Nina out on the bed, he told himself to be calm. Not to panic.

She was still talking about *now*. Still insisting that what they were about to do, with each other and to each other, wouldn't last. Everything inside him screamed in protest and he wanted her to know it, but he had no right. And nothing he could say to try to change her mind would make sense anyway.

He just knew she was important to him. That as much as he'd run from caring about her, he couldn't run anymore. Not from this.

She was in his arms. For now. And he would take it.

He would take *her*.

Even if he couldn't keep her.

With that thought in mind, he framed her face in his big hands and kissed her with everything he was feeling—tenderness, affection, lust and yes...a hint of desperation. He wanted to kiss her for hours, but, mindful that their time was limited, he also didn't want to miss out on touching the rest of her body.

Her breasts especially, he thought, remembering how sweet and right her nipple had felt in his mouth. Groaning, he pulled back and, pressing both of her breasts together, buried his face in her cleavage. Turning his head one way and then the other, he took turns sucking her nipples and simultaneously gave his hands the freedom to roam over her. From her silky-soft hair to her smooth rounded shoulders. Down her arms to her elegant fingers. Over her plush hips and then... God, yes...he clasped her thighs and pulled them up on either side of his hips, opening her so that her core pressed solidly against his upper abdomen, searing him with her heat. Between his own thighs, his erection throbbed with urgency and although he pressed it into the bedding, he found little relief.

He wanted *her*. To be inside her body. Encased by her wet, clinging heat.

Lowering his hand, he cupped her between her

thighs and carefully inserted one finger into her. She was as wet and tight as he'd imagined.

She gasped and arched, her head thrashing back and forth wildly, prompting him to add another finger to the mix. This time she didn't make a sound, but she grabbed his shoulders, her nails delivering a stinging pain that more than communicated her pleasure and ratcheted up his.

God, she was amazing. So responsive. So giving of herself.

In bed, their differences were only good ones. Two parts that looked and felt nothing alike, but fit together to create something complete and unique and good. In bed, the rest of the world disappeared, and there was no guilt, no fears for the future, just this heart-pounding pleasure that coursed through every part of his body. Invigorating and strengthening him.

After kissing each breast one last time, he slid farther down her body, stopping at her rounded belly and teasing her naval with several licks and bites, each making her squeal with delight. But when he kissed that place between her thighs, she seemed to go mute. With a silent exhalation, she surrendered to his touch, her body melting like butter into the bedding and her thighs falling to the sides.

He could feel her wetness against his face, smell the sweet musk of her womanhood, and he relished the knowledge that she wanted him. A quick glance up her body confirmed that her eyes were closed tight and that her fingers now gripped the bedsheets with every lick and thrust of his tongue. She pumped her hips against him, too, silently demanding he give her more. More of his fingers. More of his tongue. More of the blessed forgetfulness that drowned out everything but the heat and spark and push and pull of lovemaking.

He was so damn hard, hurting so bad that he couldn't stand it anymore. Pushing himself up, he crawled up her body and begged, "Touch me. Please."

Her eyes popped open and she stared at him, dazed, almost blind, before she smiled and licked her lips. When cool, slim fingers wrapped around him and began a tight-fisted stroking, his head fell back and he groaned as if overcome with pain. And in truth it was a kind of pain, one that ratcheted up his need so fast he felt dizzy. One that would only be soothed once he became part of her.

At the same time, her touch felt better than anything he'd ever experienced. His toes curled and his heart pumped hard. Blindly, he sought out her lips again and pumped his tongue into the slick cavern of her mouth just like he'd pumped it into the slick cavern between her thighs. He wondered if she could taste herself and if she liked it. He wondered if she'd want to taste him.

"Oh, God," he moaned as she pulled his cock between her legs and began grinding the head against her in slow, dragging circles. It felt like he was being dipped in warm honey, and that only added to the fantasy of her licking and lapping at him, then sucking him dry.

"Enough," he gasped out.

"No. Not enough," she said softly. "Not by a long shot."

He shook his head as he tried to make her understand. "I need to be inside you. I need a condom," he gasped.

Her hand froze, and for a second he pressed against

her, poised at her very opening, wanting so badly to thrust inside. With sheer will, he moved to the side, trying not to cry out when her hand slid away from him. Quickly, he retrieved a condom from his wallet, slid it on then covered her body again with his.

He cupped her face and stared into her eyes. "Now?" he said, his words less a question than a plea.

She nodded. "Now."

"You do it," he said.

When she looked confused, he clarified, "Put me inside you. Guide me. Show me where you want me, Nina."

Her eyes dilated and she reached down, gripped him and again guided him between her thighs. Once there, she teased him once more, this time using slow up and down strokes to drive him crazy rather than the circular motions she'd used before. He couldn't help it; every time she stroked him against her, he pushed his hips forward just a bit, until finally, finally, the tip of him slipped inside her.

They both jerked and gasped.

Dropping his forehead against hers, he murmured, "You're so hot. So wet and so damn tight."

"The more you put inside me, the tighter I'll be. And the wetter and hotter I'll get. So please…" Along with her pleading tone, she cupped his ass and pulled him closer, her thighs sawing restlessly on either side of his hips.

Slowly, steadily, he pushed into her, every fiber of his being focused on the drag of her inner tissues against his cock. When he was all the way inside, he swore he forgot to breathe. She felt fantastic. But more than that, she felt like home.

Her hips pushed up against his, urging him into a rhythm he was more than happy to start. Over and over again, he pushed himself into her. Over and over again, he pulled himself out of her. And she was right—with every movement, she got hotter. He got harder. Their moans got louder. Their embrace got tighter. And before he knew it, his thrusts got faster. Faster and harder and deeper, until he was practically pounding her into the bed, her gasps and moans and clinging arms urging him on. It was almost too fast. And not fast enough.

Too fast because he didn't want this to end so quickly.

Not fast enough because he wanted to make her come, damn it, and he wanted to come, too.

It had been so long since he'd felt this kind of pleasure, this kind of intimacy with a woman, and his body was reminding him of that fact, greedily reaching for every drop of sensation it could. And that included relishing every fine tremor that racked her body, and how her breaths grew more and more ragged as she approached climax.

"That's it," he urged. "It's gonna feel so good when you come, Nina. Come for me, baby. Let me feel you shuddering around my—"

"Simon!" she screamed as she obeyed his command and came. Her wide eyes stayed on his even as the pleasure made them go blank. Her body jerked and convulsed with the power of her orgasm, mimicking the wild spasms of her internal muscles, which were determined to pull the same response from him.

It didn't take long before they succeeded. He felt his release gather then push out of him with the force of a rocket ship, one pulse followed by another and then another and another until he finally closed his eyes in disbelief.

How much did he have to give her? How long could his pleasure go on?

And what the hell was he going to do when he was empty and their time together came to an end?

The end seemed to take a while. In her arms, clasped within her body, time ceased to exist. Eventually, however, reality began to sink in as their bodies calmed.

He had no idea what time it was. He did, however, realize that he was lying on top of Nina, making it difficult for her to breathe. Shifting to the side, he buried his face in her neck and held on as he tried to calm his racing heart and billowing breaths. Finally, when he felt capable of actually talking again, he pushed up on an elbow, pushed her hair out of her face and kissed her lightly on the lips.

Her eyes were closed, and she smiled as he kissed her, so he kept on doing it, taking the time to explore her mouth the way he hadn't been able to when the urge to get inside her had been riding him.

When he finally pulled away, it was to cradle her close once more.

But then he must have dozed off…

The next thing he knew, the space beside him had grown cold. Blinking, he sat up, fully naked since they'd kicked the bedsheets to the floor. Nina was sitting on the side of the bed and pulling her shirt on. He reached out a hand to caress her shoulder, intending to pull her back down next to him, but before he could, she turned slightly and spoke, keeping her gaze averted.

"We should get going," she said softly. "You need to work."

She was right. He did. As much as he'd love to spend the night with her—hell, the next several nights with her, all of them in bed—he couldn't put off work much longer. "Nina—"

She stood and turned to face him. She was fully dressed now. Her eyes took him in before she blushed and looked away again. Damn it, he refused to feel embarrassed by his nudity or by what they'd done. But even so, he knew her averted gaze, just like the clothes she'd donned, was meant to push him away and he felt her distance like a cold breeze.

And that was good, he thought, as he stood and began putting on his own clothes. It was exactly what he needed to remind himself that, as close as he'd felt to her, it had just been about sex. About satisfying a physical need for him. And about providing a distraction for her. Hell, if it hadn't been her, it would have been some other woman, probably one he'd picked up at McGill's. In this case, it had been her, but only because she'd needed to forget.

He'd been her drug of choice, and that was fine.

The sex had been good, but now all that mattered was keeping Nina safe, catching Davenport and solving the homeless murders. Then, life would go on. Their lives would go on. Separately, of course. They didn't have a future together, not even a professional one anymore.

But even so, even though he fully believed those things, the air chilled even more when she spoke. "You

went above and beyond the call of duty here, Simon.
Thank you for distracting me. I appreciate it."

A HALF HOUR LATER, NINA was still reeling from the
aftereffects of her time with Simon but she refused to
let him see that. She'd asked him for a distraction—
sex—despite knowing that's all it could ever be. He'd
given her what she'd asked for.

Their time on the beach had been a respite, a chance
for them to escape their worlds for a short while. Afterward, sex with him had blown her world away. Now
reality was staring them in the face in the form of the
winding Highway 1.

Now she had to stick with her side of the bargain.

Deal with the reality of the situation. And that meant
dealing with the fact their passion had been a one-
time thing.

Their time together wasn't completely over, however. Not yet. It wouldn't be until Simon caught Davenport and confirmed he'd indeed killed those two
homeless men.

Even so, although Simon was driving her back to
her house, it was only so she could pick up her clothing
and necessities. And it wasn't because he was planning
to spend the night with her, either.

As they'd prepared to go, he'd said, "I can't stay with
you, Nina. And I'll worry about you if you're at home
alone. Will you please stay in a hotel close to SIG? At
least until we get a handle on Davenport?"

She wasn't about to argue with him. Not given what
he'd told her about the murder victims, and his best
guess as to why Davenport had attacked them.

But what they knew still felt like only a few pieces in

a thousand-piece jigsaw puzzle. They needed more information. Answers. Understanding. The only way they were going to get them was if Simon found Davenport.

When Simon's phone rang, he checked the caller ID screen then picked up. "Anything new, DeMarco?"

The detective's voice came over the speakerphone. "Nothing good. Davenport's still missing. The last time he was seen was by a neighbor at his house in Charleston over a week ago."

"What?" Nina gasped.

"Nina and I both confirmed the neighbor had seen him at the beginning of this week. A friend of Nina's, a cop in Charleston P.D.—"

"I talked to him. Officer Wade King," DeMarco said. "He went back and talked to the neighbor again. She admitted she'd lied. Davenport paid her a hundred bucks to tell anyone who asked that he was still around."

Simon swore under his breath, then thanked DeMarco and hung up. "This guy has gone off his rocker but he's obviously in touch with reality enough to cover his tracks. I have reason to believe someone bribed a witness to lie to the cops about the first murder victim, Louis Cann. It's consistent with Davenport bribing his neighbor. And both bribes are evidence of his consciousness of guilt."

Anger tickled the back of her throat. Nina shifted in her seat, squaring her shoulders. "That your clinical opinion? Your official diagnosis? He's 'gone off his rocker'?"

He glanced at her with a heavy frown. "Christ, Nina, you know what I mean."

Unfortunately, even with Simon's stigmatizing language, she did. If Lester Davenport had indeed killed her cat and those homeless men, he'd gone far beyond grief. He could very well be a psychopath.

The thing was, the notion didn't jive with what she knew about the man. Lester Davenport had always seemed to be miserable. Depressed. He'd never had the hallmarks of a psychopath—grandiosity and clever manipulation. Could he instead be experiencing a late onset of schizophrenia? But schizophrenics were rarely violent and usually didn't have the organizational ability to go off the grid so thoroughly, navigate around security systems so accurately they could escape detection or even bribe witnesses to cover their tracks. Something was off, but what?

"After we get your clothes from your house and I drop you off at your hotel," Simon said, "I'll head back to SIG. You won't be shadowing me, of course, but I'd still prefer you not go into work tomorrow. If need be, I can call your boss and explain, but—"

"That's not necessary. I can call my boss myself. She's not expecting me at work until Monday anyway." She crossed her arms over her chest, and stared out the passenger window for the next fifteen minutes until they reached her neighborhood. She tried to imagine what she'd do stuck in a hotel room, her only choices to think about Davenport and the men he'd murdered, or the feel of Simon's body inside hers as he'd temporarily made her forget that pain.

Simon steered the car into her driveway, parked, turned the engine off and yanked the key out of the ignition. He rolled his head on the back of the seat before looking at her.

This time she looked back, and held his gaze. "What

happens after Davenport is caught? Will I shadow you again?"

She read his answer on his face. Not that Commander Stevens wouldn't authorize such a thing, but that Simon wouldn't want it.

"Yeah," she nodded. "Probably not a good idea." It was for the best. He'd given her what she wanted by giving her sex. She'd known it would be a one-time thing, but already she was feeling addicted to him. Not wanting him to leave her. And more specifically, not wanting him to leave her body, aching for the pleasure and fulfillment only he could give her. Yes, indeed, staying at a hotel by herself was going to be a miserable experience. Tiredly, she climbed out of the car.

He cursed, got out and stepped up to her, capturing her arms in a gentle grip when she would have walked past him. "I just don't think us working together is a good idea. You said it yourself. I care about you and I think you care about me. But nothing's going to change between us. We'll never be able to reconcile our beliefs. As much as I loved making love with you, I need to focus on my bid for management and—" Abruptly, he stopped speaking and stared through the front windows next to her front door.

"Simon—what is it?" She leaned around him but couldn't see past his broad shoulders.

"Go to a neighbor's house," he ordered. "Now. Call 911."

"What? Why?"

"I heard something from inside. Someone moving around. Give me your house keys."

She fumbled in her purse, then handed him her set of keys.

He thrust his cell phone in her hand. "Call 911. Go to a neighbors and wait for me. Now."

CHAPTER TWENTY-TWO

SIMON SLID ALONGSIDE the outer door of Nina's garage and headed to the front door, his gun in his hands, at the ready. Nina would call 911 and convey all the needed information, which would get him backup in about three minutes. But no way was he going to chance whoever was inside—and he was betting it would be Davenport—getting away and continuing to pose a threat to Nina. If he could capture Davenport, she would be safe, and so might another homeless person.

Simon quietly stepped onto Nina's porch, reached her darkened front door and grasped the handle, giving it a controlled twist. It was unlocked, leaving him no need to use the key Nina had given him. He eased the door open, then made his way inside the darkened house, following protocol by sticking to the wall and thrusting his gun out at each corner.

He covered the ground floor, but couldn't find anyone. Didn't matter. He'd heard someone moving inside and the front door had been unlocked. Davenport had probably gone up the stairwell to the second floor. Quietly, he made his way to the foot of the stairs.

In the background, he heard the familiar wail of sirens. Backup.

That meant Nina had called 911. Good girl.

He heard a bang on the ceiling above him, then footsteps in quick succession, moving away from him. Fuck—Davenport *was* upstairs. What the hell was he doing? Had he heard Simon come in? Had he thought Simon was Nina, and even now was lying in wait in her bedroom, prepared to hurt her? Maybe even rape her before he killed her?

Rage pumped through Simon's veins. He swerved around the banister and started to charge up the stairs. When he was halfway up, Simon paused, listening for hints of Davenport's location. Suddenly, he heard more footsteps, one followed quickly after another. Moving away from the stairwell.

He was running, Simon realized—but not to come back down the stairwell. He was headed to the front of the house. Probably planning on climbing through a window and onto the upper-deck balcony that stretched across the front of the house and the side of the garage. Once he was there, it would be an easy job for Davenport to clamber down to the ground below.

Where Nina might be waiting.

God damn it all!

"Police. Stop where you are!" he shouted, reversing his direction and charging back down the stairs and to the front door, desperate to reach Nina before Davenport could. He raced out onto the front porch.

Immediately, he saw him.

A man running down the long driveway toward the road.

Simon bolted after him, gaining ground quickly. "Stop. I'm with the police! Stop now!" he shouted.

The man didn't listen, but his flight would do him no good.

Simon was almost on him when the man turned to look over his shoulder. Simon had researched Lester Davenport and seen a couple of photos of the man. It was him!

His expression one of panic, Davenport raised his right arm, giving Simon a glimpse of the gun he was trying to swing around.

Before he could point it, Simon tackled him.

They hit the ground hard.

Simon immediately flipped Davenport to his stomach, wrenched his arms behind his back and snatched the gun away from him. With his knee in the man's back, Simon began reading the man his rights.

"You have the right to remain silent..." he began. "You have the right to an attorney. If you do not have an attorney..."

Simon heard a sound coming from the front of the driveway. Some distance away, patrol officers were running up to help him. Nina was there, too, her horrified gaze pinned on the man beneath Simon.

Davenport looked up and saw her, as well. All of a sudden, he began thrashing and fighting Simon's hold.

"You!" he screamed. "It's all your fault. Your fault that Beth died. And now you think you can get away with it again? Fool people into thinking you can help them? You didn't save that little girl. You put her in danger, just like her father says. Just like my Beth!"

"Shut up," Simon ordered, but no matter what he said, he couldn't get Davenport to shut up. He kept shouting his hatred at Nina until patrol officers took him away.

And from the look on her face, Nina heard every word.

CHAPTER TWENTY-THREE

THE BLUE AND WHITE LIGHTS on the last patrol car faded into the distance. Standing in her front yard, Simon turned to face Nina. She was pale and trembling. All he wanted was to bring her inside and take her into his arms, but she couldn't stay in the house. In minutes, the forensic team would arrive to process the place. In the meantime, they needed to get her stuff.

When he reminded her of that, however, she looked confused.

"Why do I still have to leave? Davenport's in custody."

Gently, he explained about the forensics team. Then said, "Besides, aside from the forensic team needing to do their job, we can't make any assumptions. Davenport's obviously guilty of breaking into your house. I think he's the man who killed two men because of his daughter's mental illness, but I don't want to make any assumptions that could put you in danger. I need to go in and interview him. Get him to confess he killed Cann and that second man. In order to do that, I can't afford to be distracted. Worried. I need to know you're safe. I can still take you to a hotel. Or better yet, to a friend's house. Is there a friend you can stay with?"

It took her a few seconds to process what he was saying, to accept that this wasn't over quite yet.

"Nina," he prompted.

She glanced up at him with shadowed eyes, then nodded. "I can stay with Karen. My boss. She's a friend, too."

"Okay. Let's go in and call her. If it doesn't look like he's messed with your things, you can grab some essentials and then I can drive you to her house."

They both went inside.

"Mud," Nina grumbled under her breath as she walked past her living room and headed for the stairwell.

"Excuse me?" Simon asked, on her heels.

She pointed to the faint impression of muddy footprints near the back patio door and automatically took a few steps toward them. "Davenport must've tracked it in."

Simon grabbed her elbow and pulled her to a halt before she could get too close to them. "Don't touch anything yet. We don't want to contaminate the scene. As soon as the techs come in to process the place, they'll photograph the prints and match them up to Davenport." Simon frowned. "But I thought he gained entry through your front door. It was unlocked. Is it possible you left it unlocked when we left this morning?"

"It's possible. More likely probable. He definitely came in through the back. See, the footprints are red, made with the mud from my backyard," Nina said slowly, drawing her words out. "I'm having a new patio put in. Right now part of the backyard is covered with this red-colored earth—fill the contractor put down as a base before laying the brick. Davenport had to have been in my backyard to get this red dirt on his feet."

Simon stroked her arm, knowing she had to be rattled by the fact Davenport had broken into her home. Hell, even he was still rattled, overcome with thoughts of what Davenport had been planning to do to Nina. None of them were pretty and even now he envisioned Nina's torso bared, her back marred with bloody initials. Fighting back nausea, he took his hand off her arm and patted her back, hoping she wouldn't notice that he was shaking. "Let's see if he touched your stuff."

She led him to her room. The last time he'd been in it, she'd cried herself to sleep in his arms. Now...

Nina's horrified cry mingled with Simon's ugly curse.

The letters *BD* were spray painted on her walls and on her pale bedspread.

Once again, he placed a comforting hand on her shoulder. "I'm sorry, Doc. But if this doesn't link him to the homeless murders, I'm not sure what will. I'll get the stuff in your dresser. You grab what you need from your closet. But if anything looks like it's been messed with, don't touch it, okay?"

Shakily, Nina nodded and headed for her closet. As she extracted a suitcase and began filling it, Simon walked over to her dresser and examined a few of the items on top of it. Framed photos of her and Rachel. A ballerina music box. A bundle of swim team ribbons. A little teddy bear with a pink bow. Like the rag doll she carried in her purse, was the bear something she'd had as a child? Maybe even something that had belonged to her sister? But he wasn't about to ask her that now, just as he hadn't pressed her for details about her sister's suicide. He already knew Rachel Whitaker had slit her wrists in the bathtub. The last thing Nina needed right now was to remember that.

He turned to her. "Bring casual and business clothes. In case you—" He broke off at the expression on her face. Her jaw had gone slack, her complexion ashen and the pupils of her eyes had dilated until they seemed almost black.

"Nina." Simon took a step forward, but she shrank back. "What is it? What's wrong?"

Nina took another step back and pointed a shaking finger. "The bear. On my dresser."

"What is it? Isn't it yours?"

She swallowed and wrapped an arm around her stomach, then bent at the knees, going into a low crouch. She gave a low moan of pain.

"Oh, Doc. Oh, no." Immediately, he went to her and gathered her in his arms. With gentle movements, he stroked her hair as she buried her head in the crook of his neck, gasping for air. He murmured her name and held her tight until her breathing regulated.

"That's how she did it," she whispered, her voice raw.

"That's how who did what?" he asked, but somehow he knew the answer.

"That's how Beth killed herself. She used a pink ribbon from a teddy bear to strangle herself to death. That bear doesn't belong to me. He brought it with him. Davenport. He left it here for me to find."

Simon wanted to rip Davenport's heart out through his rib cage, but right now Nina needed him. After she'd come close to collapsing in her bedroom, he'd held her until she stopped sobbing. Then he'd finished packing for her, throwing items from her dresser and closet into the suitcase she'd already pulled out. After that, he'd struggled with indecision. He'd been planning on leaving her in a hotel or at a friend's house and following up with Davenport.

But at that moment, Nina had needed him more. She'd trusted him with her body. He was taking responsibility for her emotional well-being, too.

He'd bundled Nina and her overnight bag into the car and had taken off for his place.

Nina hadn't argued. Didn't even ask questions. That worried him. She wasn't going to be able to take much more. Not with everything she'd already gone through.

On the way to his house, Simon called DeMarco and asked him to conduct Davenport's interview, but DeMarco said Davenport had asked for an attorney. There would be no interviewing him until at least tomorrow.

That was good. That meant Simon could give Nina his full attention.

Now, in his guest room, he unpacked her items and put them away as she sat curled up on the bed, her arms wrapped around her legs, her chin resting on her knees. For the first time since he'd met her, she looked utterly defeated. And that scared the shit out of him.

He sat next to her on the bed.

"I know he got into your house, Nina, even with the new security system in place, and I know that has to scare the shit out of you, but don't let him into your mind. Don't let him invade that space, too."

"He already has," she mumbled. "He's been there for the past three years, reminding me of what happened. How I failed to stop it."

"Then get him out. Shove him out of your mind. Put something else in there."

"Like what?"

"Hell, I don't know. Distract yourself with something."

They stared at each other, remembering what they'd done earlier that day to distract her.

"Is that an invitation?" she asked.

When she placed a hand on his chest and flattened her palm over his pectoral muscle, the rest of the world faded away. Rational thought left the building. He saw only her. Smelled only her. Felt only her.

But he still managed to keep hold of some small measure of sense. He'd worried earlier that day that making love to her would be taking advantage of her. She'd convinced him that wouldn't be the case. That she known full well what she'd wanted, and what she'd wanted was Simon. She might want him now, but this was different. She'd suffered one shock too many for him to even think about having sex with her.

"No, baby," he said even as he clasped her hand in his. "We can't. You're too upset. That's not what you need."

She tried to withdraw her hand, but Simon held on.

"Oh, yeah?" she challenged. "What do I need then?"

"You need me to hold you," he said firmly. "All night. You need me to tell you that everything's going to be okay. That you're going to be okay. And that I'm going to be here to make sure of it."

She stared at him, lips trembling, blinking to fight back tears. Eventually, she took a deep breath. Swallowed hard. Then nodded. "You're right," she said. "That's what I need."

So that's exactly what Simon gave her.

CHAPTER TWENTY-FOUR

THE NEXT DAY, SIMON interviewed Davenport at the SFPD while his attorney watched on. When Simon first walked into the small interrogation room, he did so with trepidation. He was afraid his personal feelings for Nina would prevent him from keeping his cool. That he'd want to hurt Davenport the same way the other man had hurt Nina. Not just in the recent past, but every year that he'd sent Nina a card, shattering her attempts to move on and live a happy life by reminding her again and again of his daughter's death, and the fact Davenport held her responsible for it.

Instead, as he sat across from the man, noting how pale and subdued and pathetically small he looked, Simon's anger was somehow transformed into the same professional calm that always served him well during interrogations. He began the interview by asking preliminary questions about Davenport's date of birth, place of residence and employer. Sure, Davenport was calm and cooperative now, but he had no doubt that would change once Simon started asking him the tough questions. As such, he was glad Nina wouldn't be around to hear whatever ugly accusations soon came out of Davenport's mouth.

Though she'd insisted on coming with him to the station, and had already identified Davenport's mug shot, confirming he was indeed the man whose daughter had died in her care and who had been sending her threatening cards, she hadn't even argued with Simon when he'd asked her to wait in the lobby during the interview. In a way, the ease with which she'd given in bothered him. It indicated more than anything else that she was still a little shell-shocked and not quite ready to deal with the full realities of the situation.

Still, he'd promised to keep her updated on their progress and he was going to keep that promise. Right now, however, he needed to get as much information out of Davenport as he could. Between Nina's testimony, and the fact Simon had caught him red-handed in Nina's house, had had to chase him down and had had to disarm him, convictions for making unlawful threats, burglary and resisting arrest were pretty much in the bag. However, the same couldn't be said for pinning him with the murders of Cann and John Hastings, the man and the second murder victim whose identity they'd discovered early that morning.

His preliminary questions over, Simon continued to stare at Davenport until the man squirmed. Then he stood, deliberately using his height to make the man look up at him. "Mr. Davenport, you've said you live and work in Charleston, South Carolina. Let's talk about when you arrived in California and why you're here."

Davenport looked at his attorney, who nodded, indicating he should go ahead and answer. "I drove here over the course of several days. I arrived yesterday morning."

"Did anyone accompany you on the trip?"

"No."

Of course not. So unless Davenport had some proof, such as gasoline records, it was only his word that he hadn't been in the state before yesterday. "Tell me, was the sole purpose of your cross-country trip to break into Dr. Whitaker's house?"

Again, Davenport looked at his attorney. And again, his attorney indicated he could answer. "I didn't come to break into her house. I wanted to talk to her, that's all."

"Yet you did break into her house. And you were carrying a gun with you. Do you always do that when you plan on talking to someone?" Simon asked. "Or only when you plan on talking to someone you've been sending threatening cards to? Someone you blame for your daughter's suicide?"

"She *is* to blame for Beth's death," Davenport hissed. "And the cards I've sent her were only meant to remind her of that. Beth's gone and I have to live with that loss every day of my life. Why should *she* get to move on with her life when I can't?"

Because she did everything she could to save your daughter after you obviously screwed her up, Simon thought, but he managed to keep those words to himself. "What else have you done to remind her of her guilt, as you see it?"

Davenport blinked. "Nothing."

Simon cocked a brow. "Perhaps I should rephrase my question then. Assuming you're telling the truth about not arriving in San Francisco until yesterday morning, who did you hire to terrorize Dr. Whitaker this past week?"

Davenport's brows furrowed. He glanced at his attorney, who wore a similar expression, then turned back to Simon. "What are you talking about? I haven't hired anyone to do anything."

Simon stared at the man, his stomach clenching at the man's expression and tone of voice. If he didn't know better, he'd be tempted to believe him. No, this guy was one of the best liars Simon had ever met. But he wasn't buying it. He leaned forward. "You didn't leave Dr. Whitaker a typed letter outside her front door telling her she was going to die? Didn't kill her cat and leave it in her car? Didn't kill two homeless men and carve a message into the back of one of them?"

Davenport's eyes bulged out. "Wh-what? What are you talking about? No!"

"Mr. Davenport," his attorney spoke up. "Please don't answer any more questions unless I give you the okay to do so." The man then turned to Simon. "What's going on here, Detective? My client's been arrested for burglary, assault on a police officer and possessing an unlawful firearm. Mutilation and murder of either an animal or a human isn't on the table, as far as I know."

"Not yet," Simon gritted out, "but it's gonna be. We have strong circumstantial evidence that your client is responsible for the deaths of two men."

"You're crazy!" Davenport shouted. "Crazy. I haven't killed anyone."

"But you were intending on killing Dr. Whitaker, weren't you? Isn't that why you drove to California? Broke into her house with a gun? Vandalized her home with your daughter's initials and left that bear with the pink ribbon for her to find…"

"What?" Davenport's complexion seemed to pale several shades. "No. No, I didn't do any of that. I—"

"Mr. Davenport," his attorney began, but Davenport cut him off.

"No, I won't be quiet. I didn't do any of those things. Her front door was unlocked. I let myself in, but only because I wanted to talk to her. And okay, I wanted to scare her a little. But I didn't leave Beth's initials or any damn doll. I—I wouldn't have done that. I couldn't have. I just wanted to talk to her. Tell her I knew what she was trying to do. That she was trying to convince people she'd helped that other girl, Rebecca Hyatt, but that I knew the truth, me and that reporter. That's why I came to California, so I could—"

"Reporter?" Simon interrupted. "A reporter called you about Rebecca Hyatt? When?"

"Last week."

"What was his name?"

"I—I don't know. I can't remember. Shannon something. From the *San Francisco Reporter*. He told me that a girl had almost died because of Dr. Whitaker."

Simon snorted with patent disbelief. "That's a real convenient story, Davenport. But there's no newspaper called the *San Francisco Reporter*."

Davenport looked confused. A little scared. "What? Well, then he lied about where he worked."

Simon pierced Davenport with a glare. "I totally agree someone's a liar, Davenport, but I think that person's you. But if you're going to keep to your story, why don't you tell me exactly what this phantom reporter told you."

WHILE SIMON INTERVIEWED Davenport, Nina sat in the station lobby and tried to read old magazines to pass the time. Eventually, however, after reading the same paragraph five times, she gave up. She sat there for what seemed like hours, staring at the dingy walls and entering an almost meditative state before Commander Stevens stepped up to her.

"Dr. Whitaker?"

Nina jerked to attention. "Yes?" She stood, looking for Simon. "Is the interview over?"

"Not quite yet. Simon is still in with Davenport, trying to wrap up a few loose ends. He asked me to tell you he should be out soon."

"Did—did he get the information you need?"

"Some of it. Davenport confessed to sending you a threatening card and breaking into your house, but that's it. It's to be expected," Stevens reassured her. "He's copping to those crimes since we already have the evidence we need to charge him with them. I'm not at all surprised he hasn't copped to the others, especially since he has an attorney. They'll wait to see what the DA charges him with and what kind of deal he's willing to offer prior to trial."

"But will the DA have enough to charge him with the other things? Killing my cat? Killing those two men?"

"The initials he left on the man and in your house are circumstantial evidence. We're still working on tracking down his movements. He claims he drove here and didn't arrive in California until yesterday morning. If we can confirm he was actually in the city when the victims were killed, it should be enough to charge him. Of course, the DA will want more before he's actually brought to trial, and we'll continue working on getting it for him. Unfortunately, we're going to need your help for a while longer."

Nina's eyes widened. "In what way?"

"According to Simon, you and he already discussed why Davenport might have targeted the two men that he did. However, he also said he hasn't had a chance to talk about those two men in detail, and explore whether you might have met them or otherwise know anything about them or their treatment histories."

"No. We discussed some things yesterday. Some of his theories, and the victims in general. But he—he hasn't had a chance to talk to me about them in detail yet. He said he'd speak to me after he was done with Davenport."

Stevens nodded. "Yes, well, I'd prefer another investigator go through things with you."

"Why?"

"Frankly, to cover ourselves. It's clear to me that you and Detective Granger have become…friends…and it would just be simpler all the way around if he wasn't the detective to take your official statement. Do you have any objection to Jase Tyler or Carrie Ward taking care of that?"

She hesitated and stared at Stevens. All of a sudden, she was hit by a vague sense of discomfort. As if she needed to be wary of this man. But why? What he was saying made perfect sense. And it wasn't like she'd done anything wrong. Still, she'd have felt better if Simon was here. So he could watch her back, so to speak. But that was exactly the kind of thing Stevens was trying to prevent. He didn't want there to be any appearance of favoritism or bias in case Davenport tried to fight the charges against him.

So even though she'd remain on her guard, she

needed to do what Stevens asked. She tipped up her chin. "Do I need an attorney?"

"No. You're not under suspicion for any crime, Dr. Whitaker," Stevens said. "You're not under arrest and you're free to leave at any time. We just need to explore what you might know that can connect you to Mr. Cann and Mr. Hastings, the two men to each other or more important, either of the two men to Davenport."

"Mr. Hastings. That's the second murder victim? You've identified him?"

"Yes."

"Simon said both murder victims were homeless. Have you informed their families?"

"Mr. Cann's family was contacted weeks ago. As to Mr. Hastings, we're trying to track them down right now."

Nina thought about things then took a calming breath. "Okay. I'm happy to tell you what I might know, but I doubt it will help. As I told Simon, I've never worked with the homeless population, certainly not since moving to San Francisco. But first…can I see Lester Davenport? Is that possible?"

"Why do you want to do that?"

"I knew him before he was suffering from guilt-induced crisis. I also had some interaction with him after Beth's suicide. I'm a psychiatrist. Trained in interpreting behavior and emotional states."

"Any conclusions you form about Davenport in this case can't be used by us in any formal capacity, and that includes at trial. You're one of his victims. As such, you'll be deemed a biased witness."

"I realize that. But you see, like I said, I *knew* him. Not well, but even so, even knowing how much he grieved his daughter and blamed me for her death, I would never have thought him capable of violence. Not like this."

"Would you have suspected he'd threaten you, even break into your house with a gun?"

"No," she said truthfully.

"Yet you saw for yourself that he did do that."

"Yes, but murder? Mutilation? That's far different. I just want to see him. Observe him when he doesn't know I'm there. I might be able to offer you something useful, even if it's nothing that can be used against him in court."

Stevens pondered what she'd said for several minutes, then nodded. "Come with me. You can watch the tail end of Simon's interview from a one-way mirror."

He led her to a small room with a window that looked into another small room. There, Simon sat at a long table. On the other end of the table sat a pony-tailed man in a blazer, and Lester Davenport.

Davenport was shackled to a metal chair, his forehead on the scarred metal table in front of him, his sobs echoing through the interrogation room. Despite herself, despite all the things Simon suspected he'd done, Nina's heart ached with sympathy for the man.

"Has he said anything about me?" she asked Stevens.

Stevens hesitated, and Nina reassured him, "It's okay. I've heard him blame me for Beth's death for a long time now. I'm just wondering if his accusations have remained consistent or if he's started to remember the past in a skewed way. That would give me some insight into his current mental state."

"He told Simon that you were responsible for his

daughter's death because your staff knew she was suicidal, yet you let her boyfriend give her a teddy bear with a long length of ribbon tied around its neck into a bow. He said that although your staff confiscated the bear, they failed to notice that Beth secreted the ribbon in her mouth. And he said that she used that ribbon to hang herself."

"That's exactly what happened," she said. "So he's in touch with reality."

"He said you weren't actually at the hospital at the time, though."

"That's right."

"Yet he blames you so strongly."

"Because I'd told him that Beth was getting better. That I didn't think she'd make another attempt on her life as long as she continued to improve the way she had. I was obviously wrong."

"You mean because you couldn't predict the future with perfect accuracy, you're to blame?"

"In his mind, yes."

"And in your mind?"

She startled and looked up at the commander. "Logically I know I'm not to blame. But I still can't help wondering if I could have done more to get through to Beth. Aren't you plagued by such doubts at times?"

"Of course. We all are. I just hope you remember that."

She smiled slightly. Commander Stevens was obviously trying to do the right thing by having someone other than Simon interview her, but he was compassionate about her situation, as well. He was just being objective, like he'd said. That went a long way in getting her to trust him again.

The interview concluded less than two minutes later without giving Nina much of an opportunity to observe Davenport. Stevens escorted her out of the room. As they walked farther down the hallway, she asked, "Despite what he believes about Davenport, Simon has said I shouldn't assume I'm safe now. Do you agree? Because I'd like to go home. Get on with my life."

"Does that include the shadow program with Simon?"

She shook her head. "I don't need to continue the program. I've seen enough, and I'm sure it won't come as a surprise to you that, while I find your men to have a basic understanding of mental illness consumers and de-escalation techniques, there is ample room for improvement. As such, I will be recommending SFPD and other city law enforcement undergo the MHIT training. Of course, I can shadow Simon or another detective a few more times if you insist but—"

"No," Stevens said. "You've done what I asked. If you think you have enough information to make your recommendation, I believe you. And as far as getting back to your home? Your life? I agree with Simon. We need to proceed cautiously here. However, between last night and today, the techs should have already processed your house. If you feel strongly about it, you can return home as soon as you're done here."

She nodded. "Great. Then I'd prefer to give my statement to Jase or Carrie as soon as possible."

"Of course," Stevens said. "Jase is waiting for you right now."

Stevens escorted her to another room. There, Jase greeted her in a more subdued and professional manner than normal. It set the stage. Made Nina face the fact that her friendly interactions with Simon and his team were indeed coming to an end. Methodically, Jase told her about Cann and Hastings. He showed her sanitized photos and urged her to try to remember if she'd had contact with either of them, or if she'd ever heard Davenport talk about them.

She shook her head. "No. I don't recognize them. I've never met them. You can always double-check what I'm saying by checking patient records at the hospital, see if they were ever admitted there, but other than that, I don't know what else to tell you. I'm sorry."

Jase nodded and made some notes. "That's a good idea. Looks like both men have lived in the city for the past few years. I'll check with the hospital records clerk. They won't give me any confidential information, of course, but whether a particular person has ever been a patient there should be something they can—"

Both of them jumped as the door to the interview room suddenly banged open.

From the open doorway, Simon glared at them. "What the hell is going on here?" he growled.

Jase looked at him calmly. "Take it easy, Simon. I was just asking Nina a few questions, trying to see if she could tell us anything about Mr. Cann or Mr. Hastings, or how she or Davenport might be connected to them."

"And who the hell told you to do that? The Cann and Hastings cases are mine. And DeMarco's. You have no business taking over my interviews."

"Stevens made it my business. He wanted to make sure she was interviewed by someone objective. Just to cover our asses from accusations of preferential treatment. You two have been working together. Hell, she helped you find that little girl. It's in the press. If you want charges against Davenport to be rock-solid, we need to think two steps ahead of his attorneys."

"Fine. If Stevens didn't want me interviewing her, why not DeMarco?"

"DeMarco went home. He has some kind of bug. But you're overreacting, Simon. I help you with cases all the time. Some reason you don't want me helping on this one?"

"I don't like the way you and Stevens went behind my back. You waited until I was busy with Davenport to pull her in here."

"Simon," Nina interjected. "It's okay. Commander Stevens explained and—"

"Are you done here?" he interrupted, clearly addressing Jase.

"Yeah. We just finished up."

Simon nodded. Looked at Nina. "Let's go."

AS HE DROVE NINA BACK to his house, Simon knew he was overreacting.

He trusted Stevens and Jase. He knew they trusted him.

Having Jase interview Nina about what she might know about Cann and Hastings *had* made sense. If he'd still been captain and one of his men had been in his position, he'd have maneuvered things the same way.

He knew all that. So why was he feeling so off balance and pissed? As if his own team had posed a danger to Nina when she'd already had enough to deal with as it was?

"Do you want to talk about it?" Nina asked.

He glanced at her as she sat beside him. "About what?"

"Your doubts that Davenport committed these murders."

His eyes widened in surprise. "What are you talking about?"

"I watched you questioning Davenport for the last five minutes of your interview. He denied killing those men and I could tell part of you believed him."

"Part of me found him persuasive," he corrected. "A persuasive liar. There's a difference."

"But there's part of you that believes he might be telling the truth, isn't there? Or part of you that's willing to consider it?"

He forced back his automatic denial. Forced himself to be the straight shooter he'd consistently told her he was. "Yeah," he said finally. "There is. At least until I have more, something to connect him to the two men that were murdered, some part of me has to consider that his role in all of this is limited. The theory that I posed, that he's trying to kill the mental illness that killed his daughter, is a legitimate one, but it's just that, a theory. And Davenport…well, now that I've met him…now that I've actually talked with him…"

"He doesn't seem smart enough to have pulled off these murders?" Nina nodded. "I'm afraid I have to agree."

"Everything points to him having done it. But a chain of evidence is almost never this clean. It almost seems like he's being set up. Again, I'm not saying I believe that. Eighty percent of me thinks he's good for the Cann and Hastings murders."

"But twenty percent of you doesn't. And you're not willing to risk that the real murderer is still out there.

That's why you're taking me back to your house, right? Why you don't want me to go back to my place yet?"

"Do you want to go back to your place?"

"I should. I need to get a more secure security system installed. I mean, I know DeMarco put in a good one, but Davenport managed to get around it. I really want something better. Something befitting Fort Knox would be good."

He smiled slightly. "We'll arrange for that. I can call Lana's father, Gil Archer. He runs one of the top security firms in the city, remember? As for you going back home? I'm not sure if the evidence techs have fully processed the house yet. Besides, I didn't ask if you *should* go back to your place. I asked whether you *want* to go back there."

She paused, then said, "No. I don't want to go back there. Not yet."

He looked at her. "Good." After a few seconds had passed, he reached out and placed a hand on her leg. The gesture was both comforting and arousing. "Then you'll stay at my house again." He squeezed her leg, and fire settled low in her core. Good God, did her body respond to Simon Granger's touch.

As if sensing her reaction, Simon grinned and murmured, "I'll cook you dinner. Put you in bed. Let you get some sleep."

Nina recalled how Davenport had looked in that interrogation room. She still felt sad, but she refused to wallow in it. Simon was right. They couldn't be certain that Davenport had killed Cann and Hastings, but it was the only possible explanation so far.

In the end, however, it was up to Simon, not Nina, to put all the pieces of the puzzle together. Stevens had

been right about Nina's inability to be completely objective when it came to evaluating Davenport the way
a doctor should. She was his victim, and she'd have to
leave the assessments and his treatment to someone
else. In the meantime, she refused to deprive herself
of whatever happiness she could find, no matter how
temporary it might be.

She turned until she faced Simon. "I'll go home with
you. But only if you promise you *won't* let me sleep."

CHAPTER TWENTY-FIVE

THE AIR RUSHED OUT OF Nina's lungs when her back hit
Simon's bed. Once she'd agreed to stay at his house
again, Simon hadn't taken things slow. He'd driven
her back to his place, unbuttoning his shirt as soon as
they crossed the doorway and unzipping his pants with
one hand as he led her into the bedroom with the other.
Once there, he'd stripped her, quickly and efficiently,
and then he'd pushed her onto the bed.

At first, she'd been surprised by his aggression. By
the fact that he wasn't treating her with kid gloves.
But then she realized why and she was grateful. If
he'd moved too slow or too gently, it would have made
her think about why he was doing so. As it was, she
could barely focus on anything past her own passion
and urgency.

"Condoms?" she asked, stroking her own belly and
winding her legs together in a sinuous pattern as Simon
ripped off his shoes, pants and then his shirt.

He stood before her, straight and proud, his erection
jutting out. "In the nightstand next to you," he said,
"but we won't need them for a while."

His stated intent to stretch out the foreplay made
her breath catch.

She wanted him, wanted his body on top of hers,
wanted to feel his heat inside her. And yet he just stood

there, at the edge of the bed, staring down at her. The warm, soft smile toying at his lips set her on fire, and she felt a strong urge to meet his aggression with her own. This wasn't going to be another night of her lying on her back while Simon took the lead to distract her. Of course she wanted distraction again, but he could distract her simply by being in the same room with her. Of course, it distracted her more when she was in his arms. But the biggest distraction of all? That would come when she was completely immersed and solidly focused on driving *him* wild with passion.

Starting right now.

She pulled herself onto her knees, which made his brows lift in surprise. Kneeling in front of him, she settled her hands on his shoulders and kissed him. As the kiss grew heated, however, and she sensed his intention to take over, she pulled away.

She sprinkled kisses along his firm jaw, down his throat and over his muscular chest. She savored the feel of her lips against his hot skin, but kept her hands moving. Stroking. Cupping.

He hissed as she cradled his erection in her palm. Groaned as she continued to kiss him, progressing lower and lower down his body until…

"Jesus," he hissed and tangled his hands in her hair. The slight sting as he lightly pulled her hair made her moan and she opened her mouth even wider to take in more of him. He tasted like nirvana, sweet and salty combined, and she sucked him strongly, like a particularly juicy piece of candy. When he groaned again, she glanced up and saw that he'd pulled back slightly and was now looking down, eyes hooded but open, watching her suck him off. Deliberately, she slowly pulled back, until he'd almost slipped out of her mouth, and then she twirled her tongue around the tip of his cock.

"That's such an amazing sight," he said. "Fucking beautiful."

She smiled and once again drew him deeper into her mouth. And once again, he rewarded her with a slight pull to her hair. This time, the sting sent a jolt of pleasure between her legs so sharp that she instinctively lowered one of her hands to rub at her clit. She was wet, practically dripping for him, and she worked her fingers against herself even as she continued to work him with her mouth.

"Now that's even more beautiful," he gritted out. "You touching yourself while you pleasure me. You're beautiful, Nina. I want you. Give me your mouth on mine. Now."

When she didn't comply right away, he lightly gripped her jaw and drew her mouth away from him. Then he hoisted her up and took her mouth in a deep kiss. Instinctively, she placed both hands on his shoulders again, but before she could miss the pleasure of sensation between her legs, he lowered his hand and gave it back to her. Only his touch felt so much better than her own. His fingers were bigger. Longer. Harder. And of course they made her think of another part of his body that would soon be inside her. How much bigger, longer and harder it would be, and how it would stretch her to her limits and still leave her craving more.

"Shift your legs farther apart," he commanded against her mouth. "Let me get to all these pretty pink bits and sweet, sweet heat. I want to touch every inch. And then I want to taste it, Nina."

She did as he commanded, gasping when he plunged

a finger inside her. *So good,* she thought. *This feels so good.* But he'd taken over, she realized. He was driving her crazy with pleasure, when that had been her goal for him. When she pulled back to tell him so, her words caught in her chest.

He certainly *looked* crazy with lust. His eyes were hooded, his cheeks flushed, his mouth hard and desperate. All good, but not quite good enough.

"My breasts," she gasped. "Please. Suck me. Taste me, just like you said."

Swiftly, he lowered his head, catching her right nipple in his mouth and sucking so strongly she automatically jerked and wailed, "Yes. God yes!"

He took his time there, working her with his hand, working her with his mouth and teeth, even as his hips pumped the air beside her, his cock obviously wanting some attention of its own.

She lowered her hand and gripped him. Stroked him with firm, pulling motions.

He switched to her other nipple, giving it lavish attention, as well.

And suddenly it was too much. She grabbed his ass and said, "Now. I want you inside me. Please."

"Not yet," he said.

She tried pulling him forward, but he resisted until she wanted to cry. He'd promised her lots of foreplay, but she didn't want it. She wanted him inside her, big and thick, blocking out everything else but how good they made each other feel. She was too empty. Too achy to take much more. Or rather, too achy to take anything less than all of him.

"Please, Simon. Now."

He released her breast and looked at her, and her

desperation seemed to spark his own. With a savage curse, he lowered her to the bed again, then pinned her wrists above her head.

"What are you—?" she began, startled by the erotic restraint.

"I'm going to give it to you, but we're going to go slow. You're not going to rush me. I'm going to draw this out all night. Me pumping into you again and again. You're going to beg me to give you your climax, but this time, I'm not going to give in. Not until you want it so bad, you can't think of anything else."

"I already can't think of anything else," she insisted, instinctively fighting against his hold, but stopping as his gaze became intent and, with his other hand, he began to guide himself into her body.

When he penetrated her with the tip of his cock, her head fell back with a gasp. Such a small part of him, but it brought her such intense pleasure. How was that possible?

"You want more?" he asked.

She ground her head against the bed, closed her eyes and moaned.

"Do you?" he insisted.

"Yes!"

"Then look at me. Now," he ordered, his voice going slightly hard.

Her gaze shot to his and he pushed himself inside her several more inches.

"Don't take your pretty eyes off me, Nina. I want you to look at my face when I take you. I want you to see how much pleasure you give me."

She stared at him as he'd commanded, and by the looks of things, she gave him a lot of pleasure. He looked like he was dying of it as he pushed home. He gritted his teeth. Sweat popped out on his forehead. The hands that bracketed her wrists to the bed trembled.

And inside her, deep inside her, he pulsed. Thick and hard and wonderful.

But he didn't move. He pressed in deep. Deeper.

Frantically, she wiggled her hips, and his gaze dropped to hers as he frowned. "Stay still."

She arched up even higher, working herself on him. "No! I want this. Move, damn you. I— No!" she cried as she felt him slide out of her. "What are you doing?" She fought against his hold once more, gasping when he flipped her onto her stomach, put an arm under her and lifted her until her chest was on the bed and her hips were raised to accept him.

She glanced at him over her shoulder, aroused beyond bearing, knowing that this position made her wholly vulnerable to him, wholly at his control, and that that's exactly what he wanted. To test him, she tried to lift her torso, but he pressed a hand to her back, keeping her in place.

"No," he growled. "I told you, this time you're not going to rush me." He slicked his erection against her from behind. "You want this? You want to come? Then you're going to do exactly what I say, do you understand? You're going to wait."

She shivered. He was big. Strong. Commanding. The first time they'd made love, he'd shown her so much pleasure she thought she'd die from it. But he hadn't been this aggressive. This dominating.

Even so, she had a feeling that this was his natural state as a lover. And that only made her want him more.

"Are you going to do as I say?"

"Yes," she whispered.

"Good," he said, rewarding her by pressing a kiss to her back and smoothing her hips with his palms. Then he gripped her hip with one hand and, as he had before, used his other hand to guide himself inside her.

This time, he didn't work himself into her by degrees. This time, he shoved himself in to the hilt with such force that she saw stars. And then, instead of stopping and pressing deep as he had before, he gripped her hips with both hands and started thrusting, slow and sure, but hard and powerful, starting a rhythm that had her fingers clenching in the sheets and her inner muscles gripping in a desperate attempt to keep him inside her.

But it was no use. She was at his mercy. He shuttled in and out of her for what could have been minutes, hours or days, steadily pounding her closer and closer to climax until—yes, finally!—she was almost there and then...

And then he slowed. Then stilled completely.

She wanted to scream with frustration. She wanted to flip over and slap him for denying her her pleasure. But remembering what he'd said, that if she wanted to come she'd have to wait, she forced herself to remain still.

Behind her, he waited a few seconds, obviously waiting to see what she'd do, and when she only drew in deep breaths, biting her lip to stifle her desperate moans, he said, "Good girl," and started in again.

Twice more he repeated that particular brand of torture, going at her like a jackhammer and building her to an intense orgasm only to stop and prevent her from

going over. Twice more, when he stopped, she somehow managed not to press his hand, but she couldn't
stop the words that fell from her lips.

"Please, Simon. Please. I want to come. Please make
me come."

She was babbling, almost crying with the need for
release, sure she wouldn't be able to take it if he started
and stopped again.

"Shh. I know you want it. I know you *need* it. And
this time I'm going to give it to you. Even harder than
before. But first…I said I wanted to taste you, remember?"

He slid back and pulled her legs apart, but when she
instinctively moved to turn on her back, he held her
and said, "No. Like this."

"What?" she said automatically, suddenly feeling
shy. "I don't want—"

But then his breath was on her, followed by the slick,
firm caress of his tongue. It startled her into silence.
And then drew a wail of pleasure from her as it probed
inside her. Just as he had before, he penetrated her with
slow, strong rhythmic thrusts, but this time he used another part of himself. When he wasn't penetrating her,
he was licking at her while his fingers penetrated her.
And he didn't let up until she was a shaking, sobbing
mess, her body trembling with her need for release.

Weakly, she lay there and sensed him reach into
the nightstand for a condom. She heard rustling as he
put it on. Then, once again, he gripped her hips and
positioned himself at the entrance of her body. "You
ready?" he growled.

"Yes," she breathed. "I'm ready."

"Then come, Nina. Come hard. And when you do, think of me. Only me. Me over you. Me inside you. Me," he commanded, punching his hips forward. Just like before, he rode her hard. This time, however, he reached around and put his hand between her legs, manipulating her clitoris even as he filled her.

It took less than a minute for her world to shatter. She screamed when her orgasm hit her, her hips bucking uncontrollably and her whole body shaking with spasms that seemed to go on and on. At some point, she was aware of his chest pressed against her back and his own bark of pleasure as he found his release, as well.

When it was over, he was shaking, too. So hard that she couldn't tell where her tremors ended and his began. With a groan, he moved to the side, slipped out of her and pulled her into the cradle of his arms.

NINA'S BREATHING SLOWED from harsh gasps to a more mellow rhythm. Simon kept his arms wrapped around her, enjoying the weight of her body as it lay against his, unwilling to let go. He breathed in deep, inhaling her heady scent—lilac, peppermint and sex. *Their* sex. And what incredible sex it had been. Wonderful, terrific, beautiful. Hell—to someone more sentimental, it might be described as butterflies-and-rainbows-and-glitter kind of sex. To another, it would more aptly be described as raunchy as hell. He'd been more aggressive with her than he'd ever been before. Because he'd wanted to control her. Mark her. Give her the best sex of her life, and take the kind of sex from her he knew she was capable of giving him.

The kind of sex a woman gave when she completely let go.

The kind of sex a man gave when he completely fell in love.

His heart revved up. What the hell was that word doing in his mind?

Nina shifted, as if to move away from him—as if she sensed he was upset—but he instinctively tightened his arms around her.

Love. What a loaded word. But there it was, bouncing around inside his head as if it belonged there.

He couldn't love her. He hadn't known her long enough to fall in love with her. Besides, even assuming he could love her? He'd fuck it up. Make mistakes. Just like he had with Lana.

His thoughts hit like a kick to the gut. He'd been fooling himself, thinking he didn't blame himself for Lana's death. Obviously some part of him *did* blame himself, and in the abstract, it was perfectly understandable why he would.

He'd talked to her about his concerns, warned her that she was putting herself in danger, but in the end, those words hadn't made a damn bit of difference. He should have done something. Hell, he should have kidnapped her and tied her down if that's what it had taken to keep her safe, if that was the only thing that—

Next to him, Nina shifted. In her sleep, she smiled, as if being in his arms was all she needed to be blissfully happy.

He closed his eyes and buried his face in Nina's hair. He reminded himself that Lana had been a grown woman. She would have hated him if he'd tried to control her. Just like Nina would.

Shit, Simon thought, as he finally realized just how much Nina had come to mean to him.

Even what he'd felt for Lana was different than this. *This?*

This was more powerful. More real.

And as such, it was all the more dangerous.

CHAPTER TWENTY-SIX

THE NEXT DAY, SIMON brought Nina back to work with him only to escort her, along with several files she'd picked up from her office at the hospital, to an empty room. There, she planned on preparing a formal proposal for the MHIT program, which she would eventually present to Commander Stevens and the other higher-ups. "It makes sense for me to construct the proposal," she said, "even though I won't actually be conducting any of the training or even heading up the program."

"What do you mean?" he responded with a frown. He leaned against a wall in the small office, arms crossed.

"My boss, Karen? This is really her project." Nina separated file folders, making several neat stacks. "She asked for my help to get things started, but once the proposal is approved, there will no longer be any reason for me to be involved."

"But don't you *want* to be involved?" he asked, unsettled by the feeling of distress that was suddenly rising inside him.

He'd assumed once the MHIT training began, Nina would be a critical part of it, and he'd see her, if not often, at least occasionally. Logically, a relationship between them wouldn't work, but that knowledge had been tempered somewhat by his belief she'd still be close by. Now? To realize that she never planned on coming back? It made him want to howl with rage, take her in his arms and refuse to let her go.

Instead, he simply waited for her to respond to his question.

Nina looked away and shrugged. "So long as the program is implemented, that's all that matters to me. I miss my geriatric patients. It's time I get back to them."

"You work solely with older patients?" he asked. "Like the one that gave you that skin flick? Do you ever work with younger people?"

"Not really. Not anymore. I've carved out a specialty at the hospital and it's been enough for me. Now, if you'll excuse me, I'm really looking forward to getting started on these papers. And I'm sure you have plenty to take care of yourself," she said with a bright, patently false smile.

He had a shitload of work to do, in fact. As such, he murmured a polite farewell and left. However, he did so begrudgingly, on the inside if not the outside.

He didn't like her shooing him out of the room simply because he'd been asking her personal questions, even if they'd been personal questions about her job at the hospital. It made him realize how very little of herself she'd actually revealed to him over the past week. She'd revealed some things, sure, but not a whole lot, and only when she was pushed.

To prove his point, Simon summarized what he did know about Nina and how he'd found out about it.

She'd worked with an older woman with a fondness for porn, but she'd only told him that after her purse had spilled and given him a glimpse of that porn DVD.

She'd told him about Davenport's cards and letter only after he'd confronted her about being scared.

She'd informed him that she'd inherited her house from her grandmother, but only because he'd commented that it wasn't what he'd thought a psychiatrist would own.

She hadn't told him about her sister—he'd found that out on his own. And although he knew her physically—how her body responded to his, how soft her skin was, how tight she fit around him, how heavenly her arms and scent were when they wrapped around him—he'd discovered all those things on his own, too, by touching her, tasting her, exploring her. Sure, she'd let him, of course, and she'd explored his body, too, to amazing result. But even in his arms, she'd kept herself apart from him.

Funny. Until now, he'd felt like he knew everything there was to know about her. But, man, he'd been wrong.

He didn't know the most basic things about her as a woman—her favorite color, what she liked to eat, what kind of music or movies she liked... They'd jumped right past the getting to know you stage and straight into bed, and while that was great in many ways, it also made him feel a deep sense of loss at the thought that he wouldn't be given the time to explore all of Nina's small intricacies in great detail.

He couldn't help wondering if her decision to work with geriatric patients was a result of what had happened to her sister. And to Beth. Had she decided not to work with teenagers or young people anymore because doing so brought back bad memories? It made sense.

It also made him wonder if she was truly fulfilled

with her work or if playing it safe made her feel less passionate about what she did for a living.

In the end, he could wonder all he wanted. She obviously wasn't going to volunteer the information and, really, he had no right to push her for it. Not if he wasn't planning on sticking around.

With a sigh, Simon started work by checking up on Davenport's recent credit card charges. Over the course of several days, he'd left a trail of credit card transactions for gas and food across the country. As such, the records supported his claim that he'd only recently arrived in California. "He must have hired someone to do the other things," Simon murmured to himself. "It's the only explanation." And that seemed especially true after he got a preliminary report from forensics.

The muddy footprints found in Nina's home weren't a match for Davenport, who had smaller feet and had been wearing shoes with a different tread.

Again, that didn't prove Davenport was innocent of any of the crimes Simon suspected he'd committed. After all, Simon had caught him fleeing from Nina's vandalized home and he didn't need Davenport's footprints to verify that. To the contrary, a prosecutor could easily argue the muddy footprints belonged to Davenport's accomplice, who'd left before Simon had gotten there. The presence of an accomplice would explain how someone could have left Nina a threatening letter or killed her cat even before Davenport had arrived in California.

But Simon needed additional proof of an accomplice's existence before Davenport could be convicted. He doubted Davenport would be any help on that matter. No matter how hard Simon had pushed him, Davenport hadn't been swayed from his fervent denials of working with an accomplice. According to him, he'd been alone when he'd entered Nina's home, and the house had already been unlocked. He also claimed the house had already been open and trashed by someone else. And when Simon had told him about the bear left in Nina's room, Davenport had looked genuinely shocked. Horrified. Even scared.

As Simon had already told Nina, part of him had believed Davenport's denials. Now, the credit card records and the shoe prints seemed to support them, at least in part. Simon had to consider two possibilities: Davenport was either the best actor Simon had ever met, or he was telling the truth about working alone and being lured to California by someone pretending to be a reporter. If he was telling the truth, then a murderer was still on the loose. And that murderer was someone who had targeted Nina.

At that point, however, the question would be why? And what significance the initials *BD* would have for anyone other than Davenport. Was it possible someone else—someone other than her father—might want revenge against Nina because of what had happened to Beth Davenport?

She'd had a boyfriend, Nina said. One who had given her that bear with the ribbon in the first place. He rose, intending to go to Nina and get the name of Beth's boyfriend, but just as he did so, DeMarco walked up to his desk.

"Simon," his friend said, his voice and countenance grim.

Simon narrowed his eyes and assessed his friend. The other man looked beyond tired and beyond stressed.

He looked run-down. Agitated. At the end of his rope. How the hell had that happened so quickly?

"I need to talk to you about something, Simon. Can we get that drink now?"

"Sure. But I was just going to run something by Nina. Something about who else, besides Davenport, might be responsible for carving the initials *BD* into our victims. Give me a second to do that and I'll be—"

DeMarco shook his head. "I need to talk to you now, Simon. And you'll want to hear what I have to say. Because I might know the answer to the very question you're asking."

SIMON AND DEMARCO WENT to the SIG break room and talked over coffee. Simon listened as DeMarco explained about a horrible incident he'd gone through in New Orleans six years ago, when he'd been forced to shoot a street kid named Billy Dahl.

"Man, I'm sorry. That had to be tough."

"Yes, it was."

"Given the kid's initials, I can see why you'd want to tell me about this, but there's really no reason to think what happened six years ago is motivating these crimes. Nina's the key, and we'll confirm this, but I doubt she knew Billy Dahl."

"You're assuming the murders are connected to Nina because of the initials on her cat, the cards, the letters… But what if the murders aren't connected to her at all? You have to consider them in isolation. And if you do that, you have to consider the possibility that they might be connected to Billy Dahl. Especially because of what Rita Taylor told you about someone wanting to falsely blame the murders on the police."

"Okay, let's assume you're right. Let's look at the murders independently. You think someone in Billy Dahl's family is here in San Francisco, sending you a message? But why? It's been six years. Why come after you now?"

"Because even though I shot Billy six years ago, he didn't actually die from that injury until last year."

"What the hell are you talking about?"

"Do you remember last year when I had a family emergency? Right when Jase and Carrie were in the middle of The Embalmer case?"

"Yeah. I asked you about it, but—"

"But I blew you off. I blew everyone off who asked me about it. Well, it wasn't really a family emergency. At least, not *my* family emergency. I went down to New Orleans because Billy Dahl's family was pulling him off life support. He'd been in a coma since the night I shot him and they'd hoped he'd come back to them. But he didn't and they'd decided to finally let him go."

"And they called you and told you that?"

"His sister called and told me. For some reason, she thought I deserved to know. That I'd want to know. And she was right. I—I needed to see him before they pulled the plug."

"And the rest of his family let you?"

"Yeah. They did. But not out of the kindness of their hearts. Because they wanted me to see exactly what Billy had become. Because they blamed me for what had happened to him. At least, his mother did."

"And you think his mother is the one that killed Cann and Hastings."

"No, damn it. But Dahl had brothers. Brothers with

criminal records. I don't know where they live now, but it's possible…"

"Yeah, it's possible. Anything's possible. Too many things are possible. We have so many possibilities at work here that this investigation has turned into a circus. But we have to be practical. Your theory about Billy Dahl might be a possibility, but the best possibility is still the connection to Beth Davenport. Her father. And, like I said, given the footprints found in Nina house, maybe even her boyfriend."

"So that's what you're going to check into next?"

"Yeah."

DeMarco sighed. "Okay. But you're going to have to pursue that lead without my help."

"What do you mean?"

"I've been having troubles. I have been for a while now. I thought I was handling it but things have been getting worse. I'm starting to hear things. Dream things. My memory is shot. I'm afraid…"

After a prolonged moment of silence, Simon urged, "What?"

"I'm afraid I'm losing my mind. Hell, I've even considered the possibility that *I* might somehow be responsible for the murders."

Simon couldn't help it. He snorted. "What? Like blacking out and committing murder in your spare time? Right."

"Don't dismiss it so easily, Simon. Didn't you say there were a host of possibilities in this case? Okay, so I don't think it's really true. I don't have huge memory blanks or periods of time I can't account for. But the fact that I'd even consider it scares me. I need to take some time off. Get my head together. I'm sorry to bail on you just when this case is getting more complicated, but I think it's best."

It was best that DeMarco take an extended leave from work? The situation was definitely serious, then. Simon felt nothing but concern for his friend; that and a fair amount of guilt that he hadn't realized his friend was suffering so much. He sought to reassure him now. "I understand, DeMarco. Don't worry about the case. Do what you need to do to take care of yourself and know that I'm here for you. I don't buy for one second that you're involved in these murders. And as for Billy Dahl? You did exactly what you needed to do. I'd have done the same thing. So would have Jase. And Carrie. And Mac. And any other good cop. Unless you'd blame one of us for what happened, don't blame yourself."

"I'll work on that, Simon. Until I get back, take care of yourself. And take care of your woman."

"My woman?" Of course, Simon knew immediately he was talking about Nina, and having her characterized as his felt right. *Too* right. "Nina's not my woman. She's just—she's just—"

DeMarco shot him a chiding look. "Please. I know I just told you I'm on the edge, but I haven't completely gone over the bend, Simon. She's your woman and you're damn lucky to have her, for however long it lasts. Just like she's damn lucky to have you. She's not Lana. No, there are never any guarantees in life, but you've got your second chance at happiness with her. Don't blow it because you're scared."

AFTER TALKING TO DeMARCO, Simon continued going over the evidence in the homeless murders, trying to find the chain that would link Davenport, or even the boyfriend, Leo, to them. Just like before, he came up empty. Turned out, Leo was studying overseas in Italy. Simon called and spoke to the guy himself.

After that, he followed up on what DeMarco had told him about Billy Dahl. Not because he actually believed Billy Dahl's death was connected to the homeless murders, but because no matter what he might believe, he didn't leave anything to chance. He got hold of the reports on the shooting, and did some checking on Dahl's immediate family, as well. Three of his six brothers had long criminal records, and two were in prison, one in California's San Quentin Prison. But there was absolutely nothing to suggest they'd gone on a killing spree the past week.

In other words? Dead ends all around.

But what was worse than that?

When he wasn't agonizing about how little progress he was making on the case, he was agonizing about his feelings for Nina and what he was going to do about them.

Nina had gotten bored working in the small office by herself and had decided to work at one of the empty desks across the room from Simon. At several points, he'd watched her when she hadn't known he'd been doing so, and a secretive smile had played on her lips, as if she was recalling the passion they'd shared the night before. It had made his body ache to touch her. Kiss her. Make love to her over and over again. Several times, he'd wanted to go to her, but he'd held back, wanting to prove that he could focus on the job and not her.

Now, Simon gave in to the twitchy feeling in his stomach, left his desk, headed over to where Nina sat and hitched a hip on the desk. He checked around, confirmed that they were the only two in the room and leaned in close. She looked up from the papers she was scribbling notes on and focused her gaze on him.

"Don't tell me this is one of those 'about last night' moments, is it?" she asked, an edge to her voice.

He let out a laugh and fought back the desire to cover her mouth with his, the way he had just hours before.

"Technically, it was this morning, but no, that's not why I'm here. I—I was hoping I could talk to you about something. But it would have to be off the record. Just between the two of us."

She watched him carefully. Considered what he was asking. Then nodded. "What is it?"

He struggled with his conscience. Normally, he'd never share what DeMarco had told him with another person, but Nina wasn't just anyone. She was a doctor. She'd know what he was going through. And maybe, just maybe, she'd know of a way Simon could help his friend.

Briefly, he explained what DeMarco had told him about the shooting in New Orleans. Then said, "I was hoping you might be able to give me some insight into what he's going through personally. He mentioned nightmares. That he was hearing things. That things started to go south after Billy Dahl was taken off life support."

Nina nodded. "It sounds like delayed PTSD. He's probably been dealing with the aftermath for six years, but because there was still hope—however slim—that Billy Dahl might make it, he was able to keep it out of his head. After Billy died…"

Yeah, after Billy died, DeMarco had been buried by guilt.

Cops often had a case where everything went wrong. Where innocents died. Often the wrongs happened because lieutenants or captains or commanders made a bad call, something that had weighed on Simon's mind when he'd gotten his promotion. But other times, a simple traffic stop could result in a huge mess, leaving a cop scarred for life.

"I wish he'd shared more with me," Simon said. "Maybe then I could have made him realize he had nothing to feel guilty about."

"Have you shared your feelings about Lana? Not that I'm saying you blame yourself for her death," she said quickly, "but I imagine it would be hard for DeMarco to share something so personal with you if you didn't do the same."

"Shit." Simon sighed. "You're right. I never shared my feelings with him. I've kept them to myself, just like he was doing. But I've been handling Lana's death. He hasn't." When she said nothing, he frowned. "I'm sensing you're not saying anything for a reason."

"I think unless you're willing to talk about something, you can't really know whether you're handling it or not. Have you ever talked to someone, really talked to someone about Lana's death?"

"I talked to your friend Dr. Shepard."

"You did that because you were told to. And I'm sure you didn't truly open up to Kyle about how you felt. Am I right?"

"Probably."

Nina nodded.

"So…you think I should talk to someone?"

"It might help."

"Someone like you maybe?"

"I didn't say that. But at the very least, talk to someone who cares about you. A friend." She blushed. "I mean, I care about you. And I consider you a friend. But I know you probably wouldn't feel comfortable sharing such personal thoughts with me."

"Actually," he said, "I think I'd feel most comfortable sharing personal thoughts with you."

Her eyes widened in surprise. "Oh. Well, thank you. And of course, anytime you want to talk to me, about anything, I'm here for you. As a friend."

"I'll keep that in mind. Will you do the same thing?"

"What do you mean?"

"I mean, who do you have to confide in? About Beth? About your sister? About anything else that troubles you?"

He saw her practically shut down. "I've talked to you about Beth. And my sister isn't an issue. That was a long time ago."

"You haven't talked to me about how you *feel* about Beth. And come on, Nina. I don't care how long ago it was. Your sister's death still weighs on you."

"To some extent, yes. I loved her. Of course I miss her. But I'm handling it."

"I thought you just said that if you're not willing to talk about something, you can't know you're handling it."

"Touché." She sighed.

"Does that mean you'll tell me about it—tell me about Rachel—someday?"

She looked uncertain, was clearly struggling with

an answer, and ultimately all she said was, "I'm hungry. Do you want to grab lunch?"

No, he didn't want to grab lunch. He wanted to push her, to beg her to trust him. Instead, he said, "Sure."

They gathered their stuff and were almost to the lobby when they heard a loud commotion. "Damn it, I'm looking for Nina Whitaker. I was told she was working with one of your detectives. I want to talk to her. Now."

Automatically, Simon positioned his body in front of Nina's, every nerve in his body alive and aware. A man who was speaking to the receptionist glanced up and saw Nina.

"You!" the man shouted. "You're the one who wouldn't let the cop interrogate that bastard who stole Becca. You're the reason my child can't sleep at night. The reason Becca's asthma's so bad she's been back in the E.R. three times."

Great, Simon thought, so this was Mr. Hyatt, Rebecca Hyatt's father. Just what they needed.

"Back off," Simon said. "Now."

Hyatt's gaze flew to Simon. "Are you the detective that let her hold you back? You shouldn't have let her get in the way. You should have gone after the guy who had Becca Dee."

Becca Dee? *BD.* The implications of what the man said rocked him. Simon strode toward him. "Your daughter—Rebecca Hyatt—you call her Becca Dee?"

"Yes! And it's her fault—"

Suddenly, Commander Stevens was there, striding toward them, breathing heavy as if he'd run all the way down to the lobby, which was probably the case. Accompanying him was Gil Archer, who stepped slightly to the side. "Mr. Hyatt," Stevens said. "Please don't do this. What happened to Rebecca was not Dr. Whitaker's fault. In fact, Dr. Whitaker was instrumental in finding your daughter. Without her…"

As Stevens handled the agitated father, he did so with considerable civility, which alerted Simon instantly. The guy was someone important—politically important—otherwise Stevens would be coming down on the guy more. He'd still be civil, of course, but he wouldn't condone a man who walked into SIG headquarters and started screaming at the receptionist and a civilian.

Simon's speculation was confirmed when Archer said, "Kevin, this isn't the way to handle things. Your grandfather is a friend of mine. I told you we'd bring your concerns to Stevens. That I'd set up a meeting…"

Sensing Nina shift beside him again, Simon looked at her. Damn it, she'd gone pale again. He was getting far too used to seeing that look on her face—the one where she was trying to hold things together despite getting thrown one curveball after another.

Suddenly he remembered what she'd told him the first time she'd visited him at SIG. How Rebecca Hyatt's father had focused his anger at his daughter's predicament on her. Simon reached a hand down low, out of eyesight of Rebecca's father, and grabbed Nina's fingers. Her hand trembled, but she squeezed his hand back and laced her fingers with his. Brave woman, he thought.

"No," Kevin Hyatt shouted, his face florid and filled with rage, "that other cop, Officer Rieger, said he almost had a confession out of that nut job. But this stupid shrink here decided to go all politically correct on everybody and shut down the interrogation."

Shrink. The word sounded obscene coming from Hyatt's mouth.

How many times had Simon used that word to describe what Nina did for a living? Ten? Twenty?

Had it sounded as disrespectful when he'd said it as it did now coming from this man? And hadn't that been the whole point?

How much pain had his own thoughtlessness caused Nina over the past few days? Too much, he realized.

"I understand you are upset," Stevens said. "Even enraged, and I know every father wants to protect his daughter, but this isn't the way to do it." He glanced at Simon, silently indicating he should get Nina out of here. That wasn't going to happen. Not until he made sure Stevens understood the implications this man posed given his daughter's nickname.

"I tried the regular channels. Filed a complaint, got a lawyer, but he said I could do nothing. But screw that. I'm going to the press and telling them everything I know. That you—" he pointed directly at Nina "—you did this to my daughter. Because of you, Becca Dee was out in the cold, locked in a frickin' basement for hours. She had asthma. She could have died. Don't think for a minute I'll let you get away with this."

Stevens placed his large body in front of the man, stopping his forward progression. His eyes narrowed in understanding. "Your daughter's name is Becca Dee?" he asked quietly.

His gaze met Simon's, who nodded. Then they met Archer's.

Archer sucked in a breath. "You think—" he whispered, which told Simon that Stevens had talked with his friend about the initials…and probably Nina's connection to the whole thing.

Was Archer the one who had urged Stevens to explore what Nina knew about the murders? If so, Simon had the strong urge to tell the man whose daughter he'd once dated to mind his own business.

"I need you to calm down," Stevens said to Hyatt, cutting Archer off. "And I need you to come with me. I'd like to ask you some questions. About your daughter and your grievances against Dr. Whitaker. Can we do that?"

Hyatt stared at Stevens, glared at Nina over his shoulder, then nodded. "About damn time," he muttered.

To Archer, Stevens said, "I'll have to catch up with you another time."

Archer nodded, then glanced at Nina and Simon, his gaze landing on their linked hands. Although his eyes widened in surprise, Simon didn't let go.

CHAPTER TWENTY-SEVEN

As HE LED HER OUTSIDE, Nina clung to Simon's hand as if it was a lifeline.

Such hatred. Such anger. All that intensity scared her. And, for a split second, made her question herself. Could she have wormed the information out of Michael Callahan sooner? Should she have pushed him harder?

Simon turned to her and caught her gaze with his. "It wasn't your fault," he said.

Rationally, she knew that. She knew Becca Dee's father was projecting. He hadn't been able to protect his daughter and was turning his guilt onto someone else—her. His rage had probably been bottled up inside him ever since he'd heard his daughter had been kidnapped, just waiting for a moment to explode. Waiting—

"The nickname he used... Do you think he's the one?"

Simon hesitated. "Anything's possible, remember? But given your past with Davenport and the fact he broke into your house, I'm still more inclined to believe he's the one responsible."

"Even though your theory about wanting to eradicate mental illness could apply just as equally to Hyatt as it could to Davenport? Given that Rebecca—Becca Dee—was kidnapped by a mentally ill man?"

"Even then," Simon said.

"Why?"

"The first homeless man, remember? He was killed before I met you. Before his daughter was kidnapped."

"Oh. That's right."

"You okay?"

She squeezed his hand tighter. "With you here with me? Yes. I just wish we could figure out what was going on."

"I know. But I promise, Nina. I won't stop looking until I find out."

With Simon's promise, Nina's nerves settled once more. He'd do everything he could. For her. For the two men who had been murdered. Even for Six. Right now, that was enough comfort that she was able to relax somewhat and enjoy her lunch.

That enjoyment was short-lived, however.

They were just paying their bill when a broadcast on the television set playing in the corner of the sports bar caught Nina's attention. "Simon," she said. "Look. It's Davenport."

Simon cursed, but the two of them went over to the television set and watched as Davenport held court in front of a camera crew. "He's out on bail," Simon gritted out. "And the first thing he's going to do is hold a press conference? I can just bet what he intends to say."

Illuminated by klieg lights from the news crews, Davenport's tears shone on his cheeks. He insisted that a shrink, Nina, who was working with the DOJ and SFPD, had caused his daughter to commit suicide. He admitted to sending Nina a threatening letter, and even going to her house, but claimed that he'd just gone to talk to her. According to him, she'd been angry with him and retaliated by having him arrested for a crime he hadn't committed, and that she'd corralled her boyfriend, Simon, into the mix.

After that, Davenport said, he'd been taken into police custody and treated despicably. Bullied and beaten. By Simon. Because he was engaged in a romantic relationship with Nina.

Just as he had when Hyatt had railed at her, Simon now surreptitiously grasped Nina's hand, tucking their clasped hands behind his back so no one could see. Her fingers trembled and he squeezed, hoping she'd feel his reassurance through the pressure.

The lawyer who'd obviously orchestrated the event handed the man a handkerchief. "That's all my client has to say for now," the lawyer said into the microphones. "The SFPD has blatantly disregarded this man's rights and favored one of their own. We are bringing suit to the SFPD for unlawful detention."

The interview ended. With a sick feeling, Nina turned to Simon. "I'm so sorry," she said.

"For what? This isn't your fault."

"Maybe not, but because of me, Davenport is making up lies about you. Stirring up more trouble between you and the public. That can't be good." *Can't be good for his bid to be in management,* she thought.

But Simon didn't appear concerned about that. "He's not the first suspect to make unjust complaints about me and he won't be the last, Nina. I'm not worried about it, and I don't want you to worry about it, either. You have enough on your plate as it is."

"You think?" she said as she laughed. "Besides, my plate is on the sparse side compared to yours."

"Doesn't matter. No matter how heavy our loads

look right now, we'll get through this, Nina. I will solve this case. And you will get your life back."

LESS THAN AN HOUR LATER, Simon's phone rang. It was Stevens. The two of them appeared to be discussing Davenport's interviews, as well as Rebecca's father. When Simon hung up, Nina asked, "Hyatt?"

Simon shook his head. "He filled me in on what he and Hyatt talked about, and he agrees with me. He doesn't think Hyatt had anything to do with what's been happening."

"And that upsets you? Because I can tell you're upset."

Simon ran his hands through his hair in frustration. "No. What upsets me is a request he's made of you. I don't want you to have to deal with more than you've already been forced to."

"Has there—has there been another murder?" she asked, the dread in her voice apparent.

"What? No. God no. I'm sorry. I didn't mean for you to think that. No one's been hurt."

Relief flooded her. "Then what is it?"

"After Davenport's interviews, reporters have been calling the police chief. The mayor. And Stevens. They've set up a conference that starts in less than an hour."

"To reply to Davenport's claims?"

"In part. But also to take the bull by the horns, to use your turn of phrase. To discuss how the police are responding to public concerns about its ability to deal with the homeless and mentally ill. They're going to go forward with the MHIT training, Nina. And Stevens wants you to head it up."

"Well, that's wonderful. But what does he want me to do?"

"He wants you to make a public statement at the press conference."

CHAPTER TWENTY-EIGHT

DeMarco STARED AT THE elegantly dressed woman with long black hair and a thin waist raise herself on tip-toes on a rickety chair, trying to hang a plant on a hook. He'd met Anna Wong only recently, when he'd checked out various crisis clinics in the city to determine whether Cann and the second murder victim, now identified as Hastings, had both sought counseling at the same place. She'd been able to confirm that, indeed, both men had made appointments at her clinic, the Golden Gate Crisis Center.

At the time, she'd been professional and pulled together, not a hair out of place. Now, with her guard down, Anna Wong seemed infinitely more approachable. She finally got the plant hooked up, but had leaned too far forward. She wobbled as she tried to get her balance. Despite the serious nature of his visit, he couldn't help noticing how fantastic she looked standing before him and that she possessed what was the most beautiful ass he'd ever seen.

And she was about to fall right on it.

Sure enough, her foot slipped on the chair and she squealed in alarm.

DeMarco grabbed her just as the chair teetered and slid out from under her.

Wow. She felt good. Smelled good.

"Whoa. Thank you!" the woman said.

As he gently deposited her on her feet, she turned to look at who had saved her. Her brows lifted in surprise. "Detective DeMarco. How nice to see you again. Um, did you want to talk to me about something?"

He realized she was standing on her own two feet, but his hands were still around her waist and his face was inches from hers. "Oh, sorry," he said, lifting his hands off her body and holding them up in the air, palms facing her.

She took a step back. Her silk blouse was rumpled and one of the buttons had come undone, but he wasn't about to call attention to that detail. Not when the gape gave him a glimpse of soft, rounded flesh behind the silk. She brushed her hands down, smoothing nonexistent wrinkles in a tight-fitting skirt. Then she walked to her desk and sat down.

"So…what can I do for you? As I told you before, Mr. Cann and Mr. Hastings were both seen at this clinic, but I can't disclose specifics about who they saw or what they talked about."

Damn, but in addition to a smoking body, did she ever have fine eyes, too. Almond-shaped, hot-cocoa-chocolate-colored. Bottomless. And she was staring expectantly at him.

"Actually, I'm not here to talk about either of those men. I'm—uh—I'm actually not here in an official capacity."

"Oh. Well, please. Have a seat and tell me why you are here."

He cleared his throat. Suddenly felt like bolting from the room. But the steady way she stared at him, a slight smile of encouragement on her lips, caused his racing heart to slow and his nerves to settle.

"The reason I'm here is…" He rubbed a hand against the back of his neck. Looked around the room. Then finally met her gaze again. "Well, this is a crisis center. And I'm in crisis. I need help."

CHAPTER TWENTY-NINE

THE PRESS CONFERENCE at the SFPD began at 4:00 p.m. sharp and was in full swing when Simon and Nina arrived at 4:15 just as Stevens had requested. "Given Davenport's claims, I don't want to give the press a chance to go after Nina, but I do want her to speak briefly about the MHIT training."

"Commander," a reporter spoke now, directing the crowd's attention to Commander Stevens. Simon recognized the man as an investigative reporter on the evening news. He thrust a microphone in front of Stevens's face. "Lester Davenport has filed suit against the city. This is the third lawsuit brought against the SFPD in as many weeks. Since the DOJ has jurisdiction over all law enforcement in California, can you respond to the sudden spate of lawsuits?"

"Of course," he said. "We at the DOJ take our jobs seriously, as does the SFPD. Like you, we are always concerned about the well-being of any person accused of a crime. In America, people are innocent until proven guilty. At no point during the arrest, trial or incarceration should anyone be treated unfairly."

"What about the way SFPD has been treating the mentally ill?" the reporter pressed. "We're hearing more and more about how SFPD officers are mishandling calls when someone is suicidal or delusional.

How more police brutality shows up in incidents of arrests with a mentally ill person than an arrest of citizens without compromised mental health."

"Although I cannot comment on any ongoing lawsuits," Stevens stated, "I can say that we have an ongoing study being performed to evaluate the actions police make when undertaking an arrest. We've been working with a psychiatrist, an impartial observer, to determine if the SFPD needs specialized training in how to effectively communicate with the mentally ill."

"Is this the same psychiatrist that Davenport has alleged is having an affair with one of your officers?"

"Davenport has made several claims, all of which are false. Dr. Whitaker helped us save a child, and there's plenty of press coverage on that. I believe you wrote an article about it yourself, Artie. As to whether she's dating one of my officers, her personal life isn't at issue here. She's an independent contractor, not a city employee, and she's extremely good at her job. We're lucky to be working with her."

As soon as the direction of the conversation had turned toward Nina and Davenport's claims against her, Simon had stiffened up.

"I'm fine," she whispered. She met Stevens's gaze and nodded, telling him that she was ready to speak.

"Now, Dr. Whitaker is here and has agreed to briefly speak with the press. She is here only to talk about the new program she's advocating. Keep your questions limited to that or we'll be forced to end the press conference early."

Nina glanced at Simon, smiled reassuringly and stepped forward, directly in front of the microphone. As she looked into the small gathering of reporters, she thought, *Lord, I'd rather be anywhere else than here—heck, getting a Brazilian wax would be less tortuous than staring at this crowd of rabble-rousing reporters.* But Commander Stevens had set the stage, and she needed to take action.

"Here goes nothing," she murmured under her breath and leaned closer to the microphone. The first thing she did was explain how she'd been instrumental to the Mental Health Intervention Team becoming established with the Charleston P.D. She ran through the main objectives of the program and the successes they'd encountered since the program began. "Now," she continued, "as a psychiatrist working with the SF Memorial Hospital Mental Health Division, I independently approached Commander Stevens about my desire to start a similar program here. He was very open to the idea of the program, and suggested I shadow one of his detectives in order to gather detailed information about how officers were handling encounters with the mentally ill, which would enable me to make subsequent recommendations. My observations have led me to believe that the SFPD does indeed have the basic skills to both successfully recognize when individuals are symptomatic and to handle these calls with respect and finesse. However, basic skills can always be built upon. As such, I am recommending that the MHIT program be adopted and Commander Stevens, the police chief and the mayor, have given me the green light. Over the next year..." Nina detailed what would be coming next.

A couple of reporters asked legitimate questions about the MHIT program, but then one asked, "Is the detective that you shadowed the one that you are now romantically involved with?"

Stevens raised a hand. "And that's the end of Dr. Whitaker's interview." Commander Stevens placed a hand on her elbow and moved her away from the microphone, glaring at the impertinent reporter as he did so. "If you have any other questions, ladies and gentlemen, you can direct them to me."

Grateful for his intervention, Nina wound her way back to the edge of the crowd where Simon stood waiting for her. He immediately steered her outside and toward the gated parking lot, where he'd earlier left his car.

"You okay?" Simon asked grimly.

"Yes," she said. "Speaking to reporters isn't my favorite thing to do, but I've gotten used to it. I've had to explain the program to the press before. It was a good use of my time."

"Well, I'm sure Stevens is grateful. And I know you're taking the high road by saying you're used to dealing with reporters, but given how they've dug into your personal past before—well, you know that might happen again, don't you?"

"It's okay. No matter what happens, I don't have any regrets about what's happened between us, Simon. In fact, you're the one bright spot that's been keeping me going."

He looked at her and grinned. "I feel the same way, Doc. How about we head home and I brighten your day a little bit more?"

"That sounds heavenly," she said with a smile.

He stepped up to his car, bent to unlock the passenger-side door, then froze. "Hold on." Simon held out his arm and gently nudged her back.

"What's wrong?" She gasped as she noticed the glass glinting on the ground. Someone had broken the passenger window of his car.

"Great," he murmured. "Just one more thing to deal with."

"You're in a secure parking lot next to the police department. Why would someone—"

"Probably someone drunk or hopped up on drugs. Let's go back and I'll call it in." He stooped slightly and peeked into the car, as if checking to see whether anything inside had been disturbed. "I don't want to touch—" He'd been in the middle of rising when he froze. And stayed frozen.

"Simon?" Nina asked hesitantly. "Is something wrong?"

His rib cage enlarged and his shoulders widened, as if he was drawing in a deep, deep breath.

Uh-oh. This couldn't be good. "Stay back," he ordered Nina.

Instead, she took a step forward and placed her hands on the backside of his hips. "Is it another dead cat?" she asked in a whisper.

"I told you to stay back," he said harshly.

"You don't control me, Simon," she snapped back.

"That isn't what this is about," he said, turning and trying to nudge her away from the car.

"Then what is it about? Why won't you let me see what's in the car?"

He turned then, and slid his hands down her shoulders to touch the tips of her fingers. "I don't want you to see what's inside because I'm trying to protect you."

She shook her head wearily. "My cat's been killed and mutilated. There's someone murdering mentally ill men and it might be because of me. I think we're well beyond protecting me now."

Gently, Simon placed a kiss on her forehead. "Maybe you're right. And you'll need to know this anyway. I just wish—" He shook his head. "Doesn't matter. I can't change reality. But I'm sorry, Nina. And I'm here for you. Remember that."

He stepped away from the car to allow Nina to take a look.

She hunched down, the way he had, and took in the interior. Then let out a cry.

The doll. Rachel's doll. Hanging from the rearview window by a small slip of rope tied into a noose around her neck. Attached to the doll was a photograph of a dead, naked man with the initials *BD* carved into his skin and a note. Nina fought back the urge to gag but forced herself to look closer at the note.

It read, "Life's a bitch and then you die. Like my BD."

AFTER DISCOVERING THE doll planted in his car, Simon hustled Nina into SIG and explained the situation to Jase, who arranged for the evidence techs to process the scene. Meanwhile, Simon got Nina some coffee and took her to an empty office so they could talk.

"Tell me about the doll, Nina."

Nina wrapped her hands around the coffee mug in front of her. She'd been quiet since they'd found the doll. Quiet but calm. Steady. It wasn't the reaction he was expecting and he watched her now, wary, regretting that he was having to push this but knowing he had no other choice.

"The doll belonged to my sister, Rachel, before she died."

"You had it in your purse. I saw it the day we met and your bag spilled."

"I—I'd recently taken it out. I left it in my office. I was planning on donating it. Maybe giving it to the kids' ward."

Simon jammed his hands into his hair. "You're sure it was at your office and not your house? Because I assumed that's how Davenport…"

She shook her head. "No. It was in my office. I'm positive."

"So how the hell did Davenport or anyone else get it? The door past the receptionist is normally locked. I tried it myself."

"I don't know. I can't tell you that."

"All right. Let's work on something else—how someone could know about the doll's significance to you. You say it belonged to your sister, but she killed herself twenty years ago. Did you ever talk to Davenport about it?"

"Rachel died when I was sixteen years old. Suicide. She slit her wrists in the bath. But I never told Davenport that. Of course I didn't. Why would I?"

"There was some press on it, but very little. I had to go digging for it. I suppose he could have found out about it, if he was doing research on you, but the doll… how would he make any connection with that doll?"

"He might have seen the photo."

"What photo?"

"In our local paper. A reporter caught a shot of me

sitting outside our house with my mother while the
medics worked on Rachel. I was—I was cradling the
doll. Again, the picture wouldn't be easy to find, and
pinpointing the doll would be tough, but if someone
really cared enough to look and use it against me, it's
one explanation."

"Damn it, I saw that picture in the paper, but I must
have missed the doll. But even assuming that's how
Davenport saw the doll…why would he think it's something he could use to torture you? Why would he risk
breaking into your office to get it?"

When she remained silent, he urged, "Talk to me,
Nina. Tell me why you'd blame yourself for Rachel's
death."

Her mouth twisted with resentment. "Sure. Why
not? You know every other mistake I've made in my
life. Why not this, too?"

"That's not why I'm asking and you—"

"It doesn't matter. I don't know how he knew about
it or what it meant to me. But seeing it is both a comfort and a torture."

"Why?"

"The day Rachel died? She'd come home from high
school that afternoon and was horrid to me. She'd been
going out with a boy for a year, Mason Ford, and he
treated her like dirt. He'd break up with her one day
and then demand she come back the next. I—"

Nina's words broke off as she took a deep breath.
When she spoke again, her voice was steadier. Determined. "I'd found out he was cheating on her. With not
just one but four other girls. And in the middle of a
fight about who was supposed to set the table for dinner that night, I got angry. So angry I told her about

Mason. She was devastated and thought I was lying. She charged out of the house to go tell him how horrible I'd been. Instead, he laughed in her face and told her she was his go-to girl. The one he had sex with when no one else was available. She came back to me, sobbing and begging me to help her. I held her. I said I was sorry. And I tried to say the right thing to help her. But I obviously wasn't able to find the right words. She'd tried to commit suicide twice before. And this time, she succeeded. My dad was the one who found her." She looked up at Simon with haunted eyes. "He said he blamed me," she whispered. "He apologized later. Said he didn't mean it over and over again. But at that moment, he believed it. And I believed him. Part of me still does. After all, my words drove her to something horrible and yet I couldn't find the right words later on, the ones to stop her from hurting herself."

"So you became a psychiatrist to find the right words? To save others?"

"Right. Only I failed again, didn't I? Beth Davenport is proof of that."

CHAPTER THIRTY

NINA COULDN'T STOP HER body from shaking. Her hands shook. Her knees shook. Her belly spasmed. Even with the late-afternoon sun warming the interior of the unmarked car Simon had gotten hold of, she shook as if she'd never be warm again.

As he drove to his place, he didn't speak—didn't press her to reflect on what she'd said back at SIG headquarters.

About how she'd driven her sister to suicide, only to fail Beth almost twenty years later.

Even now, years later, the memories shredded her insides. She fought to keep her eyes open, to not blink, so she couldn't imagine Rachel lying in a bathtub of water and blood. So she wouldn't see the rag doll that had been Rachel's since childhood—the one she'd been clutching in her arms as she'd sat on her own bed, being berated by an angry sister—slumped on the wet floor beside the tub. And so she wouldn't see Beth hanging from a closet rod, a pink ribbon tied around her neck.

But it didn't matter. She saw all of those things, anyway.

"My dad was already big in politics when we were young," she said, surprised by the sound of her own voice. "He expected Rachel and I to both go into law, the way he had. I did great on my SATs. Had straight

As since grade school. Captain of the debate team, class president. I broke long-standing records on the swim team."

"And Rachel?" Simon asked, his low voice rumbling through her.

She cleared her throat and tried to speak past the tension that tightened her vocal cords. "Straight Cs in high school. Flunked her first year in college. Chubby and unathletic. Desperate for my father's attention, but he lavished praise on me for my achievements and gave her the cold shoulder. She could never measure up to me in his eyes. I think that's why she'd been so desperate for Mason's attention—she wanted to be seen by a man as desirable in some way."

"Makes sense," Simon said. He flashed on the turn signal and eased the car off the main street. She didn't pay attention to the residential area they drove through. She didn't care where they were headed. Nowhere felt safe.

"Somehow this all links back to me. To something I did. But what?" she asked, her throat so tight now the words barely came out. "Which of my mistakes has come back to haunt me? And who's trying to seek justice for them?"

He whipped the car into the parking garage of his apartment complex, the sudden turn throwing Nina against the passenger-side door. "Don't say that," Simon said angrily. "Don't blame your decisions for someone else's sick vendetta. The choice to kill, to mutilate, was his, not yours. You did nothing wrong."

She smiled gamely. "No. You're right. I'm just being silly. One shock too many, I guess. This isn't my fault. Logically, I know that."

But they'd already discussed how logic didn't always match up to what one was feeling. And right now, she felt she was being punished.

And that she deserved it.

NINA AWOKE DISORIENTED, but quickly realized she still lay on Simon's living room floor, his naked body sprawled next to her, his arm under her neck. Once again, he'd given her something wonderful—not just his body but a temporary respite from unpleasant memories and the fear of what was coming next.

She was becoming addicted to him, she realized, and it had to stop. He wasn't her magic pill to make her troubles go away. If they were in a committed relationship, it would be different. She'd be entitled to lean on him once in a while. But they weren't in a relationship. They weren't going to have a happy-ever-after here. And that meant she needed to start facing the realities of her life on her own.

Sighing, she shifted and looked out the bay window to see dusk had come. Across San Francisco, lights popped on, twinkling and glowing, wrapping the city in beauty. So lovely, like the grand lady she was. But the lights were a warm and glowing facade, hiding deep dark secrets under its blanket of brilliance.

Simon stirred next to her and her body responded with a sudden and unexpected rush of desire. He'd made love to her so sweetly. So tenderly. At the same time, just like always, the sex had been powerful. Primal. And so had her response. This time, however, something had been different, too. *She'd* been different. For a few moments there, as she'd been soaring on the pleasure he was giving her, she'd felt her whole heart open up to him. For a few moments, she'd felt loved.

Love.

She hated that word.

She'd loved her parents, but had never forgotten her father's horrible accusations. She'd loved her sister, but Rachel had left her behind, choosing death instead. She'd loved her college boyfriend, but he'd cheated on her with a girl from the swim team.

And she'd loved her cat. But a sick man had taken her cat. Her stomach clenched at the memory of Six, dead in the back of her car. And she tried not to think of the two men, strangers to her, who had met a similar fate.

"You awake?" Simon whispered into her hair.

When she nodded, he placed a kiss on the top of her head.

"Want to talk about what just happened?" he asked.

"No," she said in a small voice, thoughts of love still playing in her head.

Simon rolled over until he was on top of her, framing her shoulders with his elbows. With both hands he smoothed the wayward hairs off her face, taking his time to loosen knots and to tuck her hair behind her ears. Then he lowered his head and kissed an eyebrow. Then the other. He followed up with light kisses on each temple, down her nose and up her jawline. But not her lips.

Instead, he leaned his forehead against hers, touched the tip of his nose to hers and breathed.

She sucked in his breath as if she were sucking in life itself.

"Do you remember what you said as you came?"

he asked, his voice low, sending vibrations echoing through her body.

What had she said? She could recall frantically whipping her head back and forth, could recall the building orgasm, Simon pumping hard into her. She could remember her hands on his ass, pulling him in deeper as she raised her legs high to allow him full access. She remembered panting and the sounds of his groans. And she remembered him calling her name as he came. But she couldn't remember what she'd said in response.

"I didn't say anything," she whispered.

He pulled his head up then, searching her eyes with his. "Yes, you did."

Oh, God. The memory came over her then. At the moment of her climax, she'd felt bathed in warmth. Enveloped by a sense of comfort and belonging so strong that she'd…

Embarrassment swept through her.

Love. That's what she'd felt. And that's what she'd told him. That she loved him.

And she did.

But she wouldn't admit that to him. Couldn't admit that to him.

She pushed against his shoulders until he rolled away, then got to her feet and started pulling on her clothes. "It didn't mean anything," she said, forcing the words out of her mouth. "It's just old habit. I say the words when I come hard. Take it as a compliment, but not as the truth."

He looked at her fiercely.

"What?" she said. "You don't believe me? Well, you're wrong. I was carried away by the moment,

Simon. With everything happening, it's only natural that I've become attached to you. Dependent. That's going to come to an end soon."

"You're sure of that?"

"Yes. You're a good cop."   .

"What does that have to do with anything?"

"You're going to find the man doing this. When you do, our lives will finally get back to normal. You'll get your management position. I'll go back to working with my patients."

"Have you forgotten that you're going to be heading up the MHIT program?"

"I can supervise, but I don't have to be on-site."

"Right. Is the reason you want to get back to your patients so badly because that's really where your passion lies or is it so you don't have to be responsible for life and death situations that you aren't already prepared for?"

"It doesn't take a genius to know why I'd want that kind of safety net. And you, of all people, know all about that, so don't go using that high-and-mighty tone with me."

"I wasn't. I'm not," he protested. "I just think—"

His phone rang and after a few seconds, he cursed, looked away and answered, "Simon Granger." After a minute of listening to the person on the other line, he cursed. "Call the shelter and tell the director I'm on my way." He snapped his phone shut and cursed again.

"What is it?"

"A kid's been attacked in Golden Gate Park. He's alive. But barely. I want you to come with me."

That surprised her. "Are we going to the hospital?"

"Not yet. There's an officer already there and the

victim is being treated. We're heading to the Welcome Home homeless shelter. The director specifically asked me to come see her and she said it was an emergency. That it had something to do with this latest attack."

"But why do you need me to come with you?"

"Because despite you're belief that things are coming to an end between us, I care about you, Nina. I'm not leaving you alone. And even once these murders are solved? I'm not planning on leaving you even then. Whether we decide to call it love or something else, it doesn't matter. We'll settle things between us eventually. Now let's go."

CHAPTER THIRTY-ONE

As the Welcome Home homeless shelter came into view, Nina's eyes widened.

"What the hell?" Simon exploded.

Three black-and-whites were parked zigzag up and down the street. Uniformed police officers were attempting to push back the gathering crowd on the sidewalk while two more stood directly in front of the shelter talking heatedly with Elaina Scott and a gray-haired man wearing a blue polo shirt. Simon remembered seeing the man in the office the first time he'd visited the shelter.

The shelter itself looked reminiscent of bedlam. From open windows and the doorway, the inhabitants were shouting. Some even looked to be crying.

Simon threw his car into Park. Nina had her seat belt off and the door opened even before Simon turned off the ignition.

"Stay in the car!" Simon yelled at her.

She ignored his order, and instead hit the sidewalk. "I can help," she threw out over her shoulder.

"Damn it, Nina!" He caught her arm and pulled her to a stop before she'd taken more than five steps. "What the hell do you think you're doing? Don't you ever separate yourself from me like that again. Not when we're on a call." He shook her slightly. "Do you understand me?"

She immediately looked penitent for worrying him. "Whoa. Okay, Simon. I'm sorry. I just—"

"You just were thinking of others more than you were thinking of yourself. But that is not acceptable. You do it again, and I will haul your ass out of here immediately. Got it?"

"Got it," she said quietly.

He stared at her, saw that she was serious then let her go. "I see the director. Let's go."

As Simon walked toward Elaina Scott, the man in the blue polo shirt walked inside the shelter. Of course, he immediately wondered why. If he was avoiding Simon for some reason. He'd make sure to talk to the man. But first he had to get his head on straight.

Simon took a calming breath, cursing the panic he'd felt at seeing Nina run into the crowd. All he'd been able to think about was that she would be hurt. And it would be his fault. And how he'd be grieving the loss of another woman he cared about. The loss of another woman who loved him. And no matter what she'd said earlier about having said the words during sex, Simon wasn't buying it. It hadn't been the sex talking. It hadn't even been the stress over everything that had been happening talking.

She'd meant those words at the time she'd said them.

What was crazy was they hadn't scared him. He'd wanted to hear her say them again. And again.

Only now wasn't the time to be thinking about any of this. He had a job to do, damn it. Ruthlessly, he shoved thoughts of Nina and words of love and fear of losing her out of his mind.

"What the hell's going on here?" Simon asked the patrol officer standing to Elaina's right.

"One of the officers showed up to interview the director and the residents about a 245. The occupants started getting agitated. Shouting that a cop was trying to murder them all. Backup was called. We're trying to calm the situation down, but—"

"Have all the people inside been screened for weapons?" Simon asked as he turned to Scott.

"Residents are screened for weapons before they're allowed to stay here. I told the officers that. They're upset, but they're no threat. I want these cops out of here. Now."

Simon glanced at Nina, who nodded and said, "I agree. Tell all of the uniformed officers to step back a good fifty yards. Give these people some space. This is their home—the only home they know. Police are supposed to make people feel safe, not afraid. Make them do their job."

"Right. Officer, you heard her. Let's go." Simon's orders for the officers to back off were met with a few glances of disapproval, but no one fought him. Once the police presence had been significantly withdrawn, the shouts and cries inside the house faded.

Simon turned toward Elaina. "I was told you wanted to speak to me specifically. Before I visited the victim at the hospital. Why?"

"First, tell me who this is," Elaina said, nodding toward Nina.

"Dr. Nina Whitaker. She's a psychiatrist currently working with the department."

Scott nodded. "So it's true. She helped you find that

missing girl. She's consulting with the police about how to work more effectively with the mentally ill."

"She's observing us and giving us a recommendation for a new training program. And yes, she helped us find a little girl. Now why did you want to see me?"

"I wouldn't have. Not if I hadn't heard about the work you were doing with Dr. Whitaker. But hearing that has given me hope that I initially misjudged you. That we can trust you."

"You can trust me, Ms. Scott. I only want to help."

Scott looked a Nina, who nodded. "It's true. He's a good cop, Ms. Scott."

The woman took a deep breath. "Okay. The reason I wanted to talk to you is that there's a witness. Someone who says a cop was responsible for the attack on a young man."

"A homeless man that was staying here?"

"A homeless—? No, Nelson Conrad isn't homeless. He's a volunteer here."

"The man that you were just talking to. With the blue polo shirt. Is he a volunteer, too?"

"He provides security here, but he's not the one you want to talk to. One of our residents saw the person who attacked Nelson."

A true eyewitness, Simon thought. Finally, maybe, they were going to catch a break in the case. "Okay. And where's the witness now?" Simon asked.

Scott tipped her chin, pointing toward the homeless shelter. "She's hiding inside. She'd agreed to talk to you, but after the police got here…well, she's scared. She's refusing to come out. Refusing to talk to you."

"If she's a witness to the crime, she doesn't have any choice in the matter," Simon said.

Scott narrowed her eyes. "Now, listen here—"

"He has to talk to her," Nina interjected. "You know that. It's why you called him. But we don't want to frighten this witness any more. Perhaps I can help?"

"How?"

"By gaining her trust and not adding to her fear."

She looked at Simon, who nodded.

Nina backed up two steps so she had a full view of the crowd still gathered inside the house, peering out the windows and through the door. She opened up the front of her jacket and pulled it wide, then reached inside an interior pocket and pulled out her hospital ID. She held it up over her head slowly, calmly and said in a firm yet gentle voice, "I am not with the police. I am a doctor. The man I am with—" she pointed to Simon "—he is with the police, but he's a detective. His job is to figure out who is hurting you, even if the person hurting you is a cop. My job is to make sure you are safe."

She put her ID back in her pocket and lowered her arms.

They waited.

There was jostling at the doorway as some of the residents backed away, allowing an elderly woman draped in a faded Peruvian poncho to come forward.

"You and your detective may enter. None of the others. We will tell only you," the woman said, pointing directly at Nina.

Simon felt a sense of relief and pride at the way Nina had defused the situation. He was, however, still pissed that she'd gone off half-cocked, running straight into what could have been a dangerous situation. The two of them were definitely going to have further discussion about that. First, however, he had a witness to interview.

The woman in the poncho was named Mary. Just Mary. Elaina Scott didn't know her last name and the woman refused to give it.

"I heard Nelson screaming," Mary said. "Saw the man over him and chased him off."

Simon raised his brows in surprise, which caused Mary to laugh. "I may be old and creaky, Detective, but I never smoked a day in my life, and I've got good lungs. You can hear me shout from practically one end of the park to the other."

He grinned. "So you hollered and the attacker went running?"

"Somethin' like that. Just wish I'd gotten there sooner," she added, lowering her gaze to the floor. "I was supposed to meet him. Meet him near the Japanese Tea Garden, but I was late."

"Mary, Ms. Scott told me Nelson was a volunteer here. Did you meet with him often?"

"No. But he said he was doing something near the park. And he promised to show me the Tea Garden."

"Do you know what he was doing near the park?"

"No. He didn't tell me."

"Okay. So you went to meet him. And what happened?"

"I was late. But when I got there, I saw—I saw—"

"What did you see, Mary?"

Mary brought her shoulders in closer together and curled inward. Several minutes of silence ticked by.

Simon started to speak, but silenced himself when he caught sight of Nina's subtle headshake.

Give the woman space. Distance. Time to pull herself together. Don't push.

He could practically hear Nina's unspoken words in his head.

So he waited, watching Mary breathe in and out, in and out, until her shoulders went back to square. She took one last shuddering breath and said, "He had a knife. He carved up poor Nelson. On his back. Initials. It was so bloody."

This time it was Nina who inhaled sharply and Simon who gave her the "hold back" hand gesture. He heard the murmur of voices in the distance, the squeaky sound of rubber soles on the vinyl and someone's cell phone ringing, but still he waited.

"Did you see the initials? Can you tell me what they were, Mary?"

"There were four letters."

Of course, but he had to ask anyway. "What were they?"

"BDSG."

SOMETHING WAS WRONG, Nina thought, then cursed herself.

Of course something was wrong. Someone was murdering people and carving them up like woodshop projects. What she meant was something was wrong with Simon. He'd completely withdrawn from her. Holed up inside himself and emotionally retreated from her in a way he never had before. Always before, when something traumatic like this had happened, he'd been there, a rock for her to lean on. Reassuring her that everything was going to be okay. But now that he was dealing with the realization that *he* might be personally mixed-up with these murders—at least, she assumed that was the case given Mary's revelation that the initials *SG* had been carved into Nelson Conrad's back—he was acting shell-shocked.

It was her turn to be his rock to lean on.

"Simon," she said gently. "What are you thinking?" She really wanted to ask him further what he was feeling, but she was afraid those loaded words would cause him to retreat even further inside himself.

"What?" he said, looking at her, eyes clearing as if he'd forgotten she was even there, in the car with him. "I'm thinking this has got to stop. Only I've been trying to make it stop since before I met you, and this guy has been one step ahead of me the entire time."

"This guy, meaning Davenport?"

Simon shook his head. "No. It's not him. He didn't do this. We've had an officer on him ever since he was bailed out. This is pretty much going to clear him for the other two murders, as well."

"It's still possible that he hired someone. Or that Hyatt did."

"Possible, sure. Anything's possible," he said gruffly. "But it doesn't make sense anymore. It doesn't feel right. Even before we found those other footprints in your house, it never quite did. Aside from the initials that link these crimes, my gut is telling me that Davenport and Hyatt are exactly what they appear to be. They're pissed at the world because of what happened to their daughters. Maybe my mistake has been in assuming these murders were about you in the first place."

"You had reason to believe that because of the initials he left behind. On Six. On those men."

"Yeah, well now he's left *my* initials. Given I'm the

lead detective on this case, it's obviously not coincidence. He's telling me something. And maybe what he's telling me is that I've been the wild card in this all along. That the only reason he dragged you into this in the first place was because of your work with the police. With *me*."

He probably didn't even realize it, but his expression and tone were laced with horror. Lana, she thought. His ex-girlfriend had been killed less than a year ago. He probably viewed this new threat as his nightmare come back to haunt him all over again.

They arrived back at his place and got out of the car. When they got inside, Nina took him by the arms, trying to ground him in the here and now.

She wasn't dead. She was here. Alive and protected because of him.

"Even if this person is targeting you, Simon, it doesn't make these murders your fault. You've been telling me that this whole time, and you need to listen to yourself. If you're having trouble remembering that, I'm here to remind you. You can lean on me now, just like you've allowed me to lean on you."

He stared at her with a slight frown on his face, almost as if she wasn't speaking English. Slowly, he said, "I appreciate that."

The words themselves didn't alarm her, but the way he said them, and the way he wouldn't look at her as he did so, did.

"What's going on here, Simon?"

He took several steps away from her, causing her hands to fall away from him. "You were right before, Nina. About things having to end between us. We let our mutual attraction get out of hand because of all the things that have been happening."

"And what? Now that you think you're personally connected to these murders, things are somehow different and you're suddenly willing to agree with me?"

"I don't want to pull you into this more than you already are, Nina. If someone is targeting you because of me, then the best way to protect you is to get you away from me."

His words made sense, but his timing and the detached manner with which he spoke made her instinctively rebel against them. "Are you sure that's what this is about?"

"What else would it be about?"

She threw her hands up in frustration. "I don't know. Maybe the fact that I said I loved you before. Maybe hearing that freaked you out."

"So what if it did?" he snapped, his eyes momentarily flaring with anger. "It freaked you out, too. So much so that you attributed your words to a really good orgasm."

"That's because it *scared* me. How much I was starting to care for you. But whether we call it love or not, whether it was the sex talking or not, I *do* care about you, Simon. I need you to know that."

"I do know it," he said quietly. "And you know I care about you, too."

"But you want to walk away from me. After everything we've been through together? Just like that? Before you've even caught the person responsible for the murders? You're determined to do what? Leave me alone? Hand me off to another protective detail?" *Be-*

cause I won't feel safe, Nina thought. Not the way she felt when she was with him.

"Besides the cards and letters, there hasn't been a direct threat against you," he reminded her. "I can call in favors. Talk to the members on my team. They'll help me out. For now? You mentioned your friend Karen before. Can you stay with her? I have to go to this fundraising gala, anyway. It's not social. It's work. If I can, I'll have a patrol officer drive by Karen's house to check on you."

"And what about next week? I have to go back to work, too, remember? Will there be a patrol officer checking in on me there, as well?"

"We'll do the best we can to make sure you're safe."

"Physically, yes," she said almost bitterly.

Her bitterness punched a hole in his composure. Once again, his eyes flared with emotion, but just as he had before, he quickly banked it. "Damn it, this isn't easy for me. I'm trying to do the right thing here and that means protecting you. If I have a target on my back, I don't want you anywhere near me."

"Fine," Nina said, instinctively responding to his desire for separation when before he'd sworn he wouldn't leave her alone. It didn't matter what his motivation was; her heart was bleeding. "Then I'll be sure to stay as far away from you as possible."

CHAPTER THIRTY-TWO

SIMON WOULD HAVE PREFERRED to assign a patrol officer to watch Nina, but getting her to agree to stay with her friend Karen was the best he could do right now. Still, before he left, Simon warned Nina to be careful.

"Don't take any unnecessary risks," he said. "Please." It was like the first day she'd come to shadow him all over again, when he'd warned her not to endanger herself in an attempt to help someone they encountered on a call. He hadn't known it at the time, but despite being one of the most compassionate women he knew, she wasn't foolhardy. She'd be fine, he told himself.

She smiled tiredly, as if she was remembering that first day, as well. "Don't worry yourself, Simon. I'll be fine so long as I'm not anywhere near you. At least, that's your theory, isn't it?"

She looked at a point over his shoulder, her back to Karen's front door. The other woman was waiting inside and had promised to lock the door again as soon as he left. She even had a state-of-the-art security system. There was no reason to delay his departure any longer.

Except, of course, for the fact he didn't want to leave her. But that was his heart and his body talking. His mind—that little voice he listened to when assessing life-and-death situations on the job—was telling him this was the right thing to do. He hadn't listened to that voice where Lana was concerned, and look how that had ended. This time, he wasn't taking any chances.

"I'll be at the office," he told her, "until I have to leave for the gala. Even if I'm not at the office, remember what I said before. If you need something, you can call anyone in SIG. Even Stevens. They all care about you, Nina, and won't hesitate to respond if you need them."

"How convenient for you," she said. "You can ensure I'm protected without having to put yourself out any longer."

"Damn it, don't! I'm not abandoning you. If you need me, if you call me and I can be here, I will be here. Do you understand?"

"Sure."

"Then promise me you'll call me if you need me."

She just looked at him, then turned to walk inside.

He grabbed her arm. "Damn it, Nina, promise me!"

She wrenched her arm away. "Fine," she said. "I promise. Now, is that all?"

"No," he said, before bending his head and stealing a kiss from her. He'd much rather she'd kissed him on her own, but her mouth softened under his and that was enough. He buried his hands in her hair and cradled her face, trying to communicate to her with his lips and tongue how very much he cared about her. And how scared he was about letting her down. She raised her own hands and touched his face. The contact was electric and jolted him back to reality. Already the thought of walking away from her was unbearable. He was only making it worse. He pulled away, once more said, "Be careful," and then left.

As soon as he got into his car, Jase called to tell

him he had information about the security cameras in
the SIG parking lot and the vandalism of Simon's car.
"You're not going to like it," Jase warned. And he was
totally right.

BACK AT SIG, JASE TOOK a sip of coffee, then said, "Whoever broke into your car and set up the doll did it in
exactly five minutes, between four and five after four.
That's when the security disks were tampered with, re-
sulting in a five-minute blank. This guy was smooth.
And he knew our system."

"Another cop?" Simon asked, a hollow feeling in
his gut. DeMarco? he wondered.

Impossible.

But was it really?

Davenport had gotten into Nina's house despite a
security system that DeMarco had just installed. And
then there were the initials—*BD*—that matched those
of the kid, Billy Dahl, who DeMarco had shot in New
Orleans. He couldn't bear to think that another cop—*a
friend*—could be doing such vile things, but he also
recalled his conversation with Nina, the one they'd
had on the beach before they'd made love. She'd said
that trauma could affect someone who'd exhibited no
prior signs of mental illness and skew his reality so
much that he would do things he normally wouldn't.
DeMarco had talked about some of the symptoms he'd
been experiencing, including hearing things, and if he
was hearing things, who knew what else was going
on…whether his link with reality had truly slipped.

"Let's assume it's a cop, Simon," Jase said. "Can you
think of anyone who has a personal vendetta against
you?"

He thought about it, then shook his head. "I'm not everyone's favorite person around here, but I can't think of anyone I've pissed off lately."

"How about not so lately? When you were away from SIG? When you were a captain?"

"I was captain for three weeks. The men I worked with during that time seemed to respect me. Like me, even. Of course, I wasn't there to make friends. I made some tough decisions, one in particular…" He frowned. He wondered whether it would be enough to make someone come after him like this.

"What was the decision?"

"I shut down a program for retired annuitants, retired police officers who were able to stay on the P.D.'s payroll as contract investigators. The entire program got the boot for purely budgetary reasons."

"Retired police officers would know about our security system just as much as current ones. How about I check into it? You've got to get ready to rub elbows with the bigwigs at that fundraiser, don't you?"

Simon cursed under his breath. "I should blow it off. There's no reason you should be chasing down leads while I put on a tuxedo and eat a gourmet meal. Especially when those leads might involve a dirty cop."

"No reason except the mayor and Commander Stevens will be pissed if you don't show. It's fine. I'm here anyway and I have the time to check it out."

Simon hesitated, then sighed. Being on a team was all about covering someone one moment and being covered the next. He knew he'd do the same for any member of the team, and that made it easier to accept Jase's help now. "Thanks, Jase. I'll head back as soon as I can after the gala."

"No rush." Jase hesitated. "Is Nina attending the gala with you?"

Simon briefly looked away. "No. She's staying at a friend's house."

"So you're running again?"

Simon frowned. "What?"

"Doesn't take a genius to know what you'd do once you found out you were linked to the homeless murders. To know that you'd separate yourself from her. I get it, but she has to be hurt. Especially if you two had gotten as close as I think you have."

At first, Simon resisted Jase's obvious attempts to get in Simon's business. But then he thought of De-Marco again. How *not* getting in DeMarco's business had left his friend feeling like he had to deal with his problems alone. Simon also remembered what Nina had said: that you couldn't truly know you were handling something unless you were willing to talk about it with another person. Before he knew he was going to, he confessed, "Yeah, well, we got pretty close. And yes, she's hurt. But better her feelings are hurt than she ends up dead like…"

"Like Lana?" Jase asked softly.

"Yeah. Like Lana."

"Lana was killed by a serial killer while on the job, Simon. She walked into that situation of her own accord because she was trying to help him. That's not going to happen to Nina."

"And how do you know that, Jase? 'Cause I sure don't."

Of course, Jase didn't have an answer because there wasn't one. No guarantees that Nina wouldn't die just as brutally and suddenly as Lana had one day.

Simon got up to leave, then hesitated. "Have you talked to DeMarco?"

"I touched base with him earlier today. He sounded better. Said he went and saw a counselor who is helping him figure some things out. He doesn't know when he'll be back, but he's hoping soon."

"Good." His earlier suspicions about DeMarco had vanished as quickly as they'd formed. He knew the man. No way was DeMarco responsible for any of the things that had happened over the past week. Even so, despite his renewed confidence in his friend's innocence, Simon's mind was a mess. He kept twirling one possibility after another around his head, but none of them felt right.

On his way home, he had to pass by the cemetery. The one where Lana was buried. And before he knew it, he was pulling in and walking to Lana's grave.

Simon stared at Lana's tombstone and remembered the slight breeze he'd felt the last time he'd visited her. The air was still now. Dry and uncomfortable. For a second, he almost couldn't breathe.

Had it been just three weeks ago that he'd come here to visit Lana? Even less than that since he'd met Nina? That boggled his mind. He'd known Lana for years. He'd loved her. Yet even though he'd known Nina for far less time, it was amazing how much he'd grown to care about her. And, dare he admit it…how much he'd grown to love her?

Yes, Simon thought. He loved her. He, who had never been one to fall in love quickly, had fallen in love with Dr. Nina Whitaker in less than two weeks. For the briefest moment, he felt guilty. How had Nina so thoroughly filled the place in his heart that had once only belonged to Lana?

Did I do this to you, Lana? Did you blame me, as your life left you, for failing to protect you?

Every doubt and insecurity he'd ever harbored came swamping through him. What right did he have to try to go on with his life when Lana no longer could? What right did he have to apply for a commanding role, when he'd had the role once before and given it up? When doing so had cost him Lana, had driven a wedge between them, and for all he knew, had driven her to act so recklessly that it had gotten her killed. He'd fucked everything up, just like he was fucking up this case.

He hadn't been able to stop another attack. Hadn't been able to stop Lana from being killed. Hadn't seen how troubled DeMarco had gotten. Hadn't kept Nina from being hurt again and again and again...and most recently, by *him*.

Instinctively, he moved closer to Lana's headstone. He touched the smooth surface as if doing so would grant him a physical connection with the woman he'd once loved.

The breeze suddenly picked up and swirled around him. Simon closed his eyes. Envisioned Lana's beautiful face. He could swear for a second that he smelled her. Heard her.

But it didn't comfort him. All it did was make him remember that he'd lost her.

And that, one way or another, he was going to lose Nina, too.

Help me, Lana, he thought. *Help me to understand what's going on. Who is this killer? What's motivat-*

ing him? He's killing for a reason. To prove something. But to whom?

Me? Nina? The mentally ill? The cops?

Who is he targeting?

To his surprise, the answer came to him, not in Lana's voice, but his own.

Maybe he's targeting all of us at once.

But why? And more important, who could pull off something like that? Who did Simon know that could carry out that kind of vendetta without getting caught? Whoever he was, he was dancing circles around the police, staying one step ahead of them despite the advanced security systems that had been put in place.

As the questions swirled through his mind, Simon's vision focused on the epitaph that Lana's parents had engraved on the elegant marble.

Two words on the tombstone came into stark relief.

Beloved Daughter.

BD.

It couldn't be, he thought.

But was it really that much crazier than any of the other theories he'd come up with?

He'd thought Lester Davenport's grief over losing his daughter had driven him to murder. He'd even briefly considered whether the same thing had motivated Rebecca Hyatt's father to strike out. Couldn't that same reasoning apply to Gil Archer, who'd lost his daughter, too?

What if BD didn't stand for someone's name but something else? Something like an endearment.

Beloved Daughter.

Davenport and Hyatt had blamed Nina for the deaths

of their daughters. Who did Gil Archer truly blame for Lana's?

The cops for not protecting her?

A mentally ill man for killing her?

Simon for breaking up with her before she was killed?

Nina for working with Simon, and even dating him, after his daughter no longer could?

It made sense. More sense than anything had up to this point.

If Simon was right, Gil Archer was going after all of them.

And he was winning.

AFTER LEAVING THE CEMETERY, Simon hit the ground running. After a brief stop at SFPD to put together what he needed, the first thing he did was visit Rita Taylor and show her a photo lineup that included Gil Archer's photo. Unfortunately, Rita's identification didn't go exactly as planned, and Simon was now having to move to Plan B—a plan that he needed Jase and Carrie's help to carry out.

"That's quite a theory," Jase said after whistling in amazed disbelief. He leaned back in his desk chair, hands folded against his chest. "But I have to say, given the security systems that have been tampered with, especially the parking lot security tapes, it makes sense. Archer set up our security system, did you know that?"

"I did," Simon said. "And it's something I definitely considered in wading through all this. And in formulating my plan."

"It's a good plan," Jase said, "if a little risky. You really think she'll go through with it?"

Simon thought about the woman Jase was referring to—Rita Taylor. "She said she will. Naturally, she's scared, especially after everything I've said about her needing to take her own protection seriously. But showing her the photo lineup didn't work. She said a couple of the men, including Archer, looked like the guy, but she couldn't be sure. She insists she needs to see the man up close, see him talk, get a 'feel' for him, in order to make a positive ID. She's willing to take some limited risks. According to her, it beats living in fear every day of her life."

"Well, between you accompanying her, and Carrie and I covering your back, we'll limit the risk to her. And if it turns out you're right, she'll certainly take Gil Archer by surprise, which you'll be able to witness for yourself. We'll be there right when the gala starts."

"I'll see you there, Jase. And thanks."

As he left SIG, Simon again wondered if he was thinking crazy. Did he truly believe Lana's father, Gil Archer, a respected community member and a friend of Commander Stevens, was the person behind the homeless murders?

He did. It felt right. In a way that suspecting Hyatt and even Davenport hadn't.

Besides, it was just a theory, Simon told himself. There was nothing wrong with exploring possibilities. Isn't that what Commander Stevens had said when he'd suggested Nina might know something about the murders? That a police officer had to remain objective despite personal relationships with others? Despite what he thought he knew about a potential witness or suspect?

Simon was simply taking a page from Stevens's playbook.

He had some possibilities to explore.

Covertly, he thought.

And given that tonight was the fundraising gala and that Archer was going to be there, it was the perfect opportunity for him to do so.

"So will you go with me, Nina? We both got invitations from Gil Archer to attend this fundraising gala to benefit the mentally ill. I wasn't going to go by myself, but now that you're here, it could be fun."

Nina did her best to ignore the heavy linen and embossed invitation Karen was waving in front of her face. There was no way she was going to that fundraising gala. Simon was going to be there and she didn't want him to think she was mooning over him, following him around with stars in her eyes when he'd already made it clear he wanted her to stay as far away from him as possible.

Because he wants to protect you, she reminded herself. *Because he's afraid the same thing is going to happen to you that happened to Lana. That you're going to die on him.*

It made perfect sense he'd be worried. But she couldn't help wondering if it was a convenient excuse because he'd simply grown tired of her. They'd gone to bed a few times, but so what? He'd never once said he wanted anything more from her. Never once said he loved her.

Not the way she'd said she loved him. Even though she'd told him she hadn't meant it, that it had just been the sex talking, he hadn't believed her. And she couldn't lie to herself anymore, either.

She did love him. She loved Simon Granger.

But it didn't matter. Not with a killer still out there, infecting them with fear time and time again.

In her mind, dead men carved with the letters *BD* swirled around, clashing into one another. Jarring her reality. Considering it was his job to find the killer, how much more did those images play through Simon's mind? With that kind of weight on his shoulders, it was a wonder they'd managed to get close at all.

And even once the killer was caught? There was still her career and the massive differences in their life views that would constantly drive a wedge between them.

"Nina. Are you even listening to me?" Karen said.

Focus, Nina, she told herself. What had Karen been saying? Oh, yeah. "You know how much I hate having to make small talk with strangers," she murmured.

"You could take your cop. Bet he's good on the dance floor," Karen teased.

Nina's heart twisted, and pain shot through her chest. The only dancing she and Simon had done had been in bed, and now she'd probably never feel his naked body stretched over hers again. That thought left her feeling morose.

"He's not my cop," she mumbled. "And we're not dating."

Dating was where a guy picked a girl up at her house with flowers in hand. Dating was where the guy took the girl to dinner and the movies and hoped for a kiss good-night. Dating was where a guy willingly waded through five or ten dates before getting lucky enough to get it on in the girl's bed. Dating was *not* living in the guy's house because a serial killer was after the girl. Dating was *not* using sex for distraction.

"Fine. Forget I said anything about that. You don't need a date because you have me. And if you don't want to go just for fun, think about work."

"The police have already decided to go forward with the program, Karen. We no longer have any reason to schmooze them into it."

"But we can always schmooze for money. The more money we have, the better training we'll be able to provide. Besides," she said, "how often do you and I have a chance to go to something like this? These golf club people are the richest in the city. And the ones with the most power. You never know when one of them might be willing to scratch your back because you were nice to them at a charity fundraiser. Tomorrow, you're going back to your patients. I've already agreed to take the lead on the program. Let's go have some fun. I said I'd buy you drinks when this is all over, remember?"

At that, Nina actually smiled. "The drinks at this thing are going to be free. It's an open bar, remember?"

"Is it?" Karen said with an expression of mock innocence. "Even better."

CHAPTER THIRTY-THREE

WHEN SIMON WALKED INTO the fundraising gala, several people stopped and stared. Not at him, but at the woman on his arm. She was a stunner, with her ample cleavage, wild hair, heavy makeup and short dress. She stood out among the older, more sophisticatedly dressed women, and that was perfect as far as Simon was concerned.

He'd brought Rita Taylor to this fundraising gala because he *wanted* her to be noticed. Specifically, he wanted her to be noticed by the man who'd paid her a thousand bucks to ID a cop as Cann's killer. He wanted her to be noticed by the man he was betting was Gil Archer.

"So this is how the other half lives, huh?" Rita said, her normally jaded eyes wide and glittering with no small amount of wonder. He couldn't blame her. The place looked lavish to the extreme, which again, he found a little over the top for a fundraiser for mentally ill citizens, many of them homeless.

Rita apparently felt the same way. She clucked her tongue. "Lousy bastard. By the looks of things, he could have paid me way more than a thousand bucks to lie."

Simon couldn't help it—he laughed. "Yeah," he said.

"But he probably wouldn't have been willing to negotiate with you."

She smiled back at him then looked around the room. "You're probably right. So, do you see the guy you're thinking is the one?"

Simon searched for Gil but saw no sign of him. However, he simply said, "I can't tell you that. And I can't point him out to you. You need to identify him on your own. That way, it'll be harder for someone to claim I influenced your ID."

"Right. Well, I don't see him right now and I have to go to the little girl's room."

"I'll walk you to the restroom and wait right by the door. I don't want him seeing you and getting to you before I can."

The amusement fled Rita's eyes and was replaced by something else. It wasn't quite fear, but close. "Right. Thanks for reminding me. You promised to keep me safe and I'm counting on you to keep that promise."

"I won't let you down. Just let me know the second you see him."

"I will."

NINA WAS STANDING NEXT to the bar with Karen when she saw them.

Simon and a dark-haired, overtly sexy woman wearing a short black dress. He'd arrived with a date.

And that made her feel like a complete fool.

Had she really been that wrong about him?

Had all that talk about wanting to protect her just been an excuse to get her out of his hair so he could move on to the next woman? Hurt and disbelief combined to make her breathless and slightly light-headed.

"Are you all right?" a man next to her asked.

She turned to face him. He had gray hair, but looked fit for his age. Handsome. Kind.

But then he frowned, and it made him look fairly ominous. "You look like you've seen a ghost," he observed.

Next to her, Karen had just caught sight of Simon, as well. She glanced at Nina, obviously following her train of thought.

"Oh, no, Nina. I'm sorry. Is that his date?"

Nina shrugged and smiled tightly. "Looks like it. Would you excuse me? I—I'm suddenly feeling a little claustrophobic." She turned away from Karen and the man standing next to her, noting that each of them wore identical expressions of concern as they stared at Simon and the woman by his side. Karen was her friend, not to mention a woman, so she would understand the kind of betrayal Nina was feeling. But this man was a stranger; she must really look poleaxed for him to be exhibiting such concern. "I need to get some fresh air."

"I'll come with you."

She shook her head. "No, Karen. I'd like to be by myself. Please just leave me alone."

If only everyone would leave her alone, she thought as she quickly walked out of the banquet hall and down a long corridor. Karen, Simon, grieving fathers, psychotic killers—every single one of them.

But they wouldn't. They hadn't.

And, she realized, even if they suddenly complied

and left her alone from this very moment on, the damage was already done.

Nina no longer felt safe.

She suspected she never would.

SIMON WAITED OUTSIDE the women's restroom for Rita Taylor to come out. As he did, he scanned the room, spotting Commander Stevens and the mayor at one table. Carrie and Jase were there, too, dressed to the nines and each covering different sides of the room. To his surprise, he even saw DeMarco at another table, talking to a pretty Asian woman. It was the same woman—the same *doctor,* he realized—he'd seen walking out of Welcome Home the day he'd first met Elaina Scott. Was *she* the "counselor" DeMarco had told Jase about? If so, why were they here together? For personal or professional reasons?

He decided he didn't really care. DeMarco looked more like his old self again. Relaxed. Smiling. And from where he stood, that was pretty damn amazing.

As he watched, DeMarco looked up and caught Simon's eye. He jerked his chin in greeting and Simon did the same. He couldn't talk to DeMarco now. Couldn't let down his guard. He'd sworn to give Rita Taylor his full attention, his full protection, while she was here. Once they saw Archer and she confirmed whether or not he was the man who'd paid her off, they'd be done here.

When he still didn't spot Archer, his gaze continued to roam the room.

His scan, however, came to a screeching stop when he caught sight of a beautiful blonde woman in a floor-length navy gown. Nina stood in front of the bar with her friend Karen, and an older man with graying hair and a gray suit.

What the hell was she doing here?

Almost immediately, however, his gaze returned to the man beside her. He'd seen him before…but where? For some reason, he envisioned the man wearing a blue polo shirt…

Wait! That was it. He'd seen the man at Welcome Home. He was the security guard Elaina Scott had told him about. The one who'd looked familiar to Simon the first time he'd seen him, only he hadn't been able to figure out why. Now, the knowledge tickled at his brain but still remained just out of reach. He'd never actually met the man before, Simon thought. But he'd seen his face. In a photograph? A file?

Yes, he thought. A personnel file.

The name Harold McGrogen clicked into place.

He'd been a cop. One who'd retired right around the time Simon had been promoted to captain. That's why he looked familiar. But why was he talking to Nina? How did they know each other?

He'd just stepped forward to find out when he remembered Rita Taylor and cursed. He couldn't abandon his post. Not now.

Talking to Nina would have to wait.

Even so, his gaze ate her up. She looked amazing, but she could have been wearing a cardboard box for all he cared. Her presence made him feel a thousand times better and a thousand times worse. He didn't want her anywhere near the man he now suspected of murder, yet even as he had that thought, Gil Archer walked into the room.

He was surrounded by several of his high society cronies. The man looked to be in his element, shaking hands with this person and waving at another. He reminded Simon of a politician rather than a businessman/security expert. Then again, schmoozing had always seemed to be Archer's specialty. Hopefully, it meant his guard was down and he'd react with the surprised horror Simon was expecting when he caught his first glimpse of Rita Taylor.

Something brushed against his arm and he heard a gasp.

Rita now stood by his side.

As he watched, her eyes widened and she went white. "It's him," she said. "I see him. He's here."

Dear God, Simon thought, as adrenaline surged through his veins. He automatically looked back at Archer, who was still scanning the room, likely looking for the most influential guests. When his gaze landed on Simon and the woman next to him, he frowned.

Was it really going to be this easy?

"That man over there?" Simon confirmed. "The one with the red rose pinned to his lapel? Be sure, Rita. He's a very important man."

"What?" Rita's gaze flickered to Gil Archer. "No," she said, taking Simon off guard. "Not him. Over by the bar. I saw the guy who paid me off standing over there. Talking to a blonde. I watched him talking. I watched his mouth. It's him."

Simon's gaze instantly darted back to the bar. Karen was still standing there, but Nina was gone.

And so was the man she'd been talking to.

He turned to Rita. "Do you still see him in the room?"

She glanced around them. "No, no. One minute he was here but now he's not."

"Are you *sure* he's the one that paid you the grand?"

"Believe me, I've had nightmares about his face. The photos were two-dimensional. Even seeing him now, from across the room, I recognized him. I *felt* him. I'm positive it was him."

Although he was a little skeptical of her ID, especially because it was partially based on a "feeling," Simon wasn't taking any chances. Jase and Carrie were here and would keep an eye on Archer. In the meantime…

With fear clogging his throat, he strode across the room toward Karen, Rita Taylor in tow. "Karen," he called. "Where'd Nina go?"

"She stepped out for some air," Karen said, looking slightly alarmed.

"And you let her? Damn it, she was supposed to be staying with you and lying low. What the hell is she doing here?"

"What's she doing here? At a fundraiser with the mayor, the police chief and tons of cops in attendance? Gee, seemed pretty safe to me."

"She was just talking to an older man in a suit. Did they leave together?"

"What? No. I mean, I don't know. She left, and then so did he."

"Did you see where she went?"

"Through there." Karen pointed.

Standing next to him, Rita Taylor said, "Don't you leave me, Detective. You promised to take care of me. You promised."

"Don't worry," he said. "I'm not leaving you unprotected. Several of my fellow detectives are here." His eyes found Jase, then Carrie. At his urging, they both nodded. "Do you see them?"

"Yes."

"Let's go. You're going to stay with one of them while I go after the man who bribed you. Only we have to move now or a woman I love could be hurt."

CHAPTER THIRTY-FOUR

NINA'S GAZE FRANTICALLY sought out the nearest outer door so she could indeed get the breath of fresh air she'd told Karen she needed. As soon as she spotted one, she shoved through it, stumbling into what appeared to be a narrow loading dock at the back of the building.

With a shaky hand, she propped herself up against an outer wall. Seeing Simon with that woman, leaning so protectively close to her, had wounded something inside her and she wasn't quite sure how she was ever going to heal. Here she'd been agonizing over his expressed need to stay away from her in order to protect her, and he'd been getting his jollies with another woman. He wasn't the man she'd thought he was. That was the only explanation. Otherwise, how else—

"For God's sake, don't look so damn heartbroken. Simon Granger isn't screwing another woman, he's on the job. Damn clever bastard."

At the harsh masculine words, Nina whirled around. In the faint glow of the building's outer lights, the same man who'd expressed concern for her at the bar stood glaring at her. And pointing a gun at her.

"What are you—?" She stopped herself from continuing. She knew exactly what he was doing. Threatening her. The real question was, "Who are you?"

"No one you know. This isn't personal. Not for me."

"You holding a gun to me isn't personal? You must be angry with me for some reason. Let's talk about it, please. I—"

He rolled his eyes. "Don't start with your psycho-babble mumbo jumbo. I dealt with enough shrinks while I was on the force to recognize it when I hear it."

"You're a cop? Then why—" She immediately thought of the homeless men who'd been murdered. And the allegations that Cann had been killed by a police officer.

"I *was* a cop. Now I'm a damn security guard, having to work for chump change in places like that damn homeless shelter. I have Simon Granger to thank for that."

"Simon?"

"Before he returned to the streets, he stayed a captain just long enough to cut a police department program for budgetary reasons. I got the ax."

"But you just acknowledged it wasn't for personal reasons," she said. "He was just doing his job."

He shrugged. "So was I. And I'm going to continue doing it." He motioned with the gun, clearly directing her to walk away from the building and toward the nearby street. "Come on. Let's go. Your boyfriend's going to track us down any second, and I need to get a head start on him. You're coming with me as my little insurance policy."

"He's coming after you? Because he believes you murdered those homeless men? He hasn't said anything to me about you and we were working together very closely—"

The man grabbed her arm, shoved the gun in her

side and started forcibly walking her toward the street. He snorted. "Yeah, I know exactly how close you two have been working. I've got to say, the guy impressed me. Despite everything I was throwing at you, he still managed to get you in the sack. Guess your involvement in two teenage suicides wasn't enough to kill the mood. Did you think of them while he was fucking you?"

Furiously, Nina tried to wrench away, gasping in pain when he merely tightened his hold.

"Uh-uh. None of that. I'm sure that whore Simon brought as his date has identified me already so let's just keep moving."

"The woman…she's a…"

"A prostitute. And a witness against me. That's obviously why he brought her here. To try to ID me."

"And she did," she said slowly.

"Probably, but you should have seen the look on your face when you saw them. It was priceless, really. I think he hurt you more in that moment than everything I did to you combined. Personally, that's why I'm single."

Right, Nina thought darkly. *That's why.*

"Ah, good," the man said. "There's my car just up ahead. Won't be too long now before—"

"Harold McGrogen, stop right there." Simon's voice suddenly boomed behind them.

The man holding Nina paused and stiffened. Slowly, he turned them both around until they faced Simon. "So you remember me now, huh? Too bad you didn't the first time you saw me at Welcome Home. But it wouldn't have mattered. You wouldn't have suspected me even then. You were too busy chasing Lester Davenport."

"Put down your weapon," Simon ordered.

"I don't think so," McGrogen answered. "I suggest you put down *your* weapon before I shoot your girlfriend here."

Simon looked at Nina and she tried to hide her fear. She wasn't a fool. She was terrified that she was going to get hurt. That the man was going to shoot her before Simon could stop him. But Harold McGrogen was banking on her fear and Simon's fear for her to keep them predictable. To make them mess up and enable him to get away. She could at least deny him that.

"Harold, listen to me," he said in a low voice, though it was obviously tight with tension. "I want to help you."

McGrogen laughed. "Wow, this is hilarious. Seriously, Granger? You're trying to talk me down with de-escalation techniques? Use my name? Convince me that you're not a threat? So that what? I surrender and spend the rest of my days in prison?" He scowled. "No thanks. You might as well shoot me now and get it over with. Or try to, at least," he said and laughed.

"Hey, whash—whash goin' on here?"

At the sound of DeMarco's voice behind them, Nina jerked.

McGrogen whirled, keeping his gun on Nina but turning to the side as he tried to keep an eye on both Simon and DeMarco, who was staggering slightly.

"What ya doing out here? The party's insi—inshide."

Was he drunk? Nina wondered. Or simply pretending to be?

"Get the hell out of here," McGrogen snapped, obviously believing DeMarco was drunk and apparently not realizing he was a law enforcement officer. Why would he? DeMarco was wearing a tux, was playing the drunk and it was conceivable McGrogen had never met or heard of him. Wasn't it?

She glanced at Simon, whose gaze mets hers. Instinctively, she knew he was thinking the same thing.

"Don' be like that, man. I jus' wanna—" DeMarco stumbled closer and McGrogen fired.

The retort of the gun blasted in Nina's ears and her body jerked along with McGrogen's arm.

Nina screamed as DeMarco fell to the ground.

"No!" Her cry echoed Simon's.

McGrogen still held her against him, using her as a human shield. She saw Simon look at DeMarco, who was lying still on the ground. Saw his agony at being unable to shoot McGrogen because he didn't want to risk hurting her.

"What the hell have you done, McGrogen? You just shot an unarmed man in front of me. Taking Nina with you to ensure you got away, I can understand. What do you think you're gonna do now? Shoot me, too? Kill me?"

"Shut up! He was coming at me. I had no choice, damn it."

"Of course you did! And you have a choice now. Let Nina go. She's a doctor! Let her take a look at him. Stop the bleeding. Now! Before the man dies."

She felt McGrogen hesitate, then he dragged her closer to DeMarco's body. "I'm keeping my gun on her. I swear to God if you try anything, I'll shoot her. I have nothing to lose here, Granger, and you know it."

As soon as McGrogen loosened his grip on her, Nina knelt beside DeMarco. Oh, God, there was so much blood, but at least the bullet had hit him high on the shoulder and not in any vital organs. Nina pressed her hands to the wound, trying to stanch the blood. To her surprise, when she glanced at DeMarco's face, he was gritting his teeth with pain but looking at her with clear eyes. Yes, he'd been faking being drunk. Trying to buy her and Simon some time. And what had happened? He'd been shot. Because of her.

She instantly shoved that thought from her mind.

No! DeMarco hadn't been shot because of her, but because McGrogen was a dangerous criminal. She'd taken enough blame in her life. She wasn't taking this on, too. But what could she do? How was she going to make sure she, DeMarco and Simon got out of this alive?

"Why, Harold?" Simon asked. "You were a good cop. All this because you're pissed I shut down the retired annuitant program? You know that was a decision I made for the good of the department."

"I don't give a rat's ass about the good of the department," McGrogen spit out. "I was a cop, and because of you, I'm a fucking security guard now. I was working with a bunch of crazies and bleeding hearts at the homeless shelter. How do you think that made me feel?"

"Like you were doing something worthwhile?"

McGrogen snorted in disdain just as DeMarco moved his hand toward his right pocket. His silent gaze warned her to remain silent. Still. She understood immediately. Surreptitiously, her entire body stiff and trembling with fear, ever aware that although he wasn't looking at her, McGrogen still had his gun pointed at her, she shifted her body to cover what he was doing.

Simon carried a gun in a pocket holster when he was off duty. Maybe DeMarco did, too.

Unfortunately, DeMarco had been shot in the right shoulder, his shooting arm, and even as he tried to withdraw his piece, his movements were slow. Awkward. His face was awash with sweat and he was gritting his teeth in pain. Any second and he was going to pass out. He wasn't going to be able to do it, she realized. Not before McGrogen caught him and shot them both.

Carefully, she reached into DeMarco's pocket and extracted the gun herself. His gaze shot to hers, but when she just looked steadily back, he nodded slightly, indicating he understood.

She glanced at Simon, whose gaze remained on McGrogen's. Had he seen what they were doing? She couldn't tell. All she knew was that this was her one chance to take McGrogen off guard. But could she do it? Shoot a man even though she'd taken an oath to do no harm?

She struggled with herself. With everything she believed in. She thought about Beth and Rachel and even Mrs. Horowitz and how death, while inevitable, still often came too early. Sometimes that just couldn't be helped. And right or wrong, her decision to shoot McGrogen was made easier by her belief that this man was probably a sociopath. It didn't mean she didn't feel sorry for him, but it also made her realize he was broken. Unable to be fixed. At least, she was going with that assumption until proven otherwise.

Before she could lose her nerve, Nina lifted her arm to shoot.

SIMON HAD EXTREMELY good peripheral vision and he could see everything as Nina removed DeMarco's off-duty piece from his pocket and braced herself to shoot McGrogen. *Damn it, no,* he thought. His first thought was that even if she was able to shoot him, McGrogen would automatically fire the gun he still had pointed at Nina. His second thought was he didn't want the trauma of having to shoot the man on Nina's conscience.

He'd tried, Simon thought. Even after McGrogen had shot DeMarco, Simon had tried one last time to talk him down. But seeing Nina's covert movements plainly told him something—either she didn't think he had the skill to talk McGrogen down, or she believed McGrogen couldn't be talked down. In the end, it didn't really matter.

He'd had a bead on McGrogen's face the whole time, on the space within that imaginary triangle formed by the corners of each eye and his chin. As a former cop, McGrogen would know it, yet he still looked at Simon, his gaze off of his best chance at escaping this situation—Nina.

His gaze *suspiciously* off Nina, Simon thought suddenly.

And sure enough, at that very moment, McGrogen's gun arm drifted slightly to the right, away from his hostages.

Thoughts flashed through Simon's mind. Though he hadn't actually ever met the man before tonight, he'd reviewed McGrogen's records before making the decision to shut down the retired annuitant program. As such, he knew how experienced McGrogen was. He was a seasoned cop and he'd been a good cop, too. He'd know he'd just given Simon an easy shot.

And that told Simon McGrogen *wanted* Simon to

shoot him. That McGrogen didn't want to be taken into custody. Didn't want to have to live with the consequences of what he'd done.

Suicide by cop.

But Simon wasn't giving the man that easy out.

He felt fear for them all. For Nina. For DeMarco. For himself.

But he had to take his chances. He needed to do something now.

So before Nina could fire DeMarco's piece, Simon shot first.

He shot McGrogen in his right shoulder, knowing when he did, the impact would push his weapon even farther away from Nina. Sure enough, the moment the bullet hit him, McGrogen went flying backward and landed on the pavement.

"Stay down," Simon shouted, the command meant for both McGrogen and Nina. Within seconds, he was standing over McGrogen's body, his gun trained on him. A quick glance at Nina confirmed she still crouched over DeMarco, his gun still in her hand.

Their eyes met and held for a second, but then she dropped DeMarco's gun and began ripping at his shirt and dealing with his wounds. "He shot him in the shoulder," she called over her shoulder. "The wound's not fatal but we need to get him to a hospital."

Simon felt relief swamp him. He turned back to McGrogen, who was lying on the ground, eyes closed. "Why?" the other man moaned. "Why didn't you shoot to kill me?"

So Simon had been right. McGrogen *had* wanted to commit suicide.

"Wasn't going to happen," he said to McGrogen.

"You have several crimes to answer for, including the murders of Louis Cann and John Hastings. You've got a long legal case in front of you. And I want to make sure you enjoy every single second of it."

Flipping McGrogen to his stomach, Simon cuffed him, probably taking a little too much pleasure in the man's groans of pain. "Harold McGrogen, you're under arrest for the murders of Louis Cann and…"

The door behind them banged open and several people, including Stevens, Archer, the mayor and Jase— who, along with Carrie, had been covering Simon's back inside—exited the building. Jase and Stevens immediately rushed to Nina and DeMarco's side.

"Jase?" Simon called. "Rita Taylor?"

"She's with Carrie," he said. "She took her out the front when DeMarco headed out that way. I kept an eye on things inside to make sure they didn't pose a problem for you."

Meaning he'd kept an eye on Gil Archer, just as Simon had asked him, too. He nodded his thanks to Jase, turning when Stevens said, "Granger, get your ass over here and tell me what the hell is going on."

Simon complied, but only told him part of the story. He'd tell him the rest, but only when Gil Archer was no longer within earshot. As it was now, Simon kept his guard up and his gaze on the man, but he acted normal, assisting Stevens and the others any way he could. Within minutes, the ambulance came and took DeMarco away. First, however, Simon spoke to his friend. "Thank you," he said simply, placing a hand on DeMarco's uninjured shoulder.

DeMarco nodded weakly. "I'd say anytime, but I'm really hoping that's not the case. My date's inside, probably wondering where I went. Will you let her know I'll call her?"

"I'm betting I won't have to. She's a doctor, right? She'll probably head to the hospital as soon as she knows. And I'll see you there myself," Simon said.

"Sounds good," DeMarco breathed and then was whisked away.

Simon immediately sought out Nina, who was standing next to Stevens, talking to him and Archer, the man he'd suspected of murder.

And despite everything, despite Rita Taylor's failure to identify Archer, despite what had just happened with McGrogen, Simon, in his gut, still believed it to be true.

CHAPTER THIRTY-FIVE

OVER THE NEXT FEW HOURS, Harold McGrogen was booked into jail, but he wasn't the only one having to answer to the police. Even now, Gil Archer was at the SFPD with his attorney answering some very tough questions.

After checking in with Stevens, Simon joined Nina on her living room couch. "McGrogen was more than happy to bring Archer down with him in exchange for a deal from the DA. McGrogen's worked for Archer for almost a year, and he claims that Archer paid him to send SFPD a message by killing a homeless man or two, and blaming it on a cop. That's why Archer offered to provide McGrogen as a part-time security detail to Welcome Home at a discounted rate. Of course, he made it seem like all he cared about was helping those less fortunate than him. Hell, he even had McGrogen deliver bags of his used golf clothes to the shelter on his first day there."

"So those green-and-white-checkered golf pants the second murder victim was wearing...those were his?"

"Yeah. There's gotta be something humorous in there somewhere, but I'm just not seeing it at the moment."

"So despite helping put on that big fundraising gala, he's never really cared about helping out the homeless or mentally ill. He's just seen them as weak. Potential victims. And when he needed a convenient victim, he knew exactly where to go."

"Right. He told McGrogen he blamed the police for Lana's death, and that included me in particular. That we'd failed to protect what was his. When city law enforcement started getting bad press for their recent encounters with the homeless, Archer told McGrogen to take advantage of it. Kill a homeless man. Blame it on the cops. And, just for Archer's own personal satisfaction, leave a clue that the reason Archer was doing all this was because of his anger over Lana. His beloved daughter. God, I can't believe I didn't think of it sooner."

"You focused on the more rational thing—Davenport's threat to me and the fact the initials seemed to stand for Beth Davenport. You couldn't have known how Archer's convoluted mind was working. But why did McGrogen play along?"

"Pure greed, prodded along by resentment that I'd been the man who'd axed the SFPD's retired annuitant program."

"So this all started before we ever met. What made McGrogen or Archer focus on me?"

"After Archer learned about your role in helping me find Rebecca Hyatt, he railed at McGrogen for over an hour about how unfair it was that you were alive, looking so much like his daughter and doing the kind of work Lana would be doing if only she were alive. He ordered McGrogen to up the ante and the two of them kept close contact, with Archer periodically feeding McGrogen information about you, your involvement with Beth Davenport, and the trauma of your sister's suicide."

"Unreal," Nina breathed. "But this is all assuming McGrogen is telling the truth about Archer. He doesn't have any real proof, does he?" Nina asked.

"He says Archer is the one who actually broke into your house and planted the teddy bear in your bedroom. If that's true, we should be able to get a match on those muddy footprints he left behind."

Nina winced. "To think that something so small can be used to bring down someone so big."

"Yeah, well, more often than not, that's usually how it plays out in cases like this. But you just winced.... Are you feeling sorry for Archer? Because, like Davenport, he was acting out of love for his daughter? Out of grief?" As he asked the question, Simon tried to keep his tone even so Nina wouldn't think he was criticizing her professional beliefs again. Personally, he didn't believe Archer's grief mitigated his actions any more than McGrogen's need or anger had, but the thought of Nina disagreeing with him no longer bothered him the way it once had. He wasn't trained as Nina had been trained. And, frankly, he wasn't as naturally nurturing or compassionate as she was, either. Their professional beliefs didn't mean they couldn't sustain a fulfilling personal relationship. But would she agree with him?

"No, I'm not," she said quietly, surprising him. "I don't think Archer is like Davenport. Not given what I know right now."

"What do you mean?"

"Something you just said. If we can believe McGrogen, Archer told him that Lana was *his*. I haven't heard anything about Archer crying with grief or saying how much he loved and missed his daughter. Instead, he seems to have taken the police's alleged failure to save Lana as a personal affront to him. If that's what he believes and what's motivating him, he, like McGrogen and unlike Davenport, is most likely a sociopath. I suspect it's true given how well he's been able to hide his darker side, and given how complicated and symbolic the nature of his crimes were."

"You going to follow-up on that theory? On whether he's a sociopath or not?"

"Not unless there's an important reason to. Honestly, I want nothing more to do with the man. But I assume his defense attorneys will hire a reputable mental health expert to advocate for him should he go to trial."

"I'm sure you're right," he said. Was he right about their ability to sustain a long-term relationship, he thought? God, he hoped so, but he was unsure how to present his thoughts to Nina.

"What is it? You're not buying into what he told McGrogen, are you? That you were to blame for Lana's death?"

He shook his head. "No. I mean, that's where my mind goes sometimes. Because like you with your sister, I wish I had been able to save Lana. But I suspect you'd say that just proves I'm human."

"I'm glad you see that. So, what's next? You going to start on another case right away?"

SIMON PURSED HIS LIPS as if contemplating his next move, then shook his head. "Actually, Commander Stevens has been after me to take some time off for a while and I think I'm finally going to take him up on it. Maybe go to the beach again, but this time for an extended stay."

"That's wonderful. Are you planning on doing anything special?"

"Well, I'm hoping to do something special…and do *someone* special…if she'll have me." He watched her closely, sensing that she'd caught his meaning when she blushed and fought to hide a smile.

"I can't imagine any sane woman turning you down. I know—I know I wouldn't," she whispered.

"No? Because it won't be all fun in the sack. I still have to decide if I even want a management role anymore. But I have a very personal mission to complete, too."

"What's that?"

"Ask a lot of questions. Get a lot of answers. About what makes this woman tick. What she dreams about. What makes her happy and sad. But mostly what makes her happy."

"You make me happy," she said, and he knew she'd just taken a huge risk. That they were both taking one. At least, it felt that way.

"Then we're going to make a great pair," he said. "Because I find there's very little I like more than to make you happy. Still…"

"What is it?"

"I can't help but be worried," Simon confessed. "Our entire relationship so far has been based on working together, debating your job or at least certain aspects of it, or helping you forget what's going on through sex. That's no foundation for a long-term commitment."

"You don't think so?" Nina challenged. "Because whatever the foundation of our relationship consists of, it feels like a pretty strong one to me. A *good* one. Good enough that I'm feeling strong enough to conquer some of my fears. Good enough that I'm thinking I can work with my geriatric patients, and do other things, too—like help Karen with the MHIT training and maybe do some crisis counseling on the side."

"It does, huh?" He grinned, elated that she was finding the courage to again explore the career options she'd once loved. Elated that maybe part of the reason she felt stronger was because of him. "Maybe you just need to remind me exactly *how* good it feels? And keep reminding me every...well, let's see...every decade or so?"

"That would be my absolute pleasure."

He cupped her face and grinned. "Mine, too. I love you, Doc."

"And I love you, Simon."

"That's not just your desire for me talking, is it? Because while that would be perfectly understandable, I find I want you to speak with your heart, too."

"It was never just the sex talking. Being with you was never just about distraction, either. Even so, saying I love you during sex? That felt pretty fabulous the one time I let myself do it. Wanna give it a shot?"

"Just try to stop me." He kissed her, then murmured against her lips, "On second thought..."

She laughed, pulled him closer, and together they basked in the words they each repeated again and again that night.

Words of healing. Words of respect.

Words of love.

* * * * *

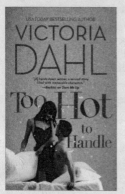

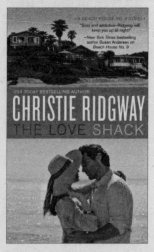

REQUEST YOUR FREE BOOKS!

2 FREE NOVELS
FROM THE SUSPENSE COLLECTION
PLUS 2 FREE GIFTS!

YES! Please send me 2 FREE novels from the Suspense Collection and my 2 FREE gifts (gifts are worth about $10). After receiving them, if I don't wish to receive any more books, I can return the shipping statement marked "cancel." If I don't cancel, I will receive 4 brand-new novels every month and be billed just $5.99 per book in the U.S. or $6.49 per book in Canada. That's a savings of at least 25% off the cover price. It's quite a bargain! Shipping and handling is just 50¢ per book in the U.S. and 75¢ per book in Canada.* I understand that accepting the 2 free books and gifts places me under no obligation to buy anything. I can always return a shipment and cancel at any time. Even if I never buy another book, the two free books and gifts are mine to keep forever.

191/391 MDN FVVK

Name	(PLEASE PRINT)

Address	Apt. #

City	State/Prov.	Zip/Postal Code

Signature (if under 18, a parent or guardian must sign)

Mail to the Harlequin® Reader Service:
IN U.S.A.: P.O. Box 1867, Buffalo, NY 14240-1867
IN CANADA: P.O. Box 609, Fort Erie, Ontario L2A 5X3

Want to try two free books from another line?
Call 1-800-873-8635 or visit www.ReaderService.com.

* Terms and prices subject to change without notice. Prices do not include applicable taxes. Sales tax applicable in N.Y. Canadian residents will be charged applicable taxes. Offer not valid in Quebec. This offer is limited to one order per household. Not valid for current subscribers to the Suspense Collection or the Romance/Suspense Collection. All orders subject to credit approval. Credit or debit balances in a customer's account(s) may be offset by any other outstanding balance owed by or to the customer. Please allow 4 to 6 weeks for delivery. Offer available while quantities last.

SUS13

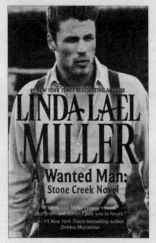

VIRNA DePAUL

77635 SHADES OF DESIRE	___ $7.99 U.S.	___ $9.99 CAN.
77674 SHADES OF TEMPTATION	___ $7.99 U.S.	___ $9.99 CAN.

(limited quantities available)

TOTAL AMOUNT	$ _____
POSTAGE & HANDLING	$ _____
($1.00 FOR 1 BOOK, 50¢ for each additional)	
APPLICABLE TAXES*	$ _____
TOTAL PAYABLE	$ _____

(check or money order—please do not send cash)

To order, complete this form and send it, along with a check or money order for the total above, payable to Harlequin HQN, to: **In the U.S.:** 3010 Walden Avenue, P.O. Box 9077, Buffalo, NY 14269-9077; **In Canada:** P.O. Box 636, Fort Erie, Ontario, L2A 5X3.

Name: _____

Address: _____ City: _____

State/Prov.: _____ Zip/Postal Code: _____

Account Number (if applicable): _____

075 CSAS

*New York residents remit applicable sales taxes.
*Canadian residents remit applicable GST and provincial taxes.

HARLEQUIN® HQN™
™ www.Harlequin.com

PHVDP0413BL